Fearless Sons of Erin and the Time Traveler Series

Book One

Back
to You

TARA NOLAN

To my Grandma Gwen, whose love of books matches my own

Thank you for always believing in me

Author's Note

Back to You contains dark content that may be triggering to some, including explicit romance, suicide, abandonment, adoption and the search of biological family, harm to a child, sexual assault, graphic violence, stalking, and murder. It is not intended for those younger than 18 years of age.

Contents

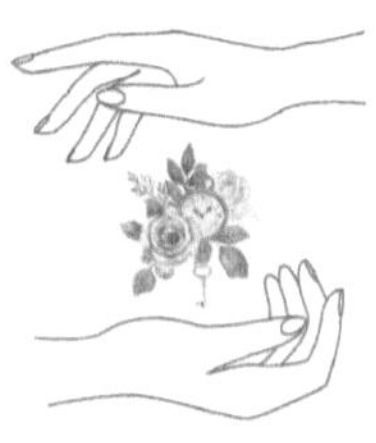

Prologue

R elativity of time.

I didn't understand much about it in school. Didn't really care to. Not until I found a way to break it. Manipulate it into a time of my choosing. Except, when I reached the other side, it had other plans I couldn't control. A world that was no longer mine. Dark. Scary. And completely antiquated. It sank its claws into me and wouldn't let go. Determined to shred me, until there was nothing left of the girl I was before.

I'm not sure I would have survived if it wasn't for him. That time suddenly became my own, and it did everything in its power to destroy me. But, little did it know, I already began to sink my own talons in. Into him. And I was holding on for dear life.

In that moment of clear certainty, I decided. I was the master of time. It did not control me.

And it could go fuck itself.

CHAPTER ONE

Emilia

PRESENT DAY

Sitting behind the large oak desk in the office above my parent's Irish pub, I stared at my adoption papers, willing them to unlock the secrets they didn't have. Of course, I knew they didn't. But that didn't stop me from searching for something I might have missed before. The curiosity hadn't eaten away at me yet.

I was content with being adopted. Ever since I could remember, I have been a part of the family. I accepted it. Even when my bronzed skin shone darker than their alabaster tones. My dark features made me stand out from them. But instead of secluding myself, I was up front and center. They adored their little Italian girl, and I loved them right back.

I flipped through the papers again, barely hearing the band below as I scanned the lines. Parents: Unknown. Last name: Long forgotten. The only thing social services knew was my first name.

Being three, that was about all *I* knew. And before I stopped talking, apparently, I was spitting out fluent Italian. I let my adoptive parents think I had forgotten it, but I still gravitated toward it as a child. They took me to Boston's Italian district to immerse me in the culture and possibly to find any family who might have known me. No one knew where I came from, and any memories of my past life were forgotten.

Eventually, I started speaking English, they stopped taking me to the Italian district as often, and I became content with the family who had taken me in as their own.

There hadn't been a reason to *want* to start looking into my biological parents. No sudden shift in circumstances. Just one day, I began to wonder how I made it onto the streets of Boston. Why hadn't they found any bodies? Or had someone taken me, and I escaped? Maybe my parents abandoned me. Kicked me to the curb like a stray dog. There were too many possibilities that I refused to wonder about any longer.

I absently looked at the old photograph on the desk, my mind going over all the possibilities as I stared at the two brothers standing outside the pub on opening day. They had opened it some years after the Civil War. The black-and-white quality made it difficult to see their features, but the bright white of their eyes made me guess that maybe they were blue. The taller one's hair was cut short, while the younger one kept his dark hair slicked back. I frowned at their stern expressions, wondering why they were so grumpy after achieving something monumental in a struggling time.

I ran my finger over the tallest one. There was something about him that always intrigued me. Even as a kid, I would find myself looking at the picture. From his fitted vest and jacket all the way down to his hands in his trouser pockets. The way he held himself as if no one could touch him. I think that's what drew me to him. He looked like he wouldn't take anyone's shit in a time that most definitely shit on his people. That, and the brothers were quite attractive.

I rubbed my forehead, thanking the stars that they weren't really *my* ancestors.

"Millie!" a familiar voice had my eyes snapping up from the picture. "What are you doing?"

I flipped the manilla folder closed and put it back in the drawer. "Nothing. What's up?" I tried to smile at my best friend as one of her dark brows raised in disbelief.

"You're on next."

I quickly glanced at the clock, gasping. "I didn't realize." I grabbed my guitar and headed toward her. "You look cute," I admitted, admiring her leather leggings and loose gold tank that accented the gold beads in her long braids.

"Thanks," Shay smiled, bumping me with her hip.

"Is a special man waiting down there, or did you dress up for me?" I joked.

We started down the stairs, and Shay slapped my ass, making me squeal as I entered the pub. "Don't tempt me, Millie Billie!"

A genuine smile spread across my face as I headed toward the stage. I started setting up as the other band packed up their instruments.

Shay whistled at one of the tables when I climbed the small platform, pounding her fists on the table like she was at a rock show. With a smile, I let go of my necklace and pushed my hair behind my shoulder, adjusting my guitar strap before stepping up to the mic.

Music had always been a part of me, and when I opened my mouth, it was as if I had left this world, traveling on the currents of the lyrics flowing from my mouth.

As requests flew in, I sang one song after another all night. From old Irish drinking songs to the latest pop hits, I sang them until they seeped from my pores. The pub always filled with family, friends, and regulars who wanted a little relief from everyday life—always counting on my family for a good time with music and plenty of drinks.

I hopped down from the small stage and snagged a glass of water.

"Hey, Emilia, girl!" A man around my dad's age and a weekly regular stopped me. "How about a Budweiser?"

"We don't sell that shit here," I laughed, our long-standing joke a comfortable familiarity. "How about a Guinness?"

"I'll take it."

"The bars that way," I smiled. "I'm off tonight!"

He groaned, and a few people that overheard us laughed.

I made my way through the crowd, looking for Shay and Dani, our friend since high school.

"Your brother won't serve us anymore," Shay pouted when she spotted me.

I raised my brows as she swayed slightly into Dani next to her. "You do look a little wasted," I laughed, noting how her dark eyes were glazed over.

"Traitor."

"Look, I got to go," Dani said, her blue eyes more focused than Shay's. She leaned in and hugged us both.

"You're good getting home?" I asked, worried she might drive. Just as I pulled back, I saw her brother by the door, waving to get her attention. Relief washed over me.

I locked my arm with Shay's and steered her toward the bar.

"You're so lame," she whined as I told her she would be consuming some water.

"You weren't saying that when I was on stage."

"Yeah, well. You were cooler then."

I laughed again and signaled to my brother, waiting for him to finish with a customer at the other end of the bar. He made his way over, green eyes rolling when spotting Shay's condition. "I told you no more," he scolded her, but his lips twitched, hiding a smile.

"Dick," she snapped as he slid the glass of water to her. My eyes met his, and we both had to turn away so she wouldn't see us suppressing laughter.

The bar started to empty out as we sipped our water and talked. I positioned myself towards Shay, ignoring the few guys our age standing close by. When I found their gazes flicking back to us, I knew it wouldn't be long until a brave one finally decided to sidle his way up to us. To my surprise, he faced me, and I had to suppress a groan. I was usually awkward whenever a boy talked to me.

"Hey, gorgeous," he said, running his hand through his golden hair. I nearly choked on my water. Did he say that to all the girls he wanted to pick up?

"I was wondering if I could buy you a drink?"

"Look at the time," Shay interrupted. "I should help Sean close up." She jumped down from her stool and gave me a wink that was so obvious I felt a blush creep over my cheeks.

I smiled politely, wishing he would just fuck off. "I'm not drinking tonight. Thanks, though." I shrugged and started to turn away.

"Oh, c'mon. Let me get you something." He held a hand up to Sean, which most definitely would annoy the shit out of my brother. That almost had me feeling a little better until Sean put two beers in front of us and winked. Actually, *winked*.

"You don't know what you're getting yourself into with her," Sean said, smirking at me as he walked away.

"Asshat," I mumbled, which had him laughing and the guy looking between us, puzzled.

"My brother," I said in explanation and tilted the bottle towards him. "Thanks." I took a long pull and tried to think of a way to leave without being rude.

He nodded while taking in my dark hair and eyes. Then, his eyes flicked toward my brother, and his brows furrowed as he noted my brother's noticeably lighter features. His frown deepened the longer he looked at Sean's pale features, blonde hair, and blue eyes, a stark contrast to mine.

When it was apparent I wasn't going to explain, he shifted toward me and leaned closer. "I saw you on stage. You're a great singer."

"Thanks."

"How did you get the gig? You play around town?"

"My parents own the pub," I said and watched as shock crossed his features as he looked back between my brother and me.

"I didn't realize—"

"Most don't." I shifted on the seat, a part of me annoyed that we even had to have this conversation. I didn't necessarily want to be just like my family, but I also didn't want to look like the odd one out. I could have been content if people had just let it be instead of constantly reminding me that my roots didn't start here. Or that maybe I didn't have any roots, to begin with. Perhaps I was just a wayward seed with nowhere to go and nothing to keep me planted.

I fiddled with my necklace while he looked around the bar and tried to figure it out. Pictures of multiple generations of our family members hung on the walls, including old furniture and heirlooms passed down through the years. It gave the pub a warm, welcoming feeling; if you were interested in old stuff, it was a great place to go and look around. And a complete culture shock to my Italian ancestry.

I decided to let him struggle as I took another pull of the beer.

"So, I was thinking..." His brown eyes landed on mine, intensifying my agitation.

I leaned against the counter as I looked him up and down, his toned arms pulling at his t-shirt, and tried to pull up some attraction to him. I wasn't shallow, and he *was* cute. I just had high standards, and most guys seemed childish to me. I held my breath as I waited for the next question.

"Can I have your number?"

A creeping, sinking sensation crawled out of my center before spreading to my limbs, weighing me down until I could not form a sentence. It took me a minute, but I turned him down gently.

When he walked away, his face was more aggravated than hurt. I rolled my eyes. *Another player bites the dust.*

I scoffed and turned back towards the counter, avoiding Shay's disappointed stare.

"Why do you do that?" she asked when they were out of earshot.

"Do what?" I smiled sweetly.

"Turn down *every* guy."

"That guy was a player."

"You don't have to marry him. Just, you know." She wiggled her eyebrows, and my mouth popped open. "Maybe you wouldn't be so cranky all the time."

"I am not cranky all the time!"

"Who knows, maybe you'd become a sex fiend, and I'd have to keep *you* from pursuing them."

A surprised laugh bubbled out of me, even as a blush rushed up my cheeks. I never said I wasn't interested. I didn't want to waste my time on a boy that just wanted in my pants before moving on to the next girl. Nah, I'd been abandoned enough in my life. I didn't need to put myself through that again. "Maybe I already am, and you don't know about my secret life." I widened my eyes for effect.

"I want proof."

I nodded like I had expected it. "I can get you the tape."

Shay made a loud guttural sound as if disgusted with me. "Who are we kidding? You're going to die an old maid with fifty cats surrounding you," she said, her red lips turned down as she imagined my bleak future. "And then I'll find them eating your carcass."

"Gee, thanks," I grimaced and ignored her while I straightened up and pushed chairs in. My dad had to leave early, so I promised I'd help Sean close up.

Shay didn't push me anymore, but I knew she just wanted me to be happy. *I* just wanted to convince her that I already was.

Wasn't I?

"Are you coming?" Sean asked sometime later, already around the corner and heading toward the back door.

"Yeah, I'll be there in a sec," I yelled, heading for the light switch.

I paused.

His black and white photo stared at me. I studied the plains of his face, his strong jaw, and the seriousness of his eyes. How his uniform pulled tight across his broad shoulders while a large rifle rested in his hand, completing his uniform. There was something about the older brother that caught my attention every time. It could have been his looks, which weren't lacking in any way, and yet, what intrigued me more was the sadness consuming his eyes. What had happened? Was it the effects of the war? Which surely would trouble anyone. Or was it something else?

I leaned in as if getting a closer look would reveal a clue about this man's life I hadn't noticed before.

"Millie?" Shay yelled from the back, startling me.

"Coming!" I shouted, flipping the light switch.

I whispered goodnight as my fingertips grazed the glass of the picture, feeling like I was leaving a part of myself behind.

Then again, I always felt that way. I'd just gotten used to it.

Or I thought I did.

CHAPTER TWO

Thomas

1859 BOSTON'S NORTH END

Thomas helped the other men unload the last box from their ship for the day. Letting it drop with a dull thud as the water lapped at the dock and the gulls' called overhead. He lifted his shirt, wiping the sweat from his face.

"Mr. O'Connor! Thomas!" A sweet voice of a young English girl ran to him.

Thomas lowered his shirt just in time to see Annie Davis bent over, catching her breath, but still admiring the plains of his muscled stomach. He raised his brow, making her blush. Though she was coming of age and Thomas no more than twenty-six, her mother would whip his Irish ass if he showed any intentions. Of course, Thomas didn't—he watched the lass grow up, for God's sake—but he was just beginning to wonder if Annie's thoughts might not be so innocent.

"What is it, lass?"

Her blush spread across her pretty features, all the way to her blonde roots as she tried to breathe slower. She must have run across town.

"It's Ms. Worth. That Hughes and Knight are looking for her. The committee is calling a meeting." Thomas bit back a snarl at the mention of the two slave-hunters from Georgia. Regular feckers in these parts, constantly making trouble.

Hiram swore behind Thomas. His friend pulled a shirt over his light-brown skin and started gathering his supplies to head out. Hiram knew first-hand how those men handled his people, and there was little time to waste.

"Ms. Worth?" Thomas tried to picture her. "Isn't that the pretty seamstress who can barely look a man in the eye?"

"Yes," Hiram confirmed. "And if they take her back—"

"Her master will put hands on her again, aye." Thomas and Hiram shared a glance while Annie looked away coyly. Everyone knew what happened to Ms. Abel Worth before she escaped and made her way to Boston.

"I'll be damned if they lay a finger—" Hiram fumed before Thomas cut him off and asked where she was while tucking in his shirt, already walking toward town.

"The courthouse. You know those two hounds will have her in no time."

"The babe, too?" Hiram asked.

"Indeed," Annie said, face draining of color.

The babe was two now and never knew slavery. According to the law, the slave master would own them both. They had to get them out of town with every bit the haste they could muster.

They rushed to Faneuil Hall, dodging those in their way.

Thomas threw his arm out, stopping Annie from crossing the street. "Careful," he told her, blocking her from the horse and buggy that came from around the corner. "Ye won't do us any good if ye're trampled."

She nodded, smoothing her hair back, trying to compose herself as they set off to cross the way to the hall.

Hiram held the door open for them to enter. They spotted Mrs. Davis almost immediately.

"I better go to Mum," Annie remarked, looking reluctant to leave Thomas' side. "I wish they'd let women join. I could help."

"Aye, lass," Thomas agreed, face falling. "But I thank ye for coming for us. Ye did your part."

Annie blushed, her blue eyes flitting between his green ones. "I hope it was enough. But I was glad it was you I was sent for."

Thomas took a step back, aware of the heavy stares from the Yankees. Thomas nodded toward Mrs. Davis and parted with sweet Annie before anyone could jump to conclusions.

"I believe she is partial to you," Hiram stated quite annoyingly as the lass walked away.

Thomas rolled his eyes, more focused on the glares directed toward them. *The poor Irishman and his mulatto friend.* He nearly snarled at the crowd as they parted before them, clearly disturbed by whatever they read on his face.

"I don't have time for women," he said offhandedly.

Hiram snorted as they rushed to the front, twisting and turning their big shoulders through the crowd. It only took a matter of minutes to get to Faneuil Hall from the docks. Yet, it was already halfway filled with abolitionists and committee members, most of whom were white elitists, of which Thomas and Hiram were most definitely not.

They were used to being outnumbered and found it easier to stick together. Hiram being one the few black members allowed to join the committee, and Thomas being the rare Irishman to join forces with a man of color, let alone the committee, were a rare sight to see and often drew the eyes of everyone.

Hiram bumped into a man.

"Pardon yourself," the man snapped at Hiram.

Thomas scowled at Mr. Adams, one of the wealthy elites who preferred donating to the cause rather than doing the hands-on work. Adams had little patience for those in the lower class and often attempted to hide his irritable disposition by bragging about how much he donated and how good it was for him to make such a sacrifice—blatantly ignoring that some donated selflessly in the hopes of truly making a difference.

Thomas's fists clenched as he suppressed the urge to punch the bastard.

"Pardon me, sir," Hiram bowed so extravagantly that there was little doubt of insult, making the man's jowls flush in anger.

Adams straightened, causing Hiram to step back to avoid Adam's ample midriff.

"Now—" Adams blustered.

"They're 'bout to begin," Thomas grabbed Hiram's arm, nodding towards Adams. "Excuse us, sir."

Thomas had Hiram turned around before either man could start a fight that wasn't productive to the support of Miss Abel.

"Here! Here!" the committee president yelled from the top of the stage, quieting the congregation. Timothy Gilbert towered over everyone, the setting sun from the windows behind him casting a glow off his balding head, giving him an ethereal appearance. "As you may have heard, one of ours—a Miss Abel Worth—has been taken to the courthouse upon the arrival of a Mr. Hughes and Mr. Knight before we could intervene. Our lawyers have notified us that the judge has declared there will be no trial."

A loud protest started around the room, and it took several minutes to calm everyone down.

"Mr. Sewall is at the courthouse in hopes of persuasion," Francis Jackson—the treasurer and only other member on the stage—stated. "But it looks like other measures will have to be taken."

"And what if he does not succeed?" a man in the back yelled out.

"On the chance that Mr. Sewall is not successful in his efforts," Gilbert addressed the crowd, "We may need volunteers for the release of Ms. Abel by a more hands-on approach."

The room went silent.

"I say we get 'er out now!" Mr. Bradley, a freeman, born in Boston, demanded.

"Count us in!" another yelled, gesturing towards the other men who worked with him in the textile mill.

Hiram's golden eyes flared with determination. Thomas nodded, silently agreeing to help him.

"Us as well," Hiram yelled, raising his hand as he and Thomas made their way down the center aisle. Others began to push their way through the chairs.

"Now, wait a minute," Gilbert said. "We should wait for word from Sewall."

"Ye know it's too late," Thomas said, looking Gilbert dead in the eye.

"Bloody Irishman," a man muttered loudly. "They'll throw you in with her before the night has fallen."

"Better me body punished than me soul, which will surely be me fate if I leave her to be taken back."

"You're already going to hell, you daft Catholic—"

Thomas took a step towards Mr. Fletcher—a small banker—and looked down at him, shutting him up almost instantly. He stood there with closed fists, waiting for the Englishman to make a move.

"Do ye have somethin' to say about me faith, *sir*?" Thomas asked when it was apparent the man wasn't going to continue.

"Not now, Tommy," Hiram whispered behind Thomas.

Thomas glared at the tiny man in front of him who was ringing his hat nervously between his hands, though Thomas had to give it to him for standing his ground.

"I think you understand me quite—quite well," Fletcher stuttered, puffing out his chest in a pathetic attempt to look more impressive in front of the crowd.

Hiram's hand clamped down on Thomas's arm, pulling him towards the other group of men gathering together. The doors burst open, causing a few women to gasp as everyone else fell silent, staring at the young boy waving his cap.

"They're taking her at dawn!" he gasped, trying to catch his breath. "I overheard they're going to take her to the docks."

The whole room exploded in commotion—torn between those who panicked, the ones who wanted to discuss their next move, and the men who were already rushing to the doors in an attempt to free her now.

Thomas swore, remembering what happened with Anthony Burns some years back. They stormed the courthouse, failing to rescue Burns. When it was time to ship Burns back to his owner, troops and guards lined the streets against anyone who opposed them. Thomas couldn't let a mob form if he wanted Ms. Abel to have a chance at freedom.

"Ye remember Burns?" he asked Hiram, shoving chairs to the side to create his own path closer to the front.

"Yeah. What of it?" Hiram asked, following Thomas.

"If we raise hell like then, they'll crack down on the guards. Let's keep it hush. Try this time on the sly, and come at them with surprise on our side. A few of us would work best." Thomas shoved the last chair aside and turned towards Hiram. "Only if we get these people to be quiet until then."

"It could work," Hiram admitted, looking around at the chaos. "Let me talk to Gilbert." He straightened; his large shoulders set in determination before he jumped the platform.

Thomas thought of the men he wanted to recruit as Hiram discussed something heatedly with Gilbert. The latter was shaking his head and grabbing the podium in frustration. Thomas watched, his heart beating to the sound of the crowd's uproar as it took Hiram another minute to talk the man down.

Then, with a stiff nod from Hiram that set Thomas's nerves on fire with anticipation, Hiram descended the stage before several gavel cracks slowed down the pandemonium. A few more, and the room quieted enough for Gilbert to speak. "I've just received delayed word from Sewall," he bellowed. "He's made some headway and wants us to leave it to him for the time being."

Protests erupted throughout the room.

With a pointed look from Gilbert, Thomas and Hiram recruited five other men to break Ms. Abel Worth and her child out of the courthouse.

"Cover your face," Hiram growled at the other men getting in the wagon, even as the darkness veiled their features from any onlookers. He wouldn't take a chance on a possible sighting.

"Piss off," a man nearly as big as Hiram grumbled as he pulled the mask over his face. Hiram ignored him, having grown up with Sam.

"Tell me why we aren't gonna be usin' more people to save Ms. Worth?" George, an older man with short cropped hair greying at the sides, asked.

"Because," Thomas explained again, "we don't need them calling more guards. If they don't think we're coming, there will be no chance to bring in troops like they did with Burns."

Thomas climbed into the seat next to Hiram and looked back at the others, ensuring their faces were covered. It didn't surprise him that he was the only white man out of the group. There were usually only a few others willing to use force to help the fugitive slaves. Their money and lawyers could only do so much. Thomas didn't have any of those, so he gave the only thing he had—himself and what he'd learned on the streets.

"I just think more will be better," George mumbled, shifting uncomfortably in his seat.

"That's your problem," Jackson said, adjusting the pistol at his hip so he could sit next to his brother, Isaac. Sitting together like that, no one could argue they weren't related. They had the same sharp features as men who didn't have an ounce of fat. But, if it weren't for Jackson putting on some muscle the last few years, a stranger could mistake them for twins. "You always want more." He patted George's stomach, which was rounding out from all the extra bit of pies his missus made for her clients.

"Watch it, boy," George growled at his son, slapping his hand away. "You may be big now, but I can still whip you."

"Hold tight," Thomas warned. With a snap of the reins, they jolted forward, throwing the men back as the wagon barreled into the street, earning Thomas a few curses from the others. He could take turns any way he pleased, not worrying about pedestrians getting in his way in the middle of the night.

They fell silent, the importance of their mission falling heavily on them. Thomas took an indirect path, planning on parking the wagon in the courthouse's rear so as not to alert the guards.

It didn't take long for the wagon to rattle through the streets. Within minutes, Thomas pulled on the reins and clattered to a stop behind the large building.

He turned around as the men prepared to get out. "Do ye remember your positions?" he asked, ignoring the adrenaline pounding in his ears.

"Yes, move over." Isaac pushed his way up front. They agreed he should be the one to wait in the wagon—it being safer for his first rescue—so they could make a quick getaway.

Thomas and Hiram jumped to the ground, adjusting their weapons and the sacks over their faces.

Thomas studied the building, looking for anyone in the windows as Sam pulled Hiram to the side. He overheard Sam ask if they needed him to go inside with them.

"We got it," Hiram responded and gripped Sam's shoulder in reassurance. "The boys will need you. Godspeed, brother."

Sam signaled to the other two men to follow him around the courthouse. They grabbed their supplies and made quick work of it, wasting no time getting to the front door.

"You sure about this?" Hiram looked to Thomas. "I can go it alone."

"And who will save your arse when ye get in a bind?" Thomas asked, pulling lock picks out of his trousers. "Bring that closer, will ye?"

"Just sayin', you don't have to risk yourself, is all." The lantern from the wagon cast deep shadows across the cover on Hiram's face, giving him the appearance of an avenging spirit.

"When has that stopped me before?" Thomas smiled, eyes flaring with mischief.

The ground shook with the resounding blast in the front of the courthouse. Given their cue, they waited for the guards to head towards the front of the building.

Hiram lowered the lantern as Thomas fiddled with the lock. A few quick turns of the picks, and the lock sprung open. Thomas shoved the door open with his shoulder, and they stumbled inside. It was dark, but with the lantern and their memory of the layout of the building, they found a staircase without incident. They made it to the second level when a rumble of footsteps came from the floor above. Thomas opened the door to the nearest room and pulled Hiram in after him. Hiram rushed to cover the lantern with his jacket before the men could see the light under the door. Hearts pounding in their ears, they waited for the men to pass.

"What do you think it was?" a deep voice drifted through the door.

"Suppose they're coming for her," another man answered, voice coming closer with each word.

"Damn fools. Why can't they leave well enough alone? Do you think they brought the whole damn committee with them?"

The footsteps passed the door without hesitation and faded down the next flight of stairs.

Hiram cracked the door and slid out, taking the lead.

They neared the third floor, where Abel and her child should have been, and drew their guns. Thomas held his hand up for Hiram to stand back with the lantern. It was brighter on this floor, the guards having candles and lanterns lit, but he didn't want to take a chance. He climbed the last few stairs and crouched down, looking around the corner to spot any of the guards.

Two were at the end of the hall, standing in front of a closed door. One was younger, fidgeting and grating on the nerves of the older guard.

"Stop it, will you?" the older man grumbled.

"I can't help it. What if they come up here?" His voice cracked, revealing his youth.

"Shite," Thomas muttered under his breath. He wanted to save Ms. Abel, but he took no joy in harming the men in his way, especially ones as young as the guard nearest to him.

He went back down to Hiram, relaying what he saw.

"We charge," Hiram said, setting the lantern on the stairs. "Like you said, 'take them by surprise'. Can't stop now that we're here."

Thomas nodded grimly and held up three fingers. When the last finger fell, they were up the stairs and running full speed down the hall before either of the guards noticed them.

"What in the bloody—" the older man started, trying to remove his pistol from his holster.

The young guard lifted his gun, hands shaking as he took off a shot. They both ducked, swearing under their breath.

The other guard raised his pistol and was about to shoot when Thomas shot the man's hand. The gun flew, and the guard grabbed his wound, screaming in pain. The younger guard dropped his gun out of fear and raised his hands.

"Stand back!" Hiram yelled, pointing his revolver at each of them. "I said stand back!"

They both stumbled away, eyes wide in shock.

"You open it. I have them," Hiram told Thomas.

Thomas wasn't surprised when he found the door locked. He took a step back, not wanting to waste any more time, and kicked—the door cracked, spraying splinters of wood as it slammed into the inside of the room.

He rushed in, looking left and right, before spotting a dark figure rocking back and forth in a chair, a small form bundled in her arms. Abel never took her eyes off her child, didn't even flinch at the commotion that was becoming increasingly louder outside.

Thomas stopped, his stomach dropping as a cold sweat broke over his skin. He took a step back, his hand finding the table next to him for support as he struggled to differentiate between what was before him and the past. It had to be the way the woman was moving. Something about the set of her features reminded him of it. There was no other explanation of why he thought of that babe, of his ma rocking his little sister on the ship to the States with the grief only a mother could feel. The babe never made it off the boat.

"What's taking so long?" Hiram yelled from the hall. "We have to go!"

Hiram's voice snapped Thomas back into action, and he ran to Abel.

"We're here to rescue ye." Thomas crouched near her, trying to better look at the little girl.

"Yer too late." Abel's southern voice was flat, void of any emotion.

"We have time, but we need to go now." He tried to urge her to stand. The soft glow from the fireplace showed a pretty face but eyes vacant of life as she stared at her child. Her hair stuck up in wild puffs where it was otherwise smoothed back, as if she had been pulling at it.

"It's too late. I wouldn't 'ave 'er suffer by that bastard's hands." Then, she looked up at Thomas, and enough hatred spread across her features that his stomach tightened. "It's better this way. My angel is in heaven."

"A Dhia!" Thomas sent a prayer up to God. Then, he glanced at the sweet, tiny face of innocence and grabbed the babe, gun still in his hand.

"Don't ya dare!" she screeched, trying to grab her baby girl.

"Hiram! Get in here!" Thomas yelled, placing the gun and toddler on the table. He put his finger under her nose, but she wasn't breathing. "Damn it, woman! We were comin' for ye!"

Hiram had his gun trained on the guards and had them shuffle to the back of the room. "What is it?"

"She's not breathing," Thomas swore, feeling the child's forehead. The girl was still warm. It couldn't have been long. "Will ye get her off me?" Thomas pushed Abel to the side and bent down, breathing into the toddler's nose and mouth.

"Ya can't do this!" Abel fumed as Hiram blocked her way. "I won't let that bastard touch my baby! It's too late!"

"Where were you when this was happening?" Hiram thundered, turning his steely glare on the guards.

"We—" the younger guard stuttered, visibly shaking. "We thought they were sleeping."

"Jesus Christ," the older one muttered, making no move to stop them. "We didn't know."

Thomas tried to resuscitate the child, ignoring everyone but that small, warm body, hoping for signs of life.

"We can still go," Hiram said, trying to calm Abel. "Let's go, Tommy."

"Not yet," Thomas growled, placing his ear on the girl's chest. What was that? "Quiet, Goddamn ye!" he yelled at Abel. He knew he shouldn't have raised his voice. She thought she was saving her child from a monster. She couldn't have known they were coming. But he sure as hell wasn't going to give up on the poor lass, and he needed her Ma to shut her gab.

Abel fell silent, no longer attempting to stop them.

"We can still get you out of here." Hiram muttered reassurances to her, trying to speed everything up so they could escape. Still, there was yelling somewhere inside the courthouse, coming closer. "Damn it, Tommy. Let's go!" Hiram turned to Thomas, losing focus on Abel.

Thomas breathed into the child's mouth again, knowing it was the last time before they tried to run. He pressed his fingers to her chest, desperate to push life into her tiny body. Was that pink returning to her cheeks?

Something flashed near Thomas, and he looked up. His heart stopped when he saw Abel with a gun pressed against her temple.

His gun. She must have lunged for it when Hiram turned towards the door.

"It's too late," she said again. "I won't go back. Thank ya, gentlemen, for tryin' to help us. But the only place safe for people like us is up above with the Almighty."

Thomas instinctively covered the child with his body, closing his eyes from the gun's blast. Hiram caught Abel before she hit the floor.

"God in Heaven," a guard whispered. "There's another stairway. If you take it, you should bypass the others."

"No!" Hiram yelled, clutching Abel to his chest, unaware of the blood soaking through his jacket.

"We swear we didn't know," the older guard muttered as the young guard turned to the side and vomited.

Footsteps sounded on the steps a few floors down: Jackson, George, and Sam could not distract them anymore. Thomas sent up a prayer for their safety.

"Let's go, comrádaí." Thomas tried to pull his big friend away from Abel with his unoccupied arm. "There are those still counting on us. Níl gach rud caillte."

Hiram finally looked at Thomas and what was in his arms. He nodded, gently setting Abel on the floor before handing Thomas his gun.

Shouts were heard from above as the snap of the reins carried them all away.

CHAPTER THREE

Emilia

The ceiling fan whirled in a monotonous procession, putting me into a trance as I laid in my bed and contemplated how to approach my parents about my past. I didn't think they knew anything. They'd made it clear that they would help me with whatever I needed, but it felt wrong. Like I was betraying the parents who really loved and raised me into the woman I became.

"What's wrong?" Shay plopped down next to me, jostling the bed and snapping me out of the steady loss of sanity.

I pulled the comforter over my face and mumbled something incoherent.

"Girl, you've been moping around here for days." We shared an apartment, so it was kind of hard to hide anything from her.

I sighed and threw off the blankets, continuing to watch the fan. "I want to find out what happened to my biological parents," I admitted, avoiding her gaze.

I could feel her stare searching my face as she thought about how to respond. "So, then we talk to your parents. Honestly, I was wondering when this would happen."

I explained my hesitancy. Shay shook her head when I'd finally finished. "We'll go see your parents today. You deserve some closure, and it would be cool to finally find out the mystery."

"Thanks." I tried to smile, finally turning towards her, even as my gut churned. If I found my family, what would even come next? *Hey, you're alive! I'm your long-lost daughter. Why did you abandon me?* I held back a groan, wanting to bury my face in the pillow. That was a conversation I wasn't sure I *ever* wanted to have.

"We'll figure this out." A look of mischief came over her dark features, and I cringed, not knowing if this new change of subject would be any better than my lost family. "Now, tell me more about the guy the other night. What was wrong with him?"

I sighed but was mildly relieved. This I could handle. "He was...okay," I hesitated, not sure how to explain the reason for not liking him.

"*Okay.*" She scrunched up her nose. "So... he's not your type. That's all you had to say. We do not settle for just *okay.*"

"We don't?" My eyebrows rose.

Her Cheshire Cat grin spread as she sat on her knees, bouncing up and down like a kid about to get some candy. "You want him to make you forget your name. If you're not terrified, then it's not the right man."

I gave her a disbelieving look.

"You'll see," she said. "One day, you'll meet the man that terrifies you, and you'll know."

"That sounds like a murder mystery, not a love story," I deadpanned.

"Just promise me you'll give it a shot with a man that piques your interest, and I'll stop bugging you."

I breathed a long, exaggerated sigh, bending my head back dramatically. "Fine. I will settle for none other than a terrifying man."

"Believe me, Millie Billie, you'll be thanking me while kissing the one who makes your knees shake!"

"No offense, but I don't think I'll be thinking of you." I laughed, throwing my hands in the air to stop her from hitting me. "Unless you want me to?"

She paused her attack as if actually considering that. I gave her a look that had her laughing loudly.

"Fine. You're not my type anyway," Shay joked.

After that, I lay there for a while, wondering for the first time if I was letting my life pass me by. That might have been part of the reason I wanted to look into my family history.

Maybe it was time to get a little out of my comfort zone. To spread my wings and soar toward whatever destiny awaited me.

Some of us jumped, while others stayed on the ground. I guess it depended on what you were leaping for.

But how did one know if it was worth the leap?

"I know you don't know where I came from but did social services say anything that might give us a hint?" I asked my mom an hour later. Shay and I had busted into my parent's small kitchen, making ourselves at home as my parents welcomed us a little exasperatedly. They usually slept in after working late at the pub, and our not-so-early intrusion offset their morning routine.

Honestly, it was remarkable how they handled our dramatics.

"I knew this day was coming." My mom shook her head sadly, her blonde hair falling into her face as she looked into her tea. "I'm sorry, honey. They found you in the street, speaking Italian and not understanding anyone. But when they had a translator come in, she said you weren't speaking entirely in Italian."

"Entirely?" I asked, looking confusedly between my parents as my heart quickened for a reason I didn't quite understand.

She shrugged. "Some of your words were from a language the translator didn't know."

I looked at Shay, my stomach turning. Something poked at the edge of my mind. I tried to focus on it. If I could just—I sighed and shook my head, the hint of a memory vanishing completely.

My mom turned towards my dad, leaning her hip on the counter as she set her tea down. "Do you remember anything the social worker said that Millie wouldn't already know, Eamonn?"

He leaned on his elbows next to my mother and cocked his head to the side in thought. I noted how his black hair was graying at the sides. "No." He shook his head and turned his attention to me. "I'm sorry, sweetie. Maybe check in the attic of the pub? There are some old papers up there. Maybe you'll find something I overlooked."

I agreed, thinking that was a good idea.

"I'm sorry we couldn't be of more help," my mom said.

"Mom, really, it's okay." I squeezed her hand, not wanting her to be upset that I needed information about my biological parents. "I promise. *You're* my family."

"Damn straight, and don't you forget it." My dad pointed at me, pretending to be intimidating. "Remember who changed your shitty diapers and spent a fortune on feeding you."

Shay choked on her tea with a laugh.

"I'm sorry, father." I rolled my eyes. Apparently, it was utterly irrelevant that I was practically potty trained when they adopted me. "However, shall I repay ye?" I mimicked the Irish accent whenever I joked with him. He used to do it to me as a kid, and after doing it for so many years—along with the help of my Boston accent—I became pretty good at it.

He shrugged. "You could bring a crowd into the pub tonight."

"If you mean by singing, sure," I said, getting up from my chair and grabbing my purse. I could use some extra tips on my night off from waitressing. "I won't be dancing on the counters tonight."

"Emilia," my mom hissed as I threw a smile over my shoulder, waving. "You mind yourself, young lady!"

"Love you guys!" I called on my way out, hearing them shout it back as I shut the door.

"So, where to?" Shay asked, following me to the sidewalk. She eyed a few men down the street, assessing their attentions rather than looks. They didn't pay us any mind.

I let out a long breath. "The attic. I can go by myself if you want to do something else."

"I'll help you," she said, and we made the short walk to the pub, enjoying the warm morning sun on our skin.

I unlocked the back door and switched the lights as we walked through. The pub was closed until lunch. We had the whole place to ourselves.

"Okay," I said, setting down my purse. "I'm not sure how dirty it is up there. This might get messy."

"If I find a dead body—" Shay glared at me. "I'm leaving your ass up there."

I laughed. "It's nice to know I can count on you."

We went up the stairs, crossing through the offices to the front room with a small bed and table. Sometimes, if my dad was working late and tired, he'd crash there. Occasionally, he'd let someone he knew stay the night if they had too much to drink.

The layout was one of an old apartment, until my grandpa turned it into an office. The first owners lived in it for a couple of years and then moved to a bigger house.

I often wondered if both of the brothers lived there or if one had a family that ran the place. My dad only said they still ran the pub but started using the upper level as housing for immigrants who needed help assimilating into America. Then, after they had their feet on the ground and had found a job and a new place to live, the immigrants would move out, and new ones would have the option of staying.

"It's just over here," I grunted as I slid a heavy chair across the floor.

Stopping just under a large rectangular door on the ceiling, I climbed the chair and pulled the string. It stuck for a second before giving way with a fresh batch of dust. I sneezed, turning my head as I pulled the stairs down.

"Yeah, that's not creepy at all," Shay muttered, eyeing the darkness above us.

I coughed out an agreement while moving the chair back. "Can you go get the flashlight out of the desk? There's a light up there, but I think we might need some more."

While she went to get the light, I climbed the stairs to look around. I couldn't see more than a few boxes and dust covering the wooden planks.

"I found two," she said, clambering up the stairs behind me. "Here."

I turned the flashlight on, revealing motes of dust billowing through the beam of light.

"Maybe you should clean it while you're up here." Shay pulled herself up after me.

I glared at her. "Let's stay on task."

"I'm just saying..." She chuckled.

The slight slope of the attic had us ducking as we walked further in. Moving the flashlight back and forth revealed a heap of boxes filled with stuff—some old lamps, odds and ends of small furniture.

I pulled the long string that turned on the bulb above us.

"Where do we even start?" Shay asked, lifting up an old brass candleholder before putting it back down.

"No idea."

"Look." She pointed to a few boxes closer to the door. "These are labeled. Look newer, too."

I went over to her. "I bet these would have some of my stuff in it." I quickly skimmed over the older dates. "1998!" I yelled, suddenly feeling excited and oddly nervous.

"This one has your name on it," Shay said, pointing to another near it.

"I'll take that one. You want to look at this one?"

"Sure." Shay grabbed the small box from me, and we set to work.

I flipped the top off of mine and started pulling out old baby clothes and my favorite stuffed animal. "Mr. Rufkins!" I yelled, shoving him in Shay's face. "They must have put him up here for safe keeping!"

Shay tried to pull back, not wanting the dog shoved in her face anymore.

"I'm glad you're reunited," she said sarcastically but smiled. "There's really not much in this one, except expenses and inventory for the pub."

"Look at this," I said, pulling out a tiny dress. Its faded blue material looked as if it was about to fall apart. It had long sleeves, buttons running down both sides of the abdomen, and flared out at the bottom. "This looks ancient." I turned it around, squinting at it as if bugs might crawl out.

"That's nothing compared to these!" Shay said, lifting out ruffled cotton pants.

"They must have gone underneath it."

We held the two parts together, trying to picture it. Every hair stood up on my body as a sense of uneasiness swept through me.

"Why would I be wearing this?" I asked Shay.

"Your mom said you were speaking Italian. It must've been your parent's style or something."

"Yeah, I guess." I put the clothes back in and shuffled some stuff to the side. "There are folders in here." I flipped through them, noting the legal papers my parents collected over the years. "I already know all of this," I grumbled my disappointment. "They knew absolutely nothing about my family. It's a dead end, Shay."

"C'mon, let's look around some more," she said soothingly, rubbing my arm.

"Maybe a box was moved or something."

"My whole existence is in this damn box." Something twisted deep inside of me that I refused to acknowledge.

"Well, it couldn't hurt." She stood up and started walking around the attic again.

I sighed and packed the box up nicely. It seemed like a lost cause, but I knew I couldn't leave that attic until I turned over every inch of it.

"Emilia, look at this." Shay stopped in the back corner, shining her light on one of the rafters. The bewilderment in her voice had me coming over immediately.

"What?"

"This." She touched something that was hanging off the rafter, and I gasped. "It's just like yours."

I glanced down at the necklace around my neck and then back up at the rosary hanging from the ceiling, the two blue stones dulled by layers of dust, but remarkably like mine.

"A lot of people have rosaries," I admitted, trying and failing to ignore the striking resemblance.

"No, these are the same beads. Same cross. It's exactly the same." She lifted it off the nail to take a closer look.

"Don't you think it's weird? What are the odds? People don't usually wear rosaries, but this one is here, just like the one you always have on. So why would it be up here?"

As she studied it, I started pushing things around, accidentally tipping over a box to the side. I bent down to pick up the contents when I saw an old, wooden chest crammed into the corner. It blended in so well that I may not have spotted it without the rosary hanging in front of it.

"And you never take that thing off," she continued. "Have you ever wondered why you're so attached to it?"

"It was the only thing I had before they found me," I said offhandedly, focusing on the chest in front of me. The truth was that I never took it off because some of me knew it was important. I just didn't know why. I always thought that maybe someone important gave it to me, and I repressed the memory.

But what was the meaning of the second one? Had my adoptive parents given it to me and just told me it was from my past? For some reason, that hurt more than not remembering.

I blew some dust off the front of the chest and rubbed the gold plaque until I could read the engraving. "Look at this."

"An old chest?" Shay asked, bending down by me.

I didn't say anything, just rubbed my thumb over the plaque again. My breath caught, and my heart rate tripled.

"Is that your name?" Shay whispered. She pointed her flashlight at it and leaned in closer. "Millie, that's your name on it! We have to open it."

I let her push me to the side while she pulled out the chest. She opened it and stopped, just staring at whatever was inside.

"This stuff looks really old," she said. "Here—" She shoved it closer to me. "—You should be the one to look through it."

"I don't understand. Why didn't my parents tell me about this?"

Shay shook her head and gave me a pointed look that seemed to say, *"Look through it, for God's sake."*

It wasn't filled to the brim, but there was enough in it that I didn't know where to start.

"These look like letters," I said, lifting up a packet of parchment, a red ribbon tied around them. I set them to the side, wanting to peruse the other stuff before I opened them. "Wow," I whispered, lifting up an old flag.

"Look at the stars." There was one large star in the middle, surrounded by a circle of tiny ones. "That's definitely not our modern flag."

"Look at this," she said, holding a green flag. The yellow words were in Irish-Gaelic. I knew that much, bordered by what looked like red banners. "28th regiment!"

"A war flag?" I asked, confused. "Why would all this old stuff and an Irish war flag be in a chest with my name on it?"

"I don't know. I guess, keep looking."

We folded the flags gently and put them to the side.

"Is this a dress?" Shay asked, lifting the green cotton out.

"Definitely," I said in awe as it unraveled. It was a plain dress cut in a style that screamed *old*, with long sleeves and a long skirt that went to the floor. I looked back at the name on the chest. Every hair stood up on my body in reaction to our discovery, and that same sensation

I felt at my parent's house. Like I was missing something that I once knew.

Shay lifted up a small white undergarment that looked like a mixture of a bra and corset, inspecting the strange thing.

I started looking through the chest some more. "How cool would it be to read this later?" I asked, showing her the leather journal.

"This is insane."

"There are more papers down here." As I tried to pick them off the bottom, my hand bumped a jar I hadn't seen in the corner, and a white powder spilled over the papers. "Shit."

I mumbled curses as I lifted the papers carefully and tried not to dump the powder in the chest. Concentrating on my task, I didn't realize how close Shay was when I blew the powder off the papers.

"Hey!" Shay yelled, coughing and flailing her hands around.

"I'm sorry," I laughed. My smile fell as soon as I saw the rosary around her neck. "Why do you have that on?" I snapped, not sure why I had a sense of uneasiness creeping through me.

"I didn't want to lose it." She coughed and wiped her face. "God, what was in that? I don't feel so good." She looked pale under her usual dark skin.

My heart pounded, and I flung myself into the trunk, removing the jar.

I shined the flashlight on the tiny glass, and my heart nearly stopped.

"I've seen this before," I whispered.

"What?" she asked. She was still trying to remove the tiny, sparkling powder from her clothes.

"I've seen this before," I said louder, beginning to panic. I stood up quickly, slamming my head into the beam above me. "You have to take that off."

"It'll be all right, piccolina," an older woman assured me as she patted my head. "It's your destiny. It'll be safer this way. Now, don't ever lose this." She placed a rosary over my neck.

I thought I was so lucky to be one of the only ones in our family to actually wear *a rosary. Even then, I knew the reverence they placed on the special talismans.*

My eyes widened, turning away from the older woman, from her long greying hair and the most colorful, long skirt I'd ever seen.

"It's so pretty," I sighed, admiring how the gold and black beads looked on my blue dress.

"I'm glad you like it," she smiled sadly. My grandmother. I remembered, and all the hair on my body stood on end. *"This next part isn't going to be easy, but remember, with this necklace, your family will always be with you."*

I nodded, not entirely understanding what she meant.

She picked up the glass jar, pulled the cork out, and sprinkled it over my head.

"I love you, piccolina," she said as my stomach started to turn.

The memory hit me hard, and I doubled over, breathing heavily. That language. It had to be the language my parents mentioned. But what was it? And how could I understand it after not hearing it for so many years?

"Millie?" Shay's voice shook. "I can't see you anymore. I don't know what's happening."

I looked up just in time to see Shay fading, almost translucent. "Take it off!" I yelled again, flinging myself at her. My arms wrapped around the open air and landed hard on the ground. I turned over quickly, crawling on my hands and knees towards the flashlight I dropped.

"Oh my God, oh my God," I kept muttering, scanning the room, hoping she would jump out at me. "This can't be happening!" And yet, I knew this was the trepidation that I'd felt. A part of me knew that the rosary was a door.

I pounced on the letters, frantically scattering them around, trying to find anything that explained why these jars would be in this chest. Finally, my eyes caught on the handwriting outside the first letter, and my throat constricted.

It was my penmanship. It was my name.

I looked at the other letters: Sean, Mom, Dad, *Shay*.

"Jesus Christ," I gasped. "What is this?"

I picked up the one with my name on it with trembling fingers and broke the sealing wax.

Millie (Me, obviously),

I know this sounds crazy, I know it's hard to believe, but you don't have time to waste. If you're reading this now, Shay has already gone.

My hand gripped my rosary so hard it nearly broke the skin.

It's scary, I know, but I already wrote the letters. Leave them out for Mom and Dad to find. It'll be hard for them for a while, but I hope my words and the proof I'd put inside them will help. Do not worry about them. We know what will ease their pain. Every detail they will need is in those letters.

I looked back at the letters and wondered why one to Shay was there.

Now, it's time to put on your big girl pants and get your ass in gear, woman.

Shay is counting on you. So, get that dress on, don't forget to wear the corset in place of your bra, don't miss the shoes on the bottom of the chest, straighten your rosary, and pour the powder over your head.

Do not look back; it will only make it worse.

Once you are ready, look for the man in the picture of the pub. You should know his face well enough by now. Yes, you will be in his time. It's too hard to explain it in this letter; you'll have to figure that out later. He will be in The North End of Boston. It might take some time, but you will be able to find him if you start asking around.

Once you find him, tell him you need to find your friend. He will know what to do from there. He's trustworthy. And, honestly, quite terrifying. But you cannot hesitate. You must endure what that time has to offer you. And just know, with some relief, that he is a force that most won't reckon with.

I read the last sentence and set the letter down, my whole body shaking.

It was all unbelievable, but too much had happened to tell me otherwise. I started to look around the attic before remembering not to. Then, with one last nod to everything around me, I began to disassemble everything I once believed.

I eyed the corset, turning it back and forth to find the best way to put it on, wiggling it around until everything seemed in place. A slip went with the garments, so I put that on before fumbling with the dress. At least the short, leather heels went on reasonably quickly. But though it fit well, the whole outfit felt wrong, disorienting me so that I had to grab onto a beam.

Steadying myself, I took everything out of the chest that I needed and dragged it over to the attic's stairs. It would be the first thing my parents saw when they came looking for me. Feeling confident that it was in the correct position, I set the letters neatly on top, along with my folded clothes. I placed my black sneakers in front of it and straightened them.

Giving a little sigh, I sat back on my heels. It was hard to part with the items when I didn't know what lay beyond. This was, by far, the scariest thing I ever had to do. I would have considered myself insane if it wasn't for Shay's disappearance right in front of me.

And I'd done this before. The memory came in bits and pieces so that I wasn't sure what I remembered and what I made up.

I swallowed past the lump in my throat and slid my fingers over the letters and my belongings one last time.

Taking a deep breath, I grabbed the jar. *What's the worst that could happen?*

I shook my head and uncorked the second jar. If it wasn't so scary, I would have delighted in the white powder falling over my head like tiny snowflakes. Instead, I coughed and waved my hand in front of my face to keep it from getting into my eyes and lungs. Nausea hit my stomach like a rock. It was as if an unseen force started pulling my skin, bones, hair, and every fiber of my being in multiple directions. It was the most excruciating thing I'd ever experienced. I was thankful I blocked the memory out when I was a kid.

I scanned the attic, trying to remember everything as my vision began to dim.

God, was it just that morning I told my parents I loved them? It seemed like a lifetime ago. Tears swelled in my eyes as I feared I would never see them again.

Someone else would need to perform in place of me tonight, I thought belatedly. My throat nearly closed with the overwhelming emotions rising in me.

It took seconds when everything went completely black, and a loud ringing pierced my ears, making me recoil in pain. It felt like the world was caving in around me as I imagined the intense eyes of the man I was supposed to find, going over every detail of the face of Thomas O'Connor.

CHAPTER FOUR

Thomas

3 December 1860

Thomas kept his head down against the frigid air, using his hat to shield his face.

"Where ye goin', Tommy?" a lanky Irishman hollered from across the street, causing Thomas to turn towards the wind.

"Feck," Thomas cursed the fierce winter that blew across the street again. He pulled his coat tighter, grateful that he had spent the last three years saving enough coin to buy it. The coat was used, but it was thicker than his last one and had no holes.

"Tremont," Thomas admitted when he was closer to who he now recognized as Joseph Murphy. Murphy smiled at him, skin crinkling around his watery brown eyes, sunken from years of hunger.

"Why would ye do that?" Murphy asked while his hand disappeared in his jacket to pull out a flask. Unscrewing it, he tilted it towards Thomas as if remembering his manners. Thomas shook his head. "Don't ye have enough problems than to be addin' their trouble in the mix?"

"Ye know where I stand, Murphy," Thomas growled, tired of hearing those complain about John Brown. The man was executed a year past, for Christ's sake. When he failed in his raid on Harper's Ferry, attempting to create an uprising in the south to end slavery, he was arrested and executed shortly after.

A memorial for him was at Tremont Temple. Some noteworthy speakers were said to speak on this and the abolition of slavery.

"Freedom should belong to all," Thomas went on.

"I'm just sayin', your people are strugglin' enough." Murphy shrugged, pulling his coat tighter as he shivered. "We don't need those negroes stealin' our jobs too. It'd be a shame if ye got caught up in all that. Don't want to be mixed in their affairs when ye're there, do ye?"

Thomas narrowed his eyes, wondering what Murphy was getting at. "If there's trouble, I suppose it'll be a concern of mine as well. Is there something ye need to be telling me?"

"Of course not, Tommy." There was something odd about Murphy's downcast eyes that Thomas couldn't put his finger on. "Just looking out for ye is all."

Thomas eyed the man, trying to calm the rage percolating beneath his skin, because he knew his people's anti-abolition beliefs were deeply rooted in fear. The Irish didn't have as many jobs as it was, and if the slaves were free, they feared they would take the few they had.

Thomas cracked his knuckles, reminding himself that Murphy was a good man struggling to feed his family after his factory closed—one of many after Lincoln was elected. "Good day, Murphy.

Tell your missus, me Ma and sister will be comin' around for a visit soon."

"She'll like that." Murphy nodded. "Caitlin always likes it when Maggie comes around. Gets her outta doin' some chores." Murphy rolled his eyes and smiled, breaking the tension. He took his hat off and offered his other hand to Thomas. "Try to keep safe out there, Tommy."

Thomas kept his head down for most of the walk to keep the wind from hitting him in the face, going around others when their big dresses or trousers came into his line of sight. And if he was being honest with himself, he didn't want to talk to anyone. Thinking of Brown and what transpired a year ago, his mood was rather glum.

The weather made the short walk feel twice as long, so the sight of the stone building was a welcome sight. Thomas stared at the imposing structure as his breath billowed like smoke and wondered how the attendees would react to an Irish abolitionist in their midst. Murphy's strange behavior had put him on edge.

"Uncle Tommy!" A curly-haired three-year-old came barreling down the sidewalk, dodging those around her and snapping Thomas out of his thoughts. She laughed loudly and leaped, knowing he'd catch her.

He grunted, pretending she was too heavy. "What have ye eaten, lass? Ye almost broke me back." Evaline was getting big, and with all her coats and skirts on, she nearly slipped out of his arms.

"You're silly," she giggled.

Evaline was one of the few that could make Thomas smile. He set her down, happy to see her cheeks pink from the cold. It always made his chest tighten in reassurance whenever he saw her full of life and joy.

"You came." Hiram put his hands in his pockets as his friend straightened.

Thomas' dark eyebrows rose in disbelief. "Did I ever give ye a reason that I wouldn't?"

"No," Hiram admitted, shrugging. They started to walk inside. "Thought your brother might have talked you out of it. But, Lord knows the rest of your people have been."

"Don't give me that shite." Thomas glared. "Ye know where I stand. Why is your head up your ass today?"

Hiram let out a rare laugh, causing a few women to stare openly at him as he walked by. One of them started preening to gain his attention, but only received giggles from the others. Thomas couldn't help but notice she was attractive and a good match. Only if Hiram's sole focus wasn't on the abolition movement. He was distracted by little else.

"You're right," Hiram answered. "My apologies, brother. Sometimes I forget there are descent Irishmen out there."

"Careful," Thomas grumbled. He had had enough of prejudice from everyone else, and didn't want to deal with it from his friend as well.

Hiram's raised his brow. "Have you forgotten your brother?"

Thomas's chest tightened as it always did when he thought of Mikey. The man was a pain in his ass, and all Thomas wanted was for him to grow the feck up. God knew Thomas had to long before he was an adult. "How can I, when I have to keep cleaning up his messes?" Thomas kept an eye on Evaline as the crowd began to surround them, all going through the open doors that led to the main hall. "Me brother doesn't represent the whole lot, though."

Hiram muttered something, but Thomas didn't catch it.

They made it through the doors and began searching for some open seats, squeezing by men and women jostling for spots before the meeting started. A man slammed into Thomas' shoulder in his rush to get to the front, and if it weren't for Hiram holding Evaline's hand, he would have knocked her over.

Thomas swore at him under his breath, and to Thomas' surprise, the man threw back a string of Irish curses over his shoulder as he barreled his way forward.

"Looks like I'm not the only one here," Thomas muttered.

"What's that?" Hiram asked, waving at their group down the row.

Thomas shook his head, thinking it was not important. "She seems to be doin' well lately." Thomas nodded towards Evaline, wanting to change the subject.

"She likes it at Rose's." Hiram glanced at the girl with the affection a father would feel. Hiram never admitted it, but Thomas knew Hiram wished he could have taken her in. Standing next to each other, one wouldn't know any different—their bronzed skin and her caramel curls reminded Thomas of Hiram's in his youth. "Rose lets her help with the baking every now and then. It keeps Eva's mind and hands busy."

"She's able to focus better now?" Thomas asked.

Evaline had been wild and always had trouble staying on one task. Hiram and Thomas often wondered if Eva's erratic behavior was due to the lack of oxygen when her mother had suffocated her or if she had been born like that. They couldn't ask anyone that may have known her—the guards told everyone that she had died at her mother's hands. George and his wife, Rose, had taken her in when they saved her that night.

Hiram shrugged. "She's getting by, and she's happy."

"Of course, she is," an older woman of a short, stocky build said, bending down to smile at the excited girl. "A little love and discipline are good for a child."

"How are you, boys?" George leaned around his wife and shook their hands. "I'm shocked I haven't heard about you getting into trouble lately."

"Give it time." Thomas chuckled, nodding toward the rest of the group.

Jackson and Isaac were there, along with their three sisters, the eldest two sitting alongside their husbands. Thomas didn't see much of them now that they had moved farther into the city. Still, they greeted him affectionately whenever passing, nevertheless.

"Good morning, gentlemen," Mira said to both of them while looking up at Hiram through her lashes. Hiram returned her greeting, and Mira smiled, dimples flashing. Thomas had to hide his grin, knowing Mira had a crush on Hiram since the girl was twelve.

Jackson and Isaac rolled their eyes.

Mira was the youngest of six siblings, the only one who still lived with their parents. Luckily, they were oblivious of their daughter's desires and still let Hiram come around the bakery. Though Hiram was a good man, and they loved him as family, they wanted their daughters to marry men who would raise their social standing, even if marginally. That meant being more selective of a man of their race working in a trade.

Not a dockworker who had to contest for a day's work or go without pay.

Commotion congregated to the podium, causing an exciting increase of chatter as someone ascended the stage. Thomas kept standing, looking over the heads of the crowd to see a wiry man shouting above the public to gain their attention. A hush fell around the Temple as the audience awaited to hear James Redpath's speech against the abolition of slavery. Running his fingers over his muttonchops, the journalist waited for Reverend J. Sella Martin to join him. Born into slavery, Martin had come far and was a well-known black preacher in their area.

Mira sat back beside her parents. Hiram picked Evaline up to see the pair, a reverent expression clouding his features as he whispered to her about their fight for freedom.

The men barely began to speak when discorded shouts started in the front row.

Adrenaline pumped through Thomas's veins before he could comprehend what was unfolding.

"Something isn't right." Thomas leaned closer to Hiram, scanning the crowd.

"What're you thinking?"

Thomas began to spot men sitting throughout the Temple that he hadn't noticed before. He couldn't put his finger on why they stood out—maybe it was the hostility on their faces or the cut of their clothing that spoke of a different class.

Whatever it was, their intentions didn't look agreeable.

Frederick Douglass pushed his way forward, intent on gaining the spot that was promised to him. Addressing the crowd, he tried to begin his speech against slavery, his broad face set sternly against those throwing out insults.

"They're not going to let him speak," Hiram growled.

A man in a nice coat and trousers pushed himself onto the stage.

"Is that Fay?" Thomas asked. Richard Fay was a well-known businessman who often spoke against the abolition of slavery.

"Looks like it."

Fay had pushed Douglass to the side. "I represent the reasoning men of the North and the South!" Fay yelled over the crowd's mixed hisses and applause, solidifying Thomas' suspicion. These were Unionists—merchants and businessmen alike—sabotaging the meeting with their outcries against secession. "Brown was a fool! Any irresponsible persons and political demagogues are to not be allowed to disturb the public peace and misrepresent us abroad!"

Douglass tried to push his way back to the front, his big mane of hair the only thing that could be seen over the crowd that now stood up. Curses rang out everywhere. Douglass yelled over the uproar, trying to give the speech intended for the meeting.

"I cannot be heard over this racket!" Fay yelled, glaring at the dark man by his side.

"When thine enemy thirst, give him drink!" Douglass retaliated.

Men and women abolitionists began to stand on chairs, trying to center the meeting on its intended purpose, a loud chant ringing through the Temple.

"Douglass! Douglass!"

"Perhaps we should go?" Mira's small hand had grabbed her father's arm, fear in her eyes.

"It wouldn't do for us to back down now, daughter," George answered, though his tone didn't lack sympathy.

Thomas' attention was drawn back to Fay as he tried to say something over the praise and insults thrown at him. The front rows began to cheer for him louder, shouting racial slurs at the darker men still standing on the stage.

"Damn them," Hiram hissed, fists clenched as he still held Evaline in the crook of his arm.

Douglass yelled louder. "... It is said the best way to abolish slavery is to obey the law. Shall we obey the blood-hounds of the law who do the dirty work of the slave-catchers?"

"Treason!"

The room burst with mixed reactions, furthering the chaos until there was no possible way for a speech. It was then that Redpath and Franklin Sanborn—a schoolmaster and known abolitionist who helped fund Brown's raid—cornered Fay, looking as if they intended to throw him out.

Cries went up around the room, the Unionists getting more violent. Men pushed one another and screamed slurs at anyone who opposed them.

"Get off the stage!" one of them bellowed, ending it with a racial profanity towards Douglass that set off curses around the room.

"I know your masters..." Douglass penetrated the crowd with his intense stare. "I have served the same master that you are serving.... Cast aside with indignation the wild and guilty fantasy that man owns property in man, even in that stout, big-fisted fellow down there, who has just insulted me."

"Go on—!" a merchant yelled the racial slur that had Thomas's jaw clenching.

"The freedom of all mankind was written on the heart of the finger of God!" Douglass retaliated.

"Was that from Exodus?" Hiram asked Thomas.

"Hell, if I'd know."

The room began to buzz like a shaken-up hive, the white Unionists turning on their black counterparts to throw them out.

Something slammed into Thomas' side, jolting him forward. He swore, steadying Rose after her husband lost balance from trying to get a man off of Isaac. He was a scruffy white man, surprisingly tougher than the businessmen closer to the stage.

Jackson was trying to calm Mira down, dragging her back so she wouldn't get hit, while his other sisters were being guided out of the chaos by their husbands.

Thomas hopped over the chair into the row behind him and grabbed the man by his shirt, tearing him away from Isaac.

"I had him!" Isaac spat, wiping the blood from his lip.

Thomas held onto the man as he tried to turn away. "Is this how ye treat your fellow countrymen?"

The man sneered and spit on Thomas. "Ye are a goddamn traitor to your race and your country!"

Thomas shoved him away in surprise, too stunned by the Irishman to stop him from causing trouble elsewhere.

Hiram had to pull a crying Evaline off him and handed her over to Rose.

"Don't leave!" she sobbed, reaching out for him. Thomas's heart squeezed as rage fueled him. That girl didn't deserve to see this. Especially after everything she'd already been through.

Hiram whispered in her ear, placating her enough to understand he'd see her later.

"Shite," Thomas grumbled. "Ye should leave before it gets any worse." He nodded to George, who started guiding Rose and a pale Mira, protecting the women the best he could through the pandemonium around them.

"They can't get away with this," Jackson growled.

Their attention was drawn back to the stage when more shouts erupted. Douglass pointed to a man in the crowd. "If I were a slave driver and got a hold of that man for five minutes, I would let more light through his skin than ever got there before."

Hiram went after a man dragging a light-skinned black woman out of her seat. Thomas saw her slap the Unionist when a sharp tug on his shirt pulled him back so firmly that he fell over a chair. Thomas pulled himself upright, fury flaming his veins. Isaac's fist collided with the man's jaw and went down.

"I had it," Thomas said, raising his eyebrows at Isaac, who only shook his head.

"We gotta help him," Isaac said, pointing to Douglass in the midst of being dragged off the stage.

"Feck!" Thomas shouted, already running up the aisle without thinking about the consequences.

Several men had Douglass by the arms. Thomas was almost there when someone's elbow slammed into his nose, causing blood to spout down his chin. He roared, slamming his fist into the man's face, propelling him forward on his way to the stage.

"Three cheers for liberty!" Douglass managed to shout.

A roar of protest met him. "Three cheers for Governor Wise!"

A new group of men entered the Temple—their black hats and long coats identifying them as the police—yelling for everyone to clear out. When people didn't move fast enough, they were ripped out of their seats, the women screaming at being treated poorly.

"All out!"

"Blow them up!"

The shouts rang around the room. Thomas looked back at the stage, and his stomach dropped, finding Douglass being dragged down the stairs by his hair. He took a step towards him when he was suddenly cut off by a prominent figure blocking his path.

"Dia duit, deartháir."

Thomas's eyes focused, and disbelief washed over him. "Mikey," Thomas rasped. "What in the bloody hell are ye doing here?" He grabbed his brother's arm, trying to drag him away as if he was still a child. It was hard to believe Mikey wasn't little anymore, even as a grown man nearly as tall as him. His brother barely budged.

"Stop!" Mikey shoved Thomas back. "Don't ye see what ye and your filthy negros are doing?"

"This has gone on long enough. Go home." He grabbed Mikey's shirt, shoving him away so that he stumbled.

Mikey's blue eyes flashed dangerously, the only warning before his fist cracked against Thomas' jaw. Thomas tackled him, and they rolled on the floor before the stage, not hearing the yelling around them. Thomas sat up first, punching Mikey in the face several times before his brother bucked him off. Mikey stood up, staggering backward as blood dripped into his eye from the split in his brow.

"What are ye doing here?" Thomas asked again.

Mikey spat to the side and squinted at the policemen gaining on them.

He began to back away. "They hired us."

"Who?" But Thomas already knew. It had been common knowledge for a while that the merchants and manufacturers were starting to worry about possible secession, and many others were impacted by stock prices decreasing rapidly. It wasn't long before they started to blame it on the abolitionists. He just couldn't believe his brother would team up with them. "They are just using ye."

Mikey smiled, throwing his hands out to encompass the room. "It's money lining me pockets. We had enough. Who gives a shite where it comes from? In me book, I'm getting paid to take them down, as I should."

"What would Ma think of ye if she heard ye were running with a hired mob?"

Mikey's smile faded to a scowl. "And what if I told Da that ye are running around with darkies? Ye think ye'd have his respect then?"

"I have nothing to hide!" Thomas yelled, moving so a man and his wife could get by. "And we are grown-ass men. It's time ye start acting like one and quit this charade. Ye are better than that, deartháir."

"Believe what ye want, Tommy boy. Ye always have." His jaw ticked, and his muscles strained as if he held back what he really wanted to say.

Thomas squinted at his brother, trying to see the young boy who used to play pranks on him as a child. He was always so happy before they'd left Ireland.

"Clear out!" an officer shouted.

"Get off me!" Thomas turned towards Hiram's voice, finding two officers struggling to remove his big friend.

"Go on," Mikey sneered. "Everyone already knows where your loyalty lies."

Thomas raised his fist, getting in his brother's face, but couldn't bring himself to do it. "We're done. Ye hear me? Don't come back home. I'm done with your shite."

Hurt flashed across Mikey's features. It happened so fast that Thomas almost didn't see it before a blank expression slammed down like an iron gate, closing himself off from Thomas like he had been doing for years. Mikey backed up. "Keep pretending ye are the good one, Tommy. But ye are just as rotten as me. Ye're fooling no one."

Thomas paled, remembering when times were harder and what he had to do to keep food on his family's table. Mikey noticed he hit a nerve, and his sneer made Thomas' stomach turn as he disappeared into the thinning crowd.

Thomas went to go after him, but curses drew him toward Hiram. Mikey was long gone, and he could still stop Hiram from causing any more trouble for himself.

"We're going," he snapped at the men holding his friend.

"Control your man, paddy." The officer spat on Thomas's feet but let go of Hiram. Hiram pulled his other arm away from the other officer.

"It's not worth it," Thomas muttered, silently praying Hiram would leave it alone.

The officers already turned away, yelling at everyone else to get out. People shoved their way out the doors, some shouting, others crying, as they all tried to escape.

A shout rang out when they emerged onto the street. It was Jackson calling them, standing off to the side with Isaac. "Where you've been?" He ran his hands over his cropped hair, agitated.

Hiram growled, punching the outside of the building. "Every time. Those bastards set us back. I'm sick of this bullshit."

"Settle, brother," Isaac said, resting his hand on Hiram's shoulder.

"Reverend Martin said we'll continue the meeting at his church this evening. We won't let them win."

Hiram stared at him, his quick breaths causing his big chest to expand quickly. Thomas watched as the words sunk in, and Hiram's breathing began to calm.

Jackson nodded, waiting for his friend to calm down. "We're not beat yet."

CHAPTER FIVE

Emilia

10 April 1861

The dark began to fade, pulled away slowly as if it were a veil—a glimmer of light blurring my vision.

"Is she alive?" a woman asked close to my face, who sounded remarkably Irish.

"Don't know," another woman answered farther away. Yes, they were most definitely Irish accents. "Any jewelry?"

Someone picked up my hand, searching.

"Don't see none." I thanked the Lord that she hadn't seen my necklace yet.

"Is there a foulness about her? Maybe take her dress."

Someone's fingers came close to my nose, and I recoiled, blinking rapidly as shapes began to appear before me.

"See that?" the one closest to me asked. Her fingers disappeared quickly.

Something sour permeated my nostrils, and I scrunched up my face, wanting to pull away, but my limbs were too heavy. A large globe swam through the darkness. I tried to focus on it. The shape slowly turned into a face as my stomach recoiled from the travel back in time. All my senses hit me at once, and I wasn't sure how much more I could take.

"What year is it?" I croaked, my dry throat screaming in pain.

"What she say?" the woman farthest from me asked.

"She asked what year it is."

They were talking to each other as if I couldn't hear them.

"How strange. Why'd she want to know that? Daft, ye think?"

They both crouched in front of me as I finally pulled myself into a sitting position. Small stones scraped my arm and dug into my hand when I pushed myself against the building behind me. My vision was almost back to normal. I was in a dirty ally with clotheslines hanging around us. And with the sun as high as it was, I guessed it was mid-day.

"I just hurt my head," I mumbled, not wanting to scare them. "I'm trying to figure out if I can remember the year is all."

"She talks strange." The woman who said that turned towards the other, ignoring me.

"What year?" I said more clearly.

"'61," the one farthest from me answered. I eyed her, remembering she was the one who wanted to take my jewelry. Her thin face was made more severe by her dark hair tied back, revealing a long neck that dipped into a dress several sizes too big. She looked older than the one nearest to me, but I couldn't tell.

I nodded, pretending this wasn't a shock to my system.

"A man did this to ye, aye?" The woman closest to me leaned in close to my face, and I could smell the sourness of her breath. I tried to breathe out of my mouth and shook my head. Her blue eyes flicked between mine as if she was trying to catch me in a lie.

"She's a pretty one." She turned to the other lady, making her dark blonde curls dance around her head. She had it tied back, but her unruly hair seemed to escape. "Think we could use her?"

"Excuse me?"

"The men would love ye." She turned back to me, running her hand through my dark hair. "You're exotic enough. You'd have men in your room every hour."

Heat rushed to my face as I realized I was talking to two prostitutes. They were dressed modestly—though their dresses were a bit worn—which surprised me. I would have expected them to show more skin.

"I'm sorry, I don't do that." I shook my head and cringed. My brain felt like it was slamming into my skull.

The brown-haired one came closer and grabbed my chin in her two fingers. She turned my head back and forth, scanning my face. "Ye sure?"

"Positive," I mumbled, pressing my hand to my stomach as a new case of nausea overtook me.

Her brown eyes narrowed. "Ye with child?"

"No!" I shouted, making them both jump. "Sorry. It just must have been from hitting my head. I'm fine. Not pregnant."

They both stared at me as if I was insane.

"Ye a virgin or somethin'?" the blonde asked. She grabbed my hands and leaned in. She did seem rather sweet, and I wondered how young she was. "Ye might bring in more customers."

I straightened, my chest tightening in embarrassment. "I don't see how that's any of your business—"

"Those will bring the men in," the brunette stated, eyeing my breasts. "Ye've been fed well. The men will love your curves."

They both stared at my figure, appraising me like a show-horse and making me the most uncomfortable I've ever been while dressed modestly. I pulled my hands out of her grip and pushed myself off the ground, standing on shaking legs. They rose with me, taking steps back, while eyeing me from top to bottom.

"I'm actually looking for a man," I stated, changing the subject.

"Is it the one who left ye in this ally here?" the blonde asked.

I tried not to think about why she came to that conclusion. "No. A friend told me he could help me. His name is Thomas O'Connor."

"Tommy boy!" The blonde clapped. "Oh, we do love our Tommy. He keeps the mean bastards away, and he's so gentle. Nessa tells me that his hands really do work wonders, and the way that he—"

I held up my hands, not wanting to hear what else she had to say about "Tommy boy" and what his hands could do. "My friend might be in trouble. I was told Mr. O'Connor might be able to help me find her."

"Why would they say that?" the blonde squinted at me and then looked at the brunette.

"I—um—" I stumbled over my words as the brunette sized me up. I felt this lady was in charge or, at the very least, well respected.

"She a negro?" the brunette asked.

"Black, yes. Why would that—"

She gave me a strange look. "He can help ye. But if ye want us to find him, ye'll have to give us a lil' somethin'."

I was hesitant to ask what that might be. "I won't have sex with anyone. I'll find him myself, if that's the case. Just point me in the direction of the North End."

They glanced at each other quickly, a silent exchange happening between them. "Shame." The brunette pursed her lips, her brown eyes sliding down my body. "Ye do us a wee favor, and we'll point ye in the right direction. What would ye suggest?"

I looked between the two, struggling to think of something that didn't have to do with my body.

"I can sing..."

"Hmm, that might do. Will ye sing in your drawers?"

"My...oh!" My heart raced when I realized they meant the weird white shorts I wore under my dress. They were loose with lace trim on the ends, ending just below my knee. I was nervous because they tied around the waist but were split down the middle. If I weren't careful, I'd be flashing my goods. "Can I wear my slip or something over them? With my corset too?"

"Aye," the blonde said. "That should work fine over your slip."

"Right," I nodded, cheeks reddening again when I realized I put my clothes on wrong. I'd have to fix that when I was alone again. All things considered, I dressed with less on in public before. Nothing too scandalous, but the usual short shorts and crop tops modern women wore. As long as these two women kept their word, I could sing without worrying about my appearance. "Okay, it's a deal."

The brunette spat in her hand and gave it to me to shake. I tried not to cringe and did the same. I couldn't help but notice how her hands were dry and calloused compared to my soft ones.

"I don't believe we properly introduced ourselves. I'm Madam Kelly, but ye can call me Nora, and this here is Bridget."

"They call me Biddy," the blonde smiled and hugged me.

"Hello, Biddy," I smiled back, realizing I might like this girl. She seemed so sweet, and I wondered what made her decide to take this path. "I'm Emilia…" I trailed off, realizing I couldn't give her my last name without her thinking I was related to Thomas. That'd be fine, except Thomas had no idea who I was and would probably think I was insane if he heard that a strange woman was looking for him *and* had his name attached to hers.

"C'mon, this way." Biddy grabbed my arm, seemingly not interested in my last name, and began to lead me out of the ally.

Stepping onto the sidewalk of the street, it was instantly brighter, the sun lighting up the brick buildings in a warm glow. It was unseasonably warm for April, for which I was grateful if I was to be singing in the streets in my underwear.

The faint odor I had smelled in the ally was increasingly pungent here, making me scrunch my nose. It took me a minute to realize it was horse manure. I silently hoped I would get used to the smell if I was to be in the nineteenth century until I found Shay. But, of course, if I found her quickly, we might be able to leave before we had to get used to any part of this time.

"Ye not from around here?" Biddy leaned in close to me, the top of her blonde head reaching my chin. She had to be just over five feet tall with her shoes on. I looked at Nora and realized she was significantly shorter than I as well.

"No." I shook my head, trying to come up with something. "My family moves around a lot…." I thought of my Italian ancestors and ignored the nagging sensation that I had forgotten something vital about them.

She nodded but didn't inquire more, and I let out a sigh of relief. I'd have to formulate a better story if everyone was going to believe it.

They led me down a road lined with tall brick and sided buildings—each tavern, store, and inn adorned with old wooden signs. The street was fascinating, radiating an outlandish, old-world feel I'd only partially felt in a museum. However, it was a bit stinky and dirtier than I'd imagined.

"Where is everyone?" I asked. The street was quiet except for a few men walking down the sidewalks and a faint click of a horse's hooves ringing against the bricks somewhere down the road.

"Don't ye worry." Biddy patted my arm. "This street will be bustlin' come nightfall."

"Oh, joy." I gave a tight smile, thinking about how many people would be leering at me later.

"Here we are," Nora said, swiveling in our direction. She stood, her back straight as she waited for us to reach a door that was only a few buildings down from the ally I woke up in. She reminded me of a raptor, constantly circling its prey until it was ready to pounce and devour it.

I approached hesitantly, walking behind Biddy as we neared the wooden door—using the small woman as if she was a shield against whatever lay beyond. Two rows of windows went three stories up—glass hazy from what looked like age and grime—concealing the deplorable acts committed behind them. I shivered, goose bumps covering my flesh as she opened the door and beckoned us inside.

The room was significantly darker, and I had to give my eyes a few moments to adjust before I made out several wooden tables and chairs scattered throughout, and a bar with no one running it. Cheap perfume, stale alcohol, and something foul that I didn't want to think too hard about filled the empty room, so strong that I fought the urge to cover my nose.

"Where's everyone else?" I asked.

"Oh, they're upstairs," Biddy smiled and patted me on the arm. "Probably getting a wee bit more rest or primping for our customers tonight."

I nodded, ignoring the rise of anxiety I was putting myself through. Maybe I could still leave and find my dad's ancestor alone.

"Ye'll join us upstairs, aye?" Nora asked, almost daring me to contradict her.

"Sure." My heart sank at the predicament I got myself into.

At that moment, a young girl ran down the stairs, dress billowing behind her in her haste to get somewhere. When she spotted us, she stumbled, quickly righting herself before straightening her hair and clothes.

"Sorry, Madam Kelly." She curtsied and kept her eyes down.

"Where ye goin' in such a fuss?" Nora snapped.

I looked at her in surprise, my suspicions answered not only by the use of her formal title but the way she scolded the young girl. I wondered whose child she was.

"Just outside, Madam."

"Go," Nora snapped, sending the girl out on quick feet lest she was scolded again.

"We're waiting for her cycle," Nora said, turning towards me. "Then maybe she'll start pulling her weight around here."

I felt the blood rush from my face, and my stomach turned. That girl couldn't be ten. If she started early, men could lie with her within the year.

"Is that necessary?" I asked, unable to keep quiet about it.

"Oh—" Biddy nodded. "She'd bring the men for sure. And if we kept quiet, we might get some more coin from others if they thought she still a virgin."

"Hush." Nora swatted Biddy's head, causing the girl to flinch.

"They just did that for me, is all I'm sayin'," Biddy mumbled, fixing her hair.

My heart pounded in my ears as I wished I could take that poor girl away.

"Her ma is upstairs, anyhow," Nora said. "She can decide what to do with her wean."

Something told me that Nora was lying, and when the time came, Nora would have every say in what would be done with the girl.

"Of course," I nodded, not wanting to cross her. It was her establishment, and I still needed to find Shay.

We headed up the stairs, the wood creaking under our feet and alerting everybody of our arrival. When we neared the first landing, quiet voices and laughter began to drift down. Nora opened the first door to the right, and the room went silent. Several women lounged on the bed and in a chair, looking as if they were enjoying a brief moment of normalcy that we suddenly interrupted.

"Meet our new act of the night, ladies," Nora said, using her hand as if she was displaying me.

They eyed me up and down, their cold stares dropping the room a few degrees. I repressed a shiver that went through me.

"What's she gonna do?" the nearest one asked. She leaned over in her chair and picked up the hem of my dress between her fingers, looking thoroughly unimpressed. "A bit boring, aye?"

"She can sing!" Biddy clapped, delighted to give them the news.

The woman scoffed, rolling her green eyes. She looked away, brushing her red hair back.

"C'mon, Nessa. Lay off her," Biddy whined. "Play nice."

"Oh, shut your gob," Nessa snapped, sitting up as if she was about to lunge at Biddy.

I took a step back, not wanting to get in between them. Nessa sneered and leaned back in her chair, obviously pleased by my unease.

"Enough," Nora snapped, causing all the women to turn towards her. "Ye will welcome Miss Emilia here, ye hear?"

"Can she even sing?" a brunette on the bed asked, fixing her shift over her legs. They were all in their undergarments, unconcerned about the skin on display.

"I'm not putting me earnings on it." Nessa smirked, causing the rest to giggle.

My cheeks flared red with anger, and I could not listen to them anymore. "I can sing now."

I looked to Nora, who raised her brow and gave a brief nod of approval. The girls sat back, looking bored.

I racked my brain for a song they might appreciate and came up with one of my favorites by Camila Cabello.

I looked at the floor and grabbed my necklace, drawing strength from its familiarity. My voice erupted throughout the room, and everyone straightened, their attention drawn to me like a moth to a flame. I smiled, finally feeling a part of myself set free, and I closed my eyes to soak it all in. I softened my voice seductively. The silence in the room hung heavy as a cloak on my shoulders, comforting me. I used its weight to unleash the rest of the lyrics with full force.

I let the last line drift through the room before opening my eyes. When I did, a few girls actually had their mouths hanging open.

I smiled and shrugged. "Would that work?"

"I told ye!" Biddy clapped, turning to each of the girls as if she had already heard me sing. "Teach ye to doubt me."

"Ye will sing that tonight, aye?" Nora asked, clasping her hands in front of her.

"Sure," I said, thinking. "Though it might sound better if the girls sang a few parts that aren't supposed to be mine."

Nora nodded, agreeing with me. "Just tell them what should be done. Get ready, ladies. Ye should be busy tonight." She left the room, closing the door behind her.

"I'm not singin' that," Nessa mumbled. "Where ye hear that? Should stick to the songs our men like."

"You don't have to," I shrugged, stepping back to let the women move around the room without getting in their way. "I'm hopefully here for just the night. I'm not trying to take any business from you. Nora thinks my singing might bring you more business, actually."

Nessa rolled her eyes. "Like ye could take any man from me." She eyed me up and down with disgust, infuriating me. I *hated* women like her.

"C'mon," Biddy beckoned, grabbing my arm before I could say anything. "Ye can get ready in me room."

I glanced back and saw them giggling together as if we were in high school. I gave Nessa the middle finger and was pleased to shut the door on her shocked face.

Biddy's room was just a few doors down.

"It's not much," she said shyly, but with a smile. I looked around, the room big enough to hold a full-size bed, armoire, small vanity table, and fireplace. It was modest in appearance and cleaner than I expected it to be. She sat down on the only chair in the room and began to take off her shoes. "Ye may sit wherever ye'd like."

I eyed the wooden bedframe with its plain sheets and wondered how often they were washed. Every unmentionable act that could have been committed on it flitted through my mind. I suppressed a cringe. I didn't want to sit on it, but my feet were unused to the shoes, and I still felt a little weak from my travel. Looking for any soil marks, I perched my butt on its edge, taking care not to touch any of it with my skin without insulting Biddy.

"Will ye like to curl your hair?" Biddy asked, stretching her feet out in front of her as if they were sore.

"Oh," I said, taken off guard. "Do you think I should?"

She eyed me up and down, more intrigued than anything. "Aye." She nodded. "Take off your dress, and we'll see what we have to work with, but I think some curl would be quite pretty. We can bring it up a bit, too."

I agreed, smiling.

"Mmm," Biddy hummed under her breath. "I wish I had your figure." She shook her head as she twisted my hair around a hot iron that she let cool a bit after having it in the fire. After the first few times she proved my hair wasn't going to burn off, I stopped flinching.

I looked down as if seeing my body for the first time. I never considered it to be the most attractive. My breasts were decent but not overly large, my waist was thin, yet it stuck out a bit when I sat down, and my hips were curvy, but not so much as to attract more attention. Yet when I compared myself to Biddy's small frame, I couldn't help but notice how much I stood out. Not only was I darker in appearance, but I was probably as tall as many of their men. And my figure was filled out where the women here were less so, all because I had proper nourishment and a healthy lifestyle.

"Your beautiful," I said, meaning it. Biddy's thin face held an innocence that couldn't be ignored, while her soft blue eyes glimmered sweetly. I had no doubt as to why the men came to her.

"Ye're too kind." She blushed, something I was surprised to see. "Where ye from?"

"Oh, well, I'm Italian," I replied honestly. "But I wasn't born there."

Biddy set down the iron. "There. Let's just..." Biddy stopped talking, putting pins in her mouth as she twisted the sides of my hair, pinning it up as the back of my hair flowed down in curls. "Just a couple here..." She pulled a few ringlets out around my neck and in front, so they delicately caressed my face and neck. Finally, she stood back, hands on hips with pursed lips, and studied me. "Mighty fine." She smiled at her work, and I couldn't help but straighten at her appraisal. "The men's eyes will be drawn to your neck here." Her hand caressed a long curl down my throat, making me shiver. I wasn't sure I wanted those men getting any ideas but refrained from telling her that.

Instead, I asked if I could see and looked around for a mirror.

Biddy's smile faded, turning serious. She went to the door and looked out, for what, I didn't know. My heart began to race at her odd behavior. Finally, the door clicked shut, and she turned to me, shoulders set straight as if on a mission.

"Can ye keep a secret?" she asked, wringing her hands together. Even with her nervousness, excitement spread across her features.

I agreed, watching her movements like a wild filly ready to bolt. That was apparently good enough for her because she quickly went to the bed, lifting the mattress until she found something underneath it. She pulled a small mirror out that couldn't be as big as my palm.

"I took this off one of the men one night. He was piss drunk, so I fumbled through his coat, curious, ye know?" She shrugged, smiling at the little mirror. "If the others found out, they'd take it for sure. Or sell it, the wee whores."

My jaw dropped at her admission, dumbfounded that an object I would probably toss without care could be so admired among them. *Cherish the small things.* I couldn't let myself to forget that again.

Biddy must have taken my look of shock as one of excitement because she shoved it at me. "Here, look."

"Can you hold it?" I asked, taking a step back so I could see more than a section of my face at a time.

"Thank you," I said, admiring her work. I would have never worn my hair this way in my time—preferring to wear it straight or in loose waves—yet it accentuated my face, while the loose ringlets drew attention to my neck. I had to give it to her; she knew what she was doing.

"Ye should take your dress off," Biddy said, hiding the mirror quickly.

"Right," I said, fumbling to remove it. "Actually, do you think I could use..." I let it drift off when I realized there might not be a bathroom here. "Do you have somewhere I can pee?" A blush spread across my cheeks at having to admit this, but I had to go for some time now, and I thought it could give me a minute to fix my dress without her noticing.

"Janey Mac!" Biddy exclaimed, looking contrite, which confused me. "Where are me manners? Ye can use me pot, I'll take it out for ye later and show ye were the privy is for next time." She bent down, pulled out a small chamber pot, and set it on the floor. She straightened with a smile before starting to get ready herself.

"Can you give me a minute?" I asked, realizing she wasn't going to leave the room.

"Oh, aye! I forget how shy ye are. Just set it outside the door when you're done. Use some of the newspaper there, if ye like."

Biddy left the room, her skirts trailing behind her, and I let out a sigh of relief. She was a nice girl, but I hadn't had a moment to myself since waking up. *What was I to do next?* I groaned as my bladder screamed at me to focus on the immediate need for action. I removed my dress and slip and inspected the pot.

"Am I supposed to squat?" I mumbled, walking around the pot as if it held the answer to some scientific equation. I eyed the newspaper, thinking she wanted me to read it when I went to the bathroom. But when I picked it up, I noticed that pieces of it were ripped off. "What in the world?" I opened it, noting that the entire right side was missing, and then looked back at the pot. Realization dawned on me, and I cringed. "Okay, there's always a first for everything." I ripped a piece off the newspaper and squatted, realizing that the split in my white drawers was used for this reason. "Good God, this is ridiculous..."

Though that first experience wasn't as hard as I thought it'd be, I was reluctant to find out what this strange, new world had in store for me next. My silent prayer was for my singing to draw Shay to me, and I wouldn't need to help Nora for more than a night.

CHAPTER SIX

Thomas

11 April 1861

"There'll be war," Hiram growled. Thomas rubbed his temples, wanting to take the liquor from his friend's hands. Hiram had always brought up the topic of war when he drank too much. In December, the secession of South Carolina from the Union awakened a deep, repressed desire in Hiram for immediate action. Even more so than Thomas, and Hiram expressed it whenever there was a lull in their day. Thomas's blood boiled with almost the same intensity as his friend's, though he dealt with it quietly and with a mind that thought three steps ahead.

Thomas stared into his ale while listening to Hiram's rant, ignoring the other lads who eyed some of the scrubbers that had just walked in. Most of the taverns on North Street were filled this time of night. Frequented by sailors and Boston's workingmen, it was common to see the prostitutes on the prowl and even more common to find the men in bed with them.

Thomas took a long pull of the ale, his muscles screaming from working all day on the docks, and leaned back in his chair, closing his eyes for a minute.

"What do we have here?" Sam muttered, elbowing Hiram into silence and pointing to the women who walked in. "Why don't you beautiful ladies come join us?"

Thomas opened his eyes just in time to see the two lasses look at each other and smile.

"Are you listening to me at all?" Hiram snapped, glaring at Sam.

"What?" Sam looked at Hiram, exasperated. "Are you gonna start the war yourself? And if you did manage that, d'you think they're really gonna let us colored fight?" He held his hands up when Hiram's golden eyes nearly flashed crimson. "C'mon, don't you think I want it as much as you, brother? I just think we need a little fun, is all."

George sat next to Thomas, staring at the table. As a freed slave straight out of the south, he wanted to fight just as severely as the younger men around him, but there was no sense in it if the government wouldn't let them. "Y'all need to shut up."

Hiram shook his head and took another pull of his drink, ignoring everyone around him.

Sam turned to the two women who joined them at the table, their perfume enveloping them. Up this close, their heavy makeup did little to cover the pockmarks inflicted on them from the pox years ago, as their usual amusement with Sam brightened their eyes.

"C'mere," Sam grabbed the brunette closest to him, making her squeal in a fit of giggles. "How are you tonight, Ellie? You're looking beautiful as always."

Ellie smacked his chest playfully, but her face fell into a pout. "There's a new lass."

"A new girl?" Sam's brows rose as he glanced at Olive, who now perched on Hiram's lap.

"Oh, that's right." Olive nodded, pushing her brown hair over her shoulder in aggravation. "That gypsy bitch gonna steal all our men," she simpered, placing her palm on Hiram's cheek to get him to look at her.

"I'm sure you have nothing to worry about," Hiram muttered while pulling her hand away from his face, the thoughts of war probably still on his mind.

"Gypsy?" Thomas asked, sitting up straight. He'd heard of a group who had left years ago.

"Aye," Ellie nodded, wanting all of the men's attention on her. "That's what the talk around town is. Foreigner, most like, with her exotic look."

"Did the lass say she was?" Thomas asked, irritated by the constant gossip.

"'Course not," Ellie replied bitterly, brushing something off her sleeve. "But she looks like 'em, I say. Said she was Italian or some such. The damned hussy is singin' the men into her bed."

"Does she keep at it while they tumble?" Thomas wondered, more intrigued than he'd like to admit.

"Well, not hers, exactly," Olive puffed. "But the wee wenches in Mistress Nora's house."

"Aye..." Thomas trailed off in thoughtful understanding. It must have given Ellie an itch knowing that her competition had just raised the stakes. "What's in it for the lass, then?"

"Dunno," Ellie pouted again, tiring of the subject. "Rather bore, she is. Who wants a lass who can sing if she doesn't satisfy his needs?" She nuzzled Sam's neck, drawing his attention away from the subject, and straight to where her hand was in his lap.

Thomas and Hiram shared a look, communicating silently as they often did. Thomas placed his coin on the table as Hiram maneuvered Olive off his lap.

"Where ye goin'?" Olive whined, holding onto Hiram's arm. He moved her small hand to his elbow and guided her around the table to George. He'd done it so skillfully that she didn't realize he was depositing her onto George's lap until the last second.

"We're calling it a night, ladies." Hiram gave a tight smile.

Thomas stood, covering his grin as George sputtered protests. George avoided the harlots, and didn't quite know where to rest his hands with Olive in his lap. Thomas patted him on the shoulder, knowing George was worried about Rose. She would surely murder him if he did anything with a scrubber. There was no doubt George would have her off his lap before they made it out the door. "Goodnight, a chara."

Olive grabbed Thomas' arm, pleading with her brown eyes. "Don't ye want to stay?"

"Maybe next time, lovely."

Olive's pale cheeks pinkened. Thomas didn't often take one to bed that wasn't Nessa, but when he did, he was well aware of the other girls appraising stares.

They left without another glance at Sam, knowing he was too preoccupied with Ellie to give them another thought.

"So, we're finding this gypsy, eh?" Hiram asked. He had his head down, hands in his pockets, not looking for the woman.

"Aye," Thomas answered, walking right towards Nora's street section.

"Why?"

"Dunno," Thomas admitted. "Curious, I guess? We can take a look and leave."

That had Hiram lifting his head. "You don't get curious." He squinted at his friend. "Why go through all the trouble?"

"Ye're saying ye're not wondering why a gypsy is in town?" Thomas asked. "Or what the lass looks like?"

The band that had occupied the city had left before Thomas arrived. He'd been interested in the traveling group since he'd heard what happened years ago. A bloody affair that left one dead and the others hightailing it out of the city. No word of who did it. Whoever it was scared the shite out of them, and they hadn't been back since.

Until now, it seemed.

Hiram shrugged. "Figured she was a foreigner. You know how people talk, start making up shit."

Thomas nodded but couldn't ignore his odd desire to find out about this woman. If she was one of them. It was a distraction from everything else, at the very least. He could worry about that later.

Several fiddlers were playing, creating a crowd so that Thomas and Hiram had to push their way through dancing bodies. It thinned out enough that they could walk freely. As they passed each door, those intoxicated could be heard hollering inside the buildings. They kept walking when a crash erupted from a tavern to their left, curses of men fighting inside.

North Street—previously known as Ann Street before it was renamed in '52, after a particularly colossal raid by Boston's police—was notoriously known for being Boston's red-light district. The change of name, however, did little to persuade the occupants to change their ways.

The street and adjoining alleys were filled with taverns, inns, and enough brothels that a man could walk into a door, and he'd indeed find a woman to take him in. From workingmen meeting in the taverns to criminals running the streets, it swarmed with people from different walks of life.

Dock Square often brought sailors from the sea, bringing profit to many businesses. Those with quiet dispositions should have avoided it entirely, and those with high morals and religious beliefs described the occupants of that territory as barbaric heathens and common criminals. Thomas didn't give one shite what they thought. The rumors were probably true anyhow.

A new crowd was up ahead, growing outside an establishment, as a husky, powerful voice broke through the chatter around them. They pushed their way through the crowd, their broad shoulders separating the men and women with little care. A few curses about their size fell on deaf ears. Thomas didn't care if the others could see, as long as he made it to the front.

The gypsy's voice pulled Thomas in like a siren, drawing his feet to her exotic beauty until he stood before her, staring straight into her dark eyes. Thomas paused, his body incapable of moving as she stared back, her wide eyes traveling over his mussy black hair, to his threadbare clothes and muddy boots. Her perusal sent a surge of adrenaline through him. His jaw clenched with annoyance at his own reaction.

A faint flush spread across her cheeks and delectably down her neck. Her voice wavered. Thomas's head cocked to the side, wondering if that was usual. Those dark eyes closed, and her voice strengthened now that she wasn't looking at him. Thomas squinted at her, trying to figure out why a woman with her reputation would be so timid.

He used that brief moment to take in her form—from the soft curve of her tan shoulders to the swell of her full breasts squeezing out of the top of the corset. Her slender waist ended in round hips that swayed to the bawdy song she sang. Thomas had never seen a woman quite like her before, standing up on a crate, a voice of honey pouring out of her mouth.

He swallowed. Even the gypsy's curves moved in ways that made his breath catch. Thomas studied her features, marveling at the possessiveness he felt for a lass he didn't know. The small fire nearby lit her skin up, revealing an unusual smoothness. She was all angles but had a softness to her curves that he suddenly wanted to cover up. He squeezed his hand into a fist, wary that it might do something stupid. Like, weaving itself through her hair.

The crowd squeezed around them, trying to get a better view of the new lass. Thomas felt an urge to pull her from the crate and away from their lewd remarks.

"Tommy?" Hiram asked by his side.

Thomas ignored him, imagining his teeth grazing over her jaw. His own clenched, threatening to break his teeth in an effort to shut down those thoughts of her. He shook his head, ashamed of himself, without really knowing why. She'd picked the profession, and he'd been with plenty of scrubbers.

There was no way she had known the band of traveling gypsies. This woman would have been a babe two decades ago. And Olive didn't mention any others. This woman was more likely a lass finding her way in this shitty city.

Thomas made himself turn away even as the expanse of golden skin flashed in his mind.

"She's a beauty," Hiram said as Thomas opened the door to Nora's bar.

Hiram's comment irritated Thomas, but he didn't know why. "Aye," he admitted, unwilling to reveal just how far his thoughts had gone.

"So, that's it?" Hiram asked, a line forming between his brows. "What now?"

"Why, isn't it our Tommy?" a sultry voice purred. Nessa pulled herself from a man's lap and lowered her skirts as she sauntered to Thomas. "What brings ye here?" She ran her hands up his chest, grasping his suspenders, and pulled him down so that his face just about grazed hers.

Thomas gently grasped her hands and extricated himself so he could straighten. The gypsy's voice fell silent outside, but he focused on the woman in front of him. "I need to speak with Madam Nora."

"Why?" Nessa lowered her hazel eyes, fluttering her lashes. "I can handle ye well enough."

Thomas caught her hands that started to explore his chest again. "Oh, I know ye can, doll," he rumbled, voice still husky from the woman outside rather than from the memory of Nessa underneath him. Nessa purred, no doubt thinking the latter. It didn't help that his eyes roamed over her creamy skin, remembering vividly what she looked like without her corset on. He pushed a stray, red hair behind her ear and let his fingers graze her neck. Nessa grinned up at him, probably thinking she had him.

"Mr. O'Connor!" Nora called out familiarly. Thomas looked over Nessa's head and smiled at Nora. "Will ye be needing a room?"

"Rather, I came to speak with ye, Madam. If ye don't mind."

"Aye?" Nora's brows rose in surprise. "What for?"

Thomas looked down at Nessa and shrugged. "Sorry, beautiful. I won't be needing a room tonight."

Nessa frowned but turned to Hiram. "What about ye, big man?"

"He could have some tension released," Thomas said as he walked towards Nora, feeling his friend's cold stare on his back. He fought a smile as he walked between tables of men gambling and drinking, here as a result of the new lass, no doubt. Nora's always had steady men flowing through, but it was never this full.

"I wanted to ask ye about your new lass," Thomas admitted, pulling his collar from his neck, feeling as if the room rose a few degrees. He was vaguely aware of Hiram and Nessa passing him, heading upstairs.

"Oh, aye?" Nora smiled, her eyes sharpening in her thin face. "She will be extra, being a virgin..."

Thomas' back stiffened. "Pardon?"

"Between ye and me," she said, folding her hands in front of her, "the lass agreed only to sing, but I believe enough coin can get her to spread her legs. She hasn't admitted as such, but I can sense this kind of thing, and that lass hasn't had a lad between those pretty legs of hers. And such nice legs, they are..."

Thomas shook his head, trying to dispel the image of the woman's legs from his head. "What is she doing here?"

"Oh..." Nora shrugged, waving her hand back and forth. "Ye know, room and board. Looking for someone or something. Nothing of import."

"Aye," Thomas nodded, looking beyond Nora in thought.

"Oh, where did that tart go?" she growled, glaring at the shut door. "She knows to sing through the night like yesterday."

"Taking a break?" Thomas snapped, suddenly feeling oddly protective of a woman he'd never met. "Who is she looking for?"

Nora's lips pinched tight, her brown eyes flaring. "Just family business."

"Are ye planning on helping her after what ye got out of her?"

"Will ye excuse me, Mr. O'Connor? If ye aren't paying for a lass, then I need to speak with someone who is." Nora looked past him, searching out her ladies. Most of them were already occupied with men and didn't need her. "Where is that wee slut?" she snapped, heading to the door.

Thomas followed Nora as he thought about what would bring a lass like that to a place like this. Aye, many good women found themselves working at a brothel to help their family, as more adventurous types did it for the thrill. But women who did it for another reason, for which most men would undoubtedly deny, was the sole purpose of being financially independent of the said men. Though he knew those of his own gender who saw their women as partners, most of them saw women as something to possess. To spit out their brats and run their household. Never to have their own opinions or make their own choices.

Thomas found himself snarling at the thought of a man making her turn to this profession. But if what Nora said was true and she was a virgin...

Thomas stopped that train of thought as quickly as it appeared.

Nora opened the door, revealing a smaller crowd and an empty crate. Laughter flowed inside, and a man by the door hiccupped, too drunk to stand up.

"Where is she?" Nora snapped at him.

"Who?"

"The lass singing, ye scut!"

"There's no lass singing..." He hiccupped again, slumping lower.

"Oh, will ye get out of here?" Nora kicked him in the leg to get him to move. "That hussy left with me money!"

Feckin' hell.

Thomas went to the small brass container and found it empty. A knot formed in his stomach, an uneasy feeling spreading throughout the rest of his body. Something didn't feel right. "Ye sure she'd up and leave?"

"I'm going to whip her until she bleeds, that ungrateful wench!"

"Are ye talking about that gypsy?" the man slurred. "Right, pretty one, she is. Especially when I'm sitting down 'ere. The way she swayed made her—"

"Did ye see her leave or not?" Thomas growled.

"She went that way," an English accent rang out. He pointed to the ally across the street. "It looked like she was following someone."

Nora huffed, puffing out her tiny chest, and began to walk towards the ally. Thomas grabbed her arm, pulling her back. "Stay here. I'll bring her back."

"Well, all right then," she said sensibly, knowing she could be walking into trouble. "Just bring her back here."

The warm night encouraged those usually in the taverns to come out and march on to their subsequent establishment. Thomas walked around several drunks who stumbled in his path and ignored a man and woman shifting in the shadows of a building. A group of men walked by, too busy whispering to each other to pay Thomas any mind, but their look had Thomas putting his hand in his pocket. The warmth of the metal of his small revolver was a comfort.

A few curses and a muffled scream echoed through the ally, spurring Thomas into action. He rounded the corner in a matter of seconds. What he saw stopped the breath in his chest as a loud ringing pierced his ears. A disconcerted rage overtook Thomas, making the edges of his vision go black.

He would come to find out that one fleeting moment could drastically change the course of a person's life.

CHAPTER SEVEN

Emilia

A FEW HOURS EARLIER

With darkness, the world came alive.

Inside the building, I wiped my sweaty palms on my shift, looking down at the entire expanse of my tan skin practically glowing against the white corset. The contrast was drastic, as was the darkness of my hair when all the other women in the brothel were fairer than I. I was sure that darker women were in the streets yesterday, but my first-night singing made it blazingly clear that I stood out.

I took a deep breath to steady my nerves and reminded myself that this outfit may be provocative for the time, but it wasn't for *my* time. I shouldn't have felt any more nervous about singing here than on the pub stage. Besides, I had nothing but good reviews the night before, and only a few men tried to touch me. I intentionally repressed the memory of the man who dared to shove money between my breasts and attempted to lift my shift before I swore at him. All the others only needed a quick swat of my hand and a sassy smile to keep them at bay.

The other women kept throwing glares, clearly thinking I would take their men tonight. The evening passed in aggravation and resistance as I had taught them their lines. Even now, though I told them I only wanted to sing, they hated me with a boiling temper that could only be the machinations of Nessa. I tried to ignore them and focus on Biddy, who, in all her natural sweetness, ignored the other women's resentment and treated me as a close friend.

"Go on," Nora mumbled by me, her hands behind her back, as she permitted me to go outside. A few men had already started to trickle in, drinking at the bar and flirting with the girls. Nora wanted me to wait until the street was good and busy outside before I started singing.

I grabbed the brass tin on the table next to me, ready to head out.

"Do you think he'll be here tonight?" I asked her.

Much to my disappointment, I hadn't seen Shay or Thomas the night before and ended up having to sing the entire night. It wasn't until near dawn, feet sore and voice weak, I was able to go in. My only choice was to bed with Biddy, and too exhausted to refuse, I gladly lay down next to her. However, somewhere in the back of my mind, my consciousness recoiled at the thought of lying on those soiled sheets, as my drained body quickly fell into a deep sleep for nearly ten hours.

I woke disoriented and panicked at the close view of my surroundings. I was alone in the room, so I regained my composure without anyone noticing. Calming down, my mood quickly shifted to a sense of despair. I had to grab my stomach, nausea overcoming me quickly.

Nora promised Thomas would come into this part of town, but what if he didn't? Should I have gone to find Shay instead of asking Nora for help? My letter—God, that sounded ridiculous considering I didn't remember writing it—said to find Thomas. But why? The situation had me nearly pulling my hair out and committing to an asylum.

Being entirely on my own in this century wore on me, and I had to hide that shaking hands from the other girls.

"Don't ye worry," Nora said, smile strained. Not for the first time, I sensed that she was keeping something from me.

"Okay," I mumbled, promising myself that this would be the last night I would try this. Nora be damned, I was going to find Shay without her or Thomas.

Heading towards the door, a man approached me, snaking his arm around my waist and causing my blood pressure to skyrocket. I pulled my face back, hit by the smell of his intense body odor and the reek of alcohol.

"Hands off!" Nora was there instantly, swatting the man away before I could react. "Mr. Clément, this lady is extra special. Ye back off, ye hear?"

"Pardonnez-moi, Madam Kelly," he said in what I assumed was French. He bowed far enough that he stumbled, almost falling on his face. "Elle est belle." Standing upright now, his eyes tried to focus on my breasts.

Feeling uncomfortable, I played with my rosary that I hid in my drawers, winding and unwinding the beads around my fingers.

"Stop that vulgarity. Speak English now, ye hear? Now, we have plenty of other pretty women over here..." Nora grabbed ahold of Mr. Clément's shoulders. She guided him to Biddy, who was all smiles, her naturally sweet charm captivating the man.

I quickly went outside and placed my tin next to the crate. The weather was chillier than the night before, but there wasn't a breeze, which allowed us to light a small fire in a rusted barrel near me. Nora said it was to keep me warm, but I knew it was for the men to see me better. So, I ascended the crate, noticing how the people passing by eyed me suspiciously.

I started singing a few old Irish songs I used to sing at the pub, and even sang a few new ones the girls had taught me the night before. But, if I was being honest, if it weren't for Shay missing, I would have enjoyed that time on my small crate much more, singing my heart out.

Singing was my outlet, escape, and refuge all rolled into one, and those two nights I sang for the small crowd were ones I would cherish for the rest of my life. Bringing joy and laughter to those struggling and trying to survive was enough to endure the stares of some men. Besides, if I remembered correctly, weren't they going to be at war soon? So, it was the least I could do while trying to find my friend. Especially since I would be gone long before then, anyhow.

About an hour later, I saw two black hats separating the crowd around them. They were taller than most, making it easier to stand out. A muttering of curses went through the gathering around me, but, to my surprise, no one stopped the two men. It was only a matter of seconds until they pushed their way through the last of the people and emerged in front of me.

A huge man with the warm tan of someone of a mixed race appeared first, admiring me with golden eyes that held more disinterest than the wanton thoughts of the other men. He stood there, hands in his trousers pockets as he waited for his friend to stand next to him, his strong brows lowering in thought. I looked toward the other, noticing first how his white skin offset his friend's and the similar way that they carried themselves. Then, he lifted his head, his hat covering most of his face while bent, and it was as if time had slowed.

It couldn't be.

My words caught in my throat, though I was able to recover with just a slight tremor in my voice.

Holy shit. I've got to be hallucinating. There's no way that he found me.

And yet, there was no denying that he was the man in the picture hanging in my family's pub.

Thomas.

It was undoubtedly him, from the short black beard on his sharp jaw, to his prominent cheekbones that framed a slightly crooked nose, probably from a break. But the most striking feature of his face was his eyes. They were green, not the blue that I suspected. The most vibrant green eyes I'd ever seen, slanted in a way that gave the impression of a predator zeroing in on their prey. And they were staring right at me.

I couldn't look away, enraptured by the man I had looked at since I was a kid. Although, I had to admit, he was a little intimidating. He was just my height while I was standing on the large crate—putting him several inches over six feet tall—and his shoulders were as broad as two of me.

The longer his eyes rested on me, the more my words began to falter. I knew I had to find him, but why was he so interested in me? I had the sudden urge to turn him around, push him away so he'd start walking somewhere else.

Instead, I closed my eyes and let every feeling trapped inside me out through my voice. I could pretend he wasn't there if I didn't look at him.

That didn't change the hyper-awareness of feeling his heated gaze upon me. His presence took up more space than his body, sweeping me into his atmosphere. And that was what convinced me that I wasn't completely losing it. That I hadn't imagined him in front of me.

The song ended, and I let out a small breath through my nose, trying to get up the nerve to talk to Thomas. At least the uneasy, prickling sensation had faded.

The crowd was still murmuring and rowdy as I tamped down my nerves. And when I finally opened my eyes...

He was gone.

I looked around, scanning the crowd for his black hair above everybody else's, but he was nowhere in sight. Had I imagined him? He vanished as suddenly as he showed up, and I found myself scrambling off the crate, running through the crowd hollering for more songs. I ignored them, sweeping my eyes left and right for Thomas.

I walked down the street, where there were significantly fewer people. I looked to my right and swore I saw a man turn down an alley. Instinctively, I followed him, wanting to catch up.

As soon as I entered the alley, a hand was clasped around my mouth, and the sharp bite of a knife pressed to my throat. I tried to scream, but only soft grunts could escape my captor's hands, and the blade dug in deeper. A warm trickle of blood began to drip down my throat, freezing me in place.

"What is a pretty lass like ye doin' out 'ere by yerself? Mmm? Lookin' for a little trouble?" The stench of the man's breath had me recoiling from him as much as I possibly could. His hand began to fumble with my shift. I tried to pull the knife away from my neck, but he was too strong.

"Stop movin', ye wench!" he hissed, lifting the thin fabric high enough to get under it. I bucked to try and get him away, but it only seemed to excite him more, and the knife started to sting. "Ye would think ye'd be used to it by now, ye whore. Too pretty to be wasted on that crate."

Something warm pressed against my flesh, causing hot tears to roll down my face. I prepared myself for what was to come next, only to hear a click of metal that stopped the man short.

"Let the lass go," a deep voice growled, sending shivers down my spine and goosebumps to erupt over my entire body. I didn't have to look to know who he was.

The man withdrew from me, and my shift fell back into place. I ran to the other side of the alley, plastering my back against the building so no one else could sneak up on me.

Thomas had a small gun pressed to the side of the greasy-haired bastard.

"C'mon, Tommy boy! Ye know I was just havin' a wee bit of fun. No need to—" Thomas cracked the man's skull with the butt of the gun, cutting off his words. The man dropped the knife and grabbed his head.

I winced, looking away.

"Ye ever touch a lass like that again, and I'll cut ye. If ye ever even look at this woman here, I'll gut ye…" Thomas began to speak in Irish, so I couldn't understand him, but whatever he said had the man visibly shaking.

With the vehemence that Thomas spoke and how he had the gun shoved underneath the man's jaw, my stomach twisted in knots. Was I wrong to go searching for this man? He did save me, but it was clear that Thomas might not be the gentleman I had imagined all these years.

A dark stain began to form on the man's pants, and I realized with a start that he had pissed himself. I couldn't blame him; I was barely holding it together and wasn't even facing Thomas' wrath. Then, with a shove from Thomas, my assailant stumbled into the street. He ran towards the crowd without looking back.

Thomas breathed heavily, looking at his feet.

"Thank you," I whispered, not knowing what to say, and frankly too scared to say the wrong thing to him.

He turned to me, looking as if he had forgotten I was there. The closer he got, the clearer his features became, several different emotions sweeping across his face before settling into indifference. Finally, he raised his hand, and I flinched, pulling away until I felt him gently sweep wayward strands of hair away from my face. I peered at him through my lashes, afraid to move.

"Ye shouldn't be here," he said. My heart nearly burst through my chest, thinking he somehow knew who I was. "Why aren't ye with your people?"

"I don't have anyone," I admitted, letting out the breath I was holding. The Italians. Of course, he thought it was odd I was in the Irish part of Boston. Where were the Italian immigrants even during this time? I raked my brain, trying to remember the history lessons they taught me in school, but I wasn't sure. "And, I can't find my friend..."

His back stiffened at my words. "That's right." He grimaced and nodded in thought. "C'mon, then."

"What?"

"I believe we need to have a talk with Madam Kelly, aye?"

"What do you know of Madam Kelly?" I asked, blushing at what he may know.

His eyes roamed my body, causing me to cover myself. I didn't want him to see me that way for some reason. It made me feel ashamed and confused in that dirty ally, though I had done nothing wrong.

He shook his head and looked upward, avoiding my gaze. "She said ye were looking for someone?"

"Yeah," I said, thinking of a way to tell him what I needed without admitting he was one of the people I needed. "She agreed to get me into contact with someone who could help me find my friend. I was going to head to The North End, but she said it was too far away—"

He glared at me, and I recoiled.

"What?" I asked.

"Madam Kelly jilted ye, she did," he growled. "Come!"

The anger in his voice made me jump just as his gentle touch on my back sent a shudder through my body. He evoked so many emotions in me that my body started to shake, overwhelmed. Yet I followed, knowing full well I was a helpless sheep navigating the wolves.

CHAPTER EIGHT

Emilia

The small crowd that was still gathered around Madam Nora's bar parted for Thomas. It was puzzling, knowing I would've struggled through them on my own, and I wondered yet again why he affected everyone. We entered the building, the door crashing into the wall so hard that everyone around the room quieted and turned in our direction. I felt myself shrink back, so Thomas's body hid most of me.

"So, ye found the wench!" Nora hollered unnaturally loud for such a small frame. She came at me, face scrunched in anger.

Thomas put his arm back and pushed me farther behind him.

"Aye, I did," he admitted. "And it's not what ye think. She didn't steal your money; she was looking for someone."

Nora's head reared back, squinting as if she didn't believe him. "Did ye check everywhere?" She looked around him, eyeing my breasts and clothes like she was about to find out herself.

"Aye," Thomas sneered, lying convincingly well.

"You know I wouldn't steal from you," I spoke up.

"I don't know ye, ye wee wench! For all I know, ye were playin' me all along!"

"Take care not to raise your voice," Thomas warned. "Your patrons are getting a free show."

Nora huffed, looking around as her nostrils flared and her mouth went tight.

"You know I needed to find my friend," I growled, just as angry. I stepped around Thomas and stood in front of Nora. "She's scared, alone, and if she's hurt, I swear to God I'm going to come after you first for not helping me." With each word spoken, my voice grew so everyone could hear me. I hadn't meant to do it, but everything that had happened built up, and I was ready to explode.

Nora's eyes widened momentarily before narrowing. "This is how ye thank me for putting a roof over your head and food in your belly?"

"It was one night!" I yelled.

"Tell me, Nora. How long were ye gonna wait to tell her she's already in The North End?" Thomas asked.

"What?" I gasped, looking to see his expression, but his hard gaze was on Nora. In my own time, I'd been in Charlestown. How had I ended up all the way in the North End?

Movement on the stairs caught my eye. Nessa just came down with the big man I had seen with Thomas earlier, sneering at me as the man looked questioningly at Thomas. Thomas just shook his head.

I looked around for Biddy and found her standing by a small man I hadn't seen before. Face pale and eyes round, the guilt was clearly written on her face.

"You lied to me?" I choked out. Though we'd just met, that betrayal had hurt the most. "After everything we talked about? I thought you were my—?" I stopped and shook my head, unable to say that I had started thinking of her as a friend.

"I'm sorry—"

"Thomas." Nessa sauntered over to us, batting her lashes at him. "Please tell me you're not siding with this gypsy filth?" Her shoulder bumped into mine as she sidled to his side, holding on to him. She looked at me, smirking.

"Gypsy?" My face paled at her accusation. I wasn't stupid; I knew gypsies had bad reputations. "I'm not a gypsy," I denied even as the memory of my grandmother had me wondering...

Could there be truth to it?

"Word around town is ye are..." She lifted a red brow.

"I'm Italian. My family—"

"Always lyin', aye?" Nessa sneered.

Thomas looked down at me, studying my face. I don't know what he saw, but the lines around his eyes deepened.

"If the lass says she's Italian, then who are we to question her?" he rumbled, looking down at Nessa. Her hand glided familiarly up his chest. His brows raised when he caught me staring.

Heat spread through me in embarrassment. It was as if Thomas had read my thoughts and tried to extricate himself from Nessa's grasp, but she set her claws in.

"I'll take ye!" a man shouted at the bar, startling us. I almost forgot we had a large audience. "Gypsy or no, ye look like a good time!"

The room erupted in laughter from the men surrounding us, breaking the tension. Everyone began talking once more, losing some interest.

"Aye, me too!" another man cut in, slamming his drink on the bar. "Always wondered what an exotic girl like ye—"

"Now, now, gentlemen." Nora raised her brows. "How much ye willing to pay for her?"

"Excuse me?" I spat. "I told you—"

"Ye'll have to work some to make me money back," Nora cut in.

Thomas growled something in Gaelic and stepped closer to Nora, simultaneously making her back up as he freed himself from Nessa. "Don't test me, woman."

For the first time since meeting Nora, fear crossed her thin features before quickly disappearing. "Nay, I want me money."

Thomas cursed under his breath, digging in his pocket for something.

"What are you doing?" his friend asked, coming closer. "Is she really worth all this?"

Thomas shook his head, ignoring him. "Here," he said, slamming some money on the bar counter.

"You can't be serious?" his friend grumbled, grabbing Thomas' arm to hold him back.

"Aye, comrádaí. Trust me." Thomas turned back to Nora. "I believe that'll give me one night with the lass. Then she's to be free."

Nora counted the money and pocketed it. "Aye, we're done. Take Biddy's room," she said to me.

I began to back away, looking between her and Thomas. My stomach dropped, instantly making me queasy. How could this be happening? How could he—

Thomas came towards me slowly, treating me like a nervous animal. I bumped into a stool behind me and almost toppled over. He caught me, moving faster than I could think, and bent his mouth to my ear. "Trust me," he whispered, sending shivers down my spine. "It's either me or those lads over there. Which would ye like?" He pulled back and I found myself lost in rich fields of Ireland, the dark green irises shrinking as his pupils expanded, enhancing the golden rim around them.

My breath caught, and I could only shake my head as his eyes flicked between my own, trying to decipher my response. He backed away, giving me space. "It's your choice."

I looked at him, then Nora, then the door. There was no way I would make it out of here without someone grabbing me.

"I'll pay double!" an Englishman yelled, slamming money onto the counter as well.

Thomas cursed under his breath, and I knew I had waited too long. His friend came to him, and they started arguing quietly. "I don't have anymore," Thomas rumbled louder than intended.

"Looks like you're mine!" the man at the bar smiled, revealing a chipped tooth on his otherwise handsome face.

He merrily elbowed a man next to him, the whole room cheering him on. Then, with enough celebration to make my stomach turn, he brushed his brown hair back and put his hat back on. He came closer, and I backed towards the door. To my surprise, the man grabbed my waist gently and started pulling me towards the back stairs. He was just my height, but years of hard work had given him the strength of a much larger man.

"Don't you worry, doll. I'll treat you nice." Strangely, I believed him. If it weren't for being sold against my will, I'd think him a good guy. Maybe he was for this time, but I wasn't planning on heading up those steps to find out.

"Wait!" Thomas snapped, slamming more coins onto the bar. What was with these damn men?

I turned quickly and found Thomas glaring at Nora, daring her to argue. His friend was staring at the ceiling, his hands in his pockets, exasperated. The only good thing about this situation was Nessa's beet-red face. I wouldn't have been surprised to see smoke coming out of her ears. The thought alone almost brought a smile to my lips.

"Can ye raise him?" Nora asked the man next to me.

This close, I had a better look at his tanned face. He couldn't be much older than I, but he had deep creases between his brows as he thought. "No, Madam. I'm afraid that was all of my coin." He let go of my waist and stepped away. "Maybe next time, doll." He tipped his hat at me and went back to the bar as the men pushed him back and forth, laughing at him.

Thomas was by me instantly, grabbing my arm and spinning me towards the stairs. I kept my head down, not wanting to make eye contact with anyone, and tried to drown all the lewd comments they threw at us. I'd never been through something so humiliating.

It wasn't until we were at the foot of the stairs that I lifted my head, hearing a familiar voice.

"I'm so sorry," Biddy cried, tears in her eyes. She grabbed my arm, pleading. "Ye got to believe me. I didn't want to lie to ye. I tried to treat ye right, didn't I? Madam Kelly said she only wanted ye for your singing." My chest tightened at the tears rolling down her face.

"Of course," I mumbled. "I know you didn't mean me harm." On impulse, I leaned in and hugged her, feeling Thomas' hand gently let go of me.

"Thank ye," she sniffed. Drying her eyes on a handkerchief she pulled out from between her breasts, she eyed Thomas and me and leaned into my ear. "I've never had him," she admitted, causing heat to spread over my face and chest. "But I've heard a lot. Ye couldn't be with a better man. Nessa steals him most times, but the other girls who'd had him say he's nice and knows what he's doin'." She stepped back and winked at me. "Ye know most men don't."

I shook my head and tried to smile back. Too nervous to say anything else, I turned to the stairs, avoiding Thomas' gaze as I passed him.

The creak of each stair seemed like a foreboding of the night ahead of me. By the time we reached the top, my whole body shook so bad that I had to hide my hands in my shift. Even the smooth beads of my rosary did little to calm me.

If I were to light the candle left on a small table, Thomas didn't give me a chance. The minute it took for him to light it was enough to hear the unmistakable creaking from the room next to us and groans across the hall. I silently sent up thanks that the darkness hid my mortification.

Thomas's hands remained steady as he held candle up to the light our way.

"Over here," my voice trembled as I stared at his shadowed feet, unable to look at his face.

We reached Biddy's door, but when I went to open it, my hands were sweaty and shaking so much I fumbled with the handle.

Thomas' large hand eclipsed mine, gently moving it away. "Let me," he said so softly that I looked up. He was looking at the door though and kept his head down even while he reached his arm out for me to go first.

The room was dark except for the red glow of the burning embers. I knew enough to put some logs on the fire.

"I'll do it, lass," Thomas said, placing the candle on the table. "Don't trouble yourself."

"I got it. I can do it," I said, desperate to keep busy. I picked up one, but my arms were so weak with nerves I dropped it. "Fuck!" I cursed and covered my mouth; shocked I said that in front of him this time.

A choking noise came from Thomas.

"What?" I snapped.

"Nothing, lass." He was laughing at me! "Just didn't know ye had it in ye."

"Will you stop calling me that?"

"And what shall I call ye?"

I waited a minute, trying to calm down. "Millie," I whispered. "My name's Emilia."

He stood there, face shadowed as the red glow reflected off his clothes, staring in my direction. "Right," he finally said, voice gravelly. "It's a pleasure to me ye, Miss Millie. I don't believe I formally introduced myself. I'm Thomas O'Connor." He took off his hat and bowed.

"What exactly do you want from me?" My voice wavered. I started putting logs on the fire so I wouldn't have to look at him.

Thomas picked up the poker and arranged it until a small flame flared. He was so close that I could smell a mixture of cigars and the fresh scent of the sea. I stepped back quickly, wanting to create distance between us.

"What do *ye* want?" he asked, straightening.

"What do you mean?" I wrung my hands. Wouldn't he just get it over with and put me out of my misery?

"Ye've never done this before, have ye?"

I threw my hands in the air, nearly at my snapping point. "What gave it away? Will you please just get this over with? I have more important matters to attend to. Just because you're horny—"

He barked out a surprised laugh. "My ye have a mouth! Did ye mother teach ye how to talk to a man that way? Or did she teach ye how to do other things with it?"

The slap rang out across the room. Thomas froze, and the air around us seemed to stand still as the fire flickered across his face, revealing emotions I couldn't discern. My chest heaved up and down while I waited for his response.

"I'm sorry," he said, completely surprising me. He sat down in the chair and leaned his head back. "Places like this tend to make men forget there are still ladies hereabouts. I shouldn't have said that to ye."

While I tried to gain control of my emotions, I stepped from one foot to the other. My feet began to throb from standing so long.

"Why don't ye sit, lass?" He eyed me. "I'm not going to hurt ye. Why do ye think I bought ye from the other men? I knew ye didn't want to be with them. And ye don't want to be with me neither. Ye have the night to relax. Sleep. Worry about everything else tomorrow."

I paused, not quite sure if I'd heard right. He couldn't have spent all that money on me without wanting something. When he remained silent, my voice cracked. "Really?"

"Really."

Relieved tears swelled in my eyes, and I swallowed past the lump in my throat. "Thank you, thank you so much."

Thomas leaned back in the chair and straightened his long legs out in front of him, placing his hat over his eyes. I wondered if he was going to sleep or giving me some privacy.

I wiped away my tears, grateful he couldn't see me, and began to take off my shoes. I didn't have many clothes on, so I lay on the edge of the bed, still not wanting to touch the sheets.

"Do ye always sleep like that?" His voice broke the silence, making me nearly fall off the bed.

"What?" I hissed.

"Sorry," he chuckled. His amusement made me want to throw something at him. "I didn't mean to startle ye. I just couldn't help but notice ye were about to fall off the bed there. And do ye always wear your stockings to bed?"

It was true; I took off the thigh-high-tights and corset last night, sleeping in only my shift with Biddy. "No," I admitted. "I just..."

He nodded and put his hat back over his face. "Do what ye want. I won't bother ye."

When I sat up, the bed squeaked, causing him to smile.

I refrained from growling my annoyance and failed to ignore how my heart sped up at his smile. "And no funny business, okay?" I said while I began taking off my stockings. "I just want to get comfortable and sleep."

His smile widened. "Of course, Miss Millie."

"Stop calling me that," I grumbled.

"Ye don't want me calling ye 'lass.' Now 'Miss Millie' either? What shall I call ye then?" He lifted his hat as I had my shift hiked up, removing my other stocking.

"No peeking!" I squealed.

He covered his face quickly, chuckling under his breath. "Sorry."

"You said you wouldn't peek," I huffed, trying to stop myself from smiling. "Just Emilia or Millie is fine. You don't need to say, 'Miss.'"

"Well, Millie. Ye have some nice legs there. Do they go with a last name?"

"You, sir, are no gentleman!" I said, throwing my stocking to the side.

Thomas rubbed his nose, hiding another grin, and shrugged. He was enjoying this way too much. "I never claimed to be one."

I opened my mouth, ready to protest, but realized he was right.

Instead, my mouth snapped shut as I tried to think of an answer to his question. The truth was, I had already given my last name a lot of thought. I was going to pick a random one. Still, another kept slithering into my consciousness, attempting to reveal a truth I wasn't ready for.

I loosened my stays and lay back down. "Moretti. Emilia Moretti."

"Mmm, good name, Emilia Moretti."

"Why did you do it?" I asked the ceiling.

"Do what?"

I turned my head and studied him, wondering what went on in his head. I swore I could see the shine of his eyes under his hat. "Buy a night with me when you don't even know me?"

A long pause had me holding my breath. Through the flickering shadows, I knew we were staring at each other. Thomas adjusted the hat lower on his face.

"Goodnight, Moretti," was my only answer, leaving me to my own assumptions.

The faint crackle of the fire did little to cover up the noises in the rooms surrounding us. I was too tired the night before to fret, but cutting my performance short this night allowed my mind to wander to what was happening beyond those walls. An awkward situation made worse because of the man sitting across from me.

I fidgeted on the bed, growing more bothered at each creak and groan. My legs pushed together, trying to relieve the pressure building deep within my core. Thomas' steady breathing eased my nerves somewhat, even as I wondered how he could be so unbothered. Instead, I focused on the fact that he was the man I needed to find Shay, and a feeling of relief washed over me. He could help me. Everything would be fine.

That was easier thought than done. My attention focused on each hitch of his breath. Something ignited inside me—a flame flickering to life, threatening to blaze. I started to wonder if his breathing was faster than before. Surely, he couldn't be as affected as me. He must have been used to this sort of thing.

My mind spun as my eyes roamed down his long, lean body. The sleeves of his shirt tightened across his biceps, defining them so that I had to swallow past the lump in my throat. I licked my lips as my gaze roamed over his vest and how it didn't even come close to concealing his broad chest. The man was built like some Celtic god I didn't know but would willingly serve diligently on my knees.

I held back a groan and made myself stare at the ceiling, refusing to indulge in any more fantasies, and wondered where they even came from.

Some time had passed, and Thomas uncrossed and re-crossed his legs, adjusting his shoulders on the back of the chair. He looked so uncomfortable that guilt extinguished my desire. He *did* save me from having to sleep with another man. The least I could do was offer him a bed to sleep on. *Right?* But that would mean he would be very close to me on the twin-sized mattress.

My traitorous eyes betrayed me again and scoured his magnificent body, making my pulse quicken as I questioned how old he was. Thomas was ruggedly attractive, and my cheeks flushed while I imagined those rough hands on my skin.

"Are ye going to sleep, or are ye going to stare at me all night?"

Heat spread across my chest and up to my roots, humiliated at being caught. "How can you even see me?" My voice wavered, giving some of my thoughts away; I silently cursed myself for speaking.

"I can feel ye."

"Feel me?" I squeaked.

He smiled and lifted his hat. "Aye."

I made a disgusted noise and turned my face towards the ceiling. "And to think I was going to let you sleep next to me."

That had him slowly sitting up, pulling his body together as if his muscles strained. "I don't know if that's wise." A clenched jaw replaced his grin as he stared into the fire.

"I just meant to sleep," I whispered nervously. "You looked uncomfortable, and I'm grateful for your help tonight. You don't deserve to sleep in that chair."

"I've slept in worse."

His tone's lack of emotion and flatness had my skin prickling with concern. I barely knew anything about his man, and I felt he hid a world of plights from me.

"Come," I said and patted the bed, more confident now. Thomas's face turned to me, eyes ablaze with the flames. "Lie down, and I promise I won't try to have my way with you."

He raised his brow.

"Joke." I smiled. "Just a joke. Apparently, not very funny."

Thomas unfurled from the chair, his immense form seeming to take up the entire room. My eyes followed as he rounded the bed, incapable of tearing my gaze from this terrifying man. Then, slowly, as if time had stilled, Thomas sat. A loud squeak rented the room as the bed sank, and I had to hold onto the edge, so I did not roll-on top of him.

He had his back to me for a few unbearable minutes, and then, when I opened my mouth to speak, he began to take off his shoes and lie down. A massive shoulder bumped mine, neither of us able to move over. My breath stilled in my chest, and I had to repress the sudden, outrageous urge to grab his hand.

"Thank ye," he grumbled.

"I hope you didn't lose much money on me tonight," I admitted. The thought had been nagging at me for a while.

"Don't worry, lass."

"But did you say you had no more?" I turned my head to him and studied the side of his face and the dark whiskers coming in. "Where did you get the rest?"

He stared at the ceiling for some time before shaking his head. His eyes roamed my face. They searched my eyes as if seeing the depths of my soul, before they grazed my nose and caressed my lips like a soft whisper.

I shivered, never overcome with such emotion by a simple gaze before. It felt as if Thomas was pulling me apart layer by layer, until he cracked me open and devoured everything that I was.

"Hiram gave it to me," he said gruffly.

"Hiram? Your friend?"

"Aye."

"Well, I hope it wasn't too much. Was it?"

"Don't—"

"I have some saved from last night."

I sat up quickly, ready to go to the trunk that held my clothes, but he grabbed my arm. Goosebumps broke out all over my body.

"Let it go, lass."

"I just don't want you to need it, is all." My eyes were trained on his hand and how it wrapped around my entire forearm.

"Sorry," he mumbled and let go of me hastily. "I'll take up a few extra jobs. And Mikey can pull in some more weight—"

"Mikey?"

"Me brother."

I shook my head, not wanting to be indebted to another man. "I'll make it up to you," I promised.

"There's no arguing with ye is there?" He sighed. "Sleep now, a ghaiscíoch bhig. We'll talk about it in the morning."

Feeling a little better, I lay down. With the relief, exhaustion weighed down on me, and my eyes drooped.

"What does that mean?" I mumbled, but enough time passed that I knew he wouldn't respond. "Goodnight, Thomas O'Connor."

When I finally succumbed to sleep, I felt a soft brush against the back of my hand.

"Oíche mhaith, little warrior."

CHAPTER NINE

Emilia

I woke up on my side, my cheek resting on something hard, wondering where my favorite cozy pillow went. My hand roamed upward, trying to get comfortable, when I felt a faint twitch underneath it. I snuggled in, and adjusted my leg over something.

I turned my face inward and inhaled, smelling smoke and the faint scent of...of a man.

I lurched backward, gasping.

Thomas looked up at me, an inscrutable expression on his face, his eyes burning through me. My breathing hitched. My hair had to be a mess and I was almost positive I had drool on the side of my face, but he didn't laugh.

"I'm sorry," I mumbled. To my horror, his shirt had a drool spot on it. "Sorry, I didn't mean to—" I waved my finger from him to me, trying to finish my sentence like an imbecile while I blushed all the way to my roots.

The heat in his eyes, and the memory of what occurred last night, had my skin tightening and warmth surging low into my belly. I panicked at my body's response and tried to get out of the bed. My leg caught on the quilt and I tumbled backwards over the edge.

He grabbed my waist and pulled me forward before I even knew that I was falling. I toppled onto his chest as he fell back onto the bed. I looked up to find his green eyes studying me. In this position, I was well aware that my breasts were pressed against him, only separated by our thin clothes. I held my breath, too afraid to move and too embarrassed by our close contact.

He cupped my face, rubbing my blush with the pad of his thumb. "Ye sure are pretty when ye wake."

My eyes widened, surprised by his remark. I let my face fall to his chest, more comfortable with the touch than having him read my expression.

The noises from the other night had fallen silent hours ago, but I knew he must have wished to spend the night with another woman. We were in a whorehouse for God's sake, and I didn't do anything for him.

"What was that?" he asked after I mumbled into his chest.

I placed my chin on his chest and stared at the buttons of his shirt. "I said you're a liar."

He brushed my hair back from my face, sending another flood of warmth to my belly and tingles up and down my limbs.

"Neamh cabhrú liom."

I never could understand Irish, but the way it sounded coming out of his mouth had my toes curling. "What does that mean?"

"Heaven help me." He smiled.

My glare made him laugh, which in turn jiggled my head up and down. I sat up, ignoring my secret desire to lie there with him all day.

"Biddy would probably like her room back," I said, rummaging through the trunk for my clothes.

"Aye?" he said a little distractedly. He placed his hands behind his head as he watched me.

Biddy's room was one of the few with a window, and the early, golden sun that shone through the dirty glass illuminated my figure beneath my shift. I dove into the shadows, though the damage was already done.

"Well, now I can describe ye to the lads," he said.

I bit my lip as my heart threatened to break through my chest, cursing myself for wondering if he liked what he saw. Without consent, my eyes drooped down and found that he did.

"You wouldn't." The words came out throaty instead of with the anger I intended. The guy in the pub didn't bring up *these* desires. That I was sure of.

"Nay." His eyes flashed as he caught me looking. I didn't let myself feel ashamed, not when he stared at me without guilt. His expression changed, closing off as he looked away first. He sat up and placed his head into his hands. "I suppose not."

I wondered about his almost instantaneous mood change, but used the time to put on as many of my clothes as I could before he looked up. I shouldn't have worried because he didn't glance at me once while I dressed. He just put his shoes on and sat in the chair, looking into the fire that died back down to embers.

"What's wrong?" I asked, adjusting my green dress.

"Hmm?"

I repeated myself and stood in front of him. He finally glanced up, taking in my conservative dress.

"Ah, now that suits ye," he admitted, appraising me from my hair—it had lost its curls from the night before, so I had pinned it up into a simple bun—down to my shoes.

"That boring, huh?" I asked, screwing up my face self-consciously.

Thomas opened his mouth and shut it quickly. "Come." He stood and opened the door for me.

"Where are we going?"

"Well, I'd grab a bite of food, but with me coin gone—"

"I can buy it!" I said a little too enthusiastically, happy that I could help. I began to dig into the pocket of my dress until he placed his hand on my arm to stop me, not meeting my gaze.

"If it'd make ye feel better." He sighed. "I'd like to take ye somewhere else though. We can talk about your friend there."

I smiled, happy that I'd finally be searching for Shay. I felt like I'd wasted too much time at Nora's, and if it wasn't for finding Thomas, I'd have never forgiven myself for not searching for Shay on my own.

We made our way downstairs, both seeking the privy out back after not going all night. I was mortified to even *think* about using the bedpan in front of him, and suspected he didn't use it to give me the privacy I clearly desired.

Most of the ladies were still sleeping, leaving the bar empty except for a couple of men eating and drinking at the counter, and the barman I now knew as Henry Walsh. I looked around, feeling odd that I would leave without saying goodbye to at least Biddy.

"Ye can come back later on, if ye're that worried," Thomas grumbled. His stiff shoulders and impatient remarks confused me. Had

I imagined his crooked smiles and quick wit? It was as if he was an entirely different man.

"Ye leaving, Miss Emilia?" Henry asked while wiping down the bar. He was a good-looking man, maybe in his forties. From what I could tell, he watched out for the girls as a father would.

"I am," I smiled. We talked for a while the first day I met him, and I'd told him my plans to find my friend.

"Well, good luck to ye. Watch yourself out there. Though ye should be in good hands." He tipped his hat to Thomas, who nodded in return.

We said our goodbyes, and I tried not to think about how well Thomas knew him. And how frequently Thomas must have gone to Nora's.

Thomas held the door open for me, revealing a gloriously bright sky. I welcomed the cool air after being in the stuffy building all night. A horse trotted by, pulling a wagon of supplies somewhere, its driver tipping his hat to both of us. I wasn't used to all the greetings, but found I liked the manners of the time.

"Ye shouldn't have been walking the streets alone," he snapped, taking off at a quick pace that had me jogging to catch up. "Why were ye even goin' down that way by yourself?" he said as we passed the alley I was attacked in. The inflection in his tone was like a slap in the face.

"I thought I saw someone I knew," I mumbled.

He raised a brow. "Your friend?"

"Just someone from my past," I mumbled, hoping he'd drop it. "Clearly I was wrong."

He nodded, letting it go. Thomas scared me when he was mad, and the way that he was acting now left me uncomfortable. Yet his actions of repeatedly saving me outweighed my fear, and I knew deep down that he was safer than any other stranger I would find. Besides, wasn't he one of my family's ancestors? Granted, I didn't know much about him other than opening the pub with his brother. There *was* that letter I'd written to myself. If you could count that. A part of me still didn't believe I wrote it, or I would write it in the future...from the past? I shook my head, unable to wrap my mind around the intricacies of time.

What I actually accomplished so quickly had me reeling, and I tripped over the uneven cobblestones. A rough hand jerked me upward, saving me from a mouth full of rocks.

"Careful," he mumbled, steadying me. We locked eyes, and I swore concern overwrought his features as if I caught him with his guard down.

"How did you know I needed help?" I asked. "In the alley I mean." I tried to think about anything other than his personal life and whether or not he had a girl.

A line creased between his eyes, as if he was angry that I asked the question. "Just passin' by and heard a scuffle," he snapped with an annoyance I didn't understand.

"If you weren't there..." My throat tightened and I couldn't finish my sentence. I was so close to being raped. Nothing like that ever happened to me, and if Thomas didn't show up...

"What's this?" he said, grabbing my arm and pulling me to a stop.

I shook my head, looking away from him so he didn't see my tears.

"Look here," he started, shifting his feet. He glanced around to see if anyone was watching, but the street was nearly empty. "A lass like ye should know better than to walk by yourself in these parts."

"Like me?" I hissed, aggravated that he was scolding me for almost getting raped.

"Ye know," he said. "Beautiful." I looked up at him, startled. That was not what I was expecting, and it made butterflies erupt in my stomach. "It's a terrible trait to have here. So just...be careful."

"Okay." I suddenly had the odd feeling that I wanted to protect myself, not only for me but for him as well.

Again, I wondered if he had a woman and tried to think about anything else.

He nodded as if the matter was decided and turned on his heel. Thomas was so abrupt and conflicting that I didn't know what to think. He acted like he both cared and was angry in one breath.

In our silence, I took the sights and sounds of the nineteenth century. It was odd to not hear cars, planes, and even music from an apartment drifting down the street. Modern technology in all its forms vanished, and had been replaced by the clip of horses' hooves, neighbors and business owners calling out to each other in greeting, the bang of pots and pans in preparation of meals, the slop of buckets thrown into the gutters with only God knew what in them. I shivered; my throat thick with repulsion at the contents.

Crates and barrels lined the streets, filled with different foods and products, depending on which store they were in front of. It was common to see vendors sitting outside of the buildings, their clothes as ragged and worn as the dwellings around them. It was amazing that some of the structures still stood as their walls crumbled, their windows shattered. It was clear we were in the poorer part of Boston, yet the farther we walked, the area improved—the buildings were a little nicer, it was a bit cleaner, and the people were dressed finer.

We walked a few blocks when an odd sense of familiarity overwhelmed me. Was that Faneuil Hall? I was used to its brick exterior, not this smooth surface adorned with classic pilasters around each floor. And Quincy Market! The strips of shops were definitely cruder, what with their dirty awnings, haphazard displays of food, animals, vendors, and merchants. I had never seen so many wagons, horses and people all in one place, especially one that was selling food.

I stopped in the middle of the sidewalk, not caring that a woman told me to watch where I was going after I bumped into her. We were near enough to the harbor that I could smell the sea. All the hair stood up on my body and I turned in a complete circle, taking in everything as I compared the changes from the twenty-first century.

I was clutching my hands to my chest, tears in my eyes when I finally heard Thomas's voice.

"What?" I asked, too overwhelmed to pay attention to him.

"I asked if something was wrong with ye."

"No," I answered, snapping back to reality as if in a trance. "I'm sorry, I just realized I've been here before, that's all."

He looked at me like I lost mind.

"It's been a while," I tried to explain. "It was just a feeling, I guess."

Thomas stood there, hands in his pockets, searching my face. I knew he must have questions and maybe he didn't trust me, but he just shook his head and told me to follow him.

Another minute and we walked right up to the marketplace; people buzzing around it like bees to a bouquet. Weaving through the crowd, Thomas grabbed my hand, sending a jolt up my arm. With his big frame in front of me I couldn't see where we were headed, but I was able to get through without being jostled too much.

We came to the front of one of the buildings when he stopped and dropped my hand.

I took a good look at the building, and my eyes widened in recognition. I looked both ways to make sure it was the right spot. "Is that Durgin Park?" Even though it was a little rough around the edges in its earlier days, it was clearly the same structure. I'd eaten there a few times when my family and I went downtown. It closed in 2019, but here it was, without its name, though I vaguely remembered that the owner named it after two of his partners died later in the nineteenth century. I couldn't remember the exact date.

Thomas looked at me quizzically. "Aye, they own it. Do ye know them?"

My eyes about bugged out of my head when I realized the two men it was named after might be inside. "They're alive?" I whispered.

His hat threw his face in shade as he looked down at me, but it didn't hide his puzzled expression. "Ye're acting strange, lass."

"Sorry." I tried to smile, back peddling. "Someone was telling me about it at Nora's."

Thomas looked like he didn't believe me, but let it go. We went inside, squeezing into a couple of seats at a long table, Thomas across from me.

A man took our order, and placed beer in front of us while we waited. I used the time to look at my surroundings, my system shot with what I was experiencing. It wasn't until I ate half of my clam chowder and a part of our cornbread that the men sitting next to us interrupted, speaking loudly and hitting fists on the table.

"You didn't hear?" the man next to Thomas asked, shocked. "They fired on Sumter!"

With those two words, the blood drained from my face and hardened into a rock in my stomach.

"What do ye think it'll mean?" Thomas asked him.

"War," I mumbled. It wasn't supposed to happen yet. How could we have had such horrible timing? Not only traveling back in time, but to a Godforsaken war to boot.

"We'll scare those rebels into submission in no time," the man said. Thomas was radiating exhilaration at the thought. I could see it in the way his eyes flared to life.

But they didn't know what I knew. They didn't know how long it'd last, how many battles that would need to be fought, nor how many men had to die before it ended. And in the middle of it all were two women who had no idea how to even survive the different timeline, one of which was an African-American amidst severe racial discrimination.

The man went on excitedly, "There was a southern ship in the harbor today bearing the Rebels flag." He shook his head in disgust. "Some demanded it be replaced with the Stars and Stripes. A friend of mine said one of ours took the flag and shredded the bloody thing." He smirked.

I sat back, feeling the pit in my stomach grow heavier.

Thomas eyed me, pushing his plate away. "Are ye feeling all right, lass?"

"No," I admitted. "I can't deal with this. I need to find my friend."

"Aye, I'm sure she'll be fine."

"She won't!" I slammed my hands on the table.

The man looked uncomfortably between us and turned to talk to someone else. Thomas sat back, examining me.

"She's black," I said. "My friend is black and all you people care about is war! They'll—"

"Hush, lass." Thomas leaned forward, worry creasing between his eyes. "Why didn't ye say it before?"

"I didn't know how," I hissed, heart pounding in worry. "And now—"

"It's just news, don't fret. I'm sure—"

"It's not. You don't understand, and I can't make you, but this is going to be a long, bloody war. I just know it is, don't ask me how—" I glared at him when he opened his mouth to interrupt me "—and my friend is out there when all this shit hits the fan. I need to find her now, and then we need to go."

"Go?" he asked, raising his brow. "Where d'ye plan to go? And how would ye know all this? Ye a spy? A gypsy like they said?" He leaned forward, green eyes flaming now. "Ye telling me ye can see the future, gypsy?"

"Don't call me tha—"

He grabbed my forearms so tightly I flinched. I tried to pull away but he pinned them to the table, holding me in place. "Answer me now," he growled.

I let my breath out on a shudder, and tried to ignore those around us. A few were staring, but didn't seem to care enough to intervene.

"We're not from around here, but we're not spies," I whispered. "I can't explain what I know, you just have to believe me. I'm sorry. I think—" I paused, not sure what I was about to say was true. But from the small flashbacks of my grandmother, her dress, the way her people were dancing around the fire, my suspicions were increasingly becoming truth. "I think I do have gypsy blood in me from my grandmother, but I never practiced their ways. I'm mostly

Italian and was raised by an Irish family who is no longer here." By now, everything was spilling out of me and I didn't know how to stop it. "Shaylah and I have been friends since we were kids. I lost her when we arrived in this part of town, and now I'm afraid for her. She's free, but with how people treat..." My words caught in my throat, and I had to choke back tears. "We're just two girls who want to go back home. Please. Please help us." The tears fell freely as I begged under his steel grip.

We sat there for a full minute, his hard eyes examining my wet ones for any lies. He sat back, letting go of my arms, and sighed. "I didn't hurt ye, did I?" he asked, looking at his plate.

"No," I admitted. Though his grip was strong, his instincts were to restrain me without hurting me. It only scared the shit out of me.

"We'll talk to Hiram. See if he's heard anything. We'll find your friend. Ye got my word."

"Thank you," I mumbled. "How much for all of this?" I gestured towards the food, wanting to change the subject and get out of there. I didn't wait for him to answer, and handed him my money, telling him to figure it out. My stomach was too sick with worry to think about anything else right then.

CHAPTER TEN

Emilia

"Where are we going?" I yelled as we weaved in and out of people on the street.

"Hiram most likely is working on the docks. We'll have to wait for the day to be done. We'll see me brother, and see if he's heard anything."

"Won't he be working?" I asked.

Thomas looked down at me, amused. "Sure, ye can call it that."

He placed his hand on my back to guide me forward.

"I'm not keeping you from work, am I?" I asked.

"Nay, ye can leave that to the nativists."

"What?"

"Never ye mind," he muttered with a shake of his head.

He pulled me down the road until we reached a street that made me pause. If I had the correct location, instead of little Italian restaurants, I was faced with what were clearly Irish tenements, for little

Irish children ran in the street while the adults yelled at them in two different languages. I had never heard Irish spoken so much. It made a warmth spread through me; this otherworldly experience made life seem as if it were a dream.

The sun was higher now, illuminating the dirty gutters, dilapidated buildings with hastily built wooden add-ons that seemed to germinate in every crevice, housing even more people, and the thin, worn faces of the struggling residents. But through it all, the children's laughter and the greetings of acquaintances lifted my heart and pulled me into their world.

A few called out to Thomas, and he tipped his hat at them, never pausing to talk. I didn't know if that was usual for him, or if they somehow could tell he was on a mission. We made it to the door of a three-story tenement and had to back up hastily as it swung open. The man pushed past us, stumbling on the top step and reeking of alcohol. Thomas grabbed my arm and pulled me closer to him as we entered.

The sudden darkness momentarily blinded me. My eyes adjusted, revealing laundry hanging around the room and small cots built into bunk beds to save some space reminding me of fungus growing against the walls. The walls, floor, and everything inside were filthy. But that was not what had me gasping and averting my eyes. A woman was in mid-dress, paying us no mind as Thomas propelled me forward. As we passed, we saw others sleeping in the room's nine other beds.

We reached a stairway that led up to the second floor. Each creak of the stair beat with my pounding heart.

"Is this where you live?" I whispered and turned to look down at Thomas while I kept climbing.

"Me brother."

"You don't live with him?" I reached the landing and turned to him again. My heart jumped in my throat when I found that I was eye to eye with him. *When did he get so close?* I took a quick step back and gasped as I tripped. Thomas grabbed my arms, steadying me.

"Are ye always this clumsy?" he asked, raising a brow.

I shook my head, unable to explain why I had lost all dexterity in my body. It had to be shock from the overwhelming input of the nineteenth century.

"Mikey moved out awhile back," Thomas explained. His fingertips grazed my arm, leaving a trail of goosebumps in their wake as he let go of me. I shivered with the loss of his warmth. "I stayed."

He stepped around me and led us past open doorways until we reached the third door.

"You didn't want to leave?" I asked.

"And leave me family to starve? Nay, that was Mikey's job."

My chest tightened at the sudden hostility in his voice.

Without knocking, Thomas went through the open door to a long room just as filthy as the rest of the house. The beds were lined up—end-to-end—filling most of the space. Thomas walked down an aisle sideways so that his broad shoulders could fit and stopped at one of the beds. I wasn't sure what he was doing until he lifted the newspaper he found and smacked a sleeping person over the head with it.

The man sat up quickly, a knife in his hand, spitting obscenities until he saw Thomas.

"Feck, Tommy. What do ye want?"

Thomas moved to the side, and I got a good glimpse of the dark-haired stranger.

"You!" I yelled, pointing a finger at him as I came into the room.

"Jesus, Mary, and Joseph," he muttered. He put the knife away and dropped his head into his hands. "Do ye have to yell? Who's the lass?"

"You don't remember me?" I fumed, remembering him from my first night at Nora's. His picture didn't do him justice. Either that or my anger clouded my recognition.

He kept his head down. "Should I?"

"Does Madam Nora's ring any bells?"

He squinted his icy blues as he looked at me for the first time.

"Did I feck with ye? No wonder I can't recall." He glanced at my dress as if it bored him.

Thomas grabbed Michael's shirt and pulled him out of bed—an awkward move in the small aisle. Michael was nearly as big as his brother.

"Watch how ye talk to the lady," Thomas growled in Michael's face.

"What would a lady be doin' at Nora's?" Michael asked, his annoyance bordering on rage.

Thomas' grip tightened.

"I was singing," I said, meeting the eyes of one of the men in a bunk. My cheeks heated with the realization that the few others in the room were no longer sleeping. "You shoved money in my breasts and lifted my shift for the whole crowd to see!"

Thomas looked at me, anger distorting his features. I had to refrain from taking a frightened step back.

"Did he hurt ye?" he asked.

I shook my head, too angry to talk.

"Feck," Thomas muttered and shoved away from his brother.

Recognition dawned in Michael's face briefly before a sneer slammed it down. "Aye, I remember ye now. How can I forget the squeal ye gave out? Made me want to know if I could get ye to do it in sheets. Turned me down, she did. Tis a shame." He looked at my clothes in disgust.

"Christ," Thomas swore, rubbing his jaw frustratedly. "Do ye have a decent bone in your body, Mikey?"

"Nay, ye got all those. Aye?" Michael's tone was flat as he sat down again, rubbing his temples. "Don't tell me ye settled for him?" He looked at me, placing his hand on his heart. "I can promise ye a better time."

His wink had me flushing with anger, but I still didn't say anything.

"Shut it, gobshite," Thomas said, the anger ebbing slowly from him. "We need your help."

"Me help? What can I help the almighty Thomas with that ye need to sink so low for me help?"

"We need to find someone."

"Why doesn't your darkie help ye?"

Thomas slammed his fist on the bed next to him. The loud crack made me jump, but Michael sat there, unimpressed. I quickly looked around and found the other men sitting up, eyes trained on Thomas. All the hairs on my body stood. Did they think they had to protect Michael?

"Really, Tommy boy," Michael tsked annoyingly. "Ye shouldn't lose your temper like that in front of some of me boys."

His boys. My eyes shot back to him.

"Believe me," I answered instead, afraid that Thomas would start a brawl with more men than he could take on, "I wouldn't be asking you if it wasn't important. She's my friend. She's tall, pretty, and she's—" I paused, trying to think of the correct term to explain her race. Then, instead of bowing to the racism of the times, I politely explained her skin tone.

"Runaway slave?" Michael scoffed, scratching at a scar that cut through one of his eyebrows.

"No," I snapped, shooting him a glare. "She's free. But she's not used to how it is here, so I'm afraid for her."

"Drop her." Michael turned to his brother, yawning. "I really don't see how this is our problem."

Thomas shook his head. "I gave the lass me word."

"And why did ye do something stupid like that?" Michael asked. He stood up, straightening his clothes and gathering things around him in preparation to leave.

"Please help me," I begged.

Desperate for help, I grabbed his arm. He pulled it out of my grasp and pushed past me.

"If ye'll excuse me, I have somewhere I need to be."

The four other men stood up, ready to go with him.

"Ní iarraim mórán, a dheartháir." Thomas muttered. Something in his tone had me looking for an explanation in his expression, but his face was guarded, staring a hole through Michael.

Michael stopped, twisting his hat in his hands, listening.

"Le do thoil," said Thomas. I wasn't sure what it meant, but it had Michael rocking back on his heels.

"And what do ye want me to do?"

"Just check the North End with your boys. The lass and I will pay Hiram a wee visit and see if any news reached him. She's free, so it should just be a matter of finding her."

Michael shook his head and sighed. "The boys will help, but they won't be happy about it."

Tension radiated from the other men. Without realizing it, I stepped away from Michael, closer to Thomas. "What boys exactly?" I asked, glancing at them quickly.

"Our Mikey here is the head of the North Boys." Thomas grabbed my shoulder and pulled me toward him. Michael's eyes followed his brother's hand, missing nothing.

"North Boys?" I asked.

"Ye mean ye haven't heard of us, lass?" Michael sneered.

"A gang. The lot of them take it upon themselves to harass the masses."

"What?" my voice shook, and I cursed myself for that reveal.

"Don't ye worry your pretty little head about it," Michael derided me. "We don't get into too much trouble. Tell her, Tommy."

Thomas' hand squeezed my shoulder, revealing his brother's lie. A chill ran through me at the thought of what crimes these men must commit. I took another step back, my back colliding with Thomas' chest.

Michael cocked his head, looking between the two of us. "How did ye two meet?"

"None of your business—" I began.

"So ye did feck the slag?"

Thomas moved so swiftly that I wasn't sure how I ended up behind him as he grabbed his brother's shirt. The men surrounding us moved closer.

"Suimiúil," Michael said, studying Thomas' face.

Thomas growled a response in Irish but let go of his brother. Michael looked at me again with an inquisitiveness that confused me.

"Let's go, lads," Michael said to his crew. "Looks like we have a job to do. What will I get in return, Tommy boy?"

Thomas clenched his fists. "One more go-around."

Michael raised his brows, momentarily surprised. He would be attractive—what with his piercing blue eyes, nearly black, slicked-back hair, and pale skin—if it wasn't for the cruelty flashing beneath it all. My skin prickled at the thought of what this man was capable of.

"Can ye describe her a bit more, lass?" he asked. "A name?" His face lost a bit of the harsh lines, reminding me more of a business-man than I expected.

I showed him how she was several inches taller than I, that she had long braids down her back, described her heart-shaped face, her small hooped nose ring, how she was thin but still had some curves, and the dark, rich shade of her umber skin. "Shaylah Banks is pretty. I don't doubt you'll have trouble recognizing her."

Thomas and Michael shared a look so severe that my stomach sank.

"You think she's okay? Right?" I asked.

Michael rubbed the back of his neck. Thomas put his hands in his pockets and stared at the floor.

"Well," Michael said, his accent heavy, "good news is we might find her easy. The bad news, another man probably already did."

"Oh, you people really can't be that bad," I said, almost hysteri-cally. "Is it really that bad here?"

"No," Thomas said, glaring at Michael. "The city is home. Ye just don't want to run into the wrong crowd. Once word spreads around who's looking for her, all should be fine. Don't worry, lass."

I wasn't sure if I quite believed him, but to my shock, Michael agreed. When he left with the others, I let out the breath I didn't know I was holding.

CHAPTER ELEVEN

Emilia

I spent the rest of the afternoon with Thomas going in and out of taverns to inquire about Shay. We stopped at a bakery owned by the sweet old man, Mr. McCusker. He hadn't seen Shay, but gave us two hot rolls to eat while we talked to him. His pleasant smile and his obvious affection for Thomas won me over, and I found myself talking to him easily while Thomas questioned a few men down the street.

"I don't know how ye did it, lass," Mr. McCusker leaned in and whispered to me conspiratorially, "but, between us, our boyo has his eyes on ye. That's no easy feat."

He patted my shoulder and winked before turning to another customer. I stood there, frozen, as I thought about what he said. The previous night Thomas laughed easily, opened up casually, and then woke up as an entirely different person. His surly attitude through-out the day had me questioning the older man's sanity. Thomas treated me with every respect you'd treat a stranger, which I'd find appropriate, except for already having a glimpse of his dark humor and quick wit. It was as if a barrier had gone up between us, making me believe his kindness to me was all an act, or that I'd imagined it entirely. If it wasn't for his help, I'd think he was more like Michael than I cared to admit. A sudden, unbidden thought that he might be using me for something wove its way obtrusively into my mind. Still, I couldn't think of what that would be and tried to ignore its tightening grip.

Thomas had me wait at the bakery, so I used the time to look around. The old baker kept his shop clean and tidy. I could give him that. The baked goods rested on racks along the walls and the front window, illuminated by the sun. I wondered how much one of the pasties was when the bell over the door rang loudly.

Thomas flew in, removing his hat as he searched for me. I stepped around the line of customers, my heart jumping at the thought that he had news of Shay.

"We need to go," Thomas said, his guarded eyes shining with excitement. "Ye were right, lass. It looks like a war has started. The papers should be spillin' out soon."

"Damn rebels!" a woman hissed in the line, crimson with rage.

The blood drain from my face, making me instantly nauseous and lightheaded. Thomas grabbed my arm when I swayed, steadying me.

"Easy," he said quietly, searching my eyes. "Are ye all right, lass?"

"What do you mean?" I silently cursed myself for not remembering more of the facts in the school paper I had written. I mainly focused on the various roles women played in the war movement. The dates and battles were all jumbled in my head. I knew that Fort Sumter had started the war, but couldn't recall what happened after that, and at what pace. Overall vital points about it did little to prepare me for Boston in the coming days, if not weeks, depending on when Shay and I could get out of the past.

"Shots were fired," Thomas responded over the commotion in the shop. "The papers should know more."

We made our way through the streets and headed to the nearest newspaper office closer to the center of town. When I saw glimpses of the far-off sea, I tried to get a clear view of the wharves, but Thomas didn't veer too close, staying on our straight path, my line of sight obstructed by the other buildings nearest to us. Just the familiarity of it calmed my frantic heart to a steady drum.

I knew we had finally reached the right street by the large crowd assembled in front of a small building. The excited voices and curses traveled to us long before we reached our destination, and people passed us in their hurry to get to the news first.

"C'mon, lass," Thomas said. He grabbed my hand, so we weren't separated, but the contact electrified my nerves all the same. I pushed the odd sensation out of my mind and concentrated on the faces around us.

We stopped when a familiar voice started speaking in front of Thomas, I peered around him to see who it was. Hiram looked down at me, surprise and confusion flashing briefly in his golden eyes.

"Good evening, ma'am," he said, taking off his hat with a bow of his head.

"Evening." I smiled awkwardly, and we both turned toward Thomas.

"So you heard?" Hiram asked.

"Aye, now ye can stop your griping. Have they released anything yet?"

"Not yet."

We started walking towards the front as they talked, easier now that I had a massive man in front of me and one behind. According to the talk around us, the newspapers would be handed out any minute. We waited, and Hiram raised his brow, looking between us.

"I need to find my friend," I blurted, more worried about Shay than the upcoming war. I quickly explained what had happened and why Thomas was helping me.

Hiram's jaw ticked, thick brows coming together in consternation. "Do you have any reason to believe she'd be in danger?"

"Well, no," I admitted, glancing at Thomas. My stomach twisted sharply. "I just have a horrible feeling."

The doors opened, and a young man came out with papers. The crowd surge pushed me forward, but Hiram grabbed the newspaper quickly, and Thomas guided me out of the way. They huddled over the paper while I waited to see.

"A demand was made at two," Thomas read slowly as if the print was hard to read.

"Look here," Hiram pointed. "The fighting is to commence at eight."

"Is that it?" Thomas squinted at the paper in disbelief.

"Let me see," I said, reaching for it. They were too busy discussing the possible scenarios that I took it from them without much notice.

The text was easy to read, with only a small section about the fort. Shots were fired, but no casualties and more details would surely come in the next few days. I handed back the newspaper, my stomach in my throat.

It didn't matter, I told myself. Shay was the only thing that mattered at that point.

I was aware of only part of their conversation. Small sections of it penetrated my ears as I looked around at the crowd, hoping I'd see a familiar face. I searched each person when someone grabbed my arm.

"Emilia." Thomas' face appeared in front of me. "I've been talkin' to ye. Hiram said he'd help. We're to go to Rose's. If anyone knows anything about anyone, it'll be ol' Rose."

I looked at Hiram and felt a weight lifted off my shoulders. "Thank you so much." I let my head drop back in relief.

"Let's just find your friend first," he said, placing his hat on his head. His grim demeanor would have drowned out my hope, but I realized that expression had dominated most of his behavior since I met him.

Putting my worries aside, I replaced them with faith in those who knew the old city. If this man couldn't find them amongst his people, then maybe the Irishman and his wayward brother could.

I silently sent up a prayer for some extra help.

CHAPTER TWELVE

Thomas

Hiram led them to a neighborhood spotted with stores and houses lining the street. They were close enough to the wharves that the soft lap of the waves against the docked ships could be heard from the next block over. Thomas lifted his head, taking in the welcome scent of the sea.

"Can I?" Emilia asked, her body already turning to go. "I just need to go by the water for a minute."

Thomas saw the set determination in her dark eyes and knew there was no changing her mind. The same look overcame her when she asked him to help her find her friend.

He nodded to Hiram. "We'll meet ye in a minute."

Hiram gave them a strange look but started back down the block, heading to Rose's Bake Shop.

The weather was warm enough on the short walk to the docks that it was almost relaxing, if it wasn't for being the wrong color in the neighborhood. From what Thomas could tell, Emilia didn't notice they were gaining far more attention than he would like. She was strange, as if she was utterly oblivious of racial segregation. Of course, Thomas was around Hiram enough that many residents recognized him, but Emilia was new, and they might not trust her.

Dodging a few pedestrians and ignoring the men unloading some cargo off one of the ships, Emilia grabbed the wooden fence near the water as a light breeze swept over her—whipping a few dark strands of hair around her face.

"What's troublin' ye, lass?" Thomas asked behind her, wishing she had chosen a different place to stand. He didn't like how one of the white dockworkers kept eyeing her. "Rose might know somethin'."

"I know, I just—" she shook her head. "I just had to get away for a minute. It's easier to breathe out here."

"Aye, I know what ye mean," he said after some time, the words coming out of his mouth almost unbidden. He didn't open up to others, and the idea of it made him uncomfortable. He stood next to her, hands in his pockets, and they watched the sun glisten off the small waves. "Sometimes I come out here just to talk to them."

"Talk to who?"

Thomas felt Emilia's gaze on him, waiting for a response. He shook his head and stared down at her, marveling at the light freckles spotting her nose before tearing his gaze away. "It was so long ago, it doesn't matter. I don't know why I brought it up."

Emilia followed his line of sight. Together they watched seagulls swoop down and fly in between the boats as the sun lowered over the water.

Thomas didn't know whether it was the rare tranquil moment or the odd woman beside him, but he found himself saying things he had long buried away. "Me sisters, Lizzie and Annie." Thomas's voice was low as he pictured a different time. "They died on the ship from Ireland. They rest on the bottom of the sea." He shrugged. "Along with all the others. When life gets hard, I talk to them and take comfort that they don't have to struggle with us. That they're at peace now."

Color spotted her cheeks, enhancing her beauty and taking the sting away from his admission. "How old were they?" she asked.

"Lizzie, no more than five, I think. Annie, just a babe."

"Why didn't you guys wait?" Tears were suddenly in her eyes, surprising him.

He squinted at her curiously, wondering how the world kept itself from this woman. How she was seemingly impacted by nothing until the loss of her friend. She was almost pure, making him want to protect her and push her away simultaneously. The deep emotions raging within him were entirely new, and that alone was enough to keep her at a distance.

"There was no food, lass," Thomas explained, clearing his throat. "Our landlord sent us out with the promise of passage to America. We didn't know to pack food and barely had enough clothes to cover us." He straightened his hat and looked everywhere but at the warm eyes staring at him. They reminded him of the rich soil back home, tugging him in ways he didn't want to understand. "Ye can guess what happened from there. It was either starve back in Ireland or starve on the ships. Not much of a choice, aye? At least America was to be better." He lowered his hat further and started walking back toward the neighborhood.

"I've never experienced anything like that." Her voice was soft. "I'm sorry."

Thomas was silent while they passed the dockworkers again. It wasn't until they crossed the street that he spoke. "Don't apologize for someone else's troubles, lass. They're my burden to bear."

"Doesn't mean you should have to do it alone."

That was where she was wrong, Thomas believed. He felt an insurmountable weight on his shoulders whenever he thought of passing his troubles on to others. It was easier to deal with life himself and not worry about anyone other than his immediate family. The fact that he was in the Vigilance Committee and was known to help runaway slaves and risked his life more than once to rescue one of them was somehow different. They were missions that he tackled. However, family they were for life. He couldn't even think about what that added weight would do to him.

"Tis better that way," he said.

"You're wrong."

Thomas shook his head, suppressing a smile at her defiance, but said no more.

Laughter carried down the street until they reached the two-story building that was Rose's Bake Shop. The boys were on the sidewalk, leaning against the shop and fooling around, when they spotted Emilia and fell silent, studying her curiously. Thomas knew Hiram must have filled them in. Still, their instinctual distrust of a new white person in their city tampered out their geniality.

"Tommy," George nodded. "Hiram said you might need some help. Is this her?" George smiled politely at Emilia.

"Aye, this is Miss Moretti," Thomas confirmed. "Emilia, this is George Wilson. George runs the shop with Rose, his wife."

"Nice to meet you." She smiled and held out her hand to everyone's shock.

Unaccustomed to shaking the hand of a woman who was not an acquaintance and a white woman at that, a look of bewilderment crossed George's features. Not wanting to be rude, he gripped her fingers lightly.

"Pleasure to meet you, Miss Moretti. These two are my sons." He gestured to Jackson and Isaac.

She shook both of their hands. Already growing used to her peculiarities, Thomas raised his brows at the other men when they looked at him. Isaac smiled freely at Emilia when he introduced himself—his easy-going nature often getting him in trouble.

"If you don't mind me saying, your mighty pretty, Miss Moretti," Isaac said, eyes gleaming with humor.

"Thank you," Emilia smiled at Isaac and took a step back toward Thomas. He bit back a grin as he wondered if she was conscious of doing it. She'd done it multiple on multiple occasions, and he found himself liking it more than he should.

"Excuse my brother," Jackson said, sharp enough that Emilia flinched. "He doesn't know how to speak to a lady."

"Oh, it's no problem," she said, worriedly looking at Thomas.

"All do respect," Jackson said, "but I wouldn't like my brother lynched. He needs to mind his mouth."

"That's enough," George said, voice unusually sharp.

Emilia went pale and looked at Isaac, who stared at the ground. Thomas disagreed with it, but Isaac knew better. If the wrong person saw, or if Emilia told someone, Isaac could be arrested, or end up with a fate much worse. The damned law made sure of it. And this woman acted like she was utterly stunned by the ordeal.

"I hope you weren't offended, Miss Moretti," Isaac said, defiance replacing the gleam in his eyes.

"No offense taken," she said weakly.

Hiram straightened from the wall, drawing their attention to him rather than the growing tension, and ushered them inside.

Emilia grabbed Thomas' arm and drew him aside.

"I hope I didn't do something wrong," she whispered, eyeing the other men talking to each other.

Thomas found it increasingly difficult to focus on her words when her warm hand gripped him. The faint trace of the rose perfume reminded him of how she'd been wrapped around him that morning.

"Your strange, lass. I give ye that. They don't know how to handle ye."

"I'm not strange!" she squealed, making the men look back at them.

"You're white."

"Not *that* white. And so are you."

"They know me."

Thomas watched understanding cross her features, and he again wondered where she grew up to make her so wildly ignorant of the racial disparities that their society upheld.

"Okay," she said, her brow furrowing together. "If I do something weird, just hit me."

"What?"

"Nudge me or something! I don't know," she hissed. "Flick me. I don't want to upset anyone. Warn me if I'm accidentally doing something stupid. Please."

Had God sent this woman to drive him mad? Thomas shook his head but agreed, if only to ease the line creasing her brows. He'd help her up to the point of finding her friend, then she would need to find her own place in the world.

Mind made up, he guided her to the counter where Rose was selling bread to a woman, Mira wrapping up the loaves while the woman paid. He greeted the two women with a smile.

"Evening, Tommy," Mira smiled back, already looking around him towards Hiram.

"Now, what are you doing here?" Rose asked, eyes narrowing as she smoothed down her apron.

"Ah, don't be like that. Can't I come for just a wee visit?"

"That's precisely why I'm asking. You're always up to something. What are you men cooking up?" She turned her critical eyes on the rest of the group, each doing their best to avoid her glare. Emilia gave her a nervous smile, making Rose purse out her big lips in thought.

"Who are you?" Mira asked, standing up from the stool behind the counter. Thomas leaned closer to see if she'd really been sitting. Mira was a petite girl about the same height standing as she was sitting on the large stool.

"Em—"

"Nevermind," Rose cut her off. "The answer's no."

"Rose, honey," George started, earning a glare that could peel paint. "Just listen for a minute."

"I don't have to listen to anything. All you boys do is get yourself into trouble, and I'm tired of it. Can't you just help your own kind? You always bring some riffraff off the streets, and I'm sick of it. She's gonna cause trouble. I'll tell you that now."

"She looks nice to me," a small voice said in the doorway that led to the back room.

Everyone turned toward Evaline. The child glowed with attention and walked into the room, her worn skirt fluttering with each step.

"Looks can be deceiving, child," Rose said, brushing crumbs off the counter.

"Uncle Hiram!" Evaline said with a big smile and ran to give him a hug.

Hiram picked her up, looking uncomfortable, but everyone knew he adored her like his own. She ran towards Thomas next and gave him just as much affection. Picking her up, Thomas tried to ignore the question on Emilia's face.

"Why are you trouble?" Evaline asked Emilia, tilting her head so that her long, dark curls tumbled over her shoulder.

"I don't mean to be," Emilia smiled tightly. "My friend is lost, and I need help finding her. She really isn't any trouble. It's just…"

"Here it is," Rose said, shaking her head.

"Well, she's like you."

"A nigger, you mean," Rose snapped, eyes flashing. "And she your property too?"

"Mama!" Mira gasped, her small hand flying to her chest. She had grown up in the North and always despaired when confronted with conflict.

"No, of course not," Emilia said. "I don't believe in that—"

Rose grunted, her agitation rising.

"Now, Rosie," George said more sternly, locking eyes with his wife. "Give the girl a chance."

"Well, she said she's not from around here." Rose's eyes still flashed but turned towards Emilia.

Mira walked around the counter, wringing her hands. "Not all whites are bad, Mama. Look at what Thomas has done—"

"Hush, child. I very well know what Thomas has done."

Mira's cheeks flared in what Thomas assumed was embarrassment from being called a child in front of everyone. Her gaze flicked to Hiram before quickly falling to the floor.

"Have ye heard anything?" Thomas cut to the chase and set Evaline back on the ground.

Her shoulders slumped in defeat, and she sat on the stool. "There's been talk about a black woman in the North End half out of her wits yesterday." Rose sighed and shook her head. "They said she was saying strange things, wearing odd clothing, and asking around. The Irish thought she was crazy and turned her out. Don't know where she is now. Didn't think much of it this morning, with the store being busy. Probably long gone by now, anyhow. Poor child. Is she dim?"

"No, we're not from around here, is all," Emilia said, turning swiftly to Thomas, hope and worry warring among her features.

"Think it's her, lass?" Thomas asked.

"It sounds like it. We can't know for sure, but it wouldn't hurt to look."

"Aye, if she's near the North End, then Mikey should be on it."

"What do you want from us?" Hiram asked, leaning near the front window.

The three other men all turned toward Thomas, knowing they needed to find Ms. Banks before she came across anyone who would do her harm. It wasn't safe for any woman to be on the city streets alone at night.

"Keep an eye out," Thomas said. "Spread word that we're looking for her and no harm is to come to her."

The three men agreed they'd take a walk around town, keeping an eye out while spreading the word. Now, she had two groups looking for her from both directions of the city. As long as she didn't travel too far, they could find her within a day of searching.

"Maybe I should walk with you?" Emilia asked, turning toward Jackson, who seemed to be taking control of the pack.

"No, you should go home, ma'am," Jackson said politely. "Wait for word."

Emilia looked up at Thomas, worry swirling in her dark eyes. "She doesn't know them. I only know what she looks like."

"Ye described her enough, lass."

Hiram stood up from talking to Evaline. "It's best you're not out after dark. A lady should stay in."

"A lady?" Emilia turned red as a beat. "I'm perfectly capable of helping. I want to go out and find my friend—ow!"

Emilia jumped, grabbed her arm, and swung towards Thomas as he lowered his hand and bit back a grin.

"You pinched me!"

"Maybe ye should stay with me."

Her lips parted as a beautiful flush spread across her features. Apparently, that flustered her enough to shut her up. Besides, she told him to stop her if she began acting strangely. Though Thomas admired headstrong women, it wouldn't be safe for her to go with them in search of her friend. He didn't regret using her social awkwardness if it meant keeping her from harm.

Hiram raised his brow at the offer of bringing a woman home, but Thomas only raised his brows in return, daring him to say something.

"All right." Jackson wiped his smile away with his hand before Emilia could see it. "Let's head out, boys."

"Wait." Isaac straightened, mischief in his eyes. "Are y'all courting or something? You should have told me before I started crushing on your woman, Tommy."

"What did I tell you?" Jackson glared at his brother and started to push him out of the bakery, but Thomas could've sworn he was trying to hold back a smile. "Sorry about that, ma'am."

"Just helping the lass, then we're parting ways." Thomas shrugged, feeling Emilia's gaze on him.

"I hope you find the girl," Rose said while they both watched Emilia and Evaline whisper conspiratorially with each other. Everyone else had left. "I just wish you boys didn't go running into trouble every other week."

"Aye," Thomas agreed, watching Emilia make Evaline laugh, so he didn't have to look at Rose. Her eyes had been narrowed on him and Emilia, and he wasn't sure he wanted to know what was on her mind.

"Here." Rose grudgingly handed him some pastries she wrapped up. "My guess is you haven't eaten?"

Thomas tried to sway her, but she wouldn't let them leave until they accepted the food.

"Ye know I'm good for it," Thomas said, promising to pay her for it later.

"Get on out of here." She ignored him, putting everything away in preparation to close the bakery.

Evaline laughed again and ran to Thomas, beckoning him with her finger so that he would bend down. "I like her," her little voice whispered into his ear. "The pretty light shines differently around her."

Even though Thomas saw no light, the hairs rose on his neck as Evaline bound into the other room, leaving him to wonder what she meant.

CHAPTER THIRTEEN

Emilia

"Where are we going exactly?" I asked, looking around at the buildings.

It didn't help that dusk faded fast, and everything was shrouded in darkness. The few gas streetlamps and the moon were the only sources of light shining down on the buildings, throwing shadows.

"Ye'll have to stay with me for tonight. Like I said back there." He must have felt my unease because he clarified. "Maggie, me sister, lives there with me, Ma and Da, too. Ná bí buartha. I told you before that I live with me family. I wouldn't save ye and drag ye around the city just to take ye for meself, lass."

"Well, that's reassuring," I mumbled, while what I really worried about was meeting his family. I wasn't going to admit that, though.

We stopped in front of a three-story brick building and Thomas turned toward me, the moon shining down on him in a way that made my breath catch. His head tilted to the side as if studying me.

"What?" I asked self-consciously.

"Nothing, just—" he shook his head and turned towards the tenements. "Just follow me."

We went around the back to the first wooden staircase. Several others led up to the other tenements. I eyed the clothes hanging on the balconies and on the multiple lines tied between the buildings. We went up two flights of stairs before stopping in front of a door worn with age.

"Thomas," I said, grabbing his arm to stop him from opening it. "Are you sure about this? Won't they, like, not want me here?"

He looked at my hand, not saying anything.

"I'm sorry," I mumbled and let go.

"Ye are with me," he said. "I will not let them deny ye."

Goosebumps spread over my body at the way he said it, as if he never took no for an answer.

I kept close to him as he opened the door, feeling oddly shy for intruding on his family. A small fire was lit, giving enough light to see a few dark figures in the small room.

Thomas stepped to the side so I could step in as well, his large body making the tiny space even smaller.

"Tommy! What have ye—" a woman began but stopped when she saw me.

"Who is this?" a gruff voice growled from one of the cots in the corner of the room. I took an involuntarily step closer to Thomas.

The man sat up, revealing a thin but large form. Even in the shadows, I could tell he had the same build as Thomas.

Thomas introduced us, giving each of our names. I guessed his sister must be on the cusp of maturity, her figure between the stages of a child and a teenager. Maggie stopped patching a pair of pants to study me beneath strands of dark hair loose from her bun. She was striking, small-boned, and delicate in a very feminine way. Still, there was something in the way she held herself that radiated strength. Even in the dark, her eyes were sharp and fierce as the fire danced in them, and for a second, it was as if I was looking into Thomas's.

Hearing his mother, Joney, whisper heatedly to Thomas, I directed my attention to her. "I'm sorry to intrude," I said a little shakily. "I can go..."

Whatever Thomas said to his mother in Irish softened the harsh lines creasing her forehead and dissolved into resignation. She skirted around a small table until she stood in front of me, surprisingly close to my height. From up close, her eyes were almond-shaped, a trait she must have passed down to her children. Her sharp features hinted at a beauty that resembled her daughter's, worn down by time and struggles.

"I don't mean to be rude." Her strong brogue—far heavier than Thomas's—rolled over me like the sky threatening a storm. "We don't have much company." She pushed her long, peppered hair behind her ear and turned to a pot hanging over the fire. "Would ye like some stew? We have a wee bit left."

"Oh, I wouldn't want to intrude..." I said at the same time Thomas presented the pastries.

"Don't be silly." She clucked, taking the offering from her son with a smile. "If Thomas is going to bring a lass home, she will be served right. C'mon, sit down." She filled a bowl and set it on the table, beckoning us to sit.

"Maggie, get a cot ready for Miss Moretti, why don't ye?" Joney kept her hands busy, trying to straighten the room up. It was relatively neat, though there was a light layer of soot on everything without proper ventilation for the fire.

"There's only Tommy's left," Maggie responded. My head jumped back a little, surprised how she didn't have an accent. But it made sense, probably having been born in America. It was just an odd contrast with the rest of the family.

Joney's pursed her lips with her hands on her hips. "Well—"

"Give it to her," Thomas said, pulling out the chair for me to sit.

"I can't—"

"Ye will," Thomas cut me off, and that was that.

The deep voice in the corner had me straightening. "I'm sure ye were expectin' better accommodations," Thomas Sr. grumbled, taking me in. I tried not to squirm under his stare. Not that it was lewd, but rather condemnatory. "Thought ye would try slummin' it with the Irish folk, aye?"

"Thomas," Joney chastised, slapping her rag down on the table. "Miss Moretti doesn't deserve to be ridiculed."

"Most people call me Millie." My smile was strained, trying to de-escalate the situation while ignoring Thomas's clenched fists as he glared at his father. "Thank you for this."

Thomas sat across from me and grabbed a small bowl for himself. "Eat," he grumbled into the bowl.

The stew was bland, filled with questionable vegetables and meat that I didn't overthink. The pastries complimented it well, though. Honestly, I was just grateful I had something to fill my stomach.

His father stood up, muttering something sharply in Irish, and grabbed a worn jacket. Joney snapped back while he prepared to leave. I couldn't help but flinch as the door slammed closed.

"I hope that wasn't about me," I mumbled.

Maggie muttered in Irish to her mother, causing Thomas to snap at her.

If I'm going to cause such strife among them, I should leave.

Joney wrung a towel in her hand, determination setting her features. "We're happy to help ye get on your feet. Don't worry, dear. Me husband will come around."

It was as if she had read my mind.

"Once we find Shay, I promise to get out of your hair, Mrs. O'Connor."

"Call me Joney." She didn't smile but kept busy. "And enough of that talk. Shall we pray? We didn't bless your food..." She lifted a small box from a shelf hidden in the corner. She removed several rosaries from it, passing them to her children.

Thomas leaned back, glancing at me oddly. "Ye don't need to worry about our prayers," he whispered while his mom was busy talking to Maggie.

"What's wrong with our prayers, Tommy?" his mom snapped, overhearing him. "I never heard ye ashamed of your religion before."

"I'm not." Thomas darkened with anger. "I don't want to make her feel uncomfortable, is all."

"I actually have one," I said, pulling out the rosary I always wore. I hadn't put it on again since arriving in this time and still had it hidden in my pocket. It was almost worth it to see the surprise on Thomas' face.

"See," Joney said smugly, "Our lass is a good Catholic." She patted my hand and smiled the first genuine smile since I arrived, making me feel like I had just won a point in her book.

"I told you I was raised by Irish parents." I shrugged, waiting for Joney to take the lead.

To my surprise, Thomas spoke first, reciting the traditional meal prayer. Then, when he was done, Joney silently prayed the Rosary with us.

We ate our meal mostly in silence.

We'd been talking about Ireland for a while—I had asked about it—when Joney made a quick movement with her hand, surprising me by wiping away a tear. She muttered an apology in Irish and cleared our empty bowls off the table.

Thomas leaned back and watched his mother. "She misses home sometimes."

"Ireland?"

"Aye. Sometimes I wonder if it would've been better just to stay."

He didn't explain more, so I stood to help his mother.

"You aren't Irish?" Maggie asked me.

"No," I admitted. "My parents are, though. They took me in when I was little. I never met my biological family, though I know they are Italian."

"Did they not want you or something?" Her words stung, but it was clear she just asked with the simple curiosity of a child.

I froze with a dish in my hand, feeling the haze of something long forgotten. Flashes came. The sudden sound of my mammina's screams as my papá yelled at someone else. My face crumpled as the memory hit me in the chest, and I had to force it down and push it far from my mind so I didn't succumb to its despair.

A prickling sensation told me it was the last memory I had with both of my parents, and it shook me to my core that it had returned after all of these years. A part of me feared what else I'd remember the longer I stayed here.

"Enough, Maggie." It was Thomas who had spoken, bringing me back into the present. "You've upset her."

Maggie's eyes widened. "I'm sorry, Miss—"

"No," I tried to smile. "Don't apologize. I was just remembering. No, I think my family sent me away because they knew they couldn't give me the life I needed." I refused to remember why my papá did it. But I remembered enough—frightened into paralysis, mammina screaming, and my papá's sense of urgency, ultimately sending me away. "I had a really good life with my adopted parents, so it all turned out."

"To give up one's own child," Joney muttered while cleaning up and fell into speaking Irish to herself.

My cheeks flamed, too embarrassed to look at Thomas. Maggie caught my eye. She stared at me in deep thought as if peeling away my layers until she understood.

"I wish my family would've given me away."

Her admission shocked me, and I instantly looked to Thomas to see if he had heard. The pain was evident on his face before he hid it behind a blank stare.

"Ye mustn't let Ma hear that." The roughness in his voice had me averting my gaze.

"It's true," she muttered, getting up to help clean.

"It should do," Joney said, thankfully not hearing our conversation as she straightened the thin cover over Thomas's cot. She eyed her son. "Don't be thinkin' ye'll share, now."

A mischievous glint lit up his eyes as he said something to her in Irish. She surprised me with a quick laugh and swat to his arm. My heart warmed at the way she clearly loved her kids. Even through the hard times, they had each other.

I turned to Maggie and asked her where I could go to the bathroom.

She squinted at me like the countless others who thought I was strange in this time. "Downstairs if you're too shy to go in the pot. I can take you."

"Thanks."

"Where ye two headed?" Thomas asked, untying his worn boot. He stood up when Maggie filled him in.

"I'll go with ye."

I felt he didn't like us going by ourselves in the dark. The thought had me nervous while we walked to the outhouses, jumping at the slightest noise. We reached a row of six wooden stalls, roughly made and smelling, frankly, like shit. I covered my mouth, wanting to turn back around.

"Haven't you ever shit before?" Maggie asked when she saw my reaction.

"Yes," I laughed.

"Mag!" Thomas snapped, more shocked than angry.

"I see bluntness runs in the family." I smiled at Thomas.

An older man shoved past Maggie and me, causing us to stumble sideways. I caught her arm, so she didn't fall.

"Are ye gonna piss or ye gonna run your gab all day?" he growled.

I began apologizing, but Thomas already had the man by the front of his shirt, pinned against the wall. The anger slipped from the man's face and instantly drained of color.

"I didn't realize they was with ye, Tommy."

"Ye didn't realize ye should be a decent human?" This wasn't the same Thomas I was with only minutes before. This Thomas was harsh, imposing, and savage—reminding me of the criminals who ran with his brother.

"Tá brón orm."

"Don't apologize to me. It's their feet ye should kiss." Thomas shoved away from the man, letting him fall before regaining his balance.

"I apologize for me rudeness," the man addressed us, side-eyeing Thomas for approval. Did he think Thomas would hurt him?

I just nodded, unable to say anything, before he quickly scampered away, apparently forgetting he had to pee.

"You're hurting me," a small voice said irritably, and I realized I had been squeezing Maggie's arms tightly.

"Sorry," I mumbled, stepping away.

I rushed by Thomas and Maggie, refusing to look at anyone lining up for the outhouses, and slammed myself into one of the small stalls. With the relief of being alone, I took a deep breath and instantly regretted it. Coughing and gagging, I nearly threw up in the hole that was considered a toilet.

"Jesus, God," I gasped, covering my mouth again. I hurried up with my business and nearly ran back out, pushing people to the side as I emerged. A few women snapped at my rudeness, but I couldn't bring myself to care.

I found Thomas and Maggie a short distance off.

"C'mon." Thomas went to guide me with his hand, and I flinched. I hadn't meant to do it. I had never experienced much violence, and the easy way he unleashed it scared me. He paused, but I could not bring myself to see if I had hurt his feelings. "Let's go up. Maybe Mikey will bring word soon."

We were halfway up the stairs when a loud bang went off down the street, I jumped and a few men yelled at each other a distance off.

"Ye can trust me, can't ye?" Thomas said gently.

"I barely know you."

Thomas clenched his jaw, but nodded. "Fair enough. Just know I'm doing me best to protect ye."

"Why *are* you helping me? Not that I'm ungrateful... It's just, you're doing a lot for a complete stranger."

Maggie was already through the door, so we were alone. Thomas looked at the building across from us as if it had an answer. "It's always been in me nature." He shrugged. "When someone needs help, I help them."

"Oh." For some reason, his answer disappointed me. "So, I'm not special or anything." Shit, that sounded pathetic out loud. I tried to laugh, but it came out fake. "Good to know, I guess."

He looked at me sharply, surprised and searching. "Ye are unlike anyone I've ever met."

I nodded. "Makes sense."

The poor man probably had no idea how to handle my mood swings just then, but honestly, the nineteenth century was beginning to wear me a little thin.

I looked down at the people walking by, when his rough fingers gently grabbed my chin. My eyes had to be saucers as he searched them, threatening to give away all my thoughts without my approval. I hoped he couldn't see them. My breath hitched with him so close, and I forgot my anxiety about what was happening around us.

"We'll find her, gaiscíoch beag."

I shivered at the endearment, which, to my embarrassment, didn't go unnoticed by Thomas. He leaned in, his entire presence filling me as the pad of his thumb caressed my lower lip. I couldn't move, could barely breathe, fearing he'd walk away. He cupped my cheek, his green eyes consuming me until I thought I'd explode if he didn't do something *more*. My tongue traced my lower lip, and I watched in amazement as his eyes turned nearly black with desire.

So, he is affected by me. Molten lava filled my belly as my body lit up like fireworks.

"Where have ye been?" Joney asked.

We sprang apart so fast I was nearly dizzy. If it wasn't for my pounding heart and the flush of my cheeks, I would have thought I'd imagined the whole thing.

I'd never experienced such heat before. And, it seemed, the rumors about Thomas were true.

It became increasingly clear that if I wasn't careful, Thomas O'Connor might possibly be my undoing.

CHAPTER FOURTEEN

Emilia

"Emilia." I tried to fight through the haze and struggled to make sense of my disoriented brain. A moment later, someone shook my shoulder. "Lass, wake up!"

I sat up groggily, my head swimming with the sudden movement. When no word had come earlier in the night, we had gone to bed. I kept my dress on, not feeling comfortable around Thomas' family. I hadn't felt tired, but I must have been more exhausted than I realized and fell asleep with little trouble.

"I need to go." Thomas' voice was hushed, and I noticed everyone else was sleeping. His dad must have come in while I was out. "Mikey found her with The Celtic Princes. I didn't want ye to wake without knowing."

My eyes cleared enough that I could see a man standing behind Thomas.

"Is she okay?" I asked Michael. "Why isn't she here?"

Michael looked down and shook his head. "I didn't think it was safe to bring her up."

Dread crushed me like a weight. "What does that mean?"

He looked at Thomas, and they had a silent exchange.

"Ye stay here," Thomas said to me, his features strained.

"No! Is she downstairs? If she's here, I'm going to her." I pushed myself to the side of the cot and put my shoes on.

"Maybe ye should wait here a minute." Thomas knelt by me. "I just didn't want ye to wake while I was gone."

"No."

"Emilia." The way he said it made me freeze. "She isn't well. I'm not sure ye should see it."

"I'm going downstairs." The words were strained as my throat constricted in terror.

Michael led the way down to an unremarkable wagon surrounded by four of his men. I tried to ignore their rough appearance and what may have been blood on their clothes. I pushed by one of them, almost in a daze, as Michael held a hand out to the man to let me pass. There were crates filled with odds and ends of supplies, some wood, piles of tools, and a dirty blanket.

"Where—" I began but stopped, seeing the blanket move. I looked to Thomas, but he only nodded grimly.

Trying to climb into the back of the wagon, I slipped on my long dress and cursed until a strong hand helped me up. I didn't have to look to know who it was.

"Shay?" I whispered, ignoring the men around us.

The blanket moved again, yet there was no response. I gently pulled back the blanket and fell backward, gasping. Tears flooded my eyes, blurring out my best friend's swollen, bloody, and almost unrecognizable face.

"You're certain it's her?" Thomas was by the side of the wagon now.

I nodded, trying to keep in a sob. I pulled myself to a kneeling position and examined her more closely. Bruises splotched her dark skin on almost every inch that was exposed. Realizing she didn't have any clothes on, I quickly tugged the blanket up around her neck.

"Shay, it's me. Millie," I whispered, gently smoothing her braids back. "Can you hear me, honey?"

Her eyes were swollen shut, unable to look at me. She began to move and a whimper of pain escaped her.

"Don't—don't move." Nausea overwhelmed me. I should have found her sooner. If I just—I shook my head, the tears falling onto the blanket. It should have been me. "I'm here now. You're safe."

Tears squeezed out the sides of her eyes as she tried to free her arm from the blanket. I grabbed her hand, lightly squeezing it to let her know I was still there.

"Who'd do this?" My voice hardened in a way I didn't recognize.

"The Celtic Princes found her."

Her hand tightened on mine, shaking.

"Okay, okay," I mumbled. "Can we take her somewhere more comfortable?" I asked Thomas. I desperately wanted to know what had happened, but she needed to be cared for first.

Thomas walked away. I distantly heard him talking to the others as I rubbed my thumb lightly over Shay's hand. Agreeing upon something, Michael climbed into the driver's seat as Thomas hopped in the back, sitting across from us. The other men walked off.

I lay down next to Shay and placed my arm protectively over her, taking special care not to hurt her. The sky was clear, thousands of stars dotting the inky black. I usually would've marveled at the brilliant view, but at this moment, all I felt was empty; an insignificant little spec in the enormous, cruel universe.

Without even thinking about it, I began singing quietly like I used to when she was upset. The wagon bumped down the road, hopefully carrying us to somewhere she could recover.

I felt Thomas watching us. It didn't matter, though. Nothing mattered except for Shay and what we had to do for her to heal so we could leave this horrible place. The sway of the wagon and the soft clomp of the horse's hooves put me in a trance until there was nothing but the two of us. The words flowed out without much thought, transporting us back to my room where we could laugh and talk easily. Where we were safe.

The wagon began to slow, the hooves' clip replaced by the reins' jingle as the horse shook itself and snorted. I pulled myself up, careful not to jostle Shay, and took in our surroundings. Rose and George waited outside their bakery, whispering. Someone must have been sent ahead of us.

"Get down, lass." I jumped, more from frayed nerves than fear. I didn't realize Thomas had come up next to me.

"I need to get her down." I tightened the blanket around Shay and tried to get my arms around her.

"Nay, I'll get her."

I lightly ran my hands over her arms, wanting desperately to heal her. "Just be careful."

"Of course."

Michael was waiting for me at the back of the wagon, holding his hand out to let me down. The gesture was oddly kind of him. Which meant that the situation must have been far worse than I thought. I swayed on my feet and grabbed hold of the wagon until I felt steady enough to walk.

"In here." Rose beckoned us through the door, though her contempt towards Michael didn't go unnoticed. "I sent the boys home. Let them get some rest while we figure out what needs to be done."

"Ná fág fós," Thomas said to his brother and followed Rose up the stairs.

I stopped and stared at Michael for the first time since he brought Shay back. His blue eyes lost all the humor from earlier that day and the arrogant way he had held himself. His clothes were ripped, dirty, and had dark red spots, making my stomach turn. The only injuries I could find on him were bruised knuckles and a split lip.

"I don't know what you had to do—" I swallowed, trying not to cry "—but I can't thank you enough." Then, without thinking, I threw my arms around him in an embrace. His body stiffened at my touch, unmoving, until I let him go.

"It wasn't for you. Nor her even," Michael admitted, slicking his dark hair back in agitation. His blue eyes wouldn't meet mine.

Thomas. He did it for Thomas.

"Well, either way. I'm grateful and won't forget what you've done for us."

I left him with George and ran up the stairs. Thomas had set Shay down on a cot, while Rose and Mira fussed around her, collecting a bucket of water and a rag to clean Shay up. The only light came from the fireplace, and a few candles were placed on the table in the center of the room. A large bed stood off to the side, along with several small cots pushed up against the walls. I vaguely remembered Thomas mentioning that all of Rose's kids were grown, Mira being the only one still at home. And Evaline, of course, but she must have been somewhere else.

"I'm going to speak with mo dhearthár," Thomas whispered. "I'll be just downstairs if ye need anything."

He turned to leave, but I grabbed his arm, feeling his forearm rippling beneath my fingers. "Thank you. So much."

"I wish we found her sooner." With a glance towards Shay, he went down the stairs.

I turned to Shay, the blanket covering her from her shoulders down.

"Wait!" I stopped Rose when she was about to wash Shay's face and carelessly pushed Mira out of the way to get to her. "Let me do it."

I wrung out the towel and sat on the side of the cot. It pained me to look at her eyes, swollen black and blue, the rims a fierce, painful red. The angles of her face were hidden under the swelling of broken capillaries and her nose had dried blood rimming the nostrils and down her chin. It looked as if her nose ring was ripped out.

"Shay," I said hesitantly, the towel hovering above her face. "Can you hear me?"

A long moment passed in silence before she nodded slightly. I let out the breath I didn't know I'd been holding.

"I'm going to clean your face now. You let me know if it hurts too much, and I'll stop. Do you think you can do that?"

Another long moment passed until she nodded again.

I began wiping her down while Rose went down to the water pump for fresh water. The idea was to fill a tub for Shay to sit in, but we found her injuries too painful for that much movement. Instead, we decided Rose would warm it up and switch out the old bucket with the new as I worked. Mira stood uselessly to the side, face pale from the shock.

I pulled back the blanket and froze, appalled by the violence committed upon my friend. My stomach turned, and I squeezed my eyes shut, wanting to burn the sight out of my memory. I made myself open them and witness everything Shay had to endure. Bruises and cuts covered her entire body. Her knees were scraped raw. Ribs tender to the touch, probably broken. The most private and sacred of places covered in blood. There was no question about what had happened to her.

Rage fueled my veins, calling for just one match to set me on fire so I could blast those bastards to smithereens. I'd never experienced so much hate. I'd never wanted to kill anyone with my bare hands just so I could see them hurt.

But I did then.

I finished cleaning Shay up and put a fresh blanket over her. It was agreed that we would try to dress her in the morning.

We sat there while I stroked the top of her head, trying to give as much comfort as I could. But, as the minutes ticked by, my anger grew until I could no longer keep quiet.

"How many?" My voice was flat, normal even. It betrayed nothing of what I felt.

Shay turned her head away.

"Shaylah, how many?"

"Maybe—" Rose began, but I held up my hand, cutting her off.

"I wouldn't ask if it weren't important. These men could hurt someone else. We cannot let them get away with this. Please."

I had to lean down so that I could hear Shay. "I don't know."

"You couldn't see or—"

"I lost count."

My stomach dropped. I stood up quickly and went to the window, hoping the fresh air would help. It was no use; I leaned over the sill and vomited.

"I'm sorry," I said to them, wiping my mouth with the back of my hand.

"I believe she's asleep," Rose said quietly. "Probably for the best."

I nodded. "Good. I'll be back. You don't mind if I stay with her tonight?"

"Of course not, sweetie. We can push one of the spare cots near her. The boys aren't here to use them anymore."

I thanked her and went downstairs, hearing the men speaking quietly around a table along one of the walls.

"How many of them did you kill?" my voice rang out.

"Maybe ye should rest, lass," Thomas suggested, pushing his chair back to stand.

I kept my eyes on Michael, who sat back, face guarded.

"How many?" I growled, unable to control myself any longer.

"Five," he responded, unflinching.

"How many are left?"

"Three."

"Why?"

Thomas stood up. "Emilia."

"I am talking to your brother," I hissed.

His eyes narrowed, but he said no more.

"The *Prancy* Princes have eight men," Michael said sarcastically. "But only five were there when we found her."

"Shay. Her name is Shay. Do you think the others had any part in this?"

"Most likely."

I nodded, thinking. "What's the next plan of action? What of the police?"

"They won't want to get in between the gangs." Michael picked at the table with his knife but stopped at George's glare. "Not with ol' Barney McGinniskin gone and them thinking us nothing but Irish rubbish. They'd need a hell lot of more reason than a negro to interfere."

"Then it's up to us." Fury rippled through me, making my hands shake. "I want to be there."

Michael's eyebrows rose, eyes taking me in critically.

"Absolutely not," Thomas snapped. "Do ye want to be harmed?"

"Look, Miss Emilia." George leaned back, looking tired. "It would be too dangerous for a woman to be near such violence."

"I think she should." The men stared at Michael as if he had grown another head. He shrugged. "Revenge would do her some good."

"Ar chaill tú d'intinn?" Thomas growled.

"Nay, but ye aren't using yours," Michael said irritably.

"Boys," George interrupted, glaring pointedly at Michael. "It's getting late. We all should get some rest."

"Look—" Michael turned toward me. "We brought your friend back. Me work is done."

"There's still three—"

"It's not me problem." He pushed his chair in and glared at us. "Goodnight."

"What happens when they find out The North Boys killed their men?" I said to his back. "Would it be your problem then?"

Michael froze but didn't turn back around. Instead, he looked at Thomas's grim face.

Thomas opened and closed his fists. "We'll meet at sunset. Bring a few of the boys."

I watched Michael walk out of the bakery and was vaguely aware of George muttering to himself as he walked up the stairs.

"So, we're going after them?" Relief washed over me.

The thoughts were so unlike me that I had to shove down my momentary hesitation. The truth was, if they were still around, I would constantly be looking over my shoulder, wondering if I would be staring into the eyes of Shay's assailants. And a part of me knew Shay couldn't fully recover without justice.

"Not we." Green eyes hardened on me. "I'll take care of this."

"God, I'm too tired to argue with you." I placed my hands over my face.

"Do ye need a place to rest?"

I shook my head. "I'll be staying with Shay tonight."

"I thought as much. I'll come by to see ye in the evening."

I stared at him. He looked like he was about to say something but changed his mind and turned to leave.

"Thomas."

He turned back to me, his face blank, but the way that the flickering candle threw shadows over him, cutting sharper edges over his nose and jaw, tightened something in my chest. Sometimes it was impossible to ignore how handsome he was.

"Thank you for everything," I managed to say. "I don't know what I would have done without you."

We stared at each other for a minute, something passing between us that I couldn't describe. Thomas was the first to turn away and leave without a word.

CHAPTER FIFTEEN

Emilia

Shay could open her eyes a little the following day, though she was still too sore to move. Rose and I managed to sit her up and cover her with a cotton nightgown. The ordeal took many minutes and left Shay panting, an excruciating experience that we believed was from the cracked ribs. We wrapped a few cotton cloths around her middle to help.

"Do you think we could ask a doctor to see her?" I asked, looking worriedly at Shay. We stood across the room, trying to be quiet after she fell asleep again.

Rose shook her head. "I'm not sure it'd do any good. Could only bring more trouble."

"I hate this!" I hissed. "This is how you guys always live?" I began to pace while running my hands through my hair. "We need some goddamn justice."

Mira flinched at my language while Rose studied me critically.

"What?" I stopped pacing.

"You remind me a lot like him."

"Who?" I snapped, frustrated.

"Mr. O'Connor. Tommy. I've heard many white men talk of abolitionism, but I haven't seen much care about a negro like him. He's always treated Hiram as a brother, choosing him even over white folk." She inhaled, her ample chest puffing out as she pointed at me. "Until you. I'm sorry for my accusations yesterday, child. I see now that you care for Ms. Banks as if she was family."

Her words were completely unexpected, springing tears from my eyes. I looked down, hoping she wouldn't notice. "Thank you for saying that."

"Just don't make me regret it. You hear?"

I gave a weak smile, wishing I was as fierce as Rose. "Of course."

The day passed slowly. Rose and Mira had to go down to the bakery while I watched over Shay. I was able to get some broth into her, and she could sit up a few times to use the chamber pot. Though she was getting fluids in her, seeing the blood in her urine frightened me. I chose not to tell her about it; she was dealing with enough already.

I found my rosary in my hand countless times, praying to God that if Shay came out of this okay, I would do anything He wished.

Shay slept most of the time, and when she woke, she refused to talk. I didn't push her. Instead, I sang to her, hummed some of our favorite songs, and ensured she was comfortable.

Finally, Rose closed the bakery and was cleaning downstairs when I heard the bell ring on the door. It had to be Thomas. Making sure Shay was asleep, I ran down the stairs to greet him, taking them two at a time, and barreled into the room to only stop short.

"Where's Thomas?" I asked Hiram.

Hiram took his hat off and wouldn't meet my eyes. "He told me to look in on you."

I could feel my blood drain from my face. "You mean he's not coming?"

"He said he'll check on you tomorrow. After it's done. How is your friend?"

"Not really good," I said, wanting to scream that she was beaten and gang raped. It wasn't fair. That she was a good person and didn't deserve it. That no one deserved that kind of fate. "But I think she will heal. Physically, at least."

Hiram nodded, worrying his hat in his hands. "I give her all my thoughts and prayers," he said kindly and pulled out a seat at the table.

"Wait. You're staying?" I stared at him, dumbfounded. It was only a matter of moments until my blood began to boil at the dawning realization. Thomas didn't send Hiram to check in on me. He sent him to watch me. I should have been unnerved by how well I understood Thomas already, but I didn't care. I growled, a deep guttural sound of frustration. "You're going to take me."

His golden eyes narrowed. "Absolutely not."

Mira gasped. "Really, Ms. Moretti. You shouldn't speak—" She stopped when I glared at her.

"Yes, you are." I stomped to the door and threw it open.

Rose and Evaline were playing some sort of game outside, stopping my rampage. She must have been with Hiram all night.

"Miss Millie!" Evaline squealed, running to me. I wondered if she was always this happy or just liked seeing people. I threw my arms out at the last second, catching her.

"How are you, sweetie?" I asked, shooting Hiram a look over her head.

"Good. Uncle Hiram said you were visiting us today!"

I set her down, exhaling slowly. She didn't know I stayed the night or about anything that happened. Suddenly exhausted, I collapsed into one of the chairs. "I guess so."

The sun had fallen, covering the earth in darkness as The North Boys walked down North Street toward McGinty's Tavern. Five men agreed to help, while the other seven scoffed—believing a darkie deserved what she got comin' to her.

"Glad to see ye come around, Tommy," Henry, one of the eldest members of The North Boys, chirped. "Did ye miss the life?"

Thomas glared at Henry—his pinched features and brown hair reminding Thomas of a weasel.

He hated the few runs he went on with his brother's gang. Sometimes it worked in his favor, though, and a part of him felt guilty for relishing in the camaraderie of his people. Most of them stuck together in the overcrowded cities for that reason. Nevertheless, Thomas wasn't afraid to break off from them if they threatened his morality. His honor was the only thing that couldn't be taken away from him. The world made sure to remind him of that.

"Nay, there's a lass involved." Mikey winked, dodging a man who tumbled out of an inn. "Remember that gypsy outside of Nora's?"

Henry's eyes widened. "The one with the big cíocha?" He held his hands up in front of his chest as if he was holding watermelons.

"Aye." Mikey and the fiery Calahan twins laughed.

Even though Thomas' anger flared, he kept his attention on their surroundings in case they came across anyone prematurely.

"How did ye end up with that shapely slag?" Henry asked.

"Did ye see the legs on her when our Mikey lifted her wee shift?" Hugh hit Henry's arm. Hugh Calahan was a small man, but where he lacked in stature, he made up for it with his exceptional skill with a blade. There were whispers among the gangs, calling him The Butcher for what he could do to a man's flesh. Thomas tried to stay clear of him, feeling unease every time he was in Hugh's company.

"Just one night under her skirts—" Henry sneered "—and she'd be screamin' me name."

Thomas' elbow collided with Henry's face so fast that he didn't realize he had done it until he saw the blood spout from his nose.

"Christ!" Henry choked, covering his face.

The other men laughed louder.

"I should have told ye that our Tommy boy was sweet on her." Mikey smiled, ignoring the dark look Henry threw at him. "Hope this doesn't trouble us with the Prancies," Mikey said more serious-ly. "Couldn't ye wait until after?"

"Feck ye." Henry spat at Mikey.

"Get a hold of yourself," Mikey said, propping his back against the front of the tavern. "Ye can't go in there like that."

Henry held his nose up, trying to lessen the blood flow. "Aye, I'll get right on it."

Thomas rolled his shoulders, the tension building while he thought about what had to be done. He could admit that he was serving justice for Ms. Banks and her people. He even could admit that he felt guilty bringing his brother into this mess. So naturally, he would want these grievances dealt with swiftly. However, he couldn't think about the primary reason why he was going to such lengths. Why he didn't want to see the pain in a particular set of brown eyes again. It made no sense; therefore, there was no sense in thinking about it either.

"I think I'm good." Henry put his head back down and looked for more blood.

Thomas was mildly disappointed when there was none and want-ed to hit him again for good measure, though he refrained from inflicting more trouble than was already necessary.

They entered the tavern The Celtic Princes frequented.

"What are you boys doing in here?" Patrick McGinty, the owner, asked. He was short but built like a bull from years of carrying barrels of liquor in and out of the place. And though he was born in the States, he carried his Irish temper. Everyone knew that only the best fighters could stand against him, and even they avoided him.

"On some business," Mikey said, heading to the bar.

The room was filled with patrons, all in various levels of intoxication. One quick sweep around revealed that The Celtic Princes were not there yet.

"Not in my place." McGinty threw a towel down on the bar. "Tommy, what in the hell are you doing here?"

Thomas shrugged, leaning against the bar. "Righting a few wrongs."

"Christ. And what the fuck happened to you?" McGinty said when seeing the blood on Henry's face.

Henry glared, mumbling curses.

"I have half a mind to throw you out now." McGinty leaned his knuckles on the bar, his blue eyes cutting them like a knife.

"The Princes had made a plaything out of a woman." The steel in Mikey's voice brought Thomas' head up. *Was that anger he heard?* "We mean to settle it."

McGinty froze. "One of ours?"

"Nay," Mikey said. "An acquaintance of our Tommy here."

"Darkie?" McGinty spat tobacco into the spittoon behind the bar. "I don't see why you bother yourself with them." He turned towards Mikey. "I'm surprised you're going through with this."

Thomas began to straighten, ready for a fight when his brother placed his hand on Thomas's chest and stepped forward.

"Ye didn't see this lass. No woman should go through that."

Thomas stared at his brother, wondering if he was serious or putting on an act to calm everyone. Then, the door opened, letting in two of the three men they were looking for.

"Out back," McGinty growled, tossing his head towards the back door. "Now, before anyone notices. I'll send them your way. Just get the fuck out of here."

"That's kind of ye," Mikey smiled, knocking his knuckles on the counter.

Thomas pulled his cap down to cover his face. He went out the backdoor first and saw a dark figure move quickly, and a sharp, searing pain shot through his shoulder. Refraining from grabbing the wound, instinct propelled him to draw his revolver. The shot was true, right through his attacker's forehead, and sprayed the bricks with gore.

"Bastard set us up," one of the twins growled.

"Feck, ye okay?" Mikey asked, but the door slammed open before Thomas could answer.

Mikey turned swiftly, slicing his knife across the man's neck before the man could raise his gun. Thomas grabbed the third man and slammed him against the building. The Calahan twins were on him before Thomas could do anything else. He stepped back as they sunk their knives into his stomach.

It was only a matter of seconds. The fight was over. They quickly pulled the bodies away from the view of the street, hiding them behind some trash and empty crates. Gunshots were often ignored, many people not wanting to get involved in any crime, but there was still a chance someone might come looking.

"What of McGinty?" Henry asked.

"He'll keep his mouth shut," Mikey answered while checking for any pulses. He nodded, confirming they were dead. "He'll know he picked wrong after I speak with him. Won't be good for business, aye?"

Thomas agreed, slumping against the bricks, suddenly drained.

"Ye're losing too much blood." Mikey pressed Thomas' hand to the wound, making him wince. "Put pressure on it." He turned to

Henry. "Run and get a few of the other boys to help ye dispose of the bodies. We'll wait here."

"Why me?" Henry spat. "Make one of them do it." He jutted his thumb at the red-headed twins.

"Are ye questioning me?" Mikey straightened, glaring down at the smaller man.

"Of course not." Henry visibly shrank and took off to find the others.

"They respect ye," Thomas said. He laid his head against the brick and closed his eyes.

"Aye, ye sound surprised."

Thomas shook his head. "I always knew ye were called to lead. It takes a certain man. I just thought ye would get better men to follow ye. Ye have so much potential." Hugh began to come at Thomas, but Georgie grabbed his arm and held him back. Thomas winked, infuriating the twins more.

"I'm doing fine," Mikey pulled out some tobacco and shoved it into his lip. "It was just last week—"

"I'm not talking about coin, Mikey. Use your power for good. Stop stealing from those who already don't have anything. Stop the murder, thievery—"

"I believe that murder just got your ass out of trouble. Aye? And that darkie would still have men—"

"Don't. Don't pretend like ye don't care when I know ye do. I saw the way ye spoke about her. Ye was rattled."

Mikey snorted. "That'd be the day. Care for a darkie." He laughed, shaking his head.

Thomas sighed, too weak to argue. "Guess I was wrong about ye then." He could have sworn his brother's features darkened.

"Ye'd guess right."

CHAPTER SIXTEEN

Emilia

My eyes began drooping as I watched the flames of the fire dance when the door suddenly slammed open, causing me to jump.

"Where is he?" I stood up, my drowsiness evaporating as my temper flared upon seeing Michael. "How dare you go without me!"

That's when two redheaded men struggled to get through the door with Thomas. I barely noted their similarities before seeing the blood staining Thomas' shoulder, and all the fight went out of me. My stomach rolled, and the world tilted.

There was so much blood.

Hiram sprang out of his chair just in time for the twins to dump Thomas unceremoniously into the seat, earning a few curses from George.

"I'm fine." Thomas swatted everyone away, but his head lolled down, and all the color drained from his face.

I could do nothing but stand there, frozen in place.

"Get Rose," Hiram commanded. "Emilia!" he said, snapping me out of it, and I ran up the stairs. It was a strange sensation—my heart beating rapidly as my body went completely numb.

My voice wasn't my own as I quietly woke Rose, careful to not disturb Evaline and Shay. Rose rifled through a small chest in one of the corners and went as fast as her older body could carry her down the stairs.

Thomas had his eyes closed, head propped against the wall like he was sleeping. My heart leaped, struck with terror that he might be dead until the squeak of the floorboards made him crack his eyes open.

I sighed in relief and stood by Rose as she pulled out a needle and string.

"I told you to let me go," I grumbled. He surprised me by chuckling, fueling my anger again. "You might not have gotten hurt!"

He laughed tiredly. "I'd be dead, lass."

"That's not funny." I frowned, his appearance scaring me more than I cared to admit.

"Cut his shirt," Rose told Michael, who surprisingly listened without sarcastic remarks.

"Anything else?" one of the twins asked, his face set in disdain. The two other men had the same look about them. I turned around and realized why when I found their attention on Hiram. Throat tight with rage, I had to keep myself from clawing their eyes.

"Ye did enough," Mikey said, while following Rose's instructions.

The others backed out of the bakery, glares still on Hiram as if they expected him to attack. Maybe they had good reason. I only noticed Hiram relax his fists when they left.

"That was me good shirt," Thomas mumbled.

"Ye have no good shirts."

"It didn't have any holes, at least."

"Well, it's got a big one now." Mikey pulled it away from his shoulder.

"You're lucky," Rose said, inspecting the wound. "It's big, but the dagger didn't hit anything."

"At least it's not me fighting arm."

She ignored him and turned to Michael. "Do you know the length of the blade?"

Michael shook his head. Without pause, Rose pulled Thomas off the wall to see if the wound had gone through his back. Thomas's face twisted in pain, but he made no protest.

"No exit point. Good. I'm fairly certain it will be okay. Lean back and I'll stitch you up." She nodded at George, who poured liquor over the wound. I cringed, but Thomas only closed his eyes tighter.

"Have you done this much?" I asked as she plunged the needle into his flesh.

"You learn a few things with these boys."

I placed my hand over my nauseated belly, wondering what world I had entered. I knew these things happened in the twenty-first century, but I'd been lucky not to experience it. Until now.

"What happened?" A voice cracked behind me, and I spun around.

"What are you doing up?" I asked, going to Shay. She was breathing hard and leaning against the railing in her nightgown and a blanket wrapped around her, staring at Thomas with swollen eyes. "Shay?"

She tore her eyes away from him to look at me. My heart broke when I saw how much she was struggling to see. "I think I'm dreaming," she whispered only to me. "Because that looks a lot like the guy in one of the pub's pictures."

"You're not dreaming," I smiled sadly. "But don't tell him that. Okay?"

I helped her down the last step and staggered under her weight. She was still so weak.

"What is she doing down here?" Michael snapped.

Shay stiffened at the sound of his voice. I grabbed her tighter, glaring at Michael.

Surprising me, Shay raised her head and looked straight at him. "I heard the commotion. Does that offend you, asshole?"

My heart filled with pride at her strength.

Michael's eyes widened in surprise, making me snort. "Ye ungrateful—"

"Deartháir." Thomas raised his head. "I will beat ye with my good arm if ye finish that sentence."

"Michael is actually the one who rescued you," I whispered to Shay. "And he's also Thomas' brother. Still an asshole, though."

Shay was shaking, either from the pain or Michael.

"C'mon, let's get you back upstairs."

"I think I have to sit down."

Hiram came to help her to one of the chairs, but she flinched away from him.

"Sorry," he mumbled, putting his hands up.

She pulled in closer to me, making tears spring to my eyes. Shay had never been one to scare easy.

"She's got it," I reassured him, and we made it to the table. "What do you need?" I asked her.

She rested her head against the wall and rolled it to the side. "I'll take some of that."

I looked at the bottle she zeroed in on. "Oh, I don't know—"

Thomas pushed it closer to us with his good arm. "Give it to her. If ye don't mind..." he said to Rose as an afterthought.

When Rose nodded, I picked it up and held it to Shay's lips. She started chugging the whiskey, so I had to take it away quickly. "Woah, there, lady. Slow down."

She just closed her eyes and laid her head back again. I stood back, overwhelmingly aware of the people in my life who sat there slumped against the wall. I pushed away the fact that I started thinking of Thomas as one of my people or important.

Besides, wasn't he the ancestor of my parents? I looked between Thomas and Michael, trying to find any clue as to which one of them would create the lineage. If one of them died because of me, would that mean my father would never be born over a century later? The weight of that would crush me. I'd still be born, but would I have been lost in the system without a family to take me in? There were so many questions left unanswered, but what it really came down to, I was starting to care for them.

Shay and I would have to leave before we messed up any more of the timeline. That daunting realization nearly doubled me over in a panic.

"Millie says you're my hero." Shay opened her eyes and focused on Michael.

"I'm nobody's hero." Michael's face twisted in disgust.

"She also agreed you were an asshole. So that makes sense."

"Shay! I'm sorry," I said, turning to Michael.

Thomas barked out a laugh, making him wince and grab his shoulder. Hiram actually cracked a smile.

"How did he get hurt?" Shay asked.

Everyone went silent; the only sound was the crackle of logs in the fireplace. I knelt in front of her.

"They're gone," I whispered. "Thomas and the boys took care of—" My throat closed, so I had to wait a moment to go on. Her skin turned a darker shade in realization. "You don't have to worry about them anymore. They can never hurt you again." I held onto her hand, but she didn't grip mine back. Her fingers were cold, and a little clammy. Her complexion drastically paled as the words set in.

"I didn't ask any of you to do that." She sat up and started to get up. Surprised, I quickly stood up and tried to help her. "I got it." Her voice lacked any emotion as she pushed by me.

"I thought it might help—"

"I'm going to bed."

"I'll help you upstairs."

"No." The fury in her voice brought me up short, and I backed off.

She winced in pain, holding her side. I started to go to her again, but a gentle hand on my arm stopped me.

"Let her go," Rose said. "She needs time."

I watched Shay until she disappeared, ignoring everyone looking at me. I turned around, and they all started to do something except for Thomas. He stared at me in a way that stripped me bare, exposing all my pain and confusion in ways I wanted to keep hidden. I tore myself away from his green gaze and started to clean up the supplies strewn about.

Rose and George went upstairs when Hiram and Michael agreed to help Thomas get home. I wrung my hands, thinking of what to say to them.

"Do you guys need me to do anything?" I asked

Hiram paused. "No, we should get him home."

"Can ye leave us alone a minute?" Thomas asked.

My heart skipped, suddenly anxious. "Thank you, guys, for helping me with Shay. I don't know what I could ever do to repay you."

"No one deserved her fate," Hiram said, rubbing his brow. "You owe me nothing."

"Tommy knows the agreement," Michael looked to Thomas, who nodded.

Agreement? Something tickled the back of my mind, but I couldn't seem to bring forth the memory.

They went outside, leaving me to run my hands nervously through my hair as I thought of what to say.

"Why are ye fretting, lass?"

I met his eyes, sighing. "I feel like this is my fault."

"Ye stabbed me in the shoulder?" His brow rose.

"No, but you wouldn't have gotten hurt if I didn't ask you to help me."

"Come here." I couldn't figure out his expression, whether the grimace was from pain or at my expense. I stood in front of him, wondering what he wanted. He gently grabbed one of my hands and watched as he rubbed his thumb across it—studying it as if he would never see it again.

"I owe you," I said, unable to tear my eyes away from where we touched. "Whatever you want, I'll do my best. I could sing for money if—"

His thumb stopped, startling me into looking at his face, but he kept his eyes on our joint hands.

"There's only one thing I need." His voice was hoarse, making my mind spin.

"Anything," I breathed.

His grip tightened, and he nodded. The muscles in his jaw clenched as he thought of the words he would speak next, and I had a horrible sinking sensation. "Go home or wherever ye find it safe. Leave this place behind."

"I—" I cleared my throat, looking away so he couldn't see my tears. Why was I about to cry? That was my plan all along. It must have been the stress of the last few days. "Rose said I could work for room and board until Shay is healed. I don't have anywhere to go yet, and with Shay hurt—"

"When she's healed. I wouldn't put you out, lass. Just promise me ye won't go looking for me." He looked up at me then, and I let the tears spill, too weak to hide my emotions. The last few days had been unbearably hard. "This will be the last time we meet intentionally. Then ye can consider me debt paid."

I found myself nodding even though I didn't want to. He stood up, making me feel as small as my following words. "Why, though?"

He placed two fingers underneath my chin and brought my face up. He swiped away my tears, and I closed my eyes, savoring his last touch. I tried to not think about what that might mean.

"I've only known ye for a short time, but even I guessed this isn't the life for ye. Ye will only get hurt if ye stay in this city."

"And you?" I searched his eyes.

"What about me?" He squinted like he was trying to read my mind.

"Nothing." I pulled out of his grasp and stepped back, despite the odd tearing sensation ripping through my chest.

He let his hand fall and grabbed his hat off the table. "It was a pleasure to meet ye," he said.

I could feel him staring at me, but I couldn't bring myself to let him see the irrational pain in my eyes. "Thanks again for helping me at Nora's and with Shay." My voice quivered as the tears rolled down my cheeks. I wanted to say more, but a sob stuck in my throat.

I only lifted my head when I heard the door shut behind him.

CHAPTER SEVENTEEN

Thomas & Emilia

Most of the morning went by in silence, the quiet solitude that often followed a battle. And one that Thomas couldn't fully enjoy after the day he had.

Thomas had gone to Long Wharf, hoping to convince one of the captains to let him work. But, unfortunately, it wasn't long until he discovered no one wanted to hire him on the docks with his injured arm.

"Get off my dock before I throw your ass in the river, damn Irish filth," the captain said, spitting on Thomas's shoes.

Thomas clenched his fist but flexed his fingers again, remembering he needed the work or his family would struggle with the rent and food.

"I can do more work with me one arm than most the men here can do with two," Thomas growled.

"I'll set this whole damn deck on fire—" The captain threw his hands out, drawing the other workers' attention. "—and the boats along with it before I hire Irish swine like you."

It took everything Thomas had not to kill the captain right then and there. He couldn't take care of his family if he went away for murder, he repeated in his mind while letting out a deep breath. The other docks provided a similar result, leaving him desolate and wandering until he found himself sitting on the crate, watching the sunrise over the water as Hiram worked.

Now, Hiram unloaded a crate off the ship, wiping his brow. The hard work took the chill out of the air. Thomas already missed the familiarity of exertion and the strain of his muscles as he pushed his body to the limit. He pulled his coat tighter.

"Are you going to ask how they're doing?" Hiram finally asked after setting down another large crate.

Hiram visited the bakery the day before. Thomas fought a grimace, knowing his friend wanted to ask why he cut himself off from the women he saved.

"Nay," Thomas admitted.

"It's been two days."

"Aye."

Hiram shook his head in annoyance and dropped the subject. Thomas knew he should explain, but he didn't know how. And he didn't want to think about it anymore.

He stood up, preparing himself for what he was about to do.

Thomas walked through the city without much thought of a destination and marveled at how it came alive. People from all types of life—nativists or immigrants, various nationalities, poor or rich, colored or white—could be spotted together on any given day. Of course, they may not get along or even like each other. And some streets may be overrun with gangs or overcrowded with new immigrants daily. Thomas lived a good portion of his life in the city, and grew to love the difficulties and contradictions that came along with such a place.

Thomas's way of thinking was rare. He knew that. It's why he never fit into one place, but found himself roaming everywhere, conversing with everyone.

He was far from perfect, though. If it came down to it, he'd burn the lot of them if they ever hurt those close to him. Tear the whole fecking system apart just to see them flounder.

Drowning in his thoughts, he was about to turn down a different street when a commotion pulled him out of his plagued thoughts and into the present. A crowd was gathering around the newspaper, men shouting and pulling the paper out of each other's hands to read it.

He went to an older man, struggling to read over his shoulder as the man kept moving. He had a hard enough time reading as it was.

"What does it say?" Thomas asked.

The man glanced at him. "Lincoln called all able-bodied men to fight for the Union," he said, spitting to the side. "Says seventy-five thousand troops needed for three months."

Thomas grabbed his wounded shoulder, feeling bitterness like he's never known blossom within his chest. He walked away without a response, feeling as if trudging through a tunnel of immeasurable pressure—suspended in a dark sea, the surface lightyears away.

His entire life, he was taller, stronger, or smarter when fighting. Most times, he was all three and used it to his advantage against bullies and oppressors. He prided himself on mastering his body, knowing it was the only thing life couldn't take away from him. And now, when the moment finally came to fight for something bigger than anything he's ever fought for, his body failed him. There was no way they'd let him enlist while his shoulder was injured. And he knew the extent of the wound would prohibit him from being able to hide it from them.

Thomas found himself on Mikey's doorstep, knowing his brother was most likely asleep. He kept his eyes from what was happening in one of the cots and went up the stairs.

The world's weight landed on his shoulders, until he could do nothing but sit on his brother's bed with his head in his hands. All he'd ever worked for and believed in slipped between his fingers as he waited for Mikey to wake.

"How long ye gonna sit there?" Mikey mumbled from under his arm.

"Christ." Thomas sat up straight. "How long have ye been awake?"

"Since ye sat your fat ass on me bed. What do ye want?"

Thomas sighed but said nothing. Mikey sat up and ran his hands through his hair—bone straight, compared to Thomas's short, slightly wavy hair.

"Well, if ye are just gonna sit there, don't mind if I piss, aye?"

Thomas flung his hand toward the pot and looked away, still lost in his thoughts.

"How's your shoulder?" Mikey asked.

"Lincoln's called for us to enlist."

Mikey grunted, shrugging. "Aye, and?"

"Me fecking arm is useless! If it weren't for—" Thomas stopped, realizing he almost said something he couldn't take back. Even if

Emilia couldn't hear it, he'd never forgive himself for taking his anger out in her name.

Mikey sat down heavily. "They'll lick the rebels in no time. No sense in signing for what is already over."

"I wouldn't expect ye to understand."

"Then why are ye here?" Mikey snapped and grabbed some tobacco, shoving it into his lip. "Stop pestering me and follow your gypsy like some lovesick mutt instead. Leave me to sleep."

Thomas stared at his hands. "I need work. With me shoulder the way it is…"

"Aye, ye are cashin' your debt in early then?"

"I'm just saying—" Thomas glared. "I'm your man until me shoulder's healed. Then we're done. Aye?"

Mikey grinned. "Aye."

Leaning over the bed, I grabbed my shoes, careful not to jostle them as I stood up. I looked back at Shay, still sleeping, and tiptoed out of the room and down the stairs.

A week of helping at the bakery had passed. I quickly learned they went to sleep pretty early, having to be up before dawn to get everything ready before opening. When I knew Shay was healing—though I worried about her mental health when she stopped talking the night Thomas was injured—I began to form a plan.

My memories had been trickling in—flashes of my parents, more of the Romani language I'd long forgotten, and my grandmother sending me across time. I knew at least one of my parents had to be Italian. But how everyone seemed to guess I was of Roma descent had me wondering. For the locals, I had to look remarkably like them to deduce my heritage. Either that or some of them had to live in the area. Or used to.

It was obvious that something had been triggering my memories. My guess was the time itself. My younger self would have recognized the customs and people. The more I immersed myself, the more my past returned.

I needed to find my grandmother or a band of Roma nearby to figure out how to get back to the twenty-first century. I couldn't be asking around the bakery for fear that it might draw too much suspicion. So instead, I would sing on North Street and ask the drunken men questions between songs. Maybe even lure one to the side to get some answers if I was desperate. Hopefully, they would be too drunk to remember it in the morning.

I made it outside without waking anyone up and put my shoes on. As I set off, I reached between my breasts, feeling the familiar metal of one of the knives I had taken for protection. It wasn't much against a gun, but I felt better for having it.

In the short time I'd been here, the streets were transformed with the promise of war. The dark cloaked most of the signs as I walked, but it was harder to ignore the small flags adorning the streets, and during the day, as companies set out for Washington D.C., the crowd cheered for their brave men. They no longer drank without purpose, but they drank for the preservation of the Union.

Just a few days before, I kept trying to see the companies marching to Faneuil Hall until Rose had enough of me constantly asking her questions. So, I searched for them, though a storm had broken, and I had to keep my head down most of the way. Finally, I made it to the hall, drenched, my borrowed hat plastered to my head.

With my heart in my throat, I scanned the crowd for familiar faces. The street was packed with men waiting to get their grey overcoats and rifles. Their faces should've been miserable in the storm. Still, they were alight, eyes blazing, ready to fight for their country and finally take down the rebels. Irish brogues mingled with mixed Bostonian accents, finally weaving together by a cause greater than their differences. The pulse of excitement was felt through the individuals I passed, their fervor sapping me hollow.

I spotted a familiar face when I was about to find refuge from the storm and my darkening thoughts. "Isaac!" I yelled, waving above the crowd. It took a few more shouts and a couple of jabs to move people out of my way before he heard.

He smiled, coming to me. "Miss Millie! How are you?"

"Your mom is putting me to work," I smiled back weakly. I tried to suppress a shiver as the rain drove down on us.

"And your friend?" he said more seriously, his smile fading. He gestured for us to talk beneath a shop's awning.

"She's getting better," I admitted. Then, grateful for the dry reprieve, I shook the water off my hat. "It was pretty bad."

Isaac frowned. "I'm sorry to hear that. You know we shouldn't be talking so freely." He looked around to see if anyone had noticed us. Thankfully, the crowd remained more interested in the newly enlisted soldiers walking down the street. "Is there something you need?"

"I was wondering if anyone we know had enlisted."

Isaac looked at me, a line forming between his dark brows, and my cheeks heated with shame and realization. He couldn't enlist nor any of the others I'd met. "I'm sure you're asking about our Tommy. But why wouldn't he tell you?"

"Just busy, I guess," I lied, not wanting to talk about it. I couldn't let him know that my worry for Thomas was what robbed me of the patriotism surrounding me.

He eyed me suspiciously but shrugged. "Hiram said they wouldn't take him. His shoulder is pretty bad. Heard he has taken up with Mikey."

"Mikey?" I gawked.

"Heard no work would take him."

"But, he can't. He doesn't even like his brother."

Isaac's dark eyes hardened while looking into the crowd. "Sometimes men have to do what they must to survive, even if they don't like it. Adapt to our surroundings or perish at the hands of those who can do what we cannot."

Goosebumps covered my flesh at the truth in his words.

"Is this darky bothering you, Miss?" A male voice made me jump.

I swung around to face a boy who couldn't be older than sixteen. "Excuse me?"

"Is he bothering you?" He jerked his thumb at Isaac. "I can get someone to take care of him."

The boy eyed Isaac in a way that made my stomach turn. He still had pimples on his face, for God's sake, and he wanted to get Isaac in trouble for talking to a woman with lighter skin. I started to fume, but instead of snapping, I took a deep breath to steady myself. I had to get Isaac out of this mess.

"Look—" Isaac began, ready for a fight.

"I asked him directions," I cut him off. "He told me, and I was just about to leave." I smiled at them both. "Thank you, sir. I'll be on my way now."

The boy mumbled something as I slid by him. I looked back, grateful that he had left, and mouthed, "Thank you," to Isaac.

He nodded and tipped his hat. Any trace of his usual humor was obliterated.

I walked away in a haze, trying to focus on the history unfolding before me; all too aware that I needed to be careful what I did in this time or I would keep getting others hurt. I looked up, rain cascading down my face as the American flag flew high.

Now, in the darkness of the night, and thankfully free of the rain, I walked quickly by myself, taking care to check my surroundings for anyone who might want to harm me. Though I had made it to North Street without trouble, I felt more comfortable with the people around me.

After some hunting, I found an empty alley and quickly stripped down to as little as possible. I ran my fingers over my hair, ensuring it was in place. I hadn't been able to curl it without drawing suspicion from Rose, so I hoped my modern long bob would be exotic enough to draw attention.

With one last wiggle of my corset, everything was in place. *God, I wish I had a mirror.* I breathed out, telling myself that my tightened corset, shapely figure, and tan skinned had to get the job done without the extra primping.

I hid my dress in part of the alley that seemed less filthy than the surrounding area and went out into the center of the street, turning in a circle to get my bearings. Then, after some consideration, I decided my act would be the same as what I did for Nora.

Placing my hat on the ground, I began singing a bawdy Irish song, immediately drawing attention. The first few onlookers gave me strange stares, but as I moved into the next song, a crowd began to form around. With each hoot and holler and dime thrown my way, my confidence grew, and I began to dance around. A brush of my fingers on a chest, a little sway with my back against one of them—I slowly drew them to me as if by magic.

It was genuinely terrifying what a woman could do with a bit of confidence. Getting my best friend home propelled me to do things I never would have done before. I would gladly welcome the shame in return for her safety.

As the night wore on, the men began to get handsy the more they drank, causing me to skirt away from them. When my feet began to hurt, and my voice became hoarse, I knew I had to quit. I stopped singing and grabbed the hat, much to the protests of men, and even some women.

I pocketed my cash and stood to the side, eyeing the people as they dispersed. Leaning up against the building, I played with the top of my corset, hoping to catch the eye of a male passerby. Most walked by without a glance, but an older man kept staring at me from across the street. I wanted to cringe, but smiled and crooked a finger at him instead.

He came to me, stumbling over his feet, and reached up to rest his hands against the building behind me, caging me in.

"Hello," I said, looking up through my lashes. I hoped to God I was doing this right.

I needn't have worried. The foul creature kept his eyes on my breasts while he licked his lips. I reminded myself of my mission and kept playing with the corset, hoping for a distraction.

"What can I help ye with, lass?" he asked, licking his lips again.

I really did cringe this time. "I saw you looking." I ran my hand down the buttons of his shirt and took a deep breath, knowing it would give him a better view. I needed this man completely at my will. "I was curious."

"Curious about what?"

I bent forward to whisper into his ear. "What you were thinking of doing to me."

He barked out a laugh. "Ye have a mouth on ye."

"So, I've heard." I smiled, trying to erase the memory of Thomas saying that to me. "Tell me," I began playing with one of his buttons, "Have you ever seen a woman like me around here?" My words were husky, seductive, all while wishing he'd just give me the needed information.

"Nay, girly. I've never seen one like you."

He leaned in for a kiss that I dodged quickly.

"Shame," I teased, ducking from under his arms. "No gypsy girls to play with?"

He made a grumbling sound, trying to come toward me. "I haven't been lucky enough until now."

I tsked, shaking my head. "I thought that might be fun. Maybe next time." I smiled and grabbed my hat. I turned to walk down the street, fear coursing through me as I prayed that he wouldn't follow.

"Where ye going?" he growled.

I swung back around flirtatiously. "I promised to meet someone." A lie. "Come find me tomorrow!" I winked at him. To my relief, a cluster of patrons exited the tavern to my left, giving me enough time to get away.

I kept walking down the street, gaining stares and whistles along the way, until doubling back around to get my stuff.

I couldn't help the sinking sensation of failure on my first night. But as I walked, the faint jingle of the coins I earned helped soothe my trepidation, and each clink helped further my resolve.

I wasn't going home empty-handed.

CHAPTER EIGHTEEN

Thomas & Emilia

"Where ye going so fast?" Nessa asked Thomas as he stood up from the bed. She didn't bother pulling up the sheet, but rather enjoyed being on display. "I thought we could lie here a bit."

Thomas struggled to button his pants—his shoulder still smarting—and gathered his belongings, avoiding the woman on the bed. He already felt guilty about what had happened between them. That was strange, considering he'd never felt that after lying with a woman.

"I have to go."

"Ye seemed distracted," she said accusatorily, surprising him into looking at her.

"Just a lot on me mind." He put his cap on and wished he'd never come to Nora's with Mikey and the crew.

Nessa stretched, her full breasts—nipples still red from his mouth just moments before—taunted him as she practically preened. She moved lazily, but Thomas knew her claws were hidden.

"I did everything ye liked, didn't I?" She pouted, batting her eyes at him.

Anger began to boil beneath his skin, though more at himself than at the woman needling him. He couldn't understand why he imagined an utterly different lass tumbling in the bed with him. Tan skin glistening instead of pearly white. He almost lost it in the beginning when he conceived the voluptuous curves in his hands. A complete contrast to Nessa's soft angles.

Thomas scowled. "Jealousy doesn't become ye. The other lads not given ye enough attention, Ness?"

"Jealous?" She scoffed, sitting up quickly. "I've never been jealous a day in me life!"

Thomas grunted and grabbed the door handle.

"Heard that gypsy wench has been whoring herself all along the street." Her words landed like an anvil, and Thomas froze in place, breathing harder as he waited for her to say more. "Guess she's not your good wee doll after all."

Thomas slammed the door shut but could not drown out her laughter as he descended the stairs.

"Where ye going so fast?" Mikey called out, putting down his cards as Thomas passed his table.

Thomas threw the door open, looking left and right as if Emilia was going to materialize before him. It had been nearly a fortnight since he'd last seen her and nearly as long since the men set out for war. For that, he was grateful—the fewer men put their hands on her, the better. What the feck was she thinking? Hadn't he saved her arse enough without her doing this dirty work? He was going to throttle her when he found her.

That thought alone should have stopped him in his tracks.

Pushing through a group, he heard Mikey yelling his name. He'd catch up whether Thomas wanted him there or not.

"What are ye doing?" Mikey snapped.

"Did ye know?"

Mikey threw his hands up in the air. "Know what, dearthir?"

"Has she been selling her body? Did ye know?" Thomas knew he sounded crazy. He also knew it was none of his business what Emilia did. He told her as much when he'd last seen her. Yet his anger drove him now, and there was no telling what it would do.

Mikey shrugged. "Thought ye didn't care?"

Thomas whirled on Mikey so fast that his brother nearly collided with him.

"Feck!" Mikey yelled. "Get ahold of yourself."

Thomas turned away from him, only able to deal with one eejit at a time. He looked down each alley at every face he passed. His ears strained to hear her voice, but she was either too far away or not on the street. He tried to expel the thought that maybe her silence resulted from being with a man. And completely ignored that he was guilty of the same crime.

Thomas began to walk faster.

"And what are ye gonna do when ye find her?" Mikey asked. "Beat the man with your one arm?"

"I'll figure it out."

Mikey grunted in disbelief. "I knew ye were doting on her, but I didn't think it was this bad."

Thomas didn't care to respond. Instead, he pushed through a small gathering in front of one of the taverns, wincing in pain as his shoulder collided with one of them.

The man hollered after him, but Thomas was already down the street. He kept walking by an alley next to one of the inns the sailors frequented when docked, when he stopped quickly and turned back around. Thomas could have sworn he saw a dark shape move in the shadows.

"Stay here," he said to Mikey.

"And miss this? Not a chance."

Thomas didn't have to go far. The two bodies were just far enough not to be seen clearly by those on the street.

"You like gypsy girls?" an all too familiar voice said seductively.

Rage went through Thomas so quickly that his whole body began shaking, a matter of seconds from detonating.

The taller form bent his head down and whispered something into Emilia's ear, making her laugh. Thomas grabbed the back of the man's shirt and yanked him off her. Emilia screamed as the man stumbled back. His stream of curses at Thomas was cut off when he felt the cut of a blade on his throat.

"I ain't lookin' for trouble," a southern voice drawled.

"What are ye doing here, ye rebel bastard?"

"Well," the man's eyes darted to Emilia.

Thomas tightened the blade until it drew blood, startling the man into silence. "Eyes on me," Thomas growled.

"I—I was hopin' to get under her sk—"

"I meant the North!" Thomas started growling at him in Irish, not caring if the man understood.

"Thomas!" Emilia shouted, hanging onto his good arm. "Please. It's not what you think."

"I just work on one of the ships," the southerner drawled, and for the first time, Thomas heard how young the man sounded. "We're supposed to set sail in the mornin'."

Thomas squinted at the man and realized he couldn't be more than eighteen.

"Ye are picking off boys now, hm?" Thomas asked Emilia. "Don't ye have any pride, woman?"

"That *boy*," Emilia fumed, "is about my age. And I told you, 'It's not what you think.' I thought you'd have more faith in me."

Flabbergasted, Thomas's grip slackened on the sailor, who in turn used the distraction to break free. Thomas let him stumble down the alley, too distracted by this new information.

"How old are ye?"

Emilia stood there, hands balled into fists, looking like she was going to spit fire.

"Twenty-one," she hissed. "Not that it's any of your business."

"It's me business if I'm dealing with a babaí!"

Mikey began a slow clap. "I didn't realize I'd have such entertainment tonight. Tell me, gypsy. How much do I have to pay for a night with a sprightly young lass such as yourself?"

"Go to hell," Emilia snapped. "You have no idea what you guys have cost me. I need to speak to your brother alone," she told Mikey.

"So ye are selling yourself." Thomas shook his head. *Had everything she'd said been a lie?* "After all that I did for ye? Were ye a cheat this whole time? Nay, you're going straight back to Rose's." Thomas grabbed Emilia's arm and began to pull her down the alley.

"Let go of me, you big, Irish, bullheaded—" She began to beat on his arm with her other hand.

"Stop!" he shouted in Irish, turning on Emilia so fast that she froze. With the light of the street lanterns enlightening her face, he could see her eyes widen in fear before squinting in a fury. That brought him back. The city was already hardening her against the world, and he couldn't decide if he was proud that she was tougher or despairing at her loss of gentility.

Thomas walked towards Emilia until her back hit the wall, and he placed a hand on each side of her head, successfully caging her in. The pain radiating through his shoulder was worth it as he watched in fascination as she swallowed, her slender throat bobbing.

"I told you, I need to explain." Her words came out hoarse. He smirked, knowing how he affected her. "I'm looking for my family."

"Ye're trying to find your family in another man's britches?" he asked sarcastically. Thomas looked into her eyes, searching for a lie.

"No! God, you're such an idiot."

Thomas refrained from flinching, though the words stung, striking too close to home.

He kept his eyes on her face as she turned it towards Mikey, demanding him to leave. Thomas was too busy tracing each curve of her profile to see if his brother listened.

Thomas grabbed Emilia's face and turned it towards him. Watched how his thumb slowly brushed over her mouth, causing a sharp gasp to escape her pretty lips.

"How many have ye graced with these lips, gypsy?"

Thomas caught her hand before it could land across his face and pinned it to the wall. Her other hand came quickly but he was faster. A rumble started deep in his chest. He had her hands pinned above her head and her gaze was absolutely feral. Thomas's grip tightened as he bent down to run his teeth over her jaw.

"What are you doing?" Emilia asked breathily, a moan threatening to break free.

She shivered as his tongue glided over the sensitive area behind her ear. Her breath quickened, and he couldn't help but look down as her breasts rose and fell. They threatened to spill out of her top, the thin fabric concealing nothing. Her body let him know she was just as aroused as him.

For fuck's sake. Where were her clothes?

"Answer the question, gypsy," he growled.

"What?"

"How many have ye entertained?"

"How many women have *you* been with, Thomas?" She snapped back. When he froze, she let out an exasperated breath. "None. I told you—"

The admission melted his shock, and his lips landed on hers, cutting her off as his hand wound in her hair, twisting it into his fingers for better access. Her mouth popped open in a gasp, allowing his tongue to sweep in. Bloody hell, she tasted divine. Thomas pulled her waist into him, her soft curves flush with his hard body.

Emilia moaned into his mouth, her tongue dancing with his as her hands traveled up his chest, making his every nerve jump at her trail of exploration.

Thomas's hand swept behind her knee, pulling her leg up around his waist. She wasn't close enough. A moan reverberated through his chest as he felt her soft thigh. Just a little higher, and he could feel the curve of her—

Thomas froze, body rigid, mouth still on hers but no longer exploring. Emilia made a soft whimper and pulled him closer.

What was he doing? Practically defiling her for anyone to see. Just after he left Nessa in the bed...

"What is it?" The way that she said it like she wanted to do every naughty thing he just imagined, made his hand slide up and squeeze her round bottom. A groan burst through his throat, never having explored a woman so well filled out. The lass was a goddess. He wanted to fall to his knees and show her how her body could be worshipped.

The thought was like a douse of cold water. His hand fisted and pulled away painfully.

Thomas felt sick. He took a step back, grabbing the ache in his shoulder. He needed to control himself. To control the situation. So, he said the first thing that came to mind, "Why didn't ye ask one of us to help ye?"

She blinked up at him in confusion, her arousal still colored high in her cheeks. Thomas watched in wonder as she pulled herself together, his words filtering through her head as she straightened her corset.

"You told me not to speak to you again, remember?" Her hostility was full force now, and if Thomas was honest with himself, he liked how feisty she appeared at that moment. It was a different side of her he'd never seen before. It made him want to punish her until she groaned his name. "And besides," she went on, oblivious of where his thoughts had gone, "You know I can't be asking just anyone about the Roma. You know what people think about them. About me. I thought, with how people talk on the docks, maybe this guy might have heard something and wouldn't be afraid to say anything." She shook her head.

"So ye really are one?"

"No. I mean...yes." She stumbled over her words, rubbing her hands together nervously. "My grandmother is, for sure. My parents—" she paused, a line forming between her brows. "They can be too, but I'm not sure. Look, it's hard to explain. I'm not from this time. I mean, I am. But I came from a different time."

Thomas leaned against the building and let his head drop, feeling a headache coming along. "Ye are speaking in riddles."

She sighed. "Look. This will sound crazy, but Shay and I are from the twenty-first century. Over one hundred and fifty years in the future."

He stared at her, trying to make her words make sense, but anyway that he put them together, they sounded wrong. Was this woman mad? Had she and her friend escaped an asylum, and that's why she had no family around?

"I know what you're thinking," Emilia whispered. "But I'm not crazy." She walked up to Thomas, desperation driving her forward. "Think about it. We're having such a hard time in this century. Think about how different I am from everyone else. Ask me anything about the future, and I'll try to tell you."

Thomas wanted to believe her; he really did. He studied her, feeling a deep sorrow growing within his chest, tightening its grip. "Maybe we should get ye back to Rose's."

"Please." Tears began to track their way down her pretty cheeks as she pleaded. "Please believe me." She pulled out her rosary, hands shaking as she showed it to him. "This. Shay has one too." Emilia's tale spewed out of her mouth, raw, painful, unbelievable. She told him of when they found the vials and everything that happened up to the point when she met him.

"Lass," his throat constricted, wishing he could believe her, "I think we need to get ye some help."

Emilia stared at him, tears falling freely now, completely despondent, and shook her head. "If you're not going to help me, then I'll do it alone. I never asked you to come back and help me. But I asked you to trust me, and you can't...or won't. It doesn't matter which, I guess." She tried to dry her face with her hands, but there was no use. Tears kept falling. "I will continue to try and get information from random men. Maybe when Shay is better, she can help me find my family a different way." She stared at him for a minute as if memorizing his face, then dropped her head and turned away. She walked back down the alley.

"Where ye going?"

"My dress is over here. You can go."

Emilia didn't look back as Thomas was rooted to the spot, uncertainty warring with reason.

I fumbled with my dress, silent sobs shaking my body. The last couple of weeks had started to wear on me, between worrying about Shay, feeling nauseated with myself while I flirted with the men for answers, and now Thomas refusing to believe me.

I couldn't even let myself think of the kiss. If that's what you could call it. I'd never been ravished so thoroughly, and we didn't even take our clothes off. My head pounded at the realization that we didn't really do anything. So, I guess it could've been a kiss.

A really, really soul-shattering kiss.

My inhalation stuttered throughout my chest after my sobs subsided. I was going to crash. Fast.

I placed one of my hands on the building to steady myself, feeling the brick's grain scrape against my skin, and took a deep breath. I needed my face to be clear before returning to Rose's.

Straightening, I patted my hip to ensure I still had my coin purse and went to the street, thankful Thomas had left while my back was turned. I was just about there when a large, dark form took up the alley's opening. I held back a scream, taking a step back.

"Excuse me," I said, hoping they'd move without a fight. I grabbed the knife I had hidden in my pocket.

"I think ye want to hear what I've got to say, lass."

"Michael?" I relaxed marginally, still wary. "How much did you hear?"

"Hear?" Amusement rang in his voice, but I chose to ignore it and went to push past. "I heard enough," he said, successfully stopping me.

"And...you believe me?"

"That doesn't matter," he said, stepping to the side. "Why don't ye come out here, and we'll have a wee chat."

We started walking down the street, heading the way I'd usually take to Rose's. The night was cool, a light breeze drying my tears as I turned my face to the sky. There was no moon that I could see, but plenty of stars.

"What do you want to talk about if you don't believe me?" I asked, feeling deflated.

"Well, the way I see it. Ye need to find someone. Aye?" I nodded, and he went on. "I have the manpower to do that. It doesn't matter if your head isn't right. If ye are right about your family living in the city, I can find them."

I glared at him, my hope morphing into suspicion. "At what price?"

He smirked, looking down at me as we walked. "You're learning quickly."

"Well, it's not very hard with you, is it?" I snapped, too tired to care.

His eyebrows raised, but he let it go. "I can help ye find them. In return, you'll give me eighty percent of your coin every night."

I stopped so fast Michael had to turn back around.

"You want me to sing?"

"Aye." He smiled, clearly thinking it was a fair trade.

I already had some money saved up, and Rose let Shay and I stay with her as long as I worked for free. So I would still take some money home at the night's end. I'd been saving it in case of an emergency, but if Michael helped me, I might be able to leave faster.

I squinted at him. "I'm not sleeping with any men or going down alleys anymore."

He nodded, as if already knowing my answer. "Believe me, it wouldn't be worth Tommy's griping. Singing will do."

"I don't give a shit what your brother thinks," I hissed. His eyes widened at my language. "I don't make much at night," I admitted.

Michael tipped his hat to me, smiling slyly. "That's where I come in. We'll arrange longer hours every night, and I'll choose the location. You'll be making enough coin in no time. And I want ye to do it until summer's end, no matter how quickly I find your family."

My excitement sizzled out at having to stay here for three more months. Not to mention, all the work I'd have to do in addition to working at the bakery. "I'll need at least one day off a week to give my voice a break and several days at the end of every month."

To my astonishment, he agreed, as long as he could pick the days. I took a deep breath and made my second demand. "And I'd like you to teach me how to fight."

"Fight?" He looked at me oddly. "What do ye need to fight for?"

"I've had a couple of instances that the guys got a little too grabby." I kept my eyes on the ground as we continued walking. "I don't want to be as scared anymore. I want to be able to protect myself if I need to."

"What do ye want to know?"

"I have a knife," I admitted. "Teach me how to use a gun. I want to know how to get out of a man's hold too. To injure him enough that I can get away."

"I can set a man by ye, if ye're that worried."

I shook my head. "I don't mind someone watching over me, but I want to be able to do it myself. I don't want to count on someone else for my safety."

Michael ran a hand down his face, looking tired. "I don't know if that's worth—"

"I'll give you one-hundred percent of my earnings for two weeks of every month. The other two weeks, I'd like to keep my twenty percent."

Michael whistled and then laughed. "Ye shock me, gypsy."

"Don't call me that," I said, my cheeks darkening. Even though I didn't grow up with my people, I vaguely knew they considered that word offensive. Though the emotions that swirled within me when Thomas said it... I guess I could say they were far from being offended.

And the way he'd said it, like fingertips skimming over my body. As if he revered that part of me. I had to hide a shiver from Michael. Yeah, only Thomas could call me that.

"I didn't mean to insult ye—" He looked down at me and stopped speaking. "Ah. I see."

"I doubt it," I mumbled. We turned down the street towards the bakery. I looked around, surprised we were almost there already. I'd been so focused on our conversation, I didn't pay much attention to the people around me.

"This is where we part ways," Michael said, his hands in his pockets.

I nodded. "Thank you for helping me."

"Ye can thank me when I actually do something." He shrugged. "So...it's a deal?" He held his hand out in front of me.

I stared at it, slightly hesitant, but seeing no better choice. My eyes set on his. "On one condition."

He raised his brow. "And that'd be?"

"You don't tell Thomas about any of this. Not the singing deal or the fighting. All he has to know is I'm still singing to find things out my own way."

"I'll admit, it's not going to be easy." He sighed, his big shoulders sagging in defeat. "But aye. Your secret is safe with me. But it's on ye if he somehow finds out. Deal?"

He held his hand out again. I spat on mine and gripped his tightly. I was rewarded with surprise and a firm shake.

"Deal."

CHAPTER NINETEEN

Emilia

MAY 1861

Shay sat at the table, up unusually late, and looked like she wasn't going to bed any time soon. I had bought her a cheap dress with my small earnings, so she could be presentable now that she could get around more.

I looked at the small clock Rose kept on the counter. My pulse quickened; I had to get her to sleep before I could go busk for Michael.

"Are you ready for bed?" I asked, not really expecting an answer. She still hadn't spoken since the night Thomas was injured.

Shay's sharp eyes pierced through me full force without the swelling. "Where have you been going at night?"

My heart soared at hearing her voice, then plummeted when I focused on the meaning of the words. "I—I don't know what you mean," I stuttered, looking everywhere but at her. I started to straighten up items that didn't need straightening.

"Don't lie to me, Emilia O'Connor. I've known you since you peed in your pants."

My head snapped up as I hushed her. "You can't say that name anymore," I whispered, going to her. "It's Emilia Moretti now. And it was one time in first grade!" I blushed. "Let it go!"

Confusion replaced her suspicion. "Where'd you get that name?"

"I remembered it," I admitted, sitting in the chair across from her. "I remember more and more lately. If anyone hears you call me O'Connor, everyone will be suspicious."

She nodded, understanding. "So, I didn't imagine that? He really is in one of the pictures?" She squinted at the blank wall as if it held all the answers. "How is that possible?"

"I don't know how any of this is possible, but when I figured out what date you were in, I was able to look for Thomas, who, yes, is my father's ancestor."

She wrinkled her nose. "He's your family."

"Well, not really," I said defensively. "I'm adopted, and he's so many generations back from being gross."

Her jaw nearly hit the floor. "You like him! I mean, from how you were talking, the both of you obviously like each other. But I didn't think you were aware of it." She shook her head, her face brightening slightly for the first time since we came here. "Usually, you're oblivious."

My face heated and a headache was most definitely coming on. "He doesn't like me." God, I sounded like I was back in high school.

Shay smiled. "That's the Millie I know." I quickly dropped my fingertips from my lips, not realizing my mind drifted to the kiss, and her eyes widened.

"You didn't," she said with a gasp.

I shook my head, unable to look her in the eye.

"Millie."

When she wouldn't look away, I relented on a sigh. "It was just a kiss. Okay?"

Her body jolted as a low screech escaped her lips. "No!"

My eyes found hers again as I tried to hide a smile.

"Oh my God! How was it?"

"It wasn't..." I paused, looking up at the ceiling. "Nice."

I looked down when she remained silent and let out a low laugh at her unhinged jaw, her features completely shocked.

"Are you telling me it was terrifying?" she whispered.

My breath came out rapidly as if I had run a mile. "He's terrified me since I first laid eyes on him."

Her gaze flicked over my face, and she sat back. "And was it worth it?"

My face fell, and I looked at my hands in my lap. "He doesn't believe me, Shay."

"Well, could you blame him? We kind of did the impossible."

I nodded. It was crazy. Actually, his reaction was probably the only sane thing in the situation. "You're right."

Shay laughed and explained when I gave her a weird look. "It's just... it took traveling through time for you to be impressed by a guy." She chuckled, shaking her head. "I should have known you couldn't be impressed with a normal guy."

I couldn't help but smile back; it was so good to see her coming out of her shell again. "I missed you so much," I said, tears springing to my eyes.

A lone tear fell from hers, and she looked down, playing with her nails. "I'm sorry I caused so much trouble since being here."

"Never apologize for that," I said, so firmly that it startled us. The rage I felt the night I wanted to kill her attackers began bubbling up inside me again. "I should have been there for you. And if it wasn't for me—" My words choked off, stuck with a sob in my throat. "God, I'm going to kill Nora." I slammed my hand on the table. "If she didn't jilt me, you might not have—"

Shay grabbed my hand, squeezing it. "You found me. You never gave up on me. I will never forget that." She paused, her dark eyes examining me. "Now, who's Nora?"

I tried to settle down so I could explain thoroughly. *That damn woman*. It took everything in me not to get up and start pacing. "She's basically a pimp," I spat. "They would call her Madam Nora, though. She was supposed to help me find Thomas but used me instead." Shay's eyes widened, getting the wrong idea.

"No, no. I sang for her. Don't worry." I squeezed her hand in reassurance as my own resolve crumbled. "I thought you hated me. Blamed me for all of this mess." I couldn't meet her eyes.

"I was mad because I wanted to do it myself."

That had me looking up. "I was mad because *I* wanted to do it!" I put my head back, remembering how Thomas tricked me. "I could have killed him when he left me behind."

"Sounds like you want to commit a lot of murder nowadays." Shay tried to smile and failed. "I'm glad you didn't. I never would've forgiven myself if you'd gotten hurt." She straightened, her pretty, heart-shaped face transforming from miserable to guarded. "Which brings me to my initial question. Where have you been going at night?"

I sighed, knowing I wouldn't get out of this if I wanted to make it on time to busk. I told Shay everything.

Dawn was frigid and miserable after being out all-night singing. Though I'd been singing for a week, it was my first self-defense lesson and a wake-up call I was already dreading. But Michael and I agreed we should do it while the city still slept. Teaching a woman how to fight would certainly draw too much attention.

Shay and I quietly crept downstairs and went out the back to a small rundown courtyard surrounded by several businesses facing the streets. Sewage and scattered trash had been thrown out back, made duller by the grey of the coming dawn.

I opened the door, so focused on finding Michael and not breathing in the stench, that I jumped when a voice came from my left.

"Didn't mean to startle ye." Michael raised his brow, spitting to the side. He stood straight from the building he was propped against—looking like he had about as little sleep as I did. When he spotted Shay, his face went completely blank. "What is she doing here?"

I looked back at Shay, then at him, and crossed my arms. "She wanted to watch. Is that a problem?"

His eyes darkened. "I'm not training one of them."

My hand shot out to slap him, but he caught my forearm, quickly blocking my assault.

"Don't," I growled, yanking my arm from his grasp.

"It's okay, Millie," Shay said, descending the stairs. "This *cracker* doesn't bother me."

"What about the other crackers I pulled you out from under?" Michael sneered.

Shay went pale and swayed on her feet as if she'd been physically hit.

"What the fuck is wrong with you?" I snapped, going to her.

She grabbed my arm. "Ignore him." She stared at Michael as if she was peeling back layers. "He didn't mean it."

"I think he did," I said. "Let's go back inside." I tried to pull her towards the door, but she didn't budge.

"No. He wasn't hateful when he saved me that night."

Michael narrowed his eyes. "I had a job to do."

"Maybe." They stared at each other long enough that I wondered just *what* had passed between them that night. She shrugged. "Maybe not. Either way, you saved me, and for that, I'm grateful." Her dark eyes focused on his light ones, making Michael's stance change, which was interesting. Did she actually make him uncomfortable? Or was she revealing some truth he didn't want us to see?

"That doesn't mean he's a good man for you to be around," I said, not liking the conflict. "It's different here."

"There's racism everywhere, Millie."

"But you know it's worse in this time," I whispered into her ear, desperate for her to understand the severity.

She wouldn't let me move her, but she shook her head as if breaking out of a trance. She suddenly looked drained.

"I'm very well aware of what they're capable of." Her words were like a slap. "But that doesn't change the fact that we need him." She turned to Michael. "Train her. I promise to just sit over here." She pointed to the steps and sat down, waiting for us to begin. I heard her mumble, "Maybe then we can get the hell out of here."

Michael kept staring at her, a mixture of hate and something else I couldn't figure out, flitting across his face. Did he expect her to fight back?

"Michael," I said. He didn't move, but his eyes landed on me. "Do we still have a deal? I'll do things my way if you're an ass to my friend."

He looked between us—broad shoulders rigid and hands clenched—but jerked his head for me to follow. I kept my distance until he told me what to do.

Michael eyed me up and down and circled around me as if appraising a show-horse. Not for the first time, I wished I had pants to practice in. But, unfortunately, the only thing I could do was tie my hair so it wouldn't get in my face and hope that the dress would do. He nodded and stopped in front of me.

"Ye're short compared to me but tall enough for a lot of the lads." He nodded, thinking. "First thing I'd want ye to try is bringing your blade across their forehead." Michael drew his knife and demonstrated with a quick slash across my face. I jumped back, startled by how quick he moved, though he didn't touch me. "With that, your victim should bleed out into his eyes, and ye can try to get away. Ye try now."

I pulled my small blade out of my corset and went closer to him.

"That's what you're working with?" Michael looked at my knife with disgust. "That's not a proper blade."

I threw my hands into the air. "I didn't exactly have the money to go buy one, Rambo. I swiped this out of Rose's shop."

"It's a cutlery knife..."

I gave him a "duh" expression, earning me a few choice curses. He lifted up his pant leg and handed me one of his. "Take this until ye can procure your own."

It was small, but it had a wicked curve to the blade. "Where am I going to put that?" I asked, imagining accidentally slicing off one of my boobs with it.

"On your leg. I'll get ye a strap to tie it down."

"Thank you." I turned the knife over, admiring the leather handle.

"Is that the hand ye will be practicing with?" He looked surprised.

I stared at my hand, wondering what he was getting at. "Is that a problem?"

"Ye're a leftie?"

I confirmed it, earning me a grunt. "Should do ye well," was all Michael said on it, but if I wasn't mistaken, he looked mildly impressed.

He had me practice my slashes, ducking and moving out of the way of his thrusts and fumbling and moving in ways my body wasn't used to. The exertion took the chill out of the air, and sweat trickled down my face as I tried to stab Michael through his shoulder. He slapped the knife out of my hand, making it fly across the ground. With a growl, he went to retrieve it. I tried not to scowl at him as I thought how spectacularly my left hand failed me.

"What?" I put my hands on my waist defiantly. Michael wasn't a patient instructor.

"That's enough for today." He handed me the knife. "I expect ye to be better prepared tomorrow."

"It was my first day," I mumbled, more to myself than to him, but he had already disappeared without a glance towards Shay.

I sat on the step next to her, wiping my sweaty face.

"What are we doing here?" Shay asked, staring at the red sunrise that had taken over the grey sky.

I hid my shaking hands in my dress and shrugged. "Surviving."

The weeks went by in a haze until I fell into a stupor every night, too exhausted to move. The early morning training and late-night singing wore on me.

However, my exhaustion didn't stop basic anatomy, and I quickly had to obtain flannel cloths for my monthly flow. Without modern, feminine products, I had to ask Mira to help me. I tried to play it off as a lack of supplies rather than a lack of nineteenth-century knowledge. With questions in her eyes, Mira showed me how to properly clean them and hang them up to dry where no one could see them. I hadn't ever felt so awkward and embarrassed from being a woman until I returned to a time when we were considered inferior.

By the time I survived the week, and another one was nearing an end, we couldn't ignore that Shay still hadn't had hers, though we didn't mention it. She began to withdraw again, staying inside and often staring at nothing, going off into her own world. I worried about her as I took orders, swept the floor, and learned different baking techniques from Rose. Shay helped when she was mentally present, but we didn't push her.

It wasn't until I came upstairs for a break one morning and found Shay heaving into a bedpan that I knew our suspicions were confirmed. Still, I went to her, hoping for the best.

"Hey, you okay?" I asked when she finished. I pulled her braids back and put a wet rag on her neck. I noticed how much her hair had grown and made a mental note to ask Rose about helping style it. My main goal was to make Shay as comfortable as I possibly could.

Shay sat back on the floor and rested against the side of the bed. "Just great." Tears fell from her closed eyes.

I sat down and grabbed her hand. "Is there anything I can do? Do you—" I paused, not sure how to go on. "Do you want me to figure out how to handle it?"

Her tears were now a flood cascading down her face. She only shook her head.

"It would be dangerous right now," I admitted. "But I could try to find someone. I don't—" I tried to keep myself from crying, wanting to be strong for her. "I don't want you to go through any more than you already did."

Shay finally opened her eyes, laying her head back to look at me. "I want to keep it."

That took me back. I scanned her face, but only found resolve. "Okay," I said, my head going through every scenario and calculating the months until her due date. "I'll push Michael to look faster. We'll try to get out before January. I mean, hopefully we're out by the end of summer, but—"

She placed her hand on my arm, and I stopped babbling. "You're doing enough, Millie."

"But—"

"It's not your fault." She straightened, always stronger than me. "Women have babies all the time. I'll be okay."

"It's dangerous, though," I whispered.

"That's why you're still looking for our way back home." She smiled sadly. Here she was, the battered one, still comforting me like she always did.

I shook my head, disgusted with myself.

"You're too hard on yourself," she said. "You're practically killing yourself trying to keep a roof over our head, while looking for our way out, and you still think you're not doing enough. Stop blaming yourself for stuff out of your control, and start looking at everything you're doing." She grabbed my hand in both of hers. "How I see it, we're stuck in this time. You're learning, adapting, and I'm useless. I'm the one you should be mad at."

I flinched as if she had struck me. "You need time to heal."

"I am healed," she said defiantly.

"Shay, these things take time..."

"I want to learn how to fight, too." She pegged me with a sharp stare when I began to protest. "If we're here for any amount of time, I need to know how to protect myself. And my baby."

I looked down and noticed her hands covering her stomach as if already protecting it.

"He's not going to like it," I admitted.

"I know."

"I don't like you having to deal with him. I know you like trying to see the good in everyone, but he's—"

"He's helping you," she pointed out.

"Yeah, after I give him all my money." I laughed darkly. "He's a racist asshole, Shay. And, if you haven't noticed, it's not uncommon here. I'd feel better if you stayed where it's safe."

"I can't hide forever. Don't you think I've noticed the war that's going on?"

"Well, yeah." I squinted at her, unsure what the war had to do with anything. "So?"

"This war is a pivotal moment in history." She said it slowly as if I was missing something vital. "After everything that's happened, I think I want to help."

"Help?" Maybe I was slower than I realized because I had no idea where this was coming from. "Help how?"

"I don't know." She shrugged. "Maybe we can find organizations to help the war effort. Or help in the hospitals or something."

"We don't know anything about nursing." But the intent on her face had me conceding. It occurred to me that she might use this as a coping method. "I'll ask around and see if there's anything we can do. You still want me to look for a way home, right?" I felt like I had entered the twilight zone, entirely blindsided by each day.

"Yeah, I just want to help while I can, you know? Make a differ-ence. I feel like maybe we're here for a reason."

As Shay rubbed her belly and stared at the wall for the first time, I wondered if I was meant to be in this time.

CHAPTER TWENTY

Thomas

JUNE 1861

A light drizzle misted Thomas as he wiped the blood off his knuckles and turned away from the unconscious man, rolling his shoulder to loosen the ache. But unfortunately, it did nothing to ease his shame.

Spring had turned into summer while he waited for the strength to return in his shoulder. Thomas kept his mouth shut as Mikey brought him farther down the rabbit hole. Of course, Thomas drew his limits, but he was desperate for cash and often followed his brother's orders. Two months in, Thomas began to think the extra money wasn't worth it.

As the contracts for the enlisted men were about to end, they still clashed with the South. Their promise of a quick victory was crumbling as the rebels fought back with more force than expected, and Thomas was more than eager to fight for his country.

With Thomas's growing strength, Mikey began using him differently. No longer was Thomas confined to thievery and blackmail. He had a natural talent for fighting and finding weak spots. A talent Mikey found invaluable when he wanted to keep his other men in the dark and one that Thomas had long tried to repress.

It was mid-June when Mikey found out one of his boys had been skimming some of the drugs off his shipments. Having been tipped off, they met on Long Wharf, where the transaction was to take place. Night had fallen, and most workers and pedestrians were already gone, so they didn't have to worry about being spotted lurking in the shadows. They waited for the two buyers to leave the warehouse before blocking Byrne's way.

Thomas threw him against the wall, stunning him with a fist to his face. He pummeled him until he was doubled over, dripping blood. Thomas shut off his consciousness and let his body do what his mind refused to accept.

Mikey grabbed the money and quickly counted it. When Thomas was nearly done, Mikey grabbed a handful of Byrne's hair, pulling his head up so he could glare into his eyes. "Ye're out, boyo. Ye can thank me for sparing your life by never showing face again."

"Mikey, it's not—"

Mikey slammed his face into the sidewalk, rendering him unconscious.

"Good work, Tommy boy," Mikey said, earning him a glare.

Mikey bent down, grabbed Byrne under the arms, and dragged him between the buildings where no one would find him until morning.

"I need to be able to trust me men," Mikey went on.

Thomas pocketed the bloody handkerchief he used to clean his knuckles. "Sounds like ye need better men."

"Precisely," Mikey smiled, holding his arms out in invitation. "With both of us, we could triple business. What do ye say?"

"No."

"I've been expanding," Mikey admitted. "Thought my interests might go beyond selling. Ye might find it beneficial. I already have a few jobs set up, bringing in some cash. Been looking into buying one of Billy Mead's saloons. I already have the entertainment bringing in some money, and—"

"Not interested."

Mikey grumbled about a lass not hesitating, but Thomas had heard enough. "Ye could help me run the saloon," Mikey persisted. "Be more on the straight and narrow, deartháir."

"Ye know ye can't be good for more than a day. And we both know it'll be swarming with crooks gambling their life away within the first year."

Mikey ground his teeth, his jaw ticking in frustration. "Think about it. I'll pull the offer at the end of summer. Just know, I'm pulling in honest money with me entertainment—"

Thomas cut him off, "What is this 'entertainment?'" A suspicious prickling sensation crawled over his skin as if he should already know the answer.

"Some lasses—"

Thomas shook his head and began to walk away. "I've heard enough," he threw over his shoulder.

"I really think it would serve ye some interest." Something in his voice had Thomas turning around. Mikey's hands were in his pockets, a cocky grin on his face. Was he taunting him?

"Aye? And why is that?"

Mikey shrugged. "Come see for yourself. Ye know where to find it."

One of the serving girls set down another pint in front of Thomas. He nodded his thanks and began to chug it.

"Are you doing all right?" Hiram asked, concern creasing his brows.

"Fine." Thomas slammed the empty pint on the table and signaled for another. He tried to ignore how Hiram and Jackson exchanged a look.

"Is it your shoulder?" Jackson asked.

Thomas glared at everyone. "Are ye going to be fussing over me like some 'ol biddies? I wouldn't have come around if ye are."

Sam tilted his head, glaring at Thomas. "We haven't seen you around much."

"Yeah?" Thomas looked into his pint as if it held all the answers. "Well, I've been busy."

"Busy running with your no-good brother?" Sam snapped.

"Aye, guess I have." Thomas looked up then and met his eye, neither wanting to break contact first.

"I saw Miss Millie a few weeks back." That drew Thomas' attention. The whole table went silent, waiting for the dime to drop. "She asked about you." Isaac leaned back in his chair, obviously pleased with himself. "Tell me, have you heard from her lately?"

Thomas scratched his whiskers, trying to hide his interest. "No, should I?"

"Enough," Hiram said, throwing Isaac a warning look.

Thomas glared at Hiram.

"I would think you would," Isaac went on, shrugging. "Since you're working for the same person."

"What is that supposed to mean?" Thomas snapped, leaning his elbows on the table.

No one answered as Thomas eyed each of his friends.

"Have ye all known something I haven't?"

Hiram sat back and ran his hand over his cropped hair. "Look, Tommy. We hear she's been singing at one of Billy Mead's saloons. The talk is that Mikey has a nice spot for her up there."

"Mikey? Me brother?" He squinted, trying to understand. Then realization dawned as Mikey's comments started to make sense. "Why would she do that?"

Hiram shrugged. "I don't know, but they've got a good deal going on. She's been bringing in a lot of men." A jolt went through Thomas. Hiram must have noticed because he quickly clarified. "Not like that, brother. She's been singing as others go through the men."

"And ye know all this how?"

Thomas eyed them, waiting for someone to respond. Isaac leaned back in his chair, looking around the room as Sam and Jackson stared at the table.

Hiram sighed. "You know we can't enter Mead's." Billy Mead was known for enforcing the Fugitive Slave Act and was one of the thugs blocking the courthouse against any attempts to rescue Anthony Burns. Even if he would let them in, they refused to enter any business of Billy's or the Mead brothers. "I heard it from some of the men on the docks."

Thomas rubbed his chest, trying to loosen the knot threatening to crush his ribcage.

"Anything else I can get you, boys?" the server asked, smiling sweetly as she set another pint in front of Thomas.

The others gave her an order, while Thomas rubbed his hands over his face, trying to gather his thoughts. Why would Emilia want to work with his brother? Thomas knew he'd hurt her when he refused to believe her, but he couldn't think of one good reason for Emilia to work with Mikey. Unless she found comfort—

No, he couldn't think about that. The rage he tried to drown in alcohol bubbled back to the surface. He slammed some money on the table, chugged the pint in one pull, and stood up to leave.

"Sit down," Hiram said, standing up as if to stop him.

"I'm just going for a look."

Hiram scrunched his face in disbelief. "If you go there, I can't go with you."

"I know," Thomas said, donning his cap. "Don't worry. It's just a look."

Hiram shook his head and sat down reluctantly. "I can't stop you. Just don't get in trouble. I won't be there to get you out of it."

"She deserves more than what your about to do, man," Isaac said seriously, putting all four legs of his chair back on the ground.

Thomas ground his teeth but nodded. Even sloshed, he could see that his friends were just looking out for him, or rather the lass he couldn't seem to keep away from. That thought drew more respect from Thomas than he was willing to admit.

He bumped into a man on the short walk there and almost lost his balance. *Feck, how much did he drink?* Thomas took a minute to orient himself, the crowd tilting as they passed him. He swallowed, wondering for the first time if he should be doing this.

Maybe the lads are right, he thought. Then, almost within the same breath, the alcohol fueled his stubborn nature, and he walked the rest of the way to Billy Mead's Saloon. He didn't stop to listen to the piano or the hypnotic voice of the woman singing. Sliding in behind a group by the door, he found a seat in the back, his cap low over his face as he took in the room.

Billy Mead's Saloon was more dignified in its style, adorned with leather seats, polished tables, and brass fixtures. At least there wasn't a pissing trough by the bar. A row of stools were propped in front of the long bar that took up the entire right side of the room, and small circular tables filled up the rest, spaced for an excellent view of the stage.

Thomas dared to look at Emilia as she leaned against the piano, bending her head back and exposing her long neck to the top of her low-cut dress. She had exchanged her plain green dress for a finer red one. Her ensemble only heightened her exotic beauty, exposing the plains of an exquisite land he'd never explored. He shook his head as if he could physically expel the images that flashed through his mind at the thought.

He looked around the room instead, wondering if the other lads were affected the same way. Nearly the whole saloon consisted of men, except for the slags peppered throughout the crowd, searching for their next target to corrupt, and the barmaids weaving in and out to take orders. Which wasn't uncommon. Most of these saloons were filled with gamblers and men trying to find a slag; the entertainment usually was a derivative. Though it looked like Emilia had a majority of the attention on her.

A strange prickling sensation overcame Thomas, making him roll his shoulders, trying to dispel his growing agitation as the other men stared at Emilia. Of course, she wasn't his, but his entire body responded with a possessiveness that he couldn't control. He let out a long breath, reminding himself that he needed to keep his distance.

The song ended, drawing hoots and hollers for more. Emilia smiled, the room brightening as she did, and looked off to the side. Thomas followed her gaze. The familiar face had him sitting straight as his brother nodded at Emilia to continue. A flash of red drew his attention back to the stage as she prepared for the next song, prompting Thomas to slide back down in his seat to avoid being seen by either of them.

Thomas glared at Mikey, thinking of all the ways he'd kill his brother. He would skin him alive if he touched one hair on her body. Just the thought of his brother spending so much time with Emilia infuriated him. It was his fault, though. Maybe she wouldn't have felt the need to work with Mikey if he had just tried to believe her.

Thomas began to stand up when Emilia started walking through the crowd, using it as a distraction for a quick escape. But the song cut short, and out of his peripheral, the red suddenly disappeared into the dull crowd. Thomas froze, trying to spot her among the laughing men. The moment he did, all his blood rushed to his throat in a fit of rage.

A man grabbed Emilia and pulled her onto his lap. Thomas went to stand again but stopped suddenly when the man stiffened. Looking closer, Thomas swore he could see a glint of metal in her hand.

Thomas' breath caught as Emilia smiled and beckoned one of the other women to him. She laughed, swaying away as if it were part of the show. If Thomas hadn't been focused on Emilia, he would have missed her slipping something into the side of her dress.

With a thump, he rocked back in his seat, exhaling his relief as dread pooled in his stomach. He hoped to see his brother standing to defend her, but he found Mikey staring at him, smirking.

Mikey looked away as Emilia began to sing a rowdy song that had the men slapping each other's backs and laughing.

Thomas clenched his fists, eyes riveted on the table before him. *Damn, the woman was good.* She adapted to the North End far beyond his expectations. Ever since he met Emilia, he saw her as someone to protect. A liability to the narrowed world Thomas made for himself. He hated that he doubted her resilience and reprimanded himself for not seeing it sooner. Emilia could handle herself. She never needed him to protect her but instead used him as a means to an end to save her friend, and now she'd found another way to get what she desired.

Thomas stood, leaving the bar, feeling in his heart that he was no longer where he belonged.

CHAPTER TWENTY-ONE

Emilia

25 June 1861

The water lapped at the docks as we walked down the waterfront, creating sweet serenity in its familiarity. It almost would have been a perfect day if it wasn't so hot. But, at least, a light breeze came off the water, stirring the hair briefly off my neck.

"Thanks for this," Shay said, turning her face towards the sun. She had been sinking into a deep depression again, and when I saw that Evaline kept getting under Rose's feet, I saw my chance to get them both outdoors.

The little girl ran a few feet before us, laughing as she scared seagulls into flight. Shay smiled at Evaline, and my insides warmed.

"You needed to get out," I agreed. "And that devil needed to burn some energy." We both turned to smile at Evaline chasing the birds as they landed, scattering them with angry squawks. I swore she never stopped.

"God, I'm starving," Shay said.

"We can—"

"You know what I want?" she asked, turning so fast that I side-stepped her. "A cheeseburger and french fries. And maybe some pizza!" She moaned and closed her eyes. "When do you think ranch was invented?"

I laughed. "I'm not sure it is yet. We could try to make it ourselves."

"That would be awesome." She sighed, and we continued walking.

I hesitated a moment. "Are you craving anything weird?"

She eyed me sideways but started to smile. I let out the breath I didn't know I was holding. We hadn't talked about her pregnancy much.

"Scrambled eggs and cheeseburgers."

"That's not too crazy."

"No," she said, smiling while she scrunched her nose. "I mean together. And maybe with some ranch on them both."

"Okay," I laughed. "Maybe it is kind of gross."

"Don't hate!" This was the happiest I'd seen her in a while, and I hoped to keep her distracted. "Just wait until you start cravings. There's no stopping them."

I looked down, my heart plummeting. Was that even something I wanted? "That's probably not happening any time soon." I forced a laugh, watching as a young couple passed us.

"Stay close, Eva!" Shay yelled. Evaline smiled back at us, her brown curls blowing in her face.

We walked a few more minutes in silence, taking in the momentary peacefulness of not having to work or worry about anything.

No one was bothering us, and it was glorious. So why had my mood suddenly gone sour?

"Have you seen him?" Shay asked.

The question took me back as if she was reading my mind. "Who?" I asked, my tone cautious.

She actually rolled her eyes. "Don't play stupid. Don't you think I noticed how you've been moping around the bakery?"

"I—I've been busy," I said. "Michael hasn't given me any news yet about my family, and with working all day and singing all night, I'm tired."

Shay's face sobered as she watched Evaline run back to us. "I know. You've been doing a lot. But you don't see how your face lights up whenever someone mentions Thomas."

"No, it doesn't." I scrunched up my nose in disbelief.

"It does," she said, smiling again. "It's quite pathetic."

I elbowed her, and she laughed. "No, I haven't seen him," I admitted. "I secretly keep hoping he'd come to see me sing, but he hasn't."

"I'm hungry!" Evaline yelled as she grabbed hold of my dress.

"Maybe he'll come around," Shay said. "Just give him time."

"I'm not sure how much time we have left," I said, looking over her shoulder. A few steamships had docked, their smoke billowing up to meet the clouds. It looked like soldiers were disembarking. "Hold on, sweetie," I said to Evaline. "We'll get something to eat after seeing who this is."

"Should we be here?" Shay asked. She had paled when seeing all the men. "What if they're from the south?"

"I don't think so," I said, hearing someone bark orders. "It might be one of the regiments that went for training. Do you remember?"

"Not really, but I haven't been paying attention too much lately."

I grabbed Evaline's hand and went closer to the marching troops. Irish brogues carried with the wind, answering my suspicions.

"I think that might be the all-Irish regiment Michael was talking about," I said.

Shay studied my face. "Was he thinking of joining?"

"No." I almost laughed at the thought of Michael joining. "He thinks it's a waste of time. I only asked him about it because…"

"Because of Thomas," Shay finished, rolling her eyes. At least I knew she was feeling better enough to be exasperated with me.

"He said Thomas didn't join, but—but wanted to." I swallowed, feeling a lump form in my throat. "Shay, you don't by chance know when the 28th Regiment forms, do you?"

"Why would I know that?"

I shook my head. "That was the regiment on the flag we found in the attic."

Understanding dawned on her features. "And that's probably the one Thomas joins." She grabbed my hand and squeezed it. "That's why you're so concerned about time? He might be gone when we finally go back home."

I looked at the blue sky and watched the clouds pass by, willing away the tears that threatened to spill. "It shouldn't matter. I don't really know him."

"Sometimes we just *click* with a person, Millie. They just make sense to you, and there's no explanation, even when it hasn't been much time. Maybe he's your person?"

I glanced at her in surprise. "Like, what? Soul mates?" I laughed nervously. "Do you really believe in that?"

"Yes." She shrugged. "Maybe you were meant to meet Thomas."

"Fate," I said, thinking hard. "You honestly believe in fate?" Actually, it shouldn't have surprised me. Shay had always been the romantic as I was more practical, leaning towards security rather than passion.

"I do," she admitted. "And I happened to find you staring at his photo more times than I can count."

I gasped, face flaming red. "I did not!"

She gave me a knowing smile as Evaline swung around, holding onto Shay's skirts.

"You talking about Uncle Tommy?" Evaline asked, breaking through our conversation.

"Yes." Shay smiled deviously. "Millie might be your Uncle Tommy's soul mate!"

"Shay!" I swatted her arm and pulled Evaline faster along. "He is not my soul mate," I said to Evaline. "Shay is just being silly."

Evaline's brows crinkled in thought as she eyed both of us. "I told him about your light, but he didn't see it."

"My light?" I asked, perplexed. I squatted down and grabbed both of her hands while I studied her sad face. "What are you talking about, honey? What light?"

"You glow." She shrugged as if it was normal. "Ms. Shay does too."

I squinted at Shay, who looked at Evaline worriedly.

"Tell me," I said to Evaline. "Have you seen anyone else glow?"

Evaline shook her head and pulled out of my grip. "Can we go eat now?"

"Just wait a second. You said Thomas doesn't see it, though?"

Her brown curls bounced with each shake of her head. "He said no."

I straightened, sharing a concerned glance with Shay. Of course, Evaline might have been making up a story, but if for some reason she could see that we were from a different time, that we didn't belong... then what did that mean?

I couldn't wrap my mind around it at the moment.

"C'mon, ladies," I said, walking back the way we came, away from the soldiers. "Let's get you something to eat."

Shay leaned in close to me. "I kind of want to follow them."

I looked over my shoulder at the men marching the opposite way. "Okay, let's drop Eva off, then we'll catch up."

Rose agreed to feed Evaline, and we grabbed a couple of slices of freshly baked gingerbread to eat on the go. We didn't know what we would find but quickly headed back out, hoping to catch up.

"This is delicious." Shay moaned rather provocatively while devouring her piece.

I couldn't hold back my smile. "They were headed that way," I pointed. "Where do you think they're going?"

"Not sure, but it sounds like an adventure."

I looked at her, amazed. "I haven't heard you talk like that in so long."

Shay shrugged. "I started focusing more on Evaline." I couldn't help but notice her hand glide over her belly. "It's got me thinking about my own and what this war means for them. Have you given any thought about helping?" She gave me a pointed look. "It might not make a difference. I'd still like to try, though."

I sighed, frustrated with myself for not helping her with it sooner. "I'm sorry, I haven't with everything going on." I looked away so she couldn't see the emotions written on my face.

"It's okay, Millie. Honestly, settle down." She laughed, grabbing my arm gently. The sweet melody of her laugh sent a thrill through me. I was finally starting to see my old friend break through her tribulations. "I already asked Rose, and she knows a few people who can point me in the right direction. Don't worry about helping me; you have enough to do."

My heart gave a solid thump, momentarily stunned.

"Miss Moretti!" A male voice shouted down one of the docks.

Shay and I froze, looking through the men and women milling about to find the familiar voice. A tall man skirted around a group gathered at one of the fruit stands and walked briskly towards us, his golden hair shining in the sun.

"Hiram!" I said, smiling at his permanently somber face. "How are you?"

"As to be expected," Hiram said, nodding to me. "Hope you two are doing well. It's nice to see you out, Miss..."

"Banks," Shay offered, giving a tight smile—her rising excitement dimmed in his presence. "Shaylah Banks."

"Miss Banks. Of course." He nodded, looking between us, suddenly looking as if he regretted calling on us. He'd visited, but Shay never felt well enough to communicate. So, her full name never came up in conversation.

I waited for a minute, wondering if there was something specific he was going to say. When he didn't, I said, "We just dropped Evaline off at Rose's for lunch."

"Oh? Good." He observed our surroundings with his hands on his hips, clearly avoiding our gaze. "I'll have to stop by to see her later."

"Okay..." I drug the word out, looking down the waterfront, knowing we probably missed our chance to see the soldiers. "Look, we were trying to follow a regiment that just disembarked not too long ago. Do you know anything about them?"

He looked at me quizzically. "The 9th Massachusetts Regiment? All Irish. Tommy wanted to join, but his shoulder was smarting too much."

I exchanged a look with Shay, my stomach sinking. "How is he?"

"Better." Hiram's golden eyes pierced through me, and I started to blush. "I'll expect he joins soon enough."

I began wringing my hands but stopped when he noticed. "Do you know where they're headed? We probably should start going."

He scratched his chin, thinking. "They should be at the State House. I could walk you there."

"Oh, you don't have to."

Hiram glanced at Shay, studying her downturned face. "I don't mind."

"Don't you have work?"

"Too many men today. They turned the rest of us away."

We headed back into the city, heading to the State House, making small talk as Shay kept her head down or took in the buildings around us.

Hiram stopped to talk to a man he knew while Shay and I stood back. We were quiet until I couldn't take it any longer. "Why'd you do that?"

She looked at me, surprised. "Do what?"

"Get weird around Hiram."

"Oh," she said, dragging her shoe through some dirt. "He knows what happened to me."

Realization ricocheted through me, and I felt my heart sink. "You have nothing to be ashamed of," I said fiercely.

"I know. It's just...embarrassing, I guess."

"You don't—"

"I know!" she snapped, face reddening with anger. "I just am. Okay? I'm sure he knows all the dirty details. That's what everyone sees when they look at me. And the bigger I get with this baby..." Her words trailed off as emotion built in her throat.

"I didn't mean to tell you how to feel," I said cautiously, swallowing my guilt. "I'm sorry. You can feel however you want. I'm just saying—" I gazed at Hiram, who kept glancing at us to check if we were still there. "I'm just saying, I don't think that's what he sees."

She huffed out her nose and looked the other way, watching the street vendors call out to those passing by.

"My apologies," Hiram said, coming up to us. "Let's go. We might still get there in time."

We walked the rest of the way, only stopping when we neared the State House, which was similar in appearance, but significantly different than what I was used to. It still had its Greek columns, proudly holding up the second-story balcony. Large arches beneath them presented the ground floor to those who walked up its significant steps. Apparently, at a later date, they would expand the building, adding the left and right wings to the sides, while the impressive gold dome was only grey here.

However, the beauty of the building was not what stopped us in our tracks, but what had to be about a thousand men standing at attention to hear a man speak.

"Hope they have better luck than the last regiment," Hiram muttered, studying the men before us.

"What do you mean?" Shay asked.

"A mob attacked the Sixth while their train went through Baltimore. They say four perished."

"That's awful!" Shay placed her hand on her chest.

My heart squeezed as fear shot through me. What if that were Thomas?

"Who's speaking?" I asked, trying to concentrate on the scene before me instead of letting my thoughts wander to the man who was avoiding me.

"Governor John Andrew," Hiram said. "He's presenting the regiment's colors."

"...In one common tide—" The governor's voice barely carried over the large sea of men. "—flows the blood of a common humanity inherited by us all, and into our hearts, by the inspiration of the Almighty, has been breathed a common understanding..."

"Is that the Irish flag?" Shay said into my ear.

I looked at the green silk fabric billowing next to the American flag. "I think so."

"Regimental," Hiram corrected.

"... I now put into your hands, as I have in the hands of regiments that preceded you, the State ensign of this Commonwealth. You already bear with you the Stars and Stripes, but I would have you recognized wherever you go as coming from this State, where you have your homes. When you look on the Stars and Stripes, you can remember that you are American citizens; when you look on this venerable ensign, you can remember your wives and families in Massachusetts."

Hiram stood rigid, his hands in his pockets as he eyed the men in front of us. We were close enough that I heard eager whispers among the ranks, their excitement radiating off them so strongly it began to penetrate my own being, urging me to fight as well. I couldn't imagine what that felt like for Hiram, to have the ability and drive to fight, but the very law prohibiting him from fighting for what he desired. For what the Union needed.

The governor's voice grew louder with enthusiasm as he finished his speech. "Take this as a pledge of affectionate care from the State of your kindred and homes and of the sincere and undying interest which its people feel and will ever feel for you. In the utmost confidence in your patriotism and valor, we send you forth as citizens of Massachusetts, assured that her honor will never be disgraced by the countrymen of Emmet and O'Connell."

A roar went up as the men hollered and pounded the ground with their feet, their fists in the air. The sight had every hair on my body standing at attention, propelling me to take a step closer to joining their ranks.

"We should go," Hiram said, grabbing my arm before quickly letting go, the propriety of the time restricting him. He eyed Shay and then the Irishmen, his brows furrowing deeper. It was then I realized he was uncomfortable around so many white men.

I looked back at the soldiers, torn between going to them and leaving. I just shook my head and turned away, not understanding what I intended to do if I stayed, anyway.

CHAPTER TWENTY-TWO

Emilia & Thomas

4 July 1861

"What will ye do now?" Michael hissed in my ear. He wrapped his arm around my neck, pinning me to his chest.

I pulled on his arm, knowing it wouldn't budge, then took a quick step to the right and swung my left fist at his groin, causing him to double over. I didn't hesitate to bring my elbow up to slam into his face.

To my surprise, my elbow actually collided with his nose this time.

"Feck!" he yelled, stepping back.

"I'm so sorry!" I spun towards him, covering my nose as if that'd somehow stop his pain.

He shook his head and smiled, pinching the bridge of his nose. "No, lass. We're finally getting somewhere. Ye're moving faster."

I smiled, triumphant, and started to do a victory dance. I stopped mid-pose when I found Shay on the back step, laughing at me while holding onto Evaline's shoulders. It was early for Evaline to be up, and the poor girl looked confused by the whole scene.

I instantly noticed Shay had on the new dress I had bought her, wanting her to have something better than her everyday brown one. I'd spent one morning searching the local thrift stores for a couple of dresses to add to our minimal wardrobe. Not having much money, I couldn't buy new ones, but I was lucky enough to find some that had slight wear. Shay's was a deep blue that complimented her dark skin nicely. The waist left some room for her growing belly—hiding the bump for now—as it flattered her figure and fell down in soft ruffles to her feet. She looked radiant.

"Why are you looking so giddy?" I asked her, suspicious.

"I'm proud of you," Shay smiled, bouncing on the toes of her feet. She ran a hand over her hair nervously. Rose had taken Shay's braids out a few weeks back, and she had started pulling it back into a bun, commonly worn by other women of that time. "And I have a surprise for you."

"Is that why you're dressed up?"

"Yes." Her grin grew, and we turned towards a figure walking towards us.

It was Hiram. My heart stuttered while I scanned the area around him, wondering if he was alone. I deflated when I saw no one else.

Hiram began to visit Shay as much as he saw Evaline in the last few weeks. Even inviting her to go with him to different events and out with people her age and color. It had a tremendous effect on her, breaking her out of her shell faster than being shut up in old Rose's place. A part of me was bitter that I couldn't do that for her, as the other part rejoiced at her recovery.

Michael had rolled his sleeves back down, buttoning the cuffs, while blatantly keeping his eyes from Shay.

Hiram stopped quickly, taking Michael in. "What are you doing here?"

Michael raised a brow. "Can't come for a wee visit with the lasses?"

Hiram stepped between Michael and the girls, his face darkening with hatred. The tension building made me sick to my stomach until Shay placed her hand on Hiram's arm and leaned around him to give a solemn smile to Michael. I didn't see why she was always so nice to him, but it seemed to break the tension.

Michael's brows drew down, eyes still glaring at her hand on Hiram's arm, then suddenly towards me. "I'll see ye tonight." Michael nodded at me, then turned to Shay. "Will ye be joining us in the morn?"

The shock on Shay's face would have been comical if the situation wasn't already so awkward.

"Yes," Shay said breathlessly, almost as if she was flustered. Her dark eyes darted between the two men. "I would like that."

Michael tipped his hat and purposefully ran into Hiram's shoulder, sauntering away without a care.

Hiram fixed his scowl and looked up at Shay on the steps. "You shouldn't be around him. Both of you." He turned to Evaline, staring at him with big eyes.

"He saved my life," Shay said, shoulders straightening in defiance.

"He *despises* colored folk," he said, picking up Evaline. She wrapped her arms around him and laid her head on his shoulder, her previous excitement evaporating quickly. "The only reason he saved you was to get Tommy in his clutches."

Shay's face fell, looking down the square where Michael had been.

"What are you guys up to?" I asked, wanting to distract them. "You look too good to be staying in."

"Well, I'm sure you know it's the Fourth of July," Shay said, brightening. "The whole city is planning festivities. Hiram had gotten us tickets to go."

"That's great!" I tried to smile through my disappointment. Unfortunately, I had to work at the bakery and hadn't had a chance to get out in weeks.

"Don't look so sad." Shay grinned. "Rose said you could go too."

"Yes," I yelled a little too loudly, surprising Hiram, and making Shay and Evaline laugh. "I'll go change really fast."

"Goodness!" Mira started on her way out the door as I pushed past her petite form.

I wore my new burgundy dress within minutes, securing my small hat to my head as I ran back down the stairs.

"Thanks, Rose!" I yelled as I darted out of the door. "You're an angel!"

The streets had been filled since early morning, clogging up the sidewalks and spilling over to every crook and cranny of the city. The hubbub grated on Thomas' nerves as it flared his nationalism. An odd contrast that he didn't know how to untangle.

Thomas lifted an apple to his mouth as he waited for Hiram at Tremont Temple, listening to The Star-Spangled Banner being played by the City Military Bands. It was faint, but he still hummed while watching the weans run by in excitement. He agreed to take Evaline and Maggie to the kid's celebration, knowing Shay would come while Emilia worked at the bakery. It was the only way he decided to come.

"When will they be here?" Maggie asked impatiently.

Thomas sighed, annoyed with his sister's dramatics these days. "Any minute."

Evaline darted in and out of the crowd down the street as Hiram followed a pursuit. It had only been seven months since the temple was ambushed by the mob, and Thomas worried that Evaline might react badly to it. However, he shouldn't have worried. The lass was so excited she didn't seem to notice it was the same building. Eva's golden curls billowed behind her with each pump of her legs, revealing her cotton pantalets under her dress. She reminded him of a bird breaking free of its cage, freedom beneath her wings.

Mira and Shay kept pace with Hiram, taking in the banners, street vendors, and all the transformations of the occasion. Shay looked healthy, filling out and glowing, and possibly even happy. Thomas sighed a breath of relief he didn't know he had been holding these last couple of months, grateful that she was improving. He began to straighten from the wall, ready to go to them, when he froze.

Emilia looked up at the building, head tipped back, exposing her thin neck while the sun kissed her tan face. He'd never seen her in the burgundy dress. It was plain and had obviously been well worn, but on her… He rubbed his chest, trying to relieve the building pressure. She was beautiful and completely oblivious to it. Thomas just stood there, transfixed by how she carried herself and her effect on those who passed her by. She had no idea how rare she really was.

Did she know he'd be there? Surely not. She had been furious with him, and he didn't expect forgiveness.

Emilia must have felt his gaze on her because her dark eyes caught his the next moment and widened. She took a step forward as if about to come to him, but stopped. Her soft expression hardened.

"Uncle Tommy!" Evaline yelled her usual greeting, colliding into his legs. The rest of them were behind her, drawing his attention away from the woman constantly in his thoughts.

Hiram introduced Shay to Maggie as everyone said hello.

Maggie leaned in close to Thomas. "You didn't tell me your mot was coming."

"She's not mine," he grumbled and turned to the group, making Maggie smirk. "Are ye ready?"

As they headed inside, Evaline squealed with glee at all the different activities, going to each one and interacting with all kids. It seemed to be going well, everyone enjoying themselves, except for the silence between him and Emilia. That was until a white mother pulled her boy away from Evaline, scowling at Eva as if the little girl was a cockroach that scuttled over her shoe. After that, Hiram decided they needed to leave.

"We'll make our way to the Common and listen to the bands," he said to Evaline, clearly annoyed.

"Oh, that would be fun, won't it, honey?" Emilia chirped.

"Am I bad?" Evaline asked, surprising everyone into a sudden silence while the room around them went on noisily.

"You are not bad," Hiram growled and set her back on her feet. "Where is—"

Shay and Mira took a step forward, but it was Shay who placed her hand on Hiram's arm, stilling him. Mira's face fell, and she seemed to dissolve into the shadows.

"You, my sweet," Shay said, squatting by Evaline, "are one of the best girls I know." Evaline's eyes flicked sadly between Shay's as if she was looking for a lie. "Sometimes people can't see that. Sometimes all people see is the color of our skin instead of our worth. Instead of the beauty living inside of us. And some are too afraid to go against what the rest of society believes."

"Why?" Evaline focused on Shay's dark hands holding her small, lighter ones. "Momma always said my daddy was a white man." She looked up then. "If I told the lady that, would she let me play with the boy, then?"

Thomas ran his fingers through his hair, scanning the crowd bitterly. Frankly, he was surprised Evaline could remember anything her mother had said. She was so young when she passed and didn't speak of her often.

Shay shook her head. "I'm sorry, sweetie. That doesn't always work. Sometimes people don't want a chance to know us."

"But we do," Emilia chimed in, kneeling down. "We think you're smart, funny, and so adventurous. And I'm seriously jealous of your beautiful curls." Emilia gently tugged Evaline's hair, making the curls spring back in place. The little girl smiled.

"You like my bow?" Evaline asked, turning to show the white ribbon tying half of her hair back.

"I love it! Honestly, I wish I had one."

"No," Evaline drug the word out, laughing. "You're too old."

"What?" Emilia laughed. "I'm still young! I could pull it off."

Evaline shook her head, smiling as if Emilia had lost her mind. "No, you're old enough to be married, not wearing ribbons." She looked up at Thomas then, making his chest seize up. "Didn't Ms. Banks say Uncle Tommy was your soul mate?"

"What? No!" Emilia's face turned ashen, and she nearly toppled sideways, catching herself at the last second. She stood up, doing everything she could to not look at him.

"Not your mot." Maggie elbowed him and giggled.

He ran his hand through his hair as the building's heat rose with his blood pressure. The idea undoubtedly flustered Emilia, while Thomas tried and failed to ignore the sudden odd rush of pleasure he felt when hearing it.

Shay hid her smile as she grabbed Evaline. "Why don't we head on out now?"

They made their way to the street, falling in with the crowd heading toward the orchestra. Ireland's national anthem rang in the distance, surprising Thomas. He vaguely remembered that it was listed on the program, yet hearing it was an entirely different experience. For so long, he'd been ridiculed, spat at, pushed to the side. He was a worthless Irish gutter rat expected to amount to nothing. And now, they were honoring the very country of the people they so intensely despised. He closed his eyes and let his pride swell at how far the Irish had come in America. Maybe the war would be good for them. The Lord knew they needed all the help they could get.

Thomas expelled his bitter thoughts from his mind and fell in step with Emilia, giving them a few paces before speaking. "Explain this soul mate business Ms. Banks speaks of."

"You never heard of a soul mate before?" She eyed him out of the corner of her eye.

He shook his head.

"Well." She sighed. "It's like you're complete with the other person. You walk through life thinking you're fine, but it's not until you meet the other person that you realize something has been missing. You just understand each other."

"Like they're the other half of your whole."

"Exactly."

Thomas grunted as if he didn't quite believe it. "Ye really believe in that sort of thing?"

"Not really, no," Emilia said, though he noted how she wrung her hands. "Shay does, though."

Thomas nodded. Before, he wouldn't have believed in it either, but these last couple of months had taught him one thing: there was far more to life than people expected. Just because a person refused to believe in something, did not mean that particular thing didn't exist. It only revealed the person's fear or, rather, inability to comprehend that there were things that might occur beyond one's understanding. Such as one's ability to travel across time, for example.

But that train of thought was pushed to the side when Thomas realized Emilia's definition fit with what he had been feeling as of late. She might not have believed in it, but...

"Ye never felt that way before?" he asked, cursing himself for letting it slip.

"No," she said. Thomas tried to ignore the sting until she pushed an imaginary hair behind her ear, fidgeting with her hat that already sat straight. Her cheeks were redder than they were moments before.

Thomas smiled. "Are ye warm?"

"What?" Her eyes looked up at his, startled. "No, not really. Why?"

He bent down to whisper in her ear. "Ye're blushing." He stroked one finger down her cheek, igniting her rosy cheeks into a bright flame down her chest. His pulse quickened at the sight.

Emilia focused ahead of them, fanning her cheeks with her gloved hand. "The afternoon's getting hotter, I guess."

"Aye, must be it." His answer propelled her to walk faster, and his grin grew as they went down the street, perfectly satisfied with watching the sway of her dress.

After listening to the orchestra for some time, they had made their way to the balloon ascension, a crowd gathering around to see.

"Wow, those aren't like ours," Shay said, shading her eyes from the sun as she looked up at the balloons still nearby.

"Right?" Emilia agreed. "These ones are kind of scary. I thought we would be able to ride them."

"Ride them?" Hiram's eyebrows created a deep 'V' between his eyes. "They're extremely dangerous."

Emilia shrugged. "I would've liked it."

There was something about the way they talked about the balloons, as if they saw a more efficient design. "What do ye mean like yours?" Thomas asked.

The women shared a worried glance.

"Oh, I just meant from where we come from," Shay said hurriedly.

"And where do ye come from?"

"Charlestown."

"That's not very far."

Emilia puckered her lips, watching the exchange. "Why don't you explain it a little more, Shay. I'm sure Thomas would be *fascinated* about where we come from. Wouldn't you, Thomas?" She turned towards him, raising her brow as if daring him to contradict her.

"Maybe this isn't the time," Thomas grumbled, noticing Hiram's questioning look. He turned back to the balloons.

"Of course, it isn't," Emilia muttered.

"I would so love to hear about the ones you saw," Mira exclaimed. "I've heard about them as a little girl, but this is the first time I've seen them in person."

Before anyone could respond, a breeze swept over the area, bringing in the smell of baked beans from one of the vendors nearby. Thomas's stomach growled but it seemed to have the opposite effect on Miss Banks. She grabbed her stomach and Emilia's arm simultaneously, paling remarkably.

Emilia whispered something to her, but Shay only shook her head, concentrating on the ground.

"What is it?" Hiram asked, setting Evaline down.

"She's going to retch again!" Evaline bellowed as if it was a common occurrence.

"Are you unwell?" Hiram grabbed her arm, naïve to the signs Thomas was beginning to see.

"The baby doesn't like her belly," Evaline said. "Auntie Rose said it's normal with pregnant ladies, though."

"Hush," Mira whispered, pulling Evaline to the side. "That is not a topic one should discuss in public."

Hiram took a step back, letting go of Shay's arm. "How long have you known?"

Thomas's stomach plummeted as he silently willed his friend to shut his gab.

"A while," Shay admitted.

"Here, sit down." Emilia guided her to a bench with one spot left.

"It's one of theirs?" There was such loathing in his voice that Shay sat back, momentarily stunned into silence.

Thomas touched Hiram's arm and said, "Let's go for a walk, comrádaí."

"Of course, it is," Shay responded icily.

Hiram punched the tree that offered the bench shade, making the women jump. His reaction drew the attention of the crowd around them. Thomas knew he had to diffuse the situation, or they'd have the coppers on their tail.

"They're not suited for normal society," a man muttered, guiding his white wife farther away from their group.

Hiram took a step toward the man, but Thomas stood in front of him, nose-to-nose, so that he was all Hiram could see. "It's not worth it. Calm down."

Thomas thought Hiram might hit him, his nostrils flaring like a bull ready to charge. It took several heartbeats before he turned on his heel and left.

Thomas glanced back at the women. Shay held her stomach, tears falling down her face as the two girls tried to distract her.

"It's not you, Miss Banks." Thomas tried to reassure her. "Hiram's temper flares when presented with such crimes. He feels he failed if one person is afflicted by a white man."

Shay's eyes pierced his, and what he saw behind them made his skin tighten with dread. Hiram had made an immeasurable mistake.

"That's ridiculous. My baby will not be given the crimes of its father. And if Hiram can't handle what I had to endure, then he can stay the fuck away from me."

A woman gasped at Shay's language and backed away, giving side glances until she disappeared through the crowd.

"I don't believe that's why he's angry. Give him some time, and he will come around."

At least, he had hoped so.

CHAPTER TWENTY-THREE

Emilia

The sky was pinking with the coming dawn, a cool breeze caressing us as we waited for Michael.

"I can't believe he acted that way," Shay said, still upset from Hiram's reaction the day before.

"I know, but I think he was angrier at what they did, Shay. He wasn't mad at you."

"No, he was *disgusted*." A tear ran down her cheek, and she wiped it away angrily. "I can't wait to get out of here."

"I'll ask Michael if he has any news." I put my arm around her, and she rested her head on my shoulder as we watched the world come to life.

"We didn't even get to see the fireworks," she mumbled.

"Why didn't ye?" Michael asked, startling us. We'd been looking in the direction of the sunrise as he seemingly materialized out of nowhere.

"No reason," Shay said, staring at her lap, hiding her tears.

Michael grunted. "Here. For both of ye."

He held out a small package wrapped in brown paper.

"What is it?" I asked, grabbing it as if it would bite me. I opened it slowly, expecting something gross, though I had no reason to think that.

"It looks like chocolate!" Shay said, grabbing it.

"Aye, I heard some people like it. My ma, with Maggie in her belly, she always craved this or that." He shrugged, looking at the buildings around us. "We never had coin for treats, though. Thought ye might need something to get ye through the morning is all."

"Isn't it expensive?" I asked, looking at it as if it were gold.

"I know a man." His blue eyes danced mischievously. "Ye don't want it?"

Shay held it in her lap. "I do," she mumbled, trying not to cry. "Why are you being so nice, though?"

"Well, if ye don't want it, then I'll—"

She snatched it away from his hand. "Thank you."

His eyes lit up with amusement.

We both broke off a piece, shoving it into our mouths. It wasn't sweet like I was expecting, but course and gritty. If Michael hadn't been watching, I would have spit it out.

Shay sucked on her piece, savoring each second of it. I almost cringed watching her, but she seemed to enjoy it.

"How'd you know about the baby?" she asked Michael.

He shrugged. "That's what usually happens, doesn't it?"

"Yeah, I guess."

He stared at her downturned face for a minute, eyes crinkled with an emotion I couldn't place. I squinted at him, trying to figure out what his game was.

"Are ye lasses ready?" He backed away, tone sharp as he said, "We don't have all day."

Shay wrapped the chocolate quickly and stood up. "Ready."

Michael drilled us relentlessly. He had me teach Shay blocks, ducks, and breaks to get out of specific holds. Michael used the excuse of me needing the practice, but I knew the asshole was avoiding touching her. It was undeniable when he would guide my hand a certain way and then turn around and snap at Shay, barking out orders about where to put hers. I could tell it was starting to wear on her, her resolve crumbling with the tightness of her jaw.

Shay's frustration finally broke, tears falling down her face. "You don't have to help me!" she snapped, turning towards him so quickly he caught her arms without thinking. He removed his hands as if burned. "I have enough people disgusted with me; I don't need to deal with your disgust too."

She ran up the stairs, stepping on the packaged chocolate, in her haste to get inside. When she was in, I snuck a glance at Michael. He was still staring at the door.

"I better go," I said.

He looked at me, nodding, but said nothing.

I made it to the stairs, picked up the package—knowing she'd want it later—and then stopped with my hand on the door. It wasn't my place to explain, but I felt a push to do so. "She had a bad day yesterday. She thinks everyone is disgusted by what happened to her. I know you're the one who saved her. Saw her at her worst. Even though you only did it to get whatever it is out of Thomas, if you could just try to treat her normally—" I paused, thinking of all his assholery, and corrected, "—At least like how a woman should be treated. That'd mean the world to us."

I looked back at Michael. He stared at the ground, running his hands through his hair. He reminded me so much of Thomas at that moment that my heart squeezed.

"I'm not," he said and looked at me. Then, seeing the puzzlement on my face, he explained. "I'm not disgusted with her."

"Then why wouldn't you touch her?"

His jaw tightened, and his Adam's apple bobbed as he swallowed. I'm not sure I ever saw such despondency in someone's eyes. "I cannot."

"Why?"

Michael scowled, either refusing to answer me or not knowing why himself, and left me to pick up the pieces of my friend.

It wasn't until he was gone that I remembered I needed to ask him if he had any word about my family.

As the weeks turned into months, my deal with Michael was coming to an end. I had kept my end of the bargain, but he strung me along, feeding me with excuses and small details that kept me put.

Kept me singing.

I knew I would have to set out on my own soon. At the same time, I felt a strong pull to stay there. Shay had picked up some of my shifts in the bakery, lightening my load considerably so that my long days became somewhat bearable. Though I was beginning to accept my new reality, I couldn't live at Rose's forever.

My moments with Thomas had stirred something inside me, pulling me towards him in ways I'd only felt marginally before. My feelings became intense, more foreign, and absolutely terrifying. As my mind told me to search for the ordinary, my heart constantly searched for the man who tilted my world upside down. I'd searched for him in the markets, the docks, and the saloons, wherever his green gaze might catch mine.

I told myself I didn't want him to see me sing. That his absence was better. I didn't need to be more attached to a man who would inevitably leave me. I'd been taught enough of that in my life. But each day, he never showed. And my soul crumbled a little with each passing moment, whispering that it was time to go.

Michael had noticed me searching one night and sat me down at the bar when I was taking a break.

"He won't come," he said.

"Who?" I played dumb, drinking my water as I glanced around at the men.

"Me thick skulled deartháir."

"Why don't you invite Shay?" I countered.

"Ye know ol' Billy wouldn't have her kind in our saloon." Ever since the day he'd given us chocolate, Michael had become politer towards her. Not so much to give away any form of affection, but in small ways. His racist remarks dropped from his speech in her company, taking on a lighter tone that held more respect. He began training her, as he did me, no longer rebuking her at every misstep. He was strict, yet kind in ways that I never expected to see from him.

Michael slicked back his hair, an agitated tell I'd come to recognize.

"Are you going to tell me why you pretend to hate them?" I asked.

He looked up sharply. "I'm not. The feckin' bastards take our jobs—"

"You don't even apply for those kinds of jobs."

He leaned elbows against the bar, staring at the barmaids weaving in and out of the men. His jaw ticked.

"Do you hate Shay? Because sometimes I think—"

"Enough," he growled.

"Fine," I snapped. "Live your life in miserable denial."

He shot me a glare that would have sent me running months ago. Now I glared right back, waiting for him to respond.

Instead, he said something that sent my mind reeling. "He won't come because ye're a threat."

I scoffed. "What is that supposed to mean?"

Michael sighed, his head falling back as if he had to give a lesson to a child. "Tommy had his path set. Always had. Ye're a distraction that'd send his carefully laid path veering into a new road. He can't afford to take ye on."

I stood up, suddenly furious, angry tears brimming my eyes. "I'm not a threat!"

"You're missing the point, *deirfiúr*."

"No, I don't think I am," I said, too angry to ask him what that word meant. Obviously, I was a path that Thomas didn't want to take. "And you're a coward who won't admit you have feelings for a black woman."

Michael stood up so fast I stumbled backward, shocked by his expression. I had become too comfortable in his company, momentarily forgetting that he was a man who killed at the drop of a dime.

"If one of me men would have heard that, I'd have to slit your pretty throat," he seethed, caging me against the bar with his arms. "Ye should get back up there and sing."

Fear streaked through me, wondering if I should tell him my suspicions. I decided no good could come of it and did as I was told.

After that, I constantly reminded myself that Shay and I didn't belong there. I needed to find a way home, back to my family and my real life—back to a time when Shay could raise her baby without as much fear.

As we fought our daily battles, the war raged on in Virginia. Then, only a couple weeks after we celebrated the Fourth of July, the First Battle of Bull Run took place. Stonewall and his confederates pushed the Union out of Manassas all the way back to D.C., proving to the rest of the nation that this wasn't going to be a short war.

Shay and I stood frozen as we heard the news. Dread pooled in my stomach at what I knew would come as those around us seethed, vehemently proclaiming that the damnable rebels would pay.

Shay did what she could, helping others pack up and send supplies to our soldiers, but there wasn't much more she could do other than that. Her belly was becoming more prominent, and she couldn't hide it when it was frowned upon for a pregnant woman to be in public.

Hiram had come around, apologizing for his actions, but their relationship was grounded in friendship rather than a blossoming love. To my surprise, she was content with the new friendship and her role in aiding the men who needed it most.

A few weeks after the retreat of our Union troops, President Lincoln called for more soldiers to join their forces. So armies on both sides added to their manpower, quickly training them and sending them to the battlefield like well-oiled machines.

It wouldn't be long before Thomas would join their ranks.

It was a cool, mid-September morning when Michael told me it was our last training session. His excuse was that I could defend myself well enough. I suspected something else. Or someone. And that woman had already stopped in August in fear of accidentally harming the baby. I was grateful that she'd learned enough to feel comfortable.

I wiped the sweat from my face, annoyed that he had sprung this upon me. "What did you find about my family?" I asked. "Are there any RomanI around or what? It's obvious our deal is ending."

"Oh, aye. They moved down south some twenty years ago."

So, they left just after they sent me away. But why? He kept hiding his knives on his body as if he didn't just drop a bomb on me. "When did you find this out?" I fumed.

"Not long after we made the deal."

My fists clenched as I resisted the urge to punch him. "Do you know where at down south? Why wouldn't you tell me this?" These last couple of months, I thought we'd been getting along. Regret coiled in my chest. *But, of course, he'd just been playing me. God, I was an idiot.*

He shrugged and finally turned his hollow gaze toward me. "The tanner said they were a traveling group. Could be anywhere by now. I saw no need for ye to know when we still had a deal, aye?"

"But I could have been asking around!" I yelled, startling some birds that pecked at trash nearby. "You have no idea what you did."

"If ye were smart, ye would have been asking around either way!"

My body jolted, stung by his words, as guilt bloomed low in my stomach. He was right. I should have been doing all I could to find them.

"Is everything all right?"

I turned around, surprised to find Shay and Rose standing on the back steps.

"He knew all along, Shay." My body shook with anger.

"Knew what?" she asked sharply, glaring at Michael.

I told her what I'd learned.

"We trusted you." She rubbed her face, trying to hide how affected she was by this.

Shay had grown close to Michael, though he remained remarkably aloof around her. It seemed the O'Connor men were hard to resist. Until now.

Shay dropped her hands and stared at him with so much betrayal written on her features that it made *me* physically sick, and Michael shifted on his feet.

All the color drained from Michael's face when she returned to the bakery without another word. He took a step forward as if he was going to go after her.

"Get that boy outta here." Rose snapped at me. "I don't know what is going on, but it can't be good if he's involved." She started down the stairs, a towel in her hands as if she was going to whip him with it. "I won't have you messing with my girls."

I turned toward him. "He was just leaving. Weren't you, Michael?"

His back straightened. "I'll see ye tonight."

"Oh, I won't be singing again."

He stepped so close that I struggled to stand my ground. "Ye will be there. Ye've been making quite a profit for me, and the saloon has been full since ye arrived. Though I will be glad to finally get rid of ye, I don't think Mr. Mead will be so understanding."

I swayed as bile rose into my throat.

"Are you all right, honey?" Rose asked, coming up beside me as we watched Michael walk away. "Should I ask George to get some of the boys to deal with him?"

I shook my head. "No, thank you." This was my problem. They'd already done enough for me, I couldn't ask them for anymore. "Just a misunderstanding. It will be okay." I tried to smile, but could tell she didn't believe me.

"C'mon," she said, guiding me by the arm. "Let's get you some breakfast."

CHAPTER TWENTY-FOUR

Emilia

I'd been singing for over an hour when a woman walked through the door, keeping her head down as a ridiculous colossal hat covered her face. It was odd that a woman was here—primarily men and prostitutes frequented this type of saloon—and that she had on a shawl that covered her neck and arms. Even with the modesty of this time, it was extravagant for the lingering heat of the summer.

My eyes trailed her as she found a seat in the back, feeling a prickling sensation of familiarity. When the woman's head disappeared behind the men in front of her, I focused on my music, momentarily forgetting about her as I did what I loved. Sadness washed over me as I thought how this would be the last time I'd sing. It seemed my regret of quitting outweighed Billy Mead's threat, which was absolutely insane.

I told myself that I could sing at the pub when I returned. That doing what I loved didn't have to be here. For some reason, that just made me sadder.

A man stood up and went to the bar instead of waiting for one of the barmaids. I turned away, flipping through the songbook Michael had given me a few months back, and reviewed one of the songs. I sipped some water when a commotion drew my attention to the back.

"Let go!" a familiar voice rang out, making my blood run cold. A man grabbed the woman and dragged her out of the seat by her arm. "Let me go!" When she tried to push him, her shawl fell from her shoulders, revealing dark skin and an all-too-familiar blue dress.

I glanced at Michael, hoping he'd stop the man, but he stood immobile, looking as if he'd just seen a ghost.

"Stop!" I yelled, afraid the man was being too rough with my pregnant friend. I descended the stage, trying to push through the men who now stood to watch what was happening. "Leave her alone!"

A man cursed, spewing out racist remarks. "What you think she's doing here?"

I pushed my way through more men, grateful I didn't have to hear the response. More men surrounded her now, pulling her by the arms as she looked around. She saw me, her eyes wild with fear, and stiffened. Shay didn't have to say anything; I knew she was pleading for help. But then her face turned, eyes widening as a man shoved people out of the way to get to her.

When they saw who it was, time seemed to still.

"Let her go," Michael rumbled.

"Mikey," a man said, bewildered. "She can't be in here."

"She's just trying to have a good time." The greasy man to her right said, knocking her hat off to smell her hair. "Aren't you, honey?"

He had a huge nose and a face scarred from a hard life. She cringed, pulling away from him. I pushed myself closer, ready to jump on one of them if they tried anything.

"Should we show her a good time out back?" said the man on the other side of her with a chuckle.

I pulled out my knife, squeezing the handle while my stomach knotted. A hand grabbed my arm, startling me. I looked up into a face covered in his hat's shadow. Relief blossomed in my chest, and I swayed with the effect of it.

Thank God. Thomas would know what to do. But when did he get here?

He shook his head slightly and pressed his finger to his lips. I must have said it out loud.

Thomas turned back towards his brother. While I'd been distracted, Michael grabbed Shay's other arm from a man who backed off. He sneered at the ugly one. "I've wanted this one for a while. I'll let ye know how she is when I'm through with her."

Michael's men laughed, but the man stared at Michael with a hard glint in his eyes. I held my breath as I waited for him to defy Michael.

Instead, a wicked grin crossed his features. "C'mon, Mikey. It looks like she already had some fun." He caressed Shay's belly. She jerked away, closer to Michael, but the man held her too tight. Even in the dim light, she clearly paled under the attention.

The crowd was getting rowdy now, pushing in to see what would happen next. I stumbled forward at their mercy.

Michael's sneer never fell, but I saw how his blue eyes flashed dangerously. "Unhand her, and I'll leave ye the leftovers. That's all she's good for, anyway. Isn't it, wench?" Michael smiled maliciously at Shay.

Shay's face crumpled in front of everyone, and my heart squeezed at Michael's betrayal.

"Nah, not this time, boyo." The man pulled Shay roughly to him.

Michael only let go of Shay long enough to land a fist across the man's face, causing him to stumble back, spittle flying as he swore at Michael.

That's when all hell broke loose—those loyal to each man going at each other in a sudden outburst of violence.

Thomas grabbed my hand, pulling me behind him to get to Michael and Shay.

I could no longer see my friend as men shoved at each other from every direction. The smell of alcohol overwhelmed me as everyone turned on one another, assumedly friends of the assaulters against any sympathizer who dared let a black woman occupy the saloon.

My stomach turned, and my eyes burned. What was wrong with people?

My grip tore from Thomas's, and I stumbled back as a pair of men barreled into me. Thomas was half a head taller than most, allowing him to look over their heads and find me easily. He began to push his way back until I waved him on.

"Get to them!" I tried to yell over the uproar. A moment of indecision crossed his face. "I'll be fine!"

His expression hardened, but to my relief, he went to help Shay.

I slowly made my way closer to them, cautious of any elbows or fists that might be thrown my way. Bumped and shoved along, I finally saw Michael fending off two men while Shay hid behind him. It looked like he was slowly backing them up toward the door.

My heart seized when Thomas took a right hook to the jaw. He staggered back but didn't go down. Instead, his face changed from anger to molten fury. He grabbed the man's shirt and slammed his forehead into his nose. I cringed as Thomas shoved him back, looking around for his next assailant.

There was an opening, and I took it. I was so focused on Shay that I screamed when a hand grabbed my arm, spinning me around to face a middle-aged man, teeth rotten as he sneered at me.

"Where ye think ye're going, lass?" he asked.

Someone pulled my hair back, and I gasped as a cold knife pressed to my throat. "Ye're Mikey's lass, aye?" The stench of his breath had me recoiling. "We've got something for ye in the back. Now be a good girl and go nicely." He removed the knife from my throat, but shoved it into my corset hard enough to make me wince as his group guided me toward the back exit.

Three men were ahead, waiting with the door open as he shoved me through. I stumbled. One caught and whipped me around, holding my arms back as the others circled. I tried to remember my self-defense lessons, going through every move I was trained to do. What I didn't consider was the blinding fear that overtook me, muddling my thoughts and nearly rendering me useless.

"Hold her still," one of the younger men said with a malicious grin that spiked paralyzing dread into me. He raised his hands, and I flinched into the man holding me. A loud tear rented the air as my body jerked forward. I let out a breath when a blow didn't land, but, to my horror, I felt a light breeze on my stomach. I looked down. He'd torn the front of my dress down to my waist, my exposed breasts on display for their entertainment.

Instinctively, I went to cover myself. They laughed as I struggled, their hungry eyes locked on my nakedness. "Keep up the show, lass." One of the men sneered.

Oh, God. I stopped moving as tears stung the back of my eyes in unleashed fury and embarrassment.

"Fuck you!" I yelled and spat at them.

"Oh," said the older one, his grin growing. "We intend to. Tell me, boys, she's even prettier than I imagined. What do you think?"

One came closer, squeezing my breast as he shoved his nose into my hair. "I imagined doing this for weeks. What makes ye think ye can sit up there and not put out? Hm?"

They all laughed again, but it was the type of laugh that sent fear straight through a person.

Michael's words filtered into my mind:

It's going to get dirty. Disgusting, even. There will come a time when no fancy moves or easy releases will get ye out. This is the street, and ye'll need to fight like ye are from the streets. It won't be pretty, lass. Survival not always is.

My body hardened as my mind detached itself, I let out a slow breath, and my body remembered its training.

The man continued to grope me, face close to mine, as he concentrated on what he was doing. I lunged, sinking my teeth into his cheek, trying to keep my dinner down as blood filled my mouth. He screamed, but I held on until the man behind me yanked me away.

We stumbled back, the groper holding his face. "Ye fecking bitch!"

I spit a chunk of his flesh at him, slammed my foot into the man behind me, and swung my head back with a satisfying crunch, breaking his nose. My knife was out instantly, and I plunged it into his neck without thinking. Blood spurted when I pulled it out, and he frantically tried to stop it.

I stood there, frozen in place, as he dropped to his knees. My momentary hesitation was a mistake. One of them charged, and we went sprawling. He ended up on top of me, holding my arms down.

"She stabbed 'im!" one of them yelled. There was a ruckus, but I was distracted by the man crushing me.

I struggled to get a breath, yanking my arms and thrashing my legs. He backhanded me, stunning me as stars sparkled behind my eyes. My dress was hastily pushed up my legs, though I couldn't seem to get my body to fight.

The other men started yelling, and one fell near me, blood running from his nose. He scrambled up, running away from something. Thomas. It had to be.

"Gypsy!" one spat. My thoughts were a muddled mess, wondering why he was yelling at me when I was clearly restrained.

I focused on the curses the men yelled, half in a daze and wondering what could be happening. If Thomas indeed came to my rescue.

The scuffle of feet scraping against the cobblestones faded into the distance.

The man on top of me was too distracted by my exposed body to notice the chaos. He fumbled with his pants and grunted, moving farther over me. My head snapped back when I felt a sharp pain and screamed, jarred back into a hideous reality.

The pain disappeared, along with the weight crushing me, as my assaulter was ripped backward and thrown against the wall. Thomas had him by his throat, a string of Irish curses rolling off his tongue as the man tried to break Thomas's grip on his neck.

I scuttled backward, pushing my dress over my legs, trying to cover my breasts with the ripped fabric. Someone crouched in front of me, and I flinched.

"It's okay, Millie. It's me." Shay grabbed my face, turning it away from Thomas and my attacker. "Did he hurt you?"

I stared at her dumbly, mind blank, not understanding her words.

She grabbed my arms and shook me a little. "Did he hurt you?"

"No," I croaked. Then I remembered the sharp pain I'd felt and looked at my lap in horror. "I don't know, maybe." I began to pull up my dress, panicking at what may have happened.

She grasped my hands, holding them down so I couldn't lift it up. "Don't. Not here. If you're not sure, then he probably didn't get far. You're okay."

Her words were meant to soothe, but I found no comfort in them. I gaped at her in terror. "Shay, I'm—"

"I know, sweetie. You still are."

I shook my head frantically. "What if—" a sob broke loose from my chest.

Her eyebrows drew down as her eyes flicked between mine. A voice rumbled close by, but I couldn't tear my eyes away from the worry in hers.

"Are ye all right?" Thomas asked again.

I couldn't bring myself to witness what he'd done to that man.

"She's okay," Shay answered for me. "Isn't that what you said?"

I nodded, head bobbing mechanically.

"Shock," he mumbled. He touched Shay's shoulder so she could move out of the way. Thomas knelt in front of me, green eyes roaming over my face. He used his thumb to try and wipe the blood off my chin. "Ye're bleeding—"

"It's not mine," I admitted.

Michael seemed to appear out of the shadows. "The one over there?"

I refused to look at the man I'd killed. "Another one was groping me while that one held my arms." Thomas's grip tightened around my chin, and Michael stiffened. "I bit his cheek off."

"Ew," Shay grimaced.

"Wait," Thomas said, sitting back on his heels. "How many were there?"

"Five. The others ran off when you—" I stopped at their looks of confusion. "I stabbed the one, but not the others. You—You weren't the ones who stopped them?"

"Stay here," Michael said and scanned the area. He came back, shaking his head. "No one. If there was, they're long gone. It was good ye fought, lass. Maybe ye scared them off."

Though he was my age, I was still his pupil, and his praise filled me with a small satisfaction, relieving some of the tension from my shoulders. And maybe he was right.

It was I who'd fought. I survived.

The feeling was short-lived when Thomas saw the right side of my face where I'd been backhanded. He sucked in a sharp breath, fury overtaking him.

Irish curses rolled off his tongue again, but he stopped mid-sentence when he saw my face crumble in panic. He sighed and lifted me up just long enough to set me on his lap, cradling me. "It's going to be okay, mo ghrá. It's over."

"As touching as this is," Michael said, running a hand through his hair, "we should head out before the coppers get here."

Thomas nodded and rested his chin on the top of my head. "Give us a moment."

Michael grunted. "One minute," he said, holding his arm out for Shay. She went to him reluctantly, face hardening with anger at him, but surprisingly didn't flinch under his guiding hand.

"I should never have let ye go," Thomas growled, arms squeezing around me protectively.

I burrowed into his neck, taking in his scent as if it was a cure. "I told you to go. Shay was more important."

His chest rumbled, mumbling something in Irish.

"What?" I asked, looking up at him. I could see the pain, regret, and wonder in his eyes. And then I didn't. He carefully closed off his emotions again, turning away from me. Making me believe I'd imagined it. Absurdly, that hurt me more than any physical pain the others inflicted upon me.

Glass shattered in front of the saloon, and loud shouts rang from one of the windows. The brawl would be out on the street within moments, and at least two dead bodies were in the alley with us.

Thomas quickly stood us up, unbuttoning his shirt as he did so.

"What are you doing?" I asked, still covering myself with my torn dress.

"Put this on," he said, handing me his shirt as he looked towards the commotion. No one had rushed out yet, but Michael and Shay were waiting down the other way. "I'd give ye me jacket, but it seems I left it in there."

I grabbed the shirt and shrugged it on, vaguely aware of Shay turning Michael for privacy. "So only two...?" I couldn't keep myself from asking and glanced up, taking in the broad expanse of his bare shoulders. Muscle rippled underneath his skin, and I swallowed, turning my concentration back on the buttons I had to fasten.

"Two are dead. The one ye stabbed and the man—" His throat seized up as if something was lodged in it "—the man on top of ye."

"I didn't mean to," I whispered, unsure if he could hear.

"It's not your fault," he said, facing the other way. "Ye did what ye needed to survive." He sounded a lot like Michael.

"I don't think the cops will care about that." My fingers were clumsy, feeling big and awkward as I tried to button the shirt. Finally, I shook so bad I gave up. "Can you help me?

He turned back around, and I openly stared at his chest, my eyes roaming down the broad plains of muscle until reaching the V teasing out of his pants. I looked up quickly and blushed when I found his eyes on my face. Thomas caught me ogling him.

"I don't think anyone saw us," he said, voice rough. "We might get out of this without suspicion."

He stepped toward me, muscles strung tight as if trying to keep control of himself.

"Here," he said quietly, buttoning from the top down as I held it closed. To my surprise, his fingers shook, though not as bad as mine. I kept my eyes on the dark hair on his chest, and reached out, unable to stop myself from running my fingers over it.

He inhaled deeply and glanced up at my face, searching my eyes. "We need to go. Can ye walk?"

I nodded as he fastened the last button, knowing I could do anything if he asked me to.

CHAPTER TWENTY-FIVE

Emilia & Thomas

"**I** know it has been a difficult night for her, but is there anything else I should know?" Rose whispered to Shay. "One doesn't vomit when—"

"No," Shay said too sharply and glanced at me. She wouldn't tell anyone I had killed a man. If Rose knew, and they found out I did it, they'd say she was willingly holding a fugitive. I could see Shay out of my peripheral, hands grasping her dress in worry.

They were in the far corner of the apartment while Evaline slept in bed. I soaked in a warm bath that Rose painstakingly heated up for me. We only used it once a week, taking turns using the same water. To freshen up daily, we'd use a primary pitcher and bowl. After seeing my condition, Rose insisted I climb into the tub and wash away the night, for which I was grateful. The warmth soothed my sore muscles.

It was apparent Rose wasn't convinced, but she let it go. "There was no blood,"

"The way she described it, I think one second more and he would have succeeded," Shay admitted, thinking I couldn't hear them. I suddenly felt a chill and ducked my head under my warm bath.

Coming up for air and water running down my face, I heard Rose say, "...should be all right. We'll keep an eye out for any afflictions—"

"What?" I howled, grabbing the sides of the tin tub. "You think he might have had a disease?"

They startled, turning towards me quickly, guilt stiffening their posture.

Rose came to me with a blanket. "Don't fret, child. Just a precaution, is all."

I stood, letting her wrap me in the knitted blanket as she guided me toward my cot. I went to lie down, but she stopped me.

"You must dress."

"Why?" I asked, wincing as I straightened back up.

"We need to discuss our plan of action," Shay said.

"Can't we do that tomorrow?"

Shay shook her head gravely. "The boys say it's not good. They're downstairs."

"They're still here?" I put my head in my hands, too tired to deal with this.

Thomas half-carried me the rest of the way home when my legs began to give out. Apparently, I began to go through shock, my mind failing me after my body gave it all. I remembered swaying into the bakery, hanging onto Thomas' arm, and Rose spiriting me up the stairs. Still, I forgot about the men after that. I'd been in a partial trance ever since.

"They are. We sent Mira down to give them something to eat."
She meant they didn't want Mira to see what had happened to me.
A bloody nose could send the girl into hysterics.

Shay helped me into my plain green dress, fussing over me like a
mother hen. She combed my wet hair as I stared at the floorboards,
following their grooves and holes with my eyes until I'd lose sight of
one and move on to the next. A way to distract my mind from what
had happened.

When she was done, she guided me downstairs. I didn't need her
help anymore, but I used it to fortify my mind for what was to come.

It was quiet, the fall of our steps on the stairs the only thing that
broke the silence. Thomas and Michael were sitting with George
around the table, a bottle of whiskey—no food to be seen—between
them as they stared at the lantern's flickering light. Mira was standing awkwardly to the side, unsure what to do with herself.

When they heard us, all three of them stood up. Thomas looked
like he wanted to come over but kept put.

"How are ye?" he asked.

I ignored his question, not knowing the answer myself. "How'd
you guys end up getting out of the saloon?"

Thomas held his chair out and gestured for me to sit, sliding
the whiskey closer. I took it gratefully, feeling drained as Shay and
Michael took their seats and took a big swig. George and Rose took
Mira upstairs, knowing they shouldn't hear the details of the night.

Thomas had created a diversion after I'd left, distracting the men
for Michael and Shay to escape out the front. The men were intoxicated enough that brawls were crashing throughout the bar, and
some surely forgot what they'd even been fighting for. Apparently,

Thomas quickly caught up to Michael and Shay, and that's when they'd found me.

Gypsy. The word still plagued me, bouncing around in my head with the same fear in the man's voice. Their reactions didn't connect with what was being done to me. Something about the whole thing just felt *off*.

And then there was the threat of the men accusing me of murder. It didn't matter that it was self-defense. This was a time when the court would take the man's side on the account that I was "asking for it." Hell, they still did that even in the twenty-first century.

"That's not all that I fear," Thomas said, drumming his fingers on the table.

My head snapped up. "What else could there be? I killed the one man." Bile rose up my throat at that admission, and I had to keep myself from swaying. I'd never forgive myself for what I'd done. I'd always question if I could have done it differently.

Thomas sighed, finally meeting my glare. "There are two dead men in that ally, whether ye killed both or not. And ye helped—" He cut over to Shay. He didn't have to say it. I helped someone of the 'wrong' race. Bile rose to my mouth. "Ye helped your friend. Everyone will be out for blood after this. Ye can't sing there anymore, and Billy will surely be looking for ye."

I held back tears when Michael agreed. I couldn't let them know how much I loved singing there.

Shay rubbed her hands over her face, clearly upset. "I'm so sorry," she moaned. "I just wanted to see you sing there once. I didn't mean for—"

"It's not your fault," I said, reaching over to grab her hand. "Don't ever apologize for other people's hate. That's on them. All of this is on them. You know I'd want you there." I glared at Michael as he scowled at the table. What did he have to be angry about?

Shay just shrugged, not meeting my eyes.

Thomas and Michael had an equal mind of me leaving the city, but it was unthinkable. I refused to leave Shay and wouldn't bring her on the road to God-knows-where while she was halfway through a pregnancy, no matter how much she agreed to the plan. The danger was too great.

Their next idea would be to hide me somewhere else, but with that came problems of its own. I'd have to hide until Shay was well enough after she had the baby. That would be for five months at the very least, which didn't even guarantee the time it'd take to actually find our way home.

After a long silence, each of us lost in our thoughts, a mischievous glint appeared in Shay's eyes. I knew that look, and it scared the hell out of me every time I saw it.

"What?" I asked hesitantly.

"They'd be looking for a pretty singer." We stared at her like she had lost her mind.

"Yeah, so..."

"What if you dressed like a man?" It was like a veil lifted, revealing many new possibilities I hadn't thought of before. "You used to wear pants all the time. It couldn't be much different now."

I straightened, my lips curling into a smile. "And I could have so much more freedom."

Thomas scoffed, his eyes roaming down my body. "No one could mistake ye for a man," he said.

"They would if the clothes were big enough, and I bound my breasts," I said excitedly. The two men looked uncomfortable with that fact. "I can cut my hair or wear it under a hat. I bet I could look like a young man!"

Shay smiled.

"I wouldn't have to do it forever. Just long enough to figure out a way to find my family."

"Ye face is as smooth as a wean's arse," Michael drawled.

"A lot of teenage boys don't have stubble on their face yet."

They argued long and hard, not believing I could pull it off. Nonetheless, my mind was already made up, and my new disguise was born.

I could no longer stay at Rose's or work at the bakery, which left me homeless, nearly broke, and overwhelmed with a desperation I hadn't felt since my first week here.

Michael tapped the table. "Tommy boy isn't going to like it," he said. "Maybe not even ye, but it's all I can think of."

"What?" Thomas and I asked at the same time.

Michael smiled. "Ye work for me. There's room to sleep at me place."

I felt my facelift as well. "Deal," I said, holding out my hand.

"Absolutely not!" Thomas snapped, pushing my hand away. "Are ye forgetting your men know the lass?"

Michael shrugged. "Not as a young lad. But if it soothes your bosom, I can hand her solo jobs."

I watched them quarrel, my head turning back and forth as they volleyed their disputes.

"Then she can work under ye," Michael admitted, leaning back in the chair, his hands relaxed behind his head while his icy eyes danced.

I held my breath, glancing at Thomas under my lashes. I might like that job.

Thomas glared, scowling at his brother but not refusing. "Fine," he grated out, surprising us all. "Only with me, and if I'm not around, with someone ye trust. And she's not staying in your cesspit of depravity. She'll stay with me. Ma and Da shouldn't mind as long as we bring in the extra coin."

My heart accelerated, and a flush spread over my body, but no one was paying attention.

I was going to live with Thomas.

Thomas held back as Mikey went down the street, and Shay went back inside.

It seemed Mikey's deception was forgiven when he saved her at the saloon. He showed up when he needed to, but the words he had said before had left a scar on her heart. I knew my friend, and though she told him he was forgiven, she would carry that pain with her forever. Not that Mikey cared, anyway...

The streetlamp burned softly, throwing a warm glow across Thomas' face as shadows danced against his sharp angles.

Before he could speak, I swallowed around a lump in my throat and started in. "I know you don't care much about me." He looked at me sharply, anger flashing. I wasn't expecting that and had to look at my feet, so I could say what was in my heart. "But tonight. To think about how that man almost—" tears fell as my throat constricted. Thomas wrapped his hand around my head, pulling me into an embrace and remarkably drawing away some of the pain. "That man almost took something from me. I'm not the whore you think I am."

"I never thought that." He pulled back to look at my face. "I knew from my first glimpse what ye were."

"But you—"

"I don't care to admit it, gypsy—" The word fell across me as a caress and sent shivers down my spine. "—But I've known a lot of slags, and ye aren't one of them."

I gave a wet laugh, ignoring the flame of jealousy, and wiped my face. My eyes dropped to his neck shyly. "I'm a virgin," I whispered, unsure why I was admitting this to him. Maybe it was more for me. Perhaps if I said it enough, I could get past this night. Or maybe I wanted him to be....

No, I stopped that thought in its tracks before it could take hold. It would hurt too much when I had to leave.

His arms tightened around me. "I'd never forget our night together, lass. Ye didn't come out and say it outright, but it was clear ye were out of your element."

"It was that obvious?" I cringed, remembering how nervous I was that night.

Thomas grabbed my face, his big palms taking up both sides, carefully avoiding the bruises. "I notice everything about ye." His thumb circled my cheek, making me close my eyes as my body buzzed. "Ye are perfect in every way."

My eyes popped open in surprise. "I know nothing could come from this," I said breathlessly, feeling time run out. "I know I have to leave, and you are probably going to enlist, but—"

He searched my eyes, waiting for what I would say next. Words failed me, so I let my eyes drop to his lips instead. He didn't move so long that I almost pulled away, embarrassed by my admission. Then slowly, so slowly that I held my breath in anticipation, he lowered his head until his warm lips pressed gently against mine.

The electricity that shot through me had me gasping, parting my mouth just a fraction, but enough to allow Thomas to slip his tongue along my bottom lip and inside.

I groaned, rising on my tiptoes to get closer, running my fingers through his hair to bring his face closer to mine. That was all the encouragement he needed to deepen the kiss, growling into my mouth as he pushed me against the wall, cradling the back of my head with his large hand.

His other hand never strayed far from my waist, but my body craved for him to explore. I could feel it in the strain of his muscles, the way his body shook against mine, that he was holding back. That he was giving my body the affection and tenderness that it needed. After all that had happened, my body didn't need rough, and Thomas knew it.

I almost couldn't believe that I was in his arms. That he wanted *me*. There were so many other women that he could have. So many other women that weren't complicated. Women who wouldn't throw his life into a complete shit-storm.

Our kiss slowed, his lips leaving soft trails across my cheekbones and down my jaw as I savored the taste of whiskey he'd left behind. I tilted my head to the side, giving him more access to my neck. My eyes fluttered closed as heat bloomed in my belly.

This. This was what I'd been missing.

He stopped, placed both hands on the building behind me, and hung his head, his whiskered cheek resting against mine as he gained control of his breathing.

I took a step forward, wrapping my arms around Thomas as I rested my head on his chest. I inhaled deeply, locking his masculine scent in my memory for later. "You got your shirt back," I said, not remembering how that happened. "Sorry about that."

"Ye didn't seem to be disappointed earlier." His chest rumbled with his laughter.

I was grateful he couldn't see my cheeks flame as I slapped his good shoulder. He caught my wrist, holding it to him, and we stood like that for a while, content to be within each other's arms. My heart slowed to a steady rhythm. My body relaxed.

"Why were you at the saloon?" I finally broke the silence.

"I've been to watch ye plenty of times."

"What?" I said, pulling back to see his face. "Why didn't I see you then?"

Thomas looked down at me, emerald eyes creased in regret. I wanted to reach up, run my hand through his whiskers, and ease every worry line on his face.

"Ye are plannin' to leave, gypsy." I watched his Adam's Apple bob up and down as he swallowed, fascinated by the strong muscles weaving through his neck. His accent came out thicker than I've ever heard it with the rise of his emotions. "And I'm fightin' in this war. Everythin' in me tells me to flee. To stay away from ye."

My chest felt like it was caving in, and the tears I'd been holding back fell over. His thumbs brushed them away. Thomas watched his skin trace mine as if in awe. "But at the same time, I cannot keep away, and I don't know why. Ye aren't like all the others."

A small breath escaped from my lips. "Like it's not even our choice? Like no matter what we do, no matter what way we turn, the world still finds a way to bring me back to you." I paused, shocked that I had let that spill from my lips. "I'm sorry—"

"Aye," he said on an exhale, eyes filled with an emotion so strong that it shot straight to my core. "Just like that."

CHAPTER TWENTY-SIX

Thomas & Emilia

AUGUST 1861

Emilia had been walking around town in her ridiculous trousers, hair pushed up in a cap for a fortnight, yet Thomas still couldn't look away. She had adapted well to her new role, quickly adapting to the lookout position and wearing man's clothing as if it were a second skin. Emilia—Eamonn, he had to remember to call her—was smart and could stick to the shadows when needed, watching for anything suspicious as they made their deals. She even fooled the others with her terrible Irish accent.

The thought brought a sad smile to his lips as they walked the deck, listening to the ocean lap softly against the ships around them. Somewhere in the distance, a seagull called.

"How long has Mikey been doing this?" she asked, peaking up from under her cap. She looked absurd, yet Thomas still found it almost impossible to keep his hands off her.

If it weren't for his family staying in the same room at night, he might have lost control weeks ago.

Thomas pocketed the money he'd been counting from the deal they'd just made.

"Five years, maybe," Thomas said with a sigh.

Emilia's eyes widened. "And he's already this high up?"

Thomas shrugged, turning his gaze to the sky's deep purple and trailing it to the bright oranges of the sunset. Of course, she'd be impressed by his brother's connections. Mikey was persistent, if nothing else. "Our parents brought us here for a better life. I told ye our sisters died on the ship, aye?" Thomas could feel her stare and nod, but he couldn't bring himself to look at her. "The conditions—" He shook his head. "Ye can imagine what hundreds of bodies on a ship can be like. A lack of food and sickness sweeping through us—"

Emilia grabbed his hand and gave it a light squeeze, quickly withdrawing it before anyone walking by could see.

"It was hell. And when we finally arrived, there was no housing to be found. So we spent our first years living in shanties. Our da was turned away from every job." Thomas balled his fists, wanting to hit something. Those first years were the hardest he ever had to endure. "Long story short: We had nothing but our small family and what was on our backs. I was big enough to scare the shite out of the bullies, but I couldn't always be there for Mikey. Eventually, he used his wit and his feckin' rebellious nature to find ways to survive." Thomas shrugged and watched understanding fill her deep brown eyes. No judgment to be found. "The weight of what we had to endure at such a young age made him nasty."

"He's not nasty." She looked about as surprised by her response as he was. "I mean, he's an asshole, and he says some awful stuff." She paused, pursing her lips as they left the dock and started walking through the city. "But I think it's an act. Obviously not the whole bad-boy, gang part, but…"

Thomas hung his head. She had known his brother briefly and had already deduced what he knew all along. Not even Hiram could see past the charade, and he'd known Mikey for nearly fifteen years.

"Am I stupid for thinking that?" She looked so sad that Thomas reached for her cheek. His hand quickly fell, remembering they were in public.

"Nay, la—" he caught himself, internally cursing for the near slip. "I think ye have gotten a glimpse of what most don't see of me dearthàir."

She looked away towards the people walking the streets rather than at him. Her following words sent a dart through his chest.

"He helped me. It may have been a deal, but he didn't have to help me. Especially with the training."

Thomas's muscles strained with guilt. "It should've been me."

"What?"

He turned to her then, not caring about the curses from those who had to walk around them. "I should have trained ye. I should've believed ye. Or, the very least, not pushed ye away." His knuckles nearly split from clenching his fists so hard. "Ye never would have the need to work at Billy's. I can assure ye that."

The look of surprise on her face was nothing compared to the shock of her next words. "I liked working there."

Thomas had to turn and start walking again to hide his expression. Jealousy was a new emotion when it came to a woman. He felt it plenty of times, bordering resentment when it came to their housing and the jobs that were turned away because he was Irish. Or every time a damn nativist turned up their nose at him as if the ground they walked on was feckin' gold.

But this. This was different.

Women were easy to attain and even easier to leave. So why did the thought of turning her away all those months ago feel like shrapnel to his abdomen? Why couldn't he purge the thought of her? The way that she moved. How her face lit up at the most mundane things. Her singing is thick like honey and just as sweet. And yet, just enough spice mixed in that sent her from unique to feckin' spectacular. There was nothing about her that didn't affect him.

"Miss the lads?" he asked sharper than he intended.

To his surprise, she snorted. "Not really. I love performing, though. Music has always been an escape for me." Her fake accent slipped, betraying her emotions. "It could be a room full of women for all I care, as long as they find enjoyment in what I'm doing."

"I'm sorry ye had to stop." And he meant it. Thomas rubbed his tightening chest.

The silence extended as they turned down another street, heading towards North Street.

"Why does your brother pretend to be racist?" Emilia blurted.

"What makes ye ask?" His brother had done questionable acts concerning the darker race, and Thomas wasn't sure why. It seemed Mikey was set out on tearing everyone down like—Thomas paused, considering. He shook his head and let out a sigh of exasperation.

"He treats Shay awful one moment and then seems to care for her in the next." She shrugged, oblivious to his inner turmoil.

"Me brother tears people down because that was done to us when we came here. I think it's his way of evening the score."

"Doesn't make it right," she scoffed. "It's not their fault people treated him shitty."

"Aye, but look around," Thomas said, eyes scanning the people passing them. Of the apparent segregation. "If it's what ye grew up believing, it's hard not to see it differently."

"You did."

"I had Hiram." He looked away, a wave of shame overwhelming him. "Ye don't know the things I did, lass." His stomach rolled as the last word came out in a whisper. "I may not have made the same choices as Mikey, but I still have done many things that I'm ashamed of."

She was quiet for a few heartbeats. "How did that happen, by the way?" She peered up at him, eyes filled with an emotion he didn't understand. "Meet Hiram?"

Sighing, Thomas explained the day he found Mikey and the Callahan twins surrounding Hiram down by the docks all those years ago. The look on Hiram's face. How they bullied him. Hit him. The despicable things they said.

"Hiram's ma fled to the north when she found out she was with child," he explained. Emilia's eyes widened. He nodded when she asked who the father was. "His father owned his mother. Because of her sacrifices and determination, Hiram could live freely in the north. It's a miracle he never found them. So many others don't make it." Thomas's thoughts returned to Miss Abel, and his stomach turned at their failure. "I'm sure ye can imagine the remarks they were throwin' around about his ma." Thomas cleared his throat and shrugged. "I intervened. It was Hiram and me against them, and it's been that way ever since."

"Is Mikey bitter about that?"

"He sees it as me choosing Hiram over him, aye." Thomas walked, quietly thinking of his brother and wishing they could have had the relationship they had in Ireland. "But I couldn't let him do it. And I don't regret me choice. I just hope he regrets his."

"Has Hiram always been so..." Her words trailed off as she thought, her head tilting back and forth. "Broody?"

Thomas let out a deep laugh, startling Emilia into looking up at him. She rewarded him with a small smile of her own. "Aye, gypsy. The man takes life too seriously. But can ye blame him after what he's been through?"

"No. But Isaac seems so happy..."

"Isaac's different. His da didn't rape his ma or own her."

Emilia's face paled considerably. "This world is so fucked up."

Thomas nodded. There were no words for how true that statement was.

They spent the next few minutes lost in their own troubled thoughts.

Her muscles visibly tensed when Emilia saw the street where they were headed. "Where are we going?"

"Mikey needs us at Nora's. Ye don't have to go in. I can drop it off quick." Thomas patted his pocket.

Thomas tried not to worry about what her silence meant the rest of the way.

I shifted on my feet outside Nora's, willing Thomas to hurry his ass up so we could go home.

Home.

My throat constricted at the thought. It wasn't my home. I needed to remember that.

I'd spent the last few weeks searching for any news about my family to no avail. Each day chiseled away more of my resolve and left me despondent. I needed to get Shay out of the nineteenth century, but I couldn't do that if I didn't have the powder. If I didn't find them soon, it was looking like I would have to go south. And just the thought of that was daunting.

Not to mention the *war* we were currently going through.

I wrung my hands and tried to divert my thoughts. Only they went to Thomas and how Nessa was probably all over him. My fists clenched, and my entire body ignited with jealousy. Thomas hadn't come out and said that Nessa was the one he'd been with, and yet it was clear the day that I saw them together. Nessa may have had many clients, but Thomas was obviously her favorite. If I had to guess, I would even say she had some feelings for him.

I scoffed as I looked at the street around me and felt a pang of nostalgia. I didn't sing here for long, but the impulse to do so now overwhelmed me. I was in the middle of watching the people go by, admiring the women's big dresses and checking out the men's fashion. Seriously, this time was far classier than ours. Even though we were in the poorer part of the city, I felt myself favoring their style. A part of me wondered if it was just a style choice or if it had to do with me being from this time as a child.

My thoughts were wondering, thankfully from the man inside the whorehouse, when my gaze fell on a familiar face. I squinted, hoping my eyes were deceiving me. Was that one of Billy Mead's men?

He was heading this way, and I couldn't deny his unmistakable broad face any longer. Frank Acker's ruddy brown hair and dull eyes may have made him easy to forget, but the man was built like a bull, with Hulk-like arms that could crush a man. If I hadn't stood by him during one of my nights singing at the saloon, I would never have noticed that he was short. The thick layers of muscle covering the man were distraction enough for any bystander.

What did he want? Surely, he was going to pass Nora's.

I fidgeted on my feet, praying that he wouldn't turn my way or look too closely at me. Otherwise, he'd see through my disguise. When he crossed to my side of the street, I couldn't take it any longer.

I slipped through the door to Nora's establishment.

The place hadn't changed since the last time I'd been there. It was a full night, with the ladies flirting their way through the men until one of them took them upstairs. The alcohol was flowing, and raucous laughter boomed throughout the room.

I made my way to the back corner, and my eyes were immediately drawn to a particularly tall man, as they always were.

Thank God Nessa was nowhere in sight.

I pushed my way through, keeping my head down so no one would spot me.

"Thomas," I said sharply, pulling on his sleeve. I ignored the way his eyes widened at my arrival.

"I was about to come out—"

"I think Frank Acker is about to come in here. What do ye think he wants?"

"Eamonn!" a familiar voice drawled a little too loudly. "It's about time I found ye in here."

I ignored Michael, who was blazingly drunk and kept my eyes on Thomas. His eyebrows creased as he looked over my head. They sharpened when the door opened, and my breath stalled in my chest. My fear had manifested.

"Eamonn, ye fancy a lass?" Michael laughed with his boys, though he was the only one in on his joke. "I'm sure a little relief would remove the stick from up your arse."

"Shut up," I growled, cutting my eyes toward him. He must have seen something in my face because he seemed to sober up a bit.

In the next second, Thomas whipped me around and shoved me up the stairs before I could even blink.

"What are ye doing?" I snapped, stumbling across one of the steps.

"Saving your arse. Whatever it is, Frank wants, Mikey can handle it."

"He's drunk." I scoffed. "Are ye sure he can?"

Amusement filled his green eyes, causing a flutter to break out in my belly.

"Ye under-estimate me, dear dearthái. He'll be fine."

"Where are we going?" I asked, reaching the top of the stairs just as two women exited one of the rooms.

I choked on my spit when I recognized Biddy and threw myself behind Thomas.

"Tommy!" her sweet voice sang. "What are ye doin' up here? Ye lookin' for Nessa?"

My hackles rose, and my lip curled, ready to snap. As if sensing my anger, Thomas's shoulders stiffened.

"How much for a room?" he asked her.

"Oh!" She sounded surprised. "The usual—"

"Nay," he said sharply, causing me to pull back and look at the back of his head as if I could read what was going on in there. "A room for me and me friend. No women. We have business that can't be overheard." Thomas pulled the cash we earned today out of his pocket and started counting the bills. "Will this cover it?"

I peeked around his arm and saw her blonde curls bob up and down. "That is grand, Tommy. Ye can have me room."

Thomas pulled out a few more bills. "And for your silence?"

She nodded, sliding the extra money between her small breasts. Her eyes flicked towards me and widened a fraction.

"C'mon, Cori," she said, her gaze still on me. "Let's head out back. It looks like we have a spare hour."

"Make it several," Thomas said, handing her extra cash.

"Are ye crazy?" I hissed with enough vehemence to scare small children.

Thomas ignored me as Biddy's, and Cori's big eyes bounced between us.

"This shall do," Biddy smiled and steered the other girl away.

I took off to her room. "Ye think it's going to take Michael *several hours* to get Frank out of here?"

"Ye never know," he said as we closed the door to the room.

"Never know?!" I yelled. I placed my hands on my hips and let my head fall back, hoping I would calm down. I dropped the accent now that we were in the room. "What are we going to do for *hours*?"

"I'm sure we can think of something." A tone I had never heard before had my head snapping in his direction. Was Thomas *teasing* me?

Oh. I shifted on my feet, suddenly nervous. Did he turn that smirk onto all the women? Because, if so, I saw why they all seemed to fall at his feet. I swallowed, shifting my eyes away from Thomas's heated ones.

"It's hot in here," I blurted, beginning to pace. "Isn't it?" I fanned my face with my hand. "Yeah, it's hot."

"Ye stated that, gypsy."

I let my hand fall so he could adequately see my glower.

He just smiled and started unbuttoning the top of his shirt.

"What are you doing?" I snapped.

One brow rose. "It's hot." He shrugged. "And ye didn't seem to mind the last time..."

I rolled my eyes and stared at the low, burning fire.

"Settle down, lass. I didn't bring ye in here to have me way with ye." He sat in the same chair he had occupied all those months ago. "We can just talk."

My nose scrunched up. Why did that leave me feeling disappointed?

I sat down on the bed with a huff. A quick glance revealed Thomas's shirt, only partially unbuttoned as he relaxed. My eyes flicked back to the fire before he could catch me staring at his chest.

"Tell me some more about your time," Thomas said.

"What do you want to know?"

Thomas shrugged. "Tell me your favorite thing about it."

"Air conditioning," I said without having to think about it.

He repeated the words slowly, making me laugh. I explained what it was, and his eyebrows almost shot through the roof.

"When did ye sell your soul for such sorcery?"

That comment had me doubling over. Then, we fell into an easy conversation, from my favorite foods to the adventures I'd been on. At some point during the conversation, I'd removed my shoes and propped myself on the bed.

"Where did you get that?" I asked, eyeing the bottle of whiskey Thomas had lifted to his lips. I hadn't seen him grab it.

"It was in the corner." One dark brow rose. "Want some?"

I reached my hand out to take it, but Thomas had stood, making my neck crane back as he walked over to me.

"Maybe just a taste," he said, pressing it to my lips. Our eyes locked as he tilted it up slowly, letting the liquid settle on my tongue as it burned down my throat. His eyes darkened as he tracked my neck with each swallow. I pulled the bottle out of his hands so I wouldn't choke beneath his stare.

"I think you've had enough." I smiled and took another swig.

His green gaze leisurely, painstakingly, trailed up my neck and across my lips until finally reaching my eyes again. A small gasp parted my lips as he rolled his bottom one into his mouth.

"All yours, gypsy."

We stared at each other until my blood heated, a thrill shooting through my limbs as the tension between us intensified.

"I should check on Mikey," he said, snapping our connection.

My eyes fell to the bottle, and I nodded, afraid to speak lest he heard the desire in my voice. I took another drink as the click of the door told me he'd left.

Sighing, I flopped back on the bed, cursing myself for thinking he might kiss me. It'd been ages since we'd kissed last, and Thomas hadn't made a move since.

CHAPTER TWENTY-SEVEN

Emilia & Thomas

It'd been several minutes since Thomas had left when a door closed in the next room, and a giggle carried its way over to me. With one glance at the door, I stood and made my way over to the wall, intrigued.

I placed my ear to the wall and heard a grunt and a curse. The woman moaned. "Yes, baby."

"Daddy," a deep voice growled. A slap had the woman gasping while loud thumps began to beat the wall next to my ear.

"Aw, daddy. Just like that. Ye always do *so* good."

Apparently, not much had changed over the centuries. I never understood the whole 'daddy' thing, though. It kind of weirded me out.

The man growled, and the tempo increased so loudly that I sprang back, irrationally thinking they'd catch me listening. He must have had her against the wall I was pressed up against.

My hand squeezed the bottle, captivated by what was happening. It wasn't hard for me to imagine the way he fucked her. The desire. How she would know all the ways to make him *beg*.

My hand trailed down my body and across my breasts until I reached my pants. Suddenly, the vest was too much.

Another swig, and I had the vest off. One more drink and I unbuttoned my pants before I could question what I was doing. I put the bottle down. I had enough and wanted to be fully aware of Thomas's reaction when he came back into the room.

I shed my boots and most of my clothes. The only thing on my body was the shirt, unbuttoned down to my breasts and only reaching my thighs. I looked down, my tan legs were scandalously displayed in this era, and with a brief feel behind me, I knew the bottom of my ass was teasing its way out.

Biting my lip, I undid another button on the shirt so that it reached my stomach. I'd taken the wrap that bound my breasts and hid it under the pile of my clothes.

The pounding picked up unbearably. The grunts and moans made me press my thighs together for relief. Unable to take it anymore, I put my hand between them, finding my center wet. I plunged them in and moaned with the couple. Increasing my pace as if I was in there with them.

My hand shot to the wall, supporting me while my eyes closed and moved like I was participating in their activities. My breathing accelerated, heat flushing my skin as our pace threatened to push us over our climax.

The door creaked open, and I twirled around. Thomas's eyes blazed down my body, searing every inch of my exposed skin.

I tried to control my breathing, but there wasn't anything I could do about my flushed face. And having him see me like this sent another intense wave of heat through me, setting my body on fire. There was no denying what I had been doing.

His boot slammed the door shut behind him.

"Don't let me interrupt," he said, gesturing for me to continue.

My heart beat against my ribcage, threatening to break out as Thomas sat down in the chair and watched me.

"I don't know what you're talking about." My voice came out breathier than I intended. I bit my lip when the prostitute started yelling repeatedly.

Thomas's darkening gaze turned absolutely feral as he leaned forward. "Ye very well know what I meant. Don't play daft now, gypsy. Put your pretty little fingers back where ye had them and finish what ye started. It would be rude of me to not let a woman finish."

On a shaky breath, I let my hand skim down my body.

"On the bed," he growled, stopping my pursuit.

Without breaking eye contact, I crawled onto the bed and lay down. My back arched as I cupped my breasts and slowly trailed them down my body before pushing them inside me. I moaned, never so turned on before.

I never did *anything* like it before.

"Faster," he rasped. His whole body tensed as if he was going to pounce. The thought invigorated me, and I moaned so loudly that I had to bite my lip to stop myself from calling out to him. "Don't stop, gypsy. It sounds like they're almost done. Wouldn't want them to finish without ye."

I circled my clit, the tension building so strongly inside me that my legs began to move, trying to find leverage to stop this maddening torture.

Thomas stood, and I froze, entirely at his mercy. And yet, I didn't have an ounce of fear in me, knowing full well that he would never hurt me. Thomas would never treat me the way those men had. No, this invigorated me and lit my body up as a heady nervousness thrummed in my veins.

"I said don't stop," he snapped, almost angrily.

I picked up the pace as he knelt by me, my breath catching as his large hand reached out and began to undo the rest of the buttons. Each skim of his fingers on my bare flesh sent a shot of electricity through me. My head flew back as I moaned, eyes screwed shut at all the sensations coursing through me.

"Yes, daddy! Yes!" her groan had me almost coming so fast that I had to stop. The slap of their bodies made me want to grab Thomas and make him show me what he could do.

My shirt fell back, exposing every inch of me except for my arms. My breathing hitched before picking up as if I had run a marathon. I opened my eyes and found Thomas's gaze trailing down my neck to pause at my breasts. All the oxygen left my body as the green of his irises disappeared.

I guess he liked what he saw, but insecurities with such undevoted attention on me sent my nerves straight through the roof.

"Breath, Emilia," he demanded, and I obeyed.

When his eyes roamed down my stomach, I moved to cover it. His hand shot out and pinned my arm to the bed.

"Don't ye dare," he growled. I wasn't usually worried about it, but the women were so skinny in this era that I felt significantly larger than them. "Ye're perfect." His other hand skimmed my thigh and over my hip until it gripped my mid-section. Could he feel that I was shaking?

His grip tightened, and I gasped as his fingers stroked my soft flesh. Both of his hands let go of me quickly as if he wouldn't be able to control himself a moment longer.

"I said, 'keep touchin' yourself,'" he rasped.

My hand found its way back, circling as he watched. I licked my lips, my mouth suddenly dry under his heated gaze.

"Faster, gypsy. I want to hear ye come with her."

His dirty words sent another flush across my skin, but I couldn't bring myself to care.

I liked them. A lot.

I drove several fingers inside me and rubbed with my palm, panting as my pace picked up. The loud banging and grunts next door became erratic, slamming into the wall as the woman screamed.

The tightening in my abdomen began to build, and my whole body tensed as Thomas watched my hand. His jaw looked like it was about to crack with the tension. I felt like I was about to levitate off the mattress. My back arched. My heels ground against the bed for purchase.

Just as the man roared with a loud bang onto the wall, the tension broke, sending me free-falling, bursts of desire shooting down my limbs. I screamed as my entire core lit up like fireworks. All the while, Thomas watched in rapture as I experienced the most intense orgasm I ever had.

"So feckin' beautiful."

My body sunk into the mattress as my soul felt like it left my body, finally sated after that torture. My eyes opened to find Thomas looking like he wanted to devour me.

"Was that your first time?" he asked.

My cheeks heated, but I shook my head. "I've done it plenty of times. First time someone watched, though." My eyes looked towards the ceiling in embarrassment. Now that the act was over, my nerves were getting the best of me.

"Has another man seen your body like this?"

My head shot towards him, surprised by the anger.

"No."

"I would very much like to touch ye," he stated, placing each hand on either side of me. The bed sank down as he leaned in. Caging me. "Is it because ye didn't want them to? Because surely, they couldn't keep away from ye. I don't know how I did for so long."

I shook my head. "I—I guess boys my age were never interesting enough. I had offers, though." The last part came out in a whisper. I watched his face transform from desire to something far more predatory.

"I am no boy, lass."

"I know," I croaked.

"Would ye like me to touch ye?"

I swallowed, unable to speak.

"Because I would very well like to, Emilia." My name on his tongue sent ripples of goosebumps over my body. He skimmed his fingers down my arm, making every nerve light up. "Do ye want me to? I need ye to say it."

Need. Thomas was giving me the option. My heart melted in my chest as my feelings grew into something I was afraid to admit.

"Yes," I breathed, unable to refuse him. In that moment, I didn't think I ever could.

"Thank fuck," he growled.

It took everything in Thomas not to pounce on Emilia as soon as she gave him permission. But, no. He wanted to take this as slow as possible. His fingers glided down her neck, and her breathing had already stopped by such a simple touch.

He was going to enjoy this very much. And yet, he paused right above her collarbone.

"Are ye sure ye don't want to save this for your future husband, lass?"

Her dark eyes found his, unraveling him with their truth before she even said the words. "I want it to be you."

His hand trailed lower, skimming the side of her breast. A shiver ran up her body, snapping his restraint. His mouth fell down, and he flicked his tongue over her nipple before sucking it into his mouth.

Emilia's head fell back, and her body arched. Thomas used the opportunity for his other hand to wrap around the back of her hip and hauled her closer. His mouth pulled from her with a pop before grabbing her breasts. They filled both of his hands completely. He marveled at their size as his thumbs brushed across them.

"This has never happened before," he admitted, raising a teasing brow at her.

Her look of confusion would have made him laugh if he wasn't so turned on. "What?"

Thomas climbed further onto the bed and spread her thighs so he could settle between them, lightly resting his weight on her. Though still fully clothed, he needed to be closer. Needed to see the way he affected her.

"It was like ye were made for me," he clarified, kneading her breasts until she gave out a heady moan. "Like these were made for me. They fit perfectly within me hands."

Emilia surprised him with a laugh. His gaze snapped back to hers, finding a mischievousness in them that went straight to his lower half. Thomas shifted so that he was fully pressed against her center, making her gasp.

"Is that funny, gypsy?"

"Maybe." She gave him a crooked smile and pressed her breasts further into his hands at the same time she rocked her hips up. It was his turn to suck air in through clenched teeth. "So, you like them?"

When he didn't answer, she raised her brow and swiveled her hips again.

As quick as a snake, Thomas's hand swiped under her knee and pulled it up around his waist as he rolled against her. Then, leaning down with his weight pressing down across all of her curves, his lips touched the rim of her ear. "Someone is being especially naughty tonight. Have ye had too much to drink?"

"No."

Thomas smiled at her throaty response. "Then shall I punish ye for coming without me?"

"You told me to!"

The slap across her ass had her gasping. As soon as her mouth opened, Thomas's was on hers so that he could devour her whimper.

"Tell me," he said into her mouth. "Did ye want to be in there with them?" She shook her head. "Did ye wish they were touchin' ye as they pleasured themselves?" She hesitated, and Thomas let out a surprised laugh. "Naughty gypsy. Put your hands above your head."

"Why?"

He raised a brow. "Your punishment. Don't ask again."

She raised her hands like a good girl and grabbed the edge of the mattress. "What are you going to do?" Her words came out shaky, but her body was moving against him. She was turned on as much as he was.

The sound of the slap registered before the sting. He could see it as her lips formed an 'O'. Thomas's fingers rubbed the sting out as he gave his answer. "I told ye no questions, but since ye want to face the consequences, I will oblige." His hand traveled back to her knee to pull her closer as he steadily rocked until she was panting. "I will drag this out until ye are beggin' for me to finish. Until ye curse me. Hate me." His tongue swiped into the hollow of her throat. "And then I will reward ye for being such a filthy lass." His hands wrapped around her hips, so the position drove her nearly mad. His mouth returned to her ear. "I am going to worship your body, lass. Tell me, do ye want Anna in here with us?"

Her eyes flashed, and Thomas had to hold back his excitement. *Was she jealous?*

"Would ye want to watch as I fuck her?"

The next slap rang out through the room, but the sting across his cheek fueled his desire instead of angering him.

"Screw you," she growled. Ah, so it *was* jealousy he saw.

He had both her hands pinned before she could blink. "Ye are going to pay for that, ghrá."

Thomas shifted so one hand pinned her hands as the other skimmed down her body, over her twitching stomach, and straight to her center. Her legs twisted as she tried to release the tension on his hand.

He spanked her again.

"Don't move," he growled, even as his subsequent strokes were slow and gentle. "So no to Anna." He couldn't help but smirk. Her jealousy pleased him more than he wanted to admit. "What about the man?" he asked, body tensing for her answer. "Would ye want him while I watched?"

Her eyes narrowed, and a sweet flush spread across her chest. "What if I wanted *them* to watch *us*?"

Thomas's hand stopped immediately. He watched Emilia bite her lip as she scanned the shock that must have been clearly written on his face.

She gave a wicked smile that he'd never seen on her before and leaned up to whisper into his ear. He had to hold back the shiver skating down his spine. "Maybe I want to take you downstairs so you can fuck me in front of everyone to show them you're *mine*." Her head fell back on the pillow, causing her dark hair to spill in a puddle around her. "Would you like that?"

Thomas still hadn't moved. Was he even breathing? This woman would assuredly be the ruin of him. His damnation. A plague of temptation explicitly made for him. It was increasingly clear that Emilia Moretti would unravel every rule he had ever made. In fact, she already was, and he wasn't sure if that bothered him anymore.

That, however, didn't change the fact that her body still shook. Her tongue might bite, but she was all timidity beneath her exterior. It made Thomas want her all the more.

His fingers began to move again while his eyes remained on hers. He watched as he slid a finger inside her. Her body tensed, but she was so wet that there was no resistance.

Thomas swallowed. He'd never been stunned like this with a woman. He should have known Emilia would be the one to completely destroy him. She was unique in every way.

The thought of claiming her in front of everyone was tempting, but Thomas was feeling uncharacteristically selfish.

"Though I want ye, we will not be 'fucking' tonight." Her movements stilled as her brows scrunched together in confusion. It was so cute that Thomas kissed her pouting mouth and said, "It is your first, Emilia. I cannot, with good conscious, take that from ye."

"Then what are we doing?" she snapped. Her anger made it hard for Thomas to hide his smile.

"I'm going to make ye scream me name, lass. But there are plenty of other ways to do that than to take your virginity." He paused, his desire fading somewhat at his following words. "That should be for your husband."

"I want you."

His eyes flashed back to hers. Emilia was chipping at his resolve, but his decision was final. He may be selfish enough to explore her body, but he would not ruin her for the man she would be with. She was worth more than a million of Thomas. He didn't deserve this gift.

"Ye have me, lass."

He slid another finger slowly into her, making her hiss at how tight it was.

"Please, Thomas." Her hips rocked, and she gasped again.

"Don't move."

His lips pressed against hers, gentle and exploring. Trying to prove all of his love in that single act.

Love?

He paused, shocked by this discovery. *For fucks sake.* Was he in love with her?

His fingers began to move in and out to distract her from his revelation. Yes, he loved Emilia for quite some time without realizing it. But she was leaving, and he was to go to war. It wasn't possible. *They* weren't possible.

This would have to be enough. It was far more than he deserved.

Thomas raised to his knees and spread her thighs. Then, very slowly, he bent down.

"What are you doing?" Her voice shook, her big doe eyes imploring.

"So many questions."

"Wait," she placed her hands on his shoulders as he lowered.

"What did I say?" he growled. "Hands above your head."

She obeyed instantly but still asked, "Maybe—" A few seconds of hesitation. Then, "Maybe don't do that?"

He raised a brow. "I don't think anything can stop me from tasting ye right now, gypsy."

And with that, he ran his tongue up her center, and they moaned together.

"Oh," she gasped. "That feels so much better than I imagined."

Thomas smiled as he slid a finger inside her. He was rewarded with a sweet purr.

He kept his mouth on her when he asked, "Who have ye imagined between your legs, a ghrá? And do ye need to be punished?"

Emilia grabbed his hair and pulled at the same time, her thighs clenched his head. Her reaction almost broke all of his self-control. Instead of taking what he wanted, he settled for his own hand. His other arm wrapped around her belly and pinned her to the bed.

"You," she breathed, and their eyes connected over the expanse of her body. "Ever since Biddy told me how good you are with the girls—" Thomas shoved in another finger, and she groaned. His hand pumped himself faster. Emilia was panting as her body arched off the bed, but she continued. "Ever since I heard what a good fuck you are, I wanted you inside me."

Thomas was on top of her within a blink, his mouth crashing onto hers when he fisted her hair, ripping her head back as his free cock rocked across her clit. Emilia gasped, eyes springing open to look between them. He watched as she realized what he had been doing.

"I can help with that," she said, licking her lips.

Thomas didn't answer. He just watched as her hand slid between them. She began to move, testing out her grip as they both watched.

"Is—" she paused, and their eyes met. "Does that feel good?"

Thomas pulled himself closer so that her movements would rub against her. "Ye tell me, lass."

"Thomas, please."

The apprehension in her tense features had him answering immediately. "Aye. Don't stop." He rocked further into her hand.

"It's bigger than I imagined," she admitted, clearly worried.

Thomas let out a dark chuckle on her shoulder. "Good thing it won't be inside ye tonight. I'm not sure if I could be gentle."

A deep breath whooshed past his ear, and her body relaxed. Suddenly, Thomas was glad of his decision. Though she said she wanted to, and she very well did, that didn't mean she was *ready*.

Pulling back, they watched each other until their hands became hurried and without rhythm. Each lost in their own desire. He curled his fingers inside of Emilia, and her pace jerked and quickened. He found the spot that would be her undoing.

Emilia's body arched off the bed, all her muscles locking up as the most intoxicating moan escaped her lips. Heat shot to the base of his spine, nearly finishing him on the spot.

Thomas groaned into her neck, body stiffening to hold off just a little longer. A woman never undid him so fast. All the while, Emilia's hand never stopped moving, bringing him over the edge right there with her.

They cursed simultaneously, and Thomas collapsed, careful to keep his weight from crushing her.

"That—" she paused, clearly dazed. "That was almost better than the one with Anna."

Thomas's gaze whipped towards her as he noticed her whole-body jiggling. Was she laughing?

"Oh, ye are going to pay for that, gypsy."

Emilia's eyes widened for a fraction of a second before Thomas stood and lifted her off the bed, causing her to squeal.

"What are you—" She was over his lap, and his hand connected to her behind before she could finish the sentence.

"Ow!" She laughed, wiggling to get free.

"Not until ye admit your lie," Thomas growled.

She wiggled again, pointing her ass farther into the air. "I don't know. Maybe we should test it out again."

The next spank was so hard that her entire ass cheek was red. Thomas rubbed the sting away and slid his fingers back inside her.

"Oh." She dragged the word out.

"I can punish ye all night, lass. But this time, I'll stop just as ye are about to come."

She sighed, relaxing into him, and he stopped his pursuit.

"It was everything," she whispered so quietly he thought he imagined it.

"Aye," he agreed, hearing the grief in his own voice. "That it was."

For the first time, Thomas didn't want to fight. Didn't want to bear arms for a country that took him in. He was happy. Truly content for the first time since he was a child. And it was entirely because of the woman in his arms. His gut propelled him to work towards this exact feeling his entire life.

So then, why did he still feel the need to go?

CHAPTER TWENTY-EIGHT

Thomas & Emilia

SEPTEMBER 1861

I t was the only way. At least, Thomas told himself that as he tied up his boots.

He wished he could show Emilia a different place. Whisk her away from everything that was happening in their world. But he couldn't take her where he was about to go next. That's why he recreated the barriers since their time at Nora's. Kept her at a distance so that it wouldn't hurt her so much when he left. He couldn't ask her to wait for a man with no promise; even if he survived the war, he couldn't give her what she deserved. She deserved everything—everything that he was not.

Maybe if he said it enough, they'd both believe it. He refused to acknowledge the prickling sensation of fear crawling across his scalp. Thomas wasn't afraid to die. No, Thomas was worried he would go with the knowledge of what he was leaving behind, and if he knew—truly accepted the depths of his feelings for her—he'd never go.

And by God, he needed to go.

Thomas reached out, about to caress a hair off her sleeping face, then stopped, hand hovering a breath from her cheek. She was beautiful, sleeping peacefully with her hair fanned around her head, a small sigh escaping her lips as they pulled into a small smile. He wondered what she was dreaming about.

Thomas looked down at the rag that was a poor excuse for a blanket. He pulled back, the shame that he had felt when he told her that was all they had. Even though all she did was thank him and smile. There was no disgust at their run-down apartment and soot-covered walls. At least the bugs weren't bad, he thought bitterly, and they didn't have to share it with any other families this time. He tried to tell himself it could be worse. It had been worse. But seeing Emilia there—she was out of place and looked like the kind of lass that slept on a real bed with the finest sheets.

It did something to him, crushed him with the knowledge that he would never be able to give her what she deserved. And if that meant he had to live without her, he'd do it. He'd give her the chance to get the hell out of this city.

Thomas sighed and ran his hand over his hair, snapping himself from his thoughts. He had somewhere to be and couldn't be around when she woke.

"Where do you think he went then?" I asked Michael.

I had caught his eye in the saloon and gestured for him to meet me outside. The night wasn't busy yet, but it would be soon, and I wanted to be out of there before anyone could recognize me.

"He hasn't been around."

Michael winked at a woman who passed by, her dress so tight her breasts squeezed out of the top. Her lips turned up in an alluring smile, even as she held the arm of another man. The man pulled her down the street, oblivious to the exchange.

"Focus," I snapped, swatting Michael's arm. "Meager spoke at the Music Hall a couple of weeks ago. I know a lot of Irishmen respect him—Oh, shut up," I hissed at his look of contempt. "Just because you don't have an ounce of patriotism in your body doesn't mean your people don't. What I'm saying is maybe Thomas finally went to enlist? He'd been distant ever since—" I stopped, cheeks flushing, realizing I had almost told him about our night. That's what I had called it. It was constantly on my mind, and I had hoped we might do it again.

A new flush spread across my body, and I prayed Michael wouldn't notice. God, the things I said that night surprised even me. Not in a million years would I have thought I'd be so daring. My new boldness was no doubt fortified by the alcohol I'd consumed. Nonetheless, the rush was exhilarating.

The high didn't last long, though, thoroughly extinguished whenever I thought of the distance Thomas had put between us. So, maybe it didn't mean to him what it did to me. He'd been with other women. What was one more? I looked away before Michael could see the sheen in my eyes.

"Since?" Michael's brow arched. When it was clear I wasn't going to explain, he said, "It hasn't even been a day, lass. Maybe he's at Nora's. Lord knows the man needs some release in that department." He watched my face and smiled as the heat flooded it again. "Unless…" He shook his head, the corner of his mouth ticking up in a cruel smile. His eyes roamed my body as if undressing me under the men's clothing. "Nay, I can see why he went seeking female companionship."

"Will you stop being an ass for once? I'd think you used it all up, treating Shay the way you do."

Michael's eyes narrowed, but he kept his mouth shut.

"Maybe I should tell her you were eyeing that lady over there." It was my turn to smile. I was poking a bear, but I had my suspicions and needed to see how he'd react. "Do you think Shay would care?"

Michael straightened from the wall, drawing the attention of a few men walking by. When they were gone, he growled, "Ye know what she is and what I am. She is not mine—"

"Really? That's not how you act whenever you're around her. Actually, it's how I'd expect Hiram to react." Michael's blue eyes darkened frighteningly, but I pushed on. "But surprise, surprise. The white, bad boy might actually have a heart. You know, if you put in some effort, she could be yours."

Michael stared at me like I had grown two heads. As if the idea was so strange that it couldn't even be a consideration. In all honesty, it would be extremely difficult in this time. I just wanted him to admit he had feelings for her. There was a big chance that he hadn't even admitted it to himself yet. Years of active racism would do that to a person.

"Do you know what they'd do to us?" he hissed. "To her?" The fear in his eyes had me clutching my stomach at the rare display of emotion. Did he even realize what he had just revealed?

"I'm sorry," I said through a tight throat. "I come from a time when you two could be together."

Michael's jaw clenched, weighing the truth in my words. "Even if that's true, I never was inclined to dally with a mot. A spent one at that."

"You don't mean that." I had to stop myself from causing him bodily harm. He was so damned stubborn. "Stop being an asshole. And stop using your assholery ways to deflect."

Michael leaned back against the wall, getting out some chew. "Nothin' to deflect, *gypsy*." He shoved it into his mouth and scanned the area, avoiding my gaze. "Your fear is probably true. Tommy most likely enlisted. And I can see why if it means getting away from ye."

I rocked back on my heels, feeling it in my bones that it was true. I think I already knew but was too afraid to admit it, and I reached out to everyone, hoping to prove it wrong.

I backed away. "You're scared."

"What do ye know about being afraid?" He glared.

"I thought I knew before. I was wrong." I pulled my hat farther over my head, hiding my expression as much as keeping up my disguise. "I can see everything I was afraid of didn't even compare to what you guys have to deal with. It only makes you weak if you let it, Michael. If you want something, fight through the fear." I stared at my boots, wishing I could take my own advice, knowing I was a hypocrite. "Fight for her if she means something to you."

I looked up to find him staring at me, face hardened by an emotion I couldn't discern.

"I know she's worth it," I said, turning. "Do you?"

As I walked around the corner, Michael yelled, "It's too late. They're both already gone!"

His words sank into me like hooks, tearing through my chest and leaving me hollow. I'd walked a couple of blocks with my head down, watching my boots scrape against the cobblestones instead of paying attention to my surroundings. It was stupid and went against everything Michael had taught me.

But honestly, I was so tired of constantly having to look over my shoulder. I was exhausted from hiding. The sexism towards women. The racism towards every possible race and culture you could conceive. Frankly, I wondered how they could keep up such hate on top of all the extra chores they had to do.

At least I didn't have to churn fucking butter.

Yet.

I didn't doubt that I'd have to if I stayed much longer. Though it must have been more necessary in the south.

I didn't know. And I was tired of having to think about the butter process. And cleaning clothes. And making sure I was in the presence of male company before walking down the street.

Maybe a male companion would have been helpful at that point. Or perhaps even Shay to just keep me aware.

Because I didn't even glance over as a wagon rumbled down the street, wheels bouncing off the road as the horse's shoes clicked a steady beat. I barely had time to look at its red paint when someone jumped off the back and shoved an abrasive bag over my head.

My scream was cut off when a knife pressed my throat.

"Make a noise, and I will slit your throat," a deep voice rasped in an accent that made goose bumps cover my flesh with an eerie, distant recognition. His hand or someone else's slid over my person and removed the knives I had hidden before wrapping a rope tight around my wrists.

I was shoved into the wagon, jarring my knee. I gasped and curled into a ball on a seat. The man sat beside me, whispering something to someone else before hitting the wagon's side. It took off down the street, swaying and bouncing so much I had difficulty staying seated.

"Who are you?" I rasped, chafing my wrists as I pulled against my bindings.

Quiet mutterings between the two men were my only answer.

"You're going to regret taking me." I paused to make sure I had their attention. "My people will come for me."

"Your people," a man spat, his rough accent barely understandable. "Those bog trotters are *not* your people." The disgust in his voice had me recoiling to the corner of the wagon as if he insulted me.

"He will kill you." I tried to sound strong, but my voice broke at the end. The truth was that I knew Thomas would find me. I had no doubt. However, I'd just been looking for *him*, and I didn't know when he would return. What if he enlisted? Would he have left immediately, or would he wait like many other recruits? A light coat of sweat enveloped my body at the thought. If he had already left, not only did he choose not to say goodbye, but there would be no way for him to know that I was taken.

A scoff and silence were my only responses as the rattle of the wheels ramped up my fear.

Freckled light peaked through the burlap bag now and then, disorienting me as I desperately tried to see something. Anything. Finding it futile, I tried to keep track of the number of turns, but wasn't familiar enough with the city's layout to remember where we were.

I took a deep breath, trying to settle myself so I could think of a way to get out of this. I wasn't completely helpless. I'd spent hours training with Michael. I knew ways to incapacitate them if only they didn't take my knives. How did they know I had them on me? Did they automatically check because they thought I was a man?

No. They seemed to recognize me.

I worried my lip.

That left me weaponless, scared, and lost. My odds of escaping, let alone fighting them off and getting back to the city, were basically zilch. That left me with the hope that Michael would start looking for me. I almost laughed out loud at the thought. It would be days before he even realized I was missing.

That's when a jolt of realization hit me. What if Billy Mead figured out my disguise and hired them? That would've made sense. An easy way to get rid of me. And using those who weren't his people would be wise. It would be harder to tie them to himself.

My breathing intensified as my heart galloped at the thought of what they would do to me. The quick inhalation of the spices around me or from the bag over my head—I wasn't sure which—turned my stomach. I pressed my head to the wall, trying to ground myself and gain control of my emotions so I could think clearly. And hopefully, not vomit with the bag over my head.

They were going to kill me. What else would they want? I had nothing.

Lost in my morbid thoughts, the time passed, seemingly taking forever, but perhaps only minutes, before the horses slowed down. My captor picked me up by my arms, and I stumbled out. I barely righted myself before I ate the ground.

"No harm is to come of her," the man still in the wagon growled.

"Then show yourselves, cowards!" The language flowed off my tongue as if I had never stopped using it. It was then that I registered they'd been speaking in Italian the entire time. My panicked brain only focused on the meaning rather than the actual words themselves.

The hood was ripped off of me, and I felt like I could finally breathe again. I blinked the hair out of my eyes, my hat nowhere to be found. Probably in the street, however many miles back.

We were just outside of the city, in what seemed to be a large meadow, the long grass swaying as we walked towards a copse of trees. The clouds overhead threatened rain, leaving the air damp and chilly.

A shiver ran through me. No one would find me here. I turned my head, only to find darkness around me and a glimpse of fire between the trees a distance off. *Where the hell was I?*

"So, you do remember?" the man closest to me asked in English. Where he lacked in height, he made up for in width. His arms were like tree trunks, straining against his threaded jacket. Even in the darkness, I could tell his hair and eyes had to be darker than mine. "You desert your people and think it's okay to come back?"

"I'm sorry. Do I know you?" I snapped, anger outweighing my fear after his insult.

The other man grabbed my arm, but I pulled free. "Come with us," he said gently, holding his hand out toward the fire. He was older than the other one and seemed a lot less hot-headed, but I still stared at him in distrust. "We were sent for you. Not to harm you."

"Who are you?"

"Your answers are waiting for you if you just come with us."

"Now I have a choice?" *Where had this sudden burst of bravery come from?* It could have been foolishness, or I possibly had enough of men pushing me around.

I followed them, weaving through the trees, until we came upon a few wagons set up in a circle around the centerfire.

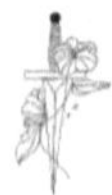

Thomas' fist pounded Rose's door so hard it rattled on its hinges, not caring that it was late. Someone yelled out a window, making him knock louder with a stream of curses out of his mouth.

George threw the door open, rubbing the sleep out of his eyes. "Christ, Tom. Is everything all right?" He stepped to the side to let him in.

"Is Emilia here?" Thomas asked, pushing past George. "She's been gone all day. Ma said she left after breakfast and may have come here."

Truth be told, it wasn't like Emilia to be gone so long, and after dark, no less. She may have been grown, but that woman always found herself in trouble, and Thomas always found himself pulling her out of it. The very thought had his stomach twisted in knots.

"She stopped by earlier," a quiet voice said by the stairs so as not to wake the rest of the house. It was a miracle anyone still slept after he'd almost broke the door down.

"When?" he asked as Shay stepped out of the shadows and into the lantern's light.

"Mid-day when you still hadn't shown up," she said, accusation clear in her tone.

"Christ," Thomas swore, running his hands through his hair. He should have told her where he'd been going. Did she think he wasn't coming back? They had no jobs today, so they were free to do what they wanted, but often found themselves in each other's company. Truth be told, they were never apart much these days. "Where'd she go after?"

"Said she was going to look for you at Michael's."

Thomas exchanged a worried glance with George.

"You don't think he'd—" George began.

"No, he cares for her." That truth struck Thomas hard. Of course, his brother didn't care about many people, but Emilia had wormed her way into his life just as much as his own. "I'll check in with him, thank ye."

"I'll go too," Shay said, already grabbing a shawl to head out.

"Maybe ye should stay."

Shay glared at him. "If my friend is missing, I will not sit on my ass. Michael will know what to do."

Thomas' head snapped back. Since when was his brother more reliable than him? "Will ye be able to keep up?" Thomas said it calmly, not wanting to worry her more than necessary even as his unease grew.

"I ran track all through high school and kept running after. A pregnancy isn't going to slow me down."

Thomas shook his head at the oddities in her speech, and let it go. He was getting used to the strange way the girls spoke, while ignoring the reason behind it.

"I'll keep her here if she comes around," George said as they walked out.

Thomas thanked him and left with Shay. To his surprise, she moved quickly for a woman well into a pregnancy, and they were at Mikey's quicker than expected.

"Get up!" Thomas kicked the side of the bed.

"Feck," Mikey groaned, rolling away from his brother.

"Have you seen Emilia?" At the sound of Shay's voice, Mikey sat up so fast he slammed his head into the bunk above him. He hissed, grabbing his head.

"Feck, woman. Ye could warn a man. What are ye doing here?"

"Emilia," Thomas growled.

"She came by Billy's asking where ye were."

Shay gasped. "She went there?"

"Did anything happen?" Thomas asked, the blood draining from his face even though Mikey didn't seem worried.

"No," Mikey leaned back, looking between them. "I'm guessing ye can't find her?"

"Do you guys think Billy did something to her?" Shay grabbed her belly, reminding them how far along she was.

Mikey stood up, carefully guiding her to sit down. Shay listened, too dazed to protest, but Thomas was all too aware of his brother's actions. There were times like this when he was a completely different man, and Thomas wasn't sure how to go about it. He couldn't quite pinpoint when it had started.

"He wasn't there," Mikey answered. "She wasn't there for long, only met me out front for a moment."

They all stared at each other, varied looks of dread on their faces as the realization sunk in.

Shay grabbed Mikey's arm, leaning into him. "Then, where is she?"

Thomas hung his head. He would have to find a way to send them home before anything else happened to these women. He hadn't looked for her family because it meant she'd be close by before he left. It was purely selfish, but now he knew he'd have to send her away if she was going to stand a chance.

This wasn't her time to live in. There was no more doubt about it.

"Ye said her family went south?" Thomas turned towards his brother.

Mikey stared at his hands, seemingly fascinated by them.

"Michael!" Thomas shouted, earning him a few curses from the men sleeping around them.

"Not precisely," Mikey admitted, avoiding Shay's shocked stare as she drew away from him. "There might be a small band of 'em not too far out of the city."

"Why would you not tell us?" Shay's voice was small, hurt at his betrayal.

Mikey looked at her, his eyebrows drawn down in what looked like guilt. "The truth might be too hard to bear."

CHAPTER TWENTY-NINE

Emilia

At least a dozen horses stood tied to hitching posts a distance off. The scene gave me déjà vu, and I paused, eyes roaming around the camp. Had I been here before? I could have sworn the wagons... I shook my head. I'd have to figure it out later.

A few women cleared plates and cleaned up the remnants of a meal. They stopped what they were doing when they spotted me, more curious than hostile. I must have been an interesting sight—hair tangled from the bag over my head and men's clothes that were disheveled and untucked from the tussle to get me here.

Or was it my complexion that raised a suspicion that I could be one of theirs? A jolt of excitement shot through my veins. Could they have been my people I was looking for? I didn't dare consider they might be my family. Not after I'd spent months in search of them. Besides, Michael said they went south. They could still be a band of the Romani, though. And if they were, they might be able to help us.

I studied them as much as they stared at me. My dark chocolate waves were lighter than theirs, as was my complexion, solidifying my suspicion about the man earlier. I had never been fair, but this group was noticeably foreign, making me wonder—not for the first time—who exactly my biological parents were. The flashes of memory revealed nothing substantial—a sudden smile from a woman, a faint call of my name, being tucked into a hard mattress. The attempts to remember more only left me irritated and with more questions, I couldn't answer.

An older woman, face lined with age and framed by wiry gray hair, looked up and met my gaze, sending a chill through me. There was something unnatural about her stare as the fire danced shadows around her. I had the absurd notion that she could see into my soul.

The soft ripple of beads sung in the night, drawing my attention to a man exiting the door to one of the vardos. *So that was the word that I couldn't place before.* My memories had been coming to me slowly since returning to this time, but this camp seemed to jump-start them. And damn, I wasn't sure I was ready for that.

The man descended the stairs, his face down, so I could only see the peppered grey of his shoulder-length hair. When he looked up, my breath caught, the surprise knocking me back a step.

I'd seen this man before from a much smaller height. The years had been hard on him, wearing lines into his broad face as deep groves framed his mouth. The contrast was so drastic that a long-forgotten memory of him smiling at my mother as she laughed resurfaced unbidden.

"Papá?" The word came out a whisper, but Manfri Moretti jerked back as if I slapped him. His frown deepened.

His eyes never left me as he neared, but mine caught on the rings on his hand as the fire's light reflected off them. He kept the other hand in his pocket, as if he was hiding something. A weapon maybe? Fear prickled along my spine. I'd have to watch him.

"Come ti chiami?" he said harshly, giving me mixed emotions of fright and elatedness at seeing him.

"Emilia Moretti," I answered. "Your daughter." I hadn't responded in Italian, but in Romani, knowing it would be uncommon for an outsider to know the language. I thanked the stars my mind retained that much.

He nodded but didn't come near as he studied me, probably wondering why I had on men's clothing. I tried to ignore the relief mixed with the pain that his distance inflicted. Just because I vaguely remembered him didn't mean I trusted him.

"I'm sure you're wondering why I'm here and dressed like this," I said, looking down at my trousers and jacket.

"We've been keeping an eye on you."

"You have?" I didn't bother trying to hide the shock and betrayal on my face. "Did you know I'd been looking for you?"

He gestured for me to sit on one of the tree stumps by the fire. "Why don't we have a seat?"

I looked around, not having noticed the disappearance of the others. The only thing between us now was the crackle of the fire, growing seemingly louder with each second he kept quiet.

"Why didn't you come to me?" I finally broke the silence.

"You were supposed to be gone." He leaned forward in his seat, spreading his hands out. Except one of them was missing, sliced clean off. Never one to be squeamish, it came as a shock when I had to swallow back bile. I averted my eyes, concentrating on the fire rather than the memory that threatened to surface. "It was so hard to let you go that I didn't want to believe you came back to us. To this."

I straightened, shoulders suddenly tense from the stress of the day. "It wasn't on purpose," I admitted. "But I think I was always meant to come back."

He stared into the fire, letting the meaning behind my words sink in. "Was it worth it?" he asked it quietly in English. I wasn't sure why he switched or if the others—wherever they were—could understand it. "Did you have a good life?"

I thought of my parents, who had adopted me, and my brother, singing in the pub and learning their family history. Then I thought of Shay and how I couldn't have done any of this without her. Hell, I couldn't have done high school without her. And everything I had learned in the twenty-first century and how it shaped me into the woman I was today. How I may have never met Thomas...

I smiled. "Yeah, it was great, actually."

His head bobbed in relief, but he didn't return the smile.

My throat tightened, and I had to force the next words out of my mouth. "Why'd you send me away?"

He tilted his head, dark eyes narrowing. "You don't remember?"

I shook my head.

"Your mother was found."

"Found?" An uneasiness weighed on me. Yet, somehow, I knew this memory was what repressed all the others.

"By her master," he said slowly as if I had forgotten something important.

My brows scrunched in confusion. "Master? What do you mean?"

He sighed, running his hand through his hair. "Before you were born, before she met me, your mother was owned and raised on a sugar plantation in Louisiana."

My pulse quickened, my heart understanding what my brain refused to admit. "She was a slave?" How was that possible? "But she wasn't—I mean. Our people are slaves?"

"Sì, figlia. The Roma have been for many centuries. Though there are not as many in this country, a number still remain enslaved, especially across seas. Your mother's people were shipped from Spain and sold in the new territory. A few generations later, her grandmother was sold to a French man when France ruled the territory. Though it was later sold to the States, your mother's family were kept on as their property."

I rocked at the revelation. God, I was so unprepared for this century. I knew basically nothing of my people other than Hollywood's misconstrued representation. History had taught us that Africans were enslaved. That was obvious. But I learned nothing about Gypsies and not enough about other races who would be considered "of color."

"Your mother could speak Romani, French, and Spanish, the latter two commonly spoken there. When she ran, she refused to speak either. So I made sure you heard nothing but Italian from me, and Romani from your mother. It does me good to hear you can still speak our language." His eyes softened.

"The women in your mother's family were kept as house servants," he explained, "away from the men in the field, for they were very beautiful, your mother especially so. When she finally had enough of him—" He stopped, looking at his stump that he rested in his other hand. "When she wouldn't let him touch her anymore, he beat her badly. Nearly died. When she healed, the other women helped her escape. She made it as far as the coast, and when she could get no farther, she searched for her people."

"And she found you." His words—the reality of it—I could barely breathe.

He nodded, head hanging low. "She found me." What should have been a happy admission was filled with nothing but grief. "It had been four years, but her *master*—" He spit the word out as if it left a bitter taste on his tongue "—finally found my Clementina in this city."

He said her name like a caress that had been withheld for too long. My chest constricted, thinking of what it would be like to have someone you loved taken away or killed. My thoughts instantly went to Thomas. I couldn't let myself consider what that meant.

"Her master searched for her for four years?" I asked.

He looked up, pain sketched into the lines of his face. "She was very beautiful. He didn't want to let her go. Had some delusion that he loved her, or maybe he just wanted to keep her as his pet. A possession that was stolen from him." He shrugged. "Her fate was the same."

My body froze as a long-forgotten scream echoed within my head. Shouts of despair, sickening curses. My smaller body trembled, the fear rolling through my stomach as the panic seized me. The same fear threatened to overwhelm me now, pebbling my skin.

"I was there." My words came out shaky. "When he took her."

He sighed, his chest heaving from emotion. "You were there when he killed her."

The whip flashed across my mother's back and then around her neck, hauling her like an animal. I covered my face as if I could hide from the images bombarding me. Her legs thrashed as she desperately tried to pull it from her neck, brown eyes wide in panic.

My father had reached for her, but a sword had come down, severing his hand. We were alone. They must have waited until we left our camp, and Papá only had enough strength to get me out of there.

"Andare!" Mammina screamed, urging Papá to do what must be done. *Go!*

It was either go after Mammina and die—leaving me at the mercy of the men—or run. It was an impossible decision, torn between saving one of the two girls he loved the most, but one that had to be made immediately.

Grabbing me with a shaking arm, Papá shoved me onto a horse, and we rode away. The last sight of my mother was her hair—several shades lighter than my own—illuminated by the building fire behind her as her dress was torn from her body. My father shielded my eyes before I could see her burn. I remembered wondering if she was a witch. That must have been why they'd done it. But surely there were rules for burning good witches. Maybe they would see that they were wrong and leave her be. God, I was so young. So naïve.

Maybe she *was* a witch, I mused. I rubbed my face, wishing I could scrape all the horror out of my head. Why did I ever want to remember?

The memories nauseated me. How did I go from naively believing her a good witch with the hope of her surviving to repressing it all together? And for so long. So many years that I could have done something. Had anyone ever punished him for his crimes? Or did he just get away with it because she was his *property*? I spit. Just the thought of the word left a sour taste on my tongue.

I didn't realize my face was wet with my tears until I looked up, my chest burning with fury. "If he wanted her so bad, why did he kill her?"

Papá looked at me sadly, rubbing his stump absently.

My throat tightened, pressure building inside me as understanding bloomed. "No," I said, standing up and backing away. "No, it can't be."

"You were only a child. You were not to blame."

"How can you say that?" I yelled louder than I intended, running my hands through my hair. "She would be alive if it weren't for me."

"No, that was on your mammina and I. I should have taken her to Europe. Canada. Somewhere he couldn't find her. You were just a creation of our love. She wouldn't want to hear you talk this way. It's on *him*. He saw her as his. As his property. And by law, you as well. He was a jealous man. Not only did I take your mother from him, but I ruined her by helping create you. I believe he considered that his right. Or the very least, he saw me as keeping an extension of his property. And if he got his hands on you..."

I stopped pacing, staring at him as my stomach turned. That man would have used me as much as my mother. An untarnished possession that could replace the tainted. I would have been his. Maybe I still was.

"What's his name?" I asked.

"It does not matter."

"The fuck it doesn't! Could he find me? Will he try to take me back?"

"You weren't supposed to come back. When I heard of a young woman in the city asking for us, I had to look into it..."

"You knew I was here the whole time?"

"I had to make sure it was you. It has been a while, figlia." When I didn't respond, he sat up straighter, resolved. "Now that you are, I wish I'd been able to teach you our ways," he paused, dark eyes boring into me. "Then again, maybe it's best this way."

"I want to know," I said, hearing the desperation in my voice. "How is it even possible? The time travel, I mean. Can we do anything else?"

"We can do many things." Guilt crossed his face. "There is not enough time, though."

"Was Mammina a witch?" I asked.

"No."

I took a deep breath. "What about Nonna?"

His eyes bore into me, making me uneasy. "She left something for you."

"But she was the one who sent me away."

He sighed, looking resigned. "She knew what was to come, though she kept it from me. She only told me of it when she was too weak to go on." He stood up and gave me his hand. "Come."

He held the beads open as I entered the vardo he had exited earlier, a horse skull hanging off the side. When I asked the significance, he told me it was to ward off the supernatural. A shiver ran down my spine.

Inside, the vardo had more room than I expected, with a bed along one of the sides, a small table with a couple of chairs in the corner, and enough room to store food and a place to cook—pots and pans hanging from the ceiling.

My Papá—it was hard to believe he was standing before me—pulled out a trunk from under the bed. While he searched in it, I asked, "Why are you still here? Why haven't you moved on?"

He sat back on his heels, staring into the trunk. "I had left for some time." He avoided my gaze, making me wonder what he was hiding. "It was your Nonna who told me I should head back."

"How could you let me struggle all these months, Papá?" I asked, my voice heavy with emotion. "I could have been hurt. Maybe even killed once."

He stood up, a small wooden box in his hand. "You are strong, even when you think otherwise. But I wouldn't have let anything happen to you, figlia."

The way he said it nagged me. "But something almost did happen to me."

His brown eyes found mine unblinking. "Danior made sure they didn't hurt you."

My cheeks reddened when I realized he knew. "Is he one of the men that brought me here tonight?" I was mortified that one of them had seen me in such a vulnerable state.

"Sì. The younger one."

"You—" I swallowed, "you weren't there, were you?"

"No, I've had Danior follow you since I heard you were asking around. When I suspected you were my daughter, I ordered him to protect you as well."

"Does he work for you or something?"

"Or something..." He hesitated. "He is my son."

"Your..." I looked around, for what I wasn't sure. I had a half-brother? "But he can't be much younger than me."

He nodded, staring at the box as if he wanted to crawl inside it. "This life is difficult, figlia. It's not meant to be done alone, and when I had lost both your mother and then you... I found another wife."

My breaths came quick, almost hyperventilating. Of course, I couldn't blame him for needing someone else, but it felt like he tossed me aside and then moved on. "Did you ever miss me? Me and Mammina?"

"Every day. Every second."

The sincerity was palpable enough for me to push past the sense of betrayal. I could think it through later. I pointed to the box and asked what was in it.

He gestured for me to sit in one of the chairs and pushed the box toward me. I flicked open the tiny clasp and lifted the mahogany lid, marveling at the beautiful craftsmanship. I almost gasped, my heart jolting in my chest at what was inside.

Five small vials reflected the light of the lantern. I lifted one with shaking fingers, examining the powdery contents, careful not to uncork it.

"What's inside?"

"Surely you recognize them."

"Sì, Papá," I said a little impatiently. "I meant specifically, what is it?"

"Crushed bone of our chovihanis."

"Our *what*?"

"Our healers—those who possess more power than the rest of us. Using the magic in their bones with the stones—our talismans—allows one to travel through time. There are very few strong enough to make them. That is why we do not walk through time as we once did."

"Stones—" I stopped when it dawned on me. I knew I needed my rosary, but I didn't realize the two blue stones inlaid between the beads enabled the powder.

He nodded, noticing my recognition. "The sapphire to break down the barriers of the mind that keep us in one plain of time, and the aquamarine for the journey."

My fist squeezed around the rosary in my pocket, my fingers trailing over the smooth edges of the stones. Pushing past my nausea about the bones, I had to ask, "This isn't Nonna is it?" I put the vial down gently, though I wanted to drop it.

"No." He sighed. "They were passed down in your Mammina's family. Her master—" He turned his face and spit his disgust "—overheard talk about them and began scouring the plantation. That's when she grabbed them and took them with her, knowing they would be weapons in the wrong hands. They are scarce, as are the talismans." He scratched the bridge of his nose with one of his fingers. "It is almost unheard of for one to possess both in a lifetime. But your Mammina's family felt it was their mission to protect them.'

'They were created in black magic, figlia. And very dangerous. When your Mammina—when she passed, I protected the vials. It was your Nonna who wanted to make sure you had them."

"Why? Why me? Why not just ship me overseas or something?"

"That truth died with her," he said gravely. "But she knew you were meant for something more than this." He gestured at the world around us. "She said you would know what to do with them when the time came."

I shut the box lid and held it in my lap as if it were about to explode. What could I possibly do other than go back to the twenty-first century?

"Your Nonna didn't always give all the answers," he explained as if he had read my mind. "A trait that comes from knowing too much. Information in the wrong hands could offset the original timeline. She knew you had to jump in time to get where you are in this instant. Without it, we don't know where you'd be today. It could be meeting someone or changing someone's life. I do not have the answers. All I know is that you are on the right road, with your destiny in your hands."

I squinted at the box, trying to make it give me the answers. It all seemed rather extravagant for a simple girl like me. I wasn't destined for anything—just a city girl who liked to sing. I was never going to go big or save lives. I was completely ordinary in every way. But I finally knew my family didn't abandon me, as I suspected. They saved me. And I wasn't sure how to process that or change the years of trust issues due to it.

"If this is my destiny," I said, looking at him. "Then why would she give me these to go back? Why send me forward to only have me come back and leave again?"

He studied my face while he rested his elbows on his knees. "There must be something that is connected between these two times." A long pause as his dark eyes scoured my face. "Or someone. Tell me, have you met anyone who is tied to your other life?"

I began to shake my head, thinking it was absurd. And then I stilled. No. That would—that would be insane. He must have read the realization on my face because he began to give me a sad smile.

"Then maybe they are your destiny."

I swallowed, my throat suddenly tight. What did Thomas have to do with anything? From what I knew—and it wasn't much—he eventually opened the pub with Michael. I didn't even know if he was ever married, though now I desperately wished I'd done some digging. Just the thought had my blood boiling. "Did Nonna say anything else?"

Papá stood up, face clearly worn from our conversation and the years between us. "Only to follow your heart. She said you often let your mind get in the way of what your heart is telling you. That and those—" He pointed to the box "—come at a great sacrifice. You will know what to do when the time comes."

"She didn't say what, when, or why?"

At that, he smiled and shook his head. "No, figlia. That is for you to figure out on your own. It is a great gift you've been given. Come now." He turned towards the open door. "It is late, and you should be heading back."

I ran my fingers through the beads as I exited the vardo, finding at least eight pairs of eyes on me. The women had returned to the camp, and I searched their faces for the one my Papá had married. When he stood by one—a middle-aged woman, tall, thin, clearly beautiful with her dark hair tied up in an intricate braid—and put his arm around her shoulders, I knew.

"Emilia, this is Bina. Bina, this is my daughter."

"Nice to meet you," I said, smiling though she didn't return it. She was too busy eyeing my pants and shirt with disgust. "You guys didn't have to leave because of me..."

"They went to the creek to wash the dishes," my Papá explained. "It is our way."

"But she wouldn't know that, would she?" Danior sneered.

I looked at him, startled by his hostility. "What is your problem with me?"

"You are a Gorger."

Not familiar with the word, I gave a questioning glance at my father.

"You are not a Romani," Papá explained. "Danior believes you have been gone too long to be one of us."

That stung. I took a step back. "Do you think that as well?" I asked my father, noticing how his wife's eyes flashed whenever she looked at me.

"No, figlia." His face was sad, but his voice was steady as he said, "I'd like you to come with us."

That had me rocking back on my heels. "You aren't staying?"

"No, we will be gone by the morrow."

The suddenness left a weight on my chest, making it hard to breathe. "Papá." My voice broke.

I glanced at the camp, watching how the men and women sat around the fire. I had a distant memory of a camp like this one, one full of laughter and dancing, not this somber scene before me.

"Will you go with us, figlia?"

My eyes returned to my papá, but it was another's face that I saw. Even as my stomach twisted, I knew the path I was about to take was the right one.

And it sure as hell would be the hardest goddamn thing I've ever done.

CHAPTER THIRTY

Thomas

I t had started drizzling hours ago, thoroughly soaking Thomas until he was nothing but a miserable shell. Mikey took Shay home in the middle of the night when he noticed she was starting to have some pain in her abdomen, but Thomas refused to stop looking. He trudged through the puddles, looked into the saloons, and went to wherever she might be. Gone without a trace. Thomas's stomach twisted with worry.

Thomas spotted Hiram down the street, his head down against the rain as he came from the direction of the docks. It was Sunday, so he must have come for Evaline or Shay; it was hard to tell which these days. Shay had started going to his church a few weeks back, so maybe the whole group was going.

"What are you doing here?" Hiram asked, surprised.

"Emilia's missing," Thomas informed him, rubbing the rain off his face. "We've been looking for her all night."

The dull sky unleashed a downpour that propelled them towards the warm confines of the bakery so quickly that Thomas didn't bother to stop and look at the unfamiliar horse tied up outside. Removing his cap, he shook his hair, sending tiny droplets everywhere while his eyes adjusted to the soft glow of the lantern. He paused, his chest loosening with relief before galloping at full speed at the sight of Emilia sitting at the table.

"For heaven's sake!" Rose exclaimed, rushing to them before he could move toward Emilia. "Give me your jackets, boys. Are you trying to kill yourself? C'mere." Rose fetched each a rag to dry off with and hung their jackets by the fire. "You'll be catchin' the cough if you're not careful."

"Aye, ma'am," Thomas mumbled, still staring at Emilia. She hadn't looked up from the small box on the table as if she hadn't even heard them come in.

Shay came to him instead. "She's been like this since she got here an hour ago," she said worriedly.

Thomas licked his lips, his mouth suddenly dry. "She say where she's been?"

Shay shook her head. "Maybe you can get something out of her."

Thomas squatted by Emilia so he could see her face. A pressure built inside him at the sight of her turmoil. Heaven help him if someone hurt her... "What happened, lass?"

She hung her head back and closed her eyes as they stared at her silently. Thomas shifted uncomfortably onto one knee and spied the bottle of whiskey on the table, and his relief at finding her faded quickly to concern again.

Just when he thought she wouldn't respond, she began talking. "Your voice is amazing. Did you know that?" Why did she sound so damned unhappy?

"Ye are the one who can sing, lass," he said offhandedly. She was slurring her words so much that he leveled the other two women with a sharp glare. "Who gave this to her?" he snapped.

Shay shrugged, shaking her head, eyes round as globes.

"She had it when I came down," Rose admitted. "George went to meet the boys before service—"

"I got it myself," Emilia said, turning her russet eyes to him. "Don't yell at them. I deserve it after the night I had." She squinted at him as she leaned closer. "C'mon, say something to me."

Thomas pulled back, hit by the strong scent of the whiskey. "Ye are drunk, lass." He took another look at the bottle and started. It was the same as the one they drank out of a few weeks back. Biddy must have sequestered Emilia away at some point in the night.

Emilia frowned. "That's not what I wanted to hear."

"What do ye want me to say? Are ye going to tell me what happened?"

"Fine, don't make me feel better."

To Thomas's dismay, her eyes swelled up with tears that began to fall. He reached up, swiping them away with his thumbs, and sighed. "Ye like me voice?" he asked, wanting to ease her pain even if it meant no answers.

She nodded, leaning into his touch. Thomas was vaguely aware of the two other women going upstairs to give them some privacy. Hiram followed them up, probably in search of Evaline.

He grabbed Emilia's chair and turned it towards him, making her gasp.

"What are you—"

He stood up and dragged a chair in front of her. "I can't kneel like that any longer." He sat, staring at his hands in thought. "Me voice wasn't always like this."

"What do you mean?" She hiccupped, covering her mouth. Thomas gave a sad smile, unable to deny how cute she was.

"I doubt ye would be able to understand me if ye heard it coming off the ship. The accent faded over the years."

"It gives me the tingles," she admitted, turning an extraordinary shade of red. To his surprise, heat replaced the tears in her eyes.

Thomas stared at her beautiful face, memorizing every freckle as his mind went to war with itself. A quick battle that his mind lost. He leaned in and cupped her face with his hands, pulling her gently toward him. Her breath caught as her eyes fixed on his mouth. He leaned in slowly and pressed his lips to hers, feather-soft, savoring the sensation. He had never enjoyed kissing a woman so much.

Emilia grabbed his jacket, pulling him closer as her kiss became more frantic. She ran her hands through his wet hair and climbed onto his lap, making him growl as he slid his hands up her back and deepened the kiss.

"Tell me you want me," she said, her lips still on his.

"Oh, I want ye, gypsy," he admitted, pulling her closer so that every inch of them was touching. "Ye don't know how badly. From the moment I saw ye singing on the street there."

She stilled for a moment, processing his words, before kissing him roughly. "Tell me I belong here," she whispered, body rigid as she rested her forehead against his. "That I made the right decision."

"What?" he asked, pulling back to look at her face, but she caught his lip between her teeth and sucked it into her mouth. He moaned even as he pulled free.

Had she noticed he'd been keeping her at a distance? She must have; the lass was no fool. If it affected her like this, though, he wasn't sure he did the right thing. Or maybe he didn't pull back hard enough.

"What are ye doing?" he growled, grabbing her arms.

"What does it look like?" she smiled and started unbuttoning his shirt.

"It looks like ye had too much to drink."

"I know exactly what I'm doing," she reassured him and ran her hands over his chest, making him shiver. "I'm not letting you push me away anymore. I choose this. I choose you."

"Stop," he said gruffly, stilling her hands as her words wrecked him. "Ye can't be serious. Ye know this won't work." He gave her a pointed look that had her flushing in anger. "I won't do this with ye now. What happened?"

Emilia sat back, hurt, scrunching up her features. She looked to the side, hiding her tears. "It will all be for nothing." Emilia turned all her anger back to him, pushing his chest. "You'll do it with any other whore. Why not me?"

His mouth hung open while he tried to find the right words, but he couldn't say them fast enough. Emilia pushed him again, propelling herself to stand up this time and walk away.

"Where ye going?" he growled, prowling after her.

"I'm leaving," she hissed, shoving her hair into her cap so fiercely that strands fell down.

"The hell ye are. Talk to me."

Emilia glared at him and stomped to the door. Thomas grabbed her arm, pulling her back. A sharp crack filled the room as the sting from the slap landed across his cheek.

"What the feck are ye doing?" Thomas yelled, grabbing her arms and shaking her until her cap fell off, her loose waves cascading around her shoulders again. "Why don't I want ye? Of course, I want ye! If ye were any other slag I'd take ye up against the wall, right here, right now." He pushed her against the wall, pinning her to it while he pulled her head back by the hair. Emilia's eyes widened, finally some sobriety in them. He ran his lips up her neck as his hand squeezed her breast, making a whimper escape her lips. "Don't provoke me, lass," he growled. His mouth found hers, ravaging her with his tongue like she wanted. He wished he was kissing her like it would be the last, but this kiss was meant to be all-consuming, desperate, punishing. If she wanted to be treated like a whore, he could make her his own personal one. Show her just how much he wanted her beautiful, full body.

He pulled back and knew she must have seen the anger in his face if the tension across her features was any indication. "The only reason I haven't is that ye mean more to me than any other woman. None of them matter!" He screamed it, throwing his hands up in the air in frustration, making her flinch with the sudden movement. "Because your first time should be special, with a man that ye marry. Not some Irish trash that isn't going anywhere. Ye deserve the world, Emilia! I can see it. They can see it!" He pointed to the stairs, knowing all three had come down when they heard the yelling. "Why don't ye, goddammit?"

"I don't know," she mumbled with an odd mix of perplexity and triumph on her face, which completely dumbfounded him. "You keep pushing me away," she went on. "I thought—"

Thomas growled, throwing the nearest chair across the room, making all of the women jump. He ran his hands through his hair and kept them there, not trusting himself to lower them or else he'd break something.

A breeze blew through the open door, sweeping Mikey in with it like an avenging angel. Thomas glared at his brother and his annoying habit of showing up at the wrong time.

"Why the feck are ye yelling?" Mikey asked, scanning the room. He raised an eyebrow when he spotted the chair.

"Not now," Thomas growled. "Why are ye even back here?"

"I couldn't sleep," Mikey said, eyes darting to the women on the stairs so quickly Thomas almost didn't see it. Mikey must have cared for Emilia more than he had realized to come in at this hour. In fact, for him to come at all was utterly bewildering. Either that or another reason brought him in...

Mikey let out a low whistle and put his hands in his pockets, cutting off Thomas's train of thought as he strolled over to Emilia. He didn't hide his perusal of her physical and mental state. "He's going to bloody war, lass. I'm sure ye can write love letters and all that. Nothing to fret about."

Emilia looked at Mikey like he was an absolute gobshite. If Thomas wasn't so angry, he would've laughed. And then the realization hit him, feeling the dread pool in his stomach. Emilia must know that he already enlisted.

"Why is your shirt open?" Mikey eyed Thomas' chest, pulling him out of his thoughts. Mikey's eyes widened, and he gave a devilish grin. "What have ye two been up to?" He crossed his arms, waiting.

Thomas growled. "Get out."

"Oh no, deartháir daor." He picked up the chair Thomas had thrown and straddled it. "I think I'm rather enjoying this."

"You don't belong here." Hiram snapped at Mikey.

"That's rich coming from ye," Mikey said with equal vehemence, pointing his chin in Shay's direction. "Tell me, where have ye gone after finding out about the baby growing inside her?"

Shay paled at Mikey's almost flippant remark.

Hiram jerked back as if Michael had struck him. "I never left," his voice rumbled dangerously. "I was just with her yesterday, matter of fact. Tell me, what have you done for her? She wouldn't be in this mess if it weren't for men like you!"

"Men like me?" Mikey stood up and took a step forward. "Tell me, what is a man like me?"

Thomas glanced at Emilia, wondering how they got here and began buttoning up his shirt while they were all distracted.

"Bigoted bastard." Hiram went nose to nose with Mikey, neither of them backing down. "A selfish, depraved prick who has done nothing but carry out unspeakable acts for his own betterment. You've never loved anyone other than yourself. And you sure as hell wouldn't know how to fight for anything other than your own gain. At least your brother fights for what is right. For a cause that goes beyond him. And has *respect* for those around him. You shouldn't even be in the same room as her!"

Though his face was pale, Mikey sneered. "At least I can look at her rounding belly and not go green in gills."

"Enough!" Thomas's voice boomed, causing the whole room to fall silent. "Do ye not see what ye are doing?"

It took a minute for the men to retreat, but they shut up at the sight of Shay's pale face.

"Ya'll are idiots." Emilia wobbled a little bit and caught Thomas' arm for balance. "Neither of you deserve her, and Rose should throw you both out. Go on," she said to Rose. "Get rid of 'em!"

Shay rolled her eyes in exasperation, but Rose straightened her shoulders, her round face set in resolve. She gave Emilia a disapproving look. "First, mind your place, child. I will turn out whoever I need to, but I didn't fight for a place of my own for another white woman to tell me what I should do."

"I didn't—" Emilia stopped, shriveling under the woman's glare, and seemed to change course. "Right, sorry, ma'am."

Rose let out a big sigh, her ample chest swelling with her subsequent reprimand. "Now, you boys get on out of here," she snapped. "I'm not going to have you talk about Ms. Shay like that."

Mikey took a step towards Shay, hesitating to go to her side. "I didn't mean to upset ye..." he said to her. Thomas rocked back on his heels. That was the closest to an apology he'd ever heard from his brother.

Hiram snorted. "That's because you don't give a shit."

"Stop!" Shay barked, and to Thomas' astonishment they shut up. "I don't know what is wrong with you two, other than you need to get over hating each other. I'm done with it. Hate each other all you want, but leave me out of it."

"Why's everyone yelling?" A soft voice floated down the stairs.

Shay turned around quickly, scooping up the little girl into a hug. Mira had come down with her, hands balled into fists as she took in the situation.

"I'm sorry, sweetie," Shay said to Evaline. "Were we being too loud?"

Evaline nodded and stared at everyone. Then, "Uncle Tommy!" she squealed, squirming out of Shay's arms to run to him.

"Good morning, mo stoirín," he said, while picking her up.

Her big brown eyes looked up at him, melting his heart a little more. There was no doubt that every time he saw her, he was reminded that saving her was the best thing he'd ever done. He looked over at Emilia. One of the best things, he corrected.

"Are you coming to church with us?" she asked, wiggling down again. "Why are your clothes so wet?"

"Nay, lassie. Ye know I go to a different service."

"We should be going," Rose said, grabbing everything she needed. "C'mon, Eva. Why don't you go out with Mira and Hiram, hm?"

Evaline frowned. "But I want to stay with everyone."

Mira skirted around Shay and descended the rest of the stairs. She went to grab Hiram's arm, but Hiram was already sweeping Evaline up, making her squeal and giggle as he carried her out of the room.

Mira shoved her hat on her head, tying it angrily as she turned to Shay. "You've caused nothing but trouble since you arrived. Why don't you just leave?"

"Mira!" Rose said, slapping her hand down on the counter. "How dare you—"

"It's true, Mama! And I'm sick of it." Mira straightened, the top of her head barely reaching Shay's chin, but her shoulders were back, resolute, her hands clasped in front of her. "You told her she could stay until she was well. Well, she's fine now, Mama."

"I didn't know you felt this way," Shay said, looking at Rose. "I'm sorry if I over stayed—"

"Nonsense," Mikey said, sneering at Mira. "Our wee lass here has her eyes on a particular man, and ye are in the way."

Mira blushed, darkening her umber skin all the way down her neck, sputtering her denial.

"Is this true?" Rose asked her daughter.

"We're going to be late," Mira said, beginning to fidget.

Shay went to her, grabbing Mira's hands, surprising her still. "You have nothing to worry about. Hiram and I are just friends." Shay met Mikey's eyes, something passing between them. "If you have feelings for him, you need to tell him. I won't get in your way."

Mikey's hands balled into fists, his knuckles turning white as every muscle in his body tensed.

Mira slowly pulled her hands free and backed away.

"Mira?" Rose snapped. "Why haven't you mentioned this before?"

Mira wouldn't look up, but she was clearly trying to hold back tears.

"Can we talk about this later, Mama?" Her heels softly clicked away before her mother could respond.

Rose watched her daughter leave as if she didn't recognize her. After a few quiet moments, she turned towards Shay. "Are you coming, honey?"

Shay shook her head. "Tell Hiram I will see him tomorrow." She glanced at Emilia out of the corner of her eye. "I think I have some things to figure out today."

Rose nodded, a look of understanding on her face. "You can stay as long as you need. I will talk to my daughter."

Shay smiled sadly. "Thank you so much. For everything. I mean it."

"And as for you, girl," Rose said to Emilia. "I don't know what happened last night, but you need to get your head on straight."

"Yes, ma'am," Emilia muttered.

Rose took in Emilia's sad state and softened a bit. "Don't look so down, dear. You'll figure it out."

She patted Emilia's arm, then turned her glare at Mikey before leaving.

"Lovely, woman." Mikey rolled his shoulders, unphased by the hostility. "I think I'm growing on her."

Shay scoffed, giving him a disbelieving glare.

"Jealous?" He smiled unexpectedly, and Shay's glower fell, seemingly at a loss for words.

Thomas tried to ignore the shock of his brother flirting with a colored woman. It was so unlike Mikey that Thomas worried about his intentions. But that was an entirely different conversation they would need to have later.

Thomas pulled Emilia to him, ignoring his brother. "Don't think ye are getting out of telling me where ye were all night, gypsy."

Emilia tried to pull away, not meeting his eyes.

Thomas held on tighter. "Tell me what is bothering ye, lass. That I enlisted?"

"I always knew you were going to enlist." Emilia sighed, rubbing her eyes. "It's not that. Though it was how I started the day. Looking for you."

"I'm sorry," he said. When she didn't respond, he hesitated, waiting a moment before he squeezed her into a hug and rested his chin on her head. He couldn't remember the last time he'd been gentle with someone, it wasn't in his nature, and yet, holding Emilia like this, tucked against his body, it was like he'd been doing it his whole life. It felt natural as breathing. Emilia was familiar in a way that no other woman had been. "I should have told ye. I just knew if I told ye before, I wouldn't be able to make myself sign those papers."

She rested her cheek on his chest and took a shuddering breath. "It's not that. But I have to ask—" she said it quietly so the others couldn't hear and turned her dark eyes up to search his. "Did you mean all those things? You—" she paused, and he brought up his hand to lightly pull her bottom lip down, releasing it from her teeth while forgetting about everyone else in the room. "You don't really think about yourself like that, do you?"

Thomas was entranced by her, eyes staring up at him adoringly. His heart swelled with an unfamiliar feeling that left him uncomfortable. She couldn't look at him like that. He couldn't feel like *this*. It went against everything he was working toward. "It's the truth. I'm no good."

"But you are good!" She squeezed his abdomen with purpose. "Thomas, you are one of the best men I know. You fight for others. Always put yourself last. You love your family. You saved me in ways that you could not even understand. Your people may not have a lot in this city, but I've come to love them as much as my family. They're so resilient, strong, and bull-headed. Just like you. How do you not see that?"

He just shook his head. "I have done unimaginable things, lass. If ye knew half of them, ye would never look at me again."

"Nothing could make me love you less, Thomas."

She said it easily, as if she had known it all along. As if it the words had been an extension of them both, entangling her so much with Thomas that he knew there was no going back. It took her a moment to realize what she'd admitted. Emilia's face paled and she let go of Thomas, taking a step back. The loss of her in his arms doused the flame of pleasure that flared from her words.

"I'm sorry," she said, looking at the floor. "I shouldn't have said that."

Thomas rubbed the back of his head, suddenly self-conscious in front of the others. Was he nervous? Thomas hadn't been feckin' nervous since he was a damn lad. And yet, right here, right now, he couldn't deny it. His nerves coiled tight in his belly like snakes.

"Well, don't keep us in suspense, Tommy boy," Mikey mumbled, breaking the silence.

Thomas stared at Emilia in her ridiculous clothes, baggy shirt, and pants to hide her curves. Her hair was still messy from shoving it in a hat for days, cheeks flushed from the alcohol.

He never saw a woman more beautiful.

"Did ye mean it?" he asked.

"Well…" she paused, looking worriedly at Shay, and fidgeted on her feet. "Yes, I meant it."

Thomas nodded, taking two significant steps to get to her. "I tried not to," he said, cupping her face. "Me whole life, I had no problem turning a woman away. Forgetting them. Ye have plagued me since I met ye. Entrapped me with your singing. Snared me so many times I lost count."

"I—"

Thomas put a finger to her mouth. "There is no choice in this for me. Whether ye entrapped me or from my own heart's betrayal." He bent down to whisper in her ear. "I didn't know what love was until I met ye. Ye are every definition of the word, and I know just why no other made me risk it all." His thumbs traced her cheekbones and spread out around her face. She tilted into his hold. "They weren't ye. I've been waiting for ye, Emilia Moretti, without even knowing it. I love ye more than life itself."

She squirmed with the sensation, either reacting to what he said or from the tickle of his breath. Either way, it made him smile as he snaked an arm around her waist, pulling her in.

"You mean it?" Emilia asked, blinking up at him.

"Lord knows I tried not to. Ye're a damned infuriating siren if I ever met one."

Thomas wound one hand into her thick hair and tilted her chin up with the other. Then, as soft as a whisper, he pressed his lips against her silky ones. Fire burst through his body, consuming him. It took everything he had not to carry her away somewhere they could be alone. It didn't help his resolve that Emilia latched onto him as if she feared he'd vanish, pressing all her sweet curves—

"Are ye gonna give us a show?" Mikey asked.

Their bubble burst, and they pulled apart, remembering they had an audience. Shay was nearly bouncing on her toes in glee.

"Don't," Emilia said, giving her a mock glare but unable to hide her smile.

"I'm glad you guys sorted that out." Shay swayed with barely controlled excitement.

Mikey snorted. "Not that I don't love all this romantic..." He waved his hand and looked at them dubiously, "shite, are ye going to tell us where ye've been? Or do ye expect us to stay up all night looking for your arse without an explanation?"

A heavy blanket fell over the room, reminding them what had brought them there in the first place.

CHAPTER THIRTY-ONE

Thomas

Emilia paled as the night's troubles came crashing down on her again, and Thomas glared at his brother. Mikey only shrugged, never one to beat around the bush.

"We were really worried about you," Shay said, coming to Emilia.

"I'm so sorry you guys were looking for me," Emilia said, looking as if she wanted to sink into the ground. "It wasn't my intention; it was actually entirely against my will until I knew what was happening." She looked at the small box on the table and sighed. "I guess I should tell you guys about this then." She pushed the box towards Shay with shaking fingers. "I don't trust myself to pick it up right now."

Shay lifted the lid and gasped, placing her hands over her mouth. Thomas leaned in, finding five glass vials filled with—

"What is it?" he asked, lifting one of them in front of the lantern. The contents were too light to be dirt and too inconsistent to be sand.

Emilia sighed. "The ashes of my people, apparently." Her voice was flat, causing him and Michael to laugh until they saw how serious she was.

"What the feck?" Mikey blurted.

"Ew!" Shay squealed, stepping back. "That was on my face?" She looked like she might vomit. Thomas kept an eye on her so he could move out of the way in case she did.

"Yes," Emilia gave a reluctant smile and explained how it worked.

Shay's eyebrows drew down. "But how did you find out all of this?"

To Thomas' surprise, Emilia's eyes began to fill with tears again. Whatever she had gone through really did a number on her. "They left," she said, bowing her head.

"Who left?" Thomas asked, rubbing her back.

"My papá." Tears cascaded down her face now. Thomas's jaw tightened, feeling helpless. "They found me yesterday. Well, I guess they knew I was here for a while. I—" She swallowed, stealing herself for whatever she was about to tell them. "They left today. I chose to stay behind."

Shay sat down, holding onto the small box tightly. "I don't understand, Mill."

Thomas stared at Emilia, his chest constricting as he realized what she was saying. What she may be admitting. Had she refused her family for him? That couldn't be it. Why would she want to give up her family for a man like him? He had nothing to his name. Nothing he could offer her. It had to be for Shay. But that didn't explain her reactions when she saw him. It was as if she was pushing him... Thomas's hands balled into fists. She'd been forcing him to acknowledge their connection. To fight for it.

"My family had been in town. They asked me to go with them." Her dark eyes found him, and his whole body jolted by the silent admission.

As if in a daze, Thomas sat with them around the table as Emilia recounted the night's events. With each word she spoke, his heart pumped faster, realizing how much she had given up. For him. But that wasn't entirely true. He looked at Shay, the tightness in her features, and how this was affecting her. Emilia had chosen not only him, but also those she had grown close with. Those who had chosen *her*.

And what completely confounded him was how during some of it, Emilia fell into speaking Italian without even realizing it. At one point, Shay told her to slow down because she couldn't understand her friend. He would've considered it natural—he did it with his native tongue—except Shay looked as if she was seeing someone she didn't recognize. The language seemed to come back faster to Emilia the more she spoke it.

During a pause, Shay leaned in and grabbed her friend's hand. "You'd been looking for them, Millie. It's what sent us on this whole path. Are you sure you don't want to go with them?"

Emilia shook her head and gave a humorless laugh. "My half-brother may be an ass, but he was right about one thing. I don't belong with them."

"But—"

"Honestly, Shay." Emilia pulled her hand free and ran it through her hair. "I'm not one of them anymore. I feel more at home here."

She smiled, looking at each of them at the bakery. "With you guys and my family back home. I'm not sure if I could ever fit in with the Roma anymore—even with the memories I have. I could try, but—" She shook her head. "I don't know. They seemed to have moved on without me. My papá has a new family." She blew a gust of air out of her mouth, her cheeks puffing out. Thomas had to fight the urge to kiss her again. "And I can't do what I have to do next if I'm with them."

Shay's brows scrunched together in confusion. "Next? What—"

"You should go," Emilia interrupted and tapped the box. "You have everything you need."

"You're saying it like you're not going, too." Shay's dark eyes flicked towards Mikey, but he looked down, suddenly fascinated with his hands.

Emilia sighed, leaning her head back. The flush had faded from her cheeks, and her eyes sharpened, losing some of the effects of the alcohol along with the ease with which she spoke.

"I'm going to stay," she admitted, shocking the room into silence. "For now. They killed my mammina, Shay. I can't go. Not yet. But I need to know you'll be okay. That you're in safe hands back home."

Emilia looked at Thomas, her eyes so serious that it made him uneasy. They sat quietly like that, no one speaking.

What was she thinking? She had her ticket home. A way to finally get out of this godforsaken place. If he had the chance, he'd take it in a heartbeat.

Wouldn't he? Thomas ground his teeth. He feckin' wouldn't, and he knew it. He could have left; instead, he decided to stay with his people. To fight for something bigger than himself. Wasn't that what Emilia was doing?

Still, Thomas shifted in his seat, stubbornly ignoring the truth. "Ye should go home."

"I know it's not what you want to hear—" Emilia began to protest.

"What of the man who killed her?" Shay asked. "Will he look for you, too?"

Thomas's blood chilled as he turned toward Emilia. "He'll need to get by me first," he growled.

Emilia threw him an exasperated smile. "Before I left, I made sure I knew the name of the man who killed her. A Louisiana Frenchman—Marcel Pierre Bouderaux." Emilia's face contorted in rage as she said it as if the very words left a bitterness in her mouth. "He went by Pierre and was apparently shot in a hunting accident years ago." The exaggerated widening in her eyes made little doubt that it was an accident.

Thomas sat back, not feeling the least bit guilty about the relief from another man's death. The type of monster who could own and abuse another person should be in the ground. But still, he had to ask, "Are ye sure?"

Emilia nodded. "My papá did it himself."

"Okay." Shay looked as relieved as Thomas felt and tucked the box into her arm. "We stay for a while. You did so much for me. I want to do this for you. We'll do some volunteering, deal with whatever you need to do to get through this. We can—"

"I can't ask you to do that," Emilia interrupted. "It's not safe here. You should have modern doctors that can—"

"I'm staying." Shay straightened and grabbed her friend's hand. "I love you, Millie. If this is what you need, then I'll wait. We have our ticket home, but I don't want you to regret it if we leave. We'll stay until you get everything sorted out."

"But the baby—"

"Rose knows how to bring a baby into the world. Relax, Mill. Trust me when I say I can do this. You know I can."

"I know," Emilia said, face still tight with worry. "You're the strongest woman I know."

Shay smiled, tearing up a little. "Damn straight."

Mikey leaned forward. "So ye two aren't leaving then?" His voice was level, but Thomas noticed the tick in his jaw.

Thomas remained still, not wanting to betray his own unease.

"The thing is, I don't think I will be around for the birth." Emilia fidgeted nervously under their stares. "I know I said I would be—and I really want to—but now you have the chance to go home. And I need to do something first, and it might take a while. That's why I want you to really think about this. If you need to go, you should."

Shay sighed, running her hands over her belly. "I told you, I'm staying. Go do what you got to do, and I'll be fine here with Rose. I wanted to volunteer some more anyway."

"Do ye really think ye should be out and about—" Mikey began until Shay glared at him. He held up his hands. "I'll keep an eye on her," he said to Emilia.

Emilia nodded with an understanding that made Thomas wonder what he'd missed between her and his brother. Their budding friendship—if you could even call it that—was almost as surprising as his interest in Shay.

"You've been quiet." Emilia's brown eyes finally landed on him. She was worried. He could see in her gaze, the tension in her shoulders, and how she kept wringing her hands.

He shrugged. "I said ye should go, and I stand by that. But I learned some time ago that ye will just do what ye want." Thomas couldn't tell her that he wanted her to stay when he believed she should go. It wouldn't do him any good, anyway.

She gave a shy smile and looked at all of them in turn. "The thing is, you probably aren't going to like what I have planned. But I've been thinking about it all night, and I feel like my life has been leading up to this moment. I need to do it."

Shay leaned back in her chair and rolled her eyes. "I should've known it wouldn't be easy."

"And it might be a little dangerous..."

"Christ, lass," Thomas swore under his breath. "What exactly do ye have planned?"

Emilia cringed. "Can any of you give me a good haircut?"

"What in the bloody hell?" Mikey raised his brow. "Do I look like a barber?"

"How much are you planning on cutting off?" Shay narrowed her eyes in suspicion.

Emilia sighed so profoundly that Thomas almost felt it in his soul.

Her following words drifted over to him as if going through a deep fog. *All of it.*

Time seemed to stand still. Surely, he hadn't heard right.

A heavy weight of dread fell onto Thomas, far heavier than the mixture of guilt and relief that overwhelmed him when he found out she was staying. For Thomas knew Emilia far better than he'd admit.

The information she had received and her subsequent actions told him two things: Emilia was no longer running from her past. And if war threatened those she cared for, Emilia planned to fight.

He knew, for she was so much like him when it came to those they loved, and it terrified the shite out of him. Because she would sacrifice everything, including herself.

Just the thought of that alone raised such fear and fury in him that he knew what he would do. Thomas would take the whole feckin' Confederacy down with him before that happened.

CHAPTER THIRTY-TWO

Emilia

"Where are we going?" I asked when I nearly tripped over the cobblestones as Thomas propelled me down the street, my hands over my eyes the last block of the walk. Thank God it was late enough that most people were home or heading there and not staring at me, making a fool of myself.

At least I was in my best burgundy dress and still had all my hair. I was supposed to cut it off that evening, but Thomas implored me to hold off, with the only explanation that we were going somewhere.

It would be my last outing as myself, let alone a woman, and Thomas told me not to worry. It'd only be for the night. Then I could go back into disguise. He'd have me hidden away before someone could see me.

"Are you sure this is okay?" I asked, still nervous about one of Billy Mead's men potentially spotting me.

"Mikey has it taken care of, lass."

I stopped in my tracks and Thomas cursed as his arm pulled free of my hand. "What do you mean he has it taken care of?" I lowered my other hand from my eyes, but he stopped me.

"We're almost there, don't look." His deep sigh almost had me smiling. "He just has the boys watching Mead's men. That is all, gypsy. Now can we get off the street before we draw more of a crowd?"

My hand fell, and I gasped, looking around to find the street almost empty. I irrationally thought that people were watching me flounder. I raised my lip and growled at him, earning a wicked grin. I tried to keep up my ferocity, but I failed miserably as we continued to walk, my hand over my eyes again.

It still amazed me how different the sounds of the nineteenth century were from the twenty-first. No cars driving by or planes overhead. The lack of modern machinery. It quieted the world and filled it with *life*. A woman banging pots in the apartments above, kids hollering down the street, the clop of horse hooves in the distance. The sounds of the city invigorated me, and I often wondered if the south would be the opposite. More relaxing.

The smells, on the other hand, those I could have lived without. Modern sewage systems and streets free of horse manure had to be two of the top five things I missed about the future. Number one: hot, running water. The second... air conditioning. God, did I miss air conditioning. Heat slowly moved to third place on the list as the summer cooled into fall.

With my eyes closed and Thomas silent, my mind wandered to all the differences between the two centuries. To my surprise, I found myself...content. I was okay with lacking those things, because I had gained so many others. I had learned how to protect myself. How to fight for those I loved and what I believed in. I gained so many friendships and those who were quickly becoming family. Though, my heart squeezed when I thought about the family I'd left behind.

And then there was Thomas. I bit my lip, my hand squeezing his arm as I tried to control myself. I very much wanted to spin him towards me, raise on my toes, and kiss him. Maybe he was taking me somewhere we could be alone. If that were the case, I would...

"We're here," Thomas said, his oddly hushed words by my ear interrupting my indecent thoughts.

I lowered my hand to find myself standing in front of a two-story brick building with various instruments displayed in the front window. My eyes widened, finding Thomas again as my hand squeezed his jacket.

"What are we doing here?" I asked.

Shifting on his feet, he looked at me under the brim of his hat, face void of all emotions and body rigid. I never thought I would witness what was unfolding before me.

"I thought ye may want to enjoy yourself on the last night of your womanhood."

I narrowed my eyes at him, trying to keep myself from smiling. "Enjoy myself. How?"

I expected my flirtatious tone to draw heat from his eyes, but he only rocked back on his heels and looked down the street.

Oh, my God. He is nervous. The realization almost had me dancing, if it weren't for the sudden tightening in my chest at seeing this side of Thomas for the first time. God, I loved this man so much. All towering frame and brooding muscles. Just looking at him made my body tingle. And yet, here he was, nervous at taking me on a date—if that's what this was—as if his hands didn't know how to make my body ignite beneath them. Because what was between us went far beyond just the physical, and I knew, *I knew*, he was trying to prove that to me.

Though that part was rather remarkable as well. I wouldn't have minded doing more of that.

This, however, was... sweet. No one had done anything like it for me. I looked away, not wanting him to see the tears threatening to spill over.

"It's no E.G. Wright, but I thought maybe ye would like to take a look around..." he trailed off.

My gaze connected with an older man down the street before he turned and went around the corner. Good. Not many people saw us then.

I nodded, smiling through my tears as I turned back towards the building, excitement rising inside me.

"Yes, of course."

Thomas ascended the stairs as I waited below, bouncing on my toes while trying to keep the rest of my giddiness under check. Maybe it wasn't a date. Nevertheless, it was a nice gesture, and I refused to tamper with my happiness.

Thomas had the door unlocked and gestured for me to go in.

"Why did you do this?" I asked when I stood by his side. I eyed the keys in his hand. "*How* did you do this?"

"Ye were going to cut your hair off, a ghrá." His fingers brushed my hair back, nearly making me purr. "I thought I should court ye as a woman at least once before ye weren't yourself anymore..."

A warmth spread through my body at his consideration, at all he wasn't saying out loud. That we might not get another chance if we were both to go to war. It meant everything to me. Of course, I'd still be the same person, even dressed as a man, but he was right. I was far more comfortable flirting with him while I still looked myself.

Thoughts of how I could torture him on this date surfaced. I had to bite my tongue before I used it on him as images of different techniques that I wanted to try flashed through my mind.

"As for how..." Thomas shrugged a crooked grin on his face, making my heart pleasantly fall into my stomach. "A guy owes me brother. With some negotiating, business was resolved, with the keys landing in me hands tonight."

An exhilarating nervousness simmered inside of me as Thomas pulled me inside. A lantern by the front door softly lit the dark room. Thomas grabbed it and guided me through the tables and stands filled with different second-hand instruments.

My fingers skimmed a beautiful piano as my eyes landed on a violin. I didn't know how to play, but I always wished I had taken lessons.

"I know it's not much—"

"It's perfect." I cut him off. And it was. The E.G. Wright company was known for the new instruments they made, but this—this store told a story. Every scratch and scuff was the history of past lives. A loving caress from its owner.

A slight ache pierced my chest. I hadn't played my guitar in months. I did a complete three-sixty, my eyes landing on each instrument before flicking to the next. Weaving through the tables, I ensured my long skirt didn't catch on anything as I carried out my new mission.

"Can I have that?" I asked Thomas, not even looking his way as my hand reached for the lantern he was holding.

"Aye, lass. Are ye going to tell me why ye look like you're about to start foaming at the mouth?"

"Oh my God!" I squealed loudly, making Thomas curse as I ran to the small guitar in the corner. I sat the lantern down to get a better look at it. The guitar was obviously well-used and smaller than what I was accustomed to, but as I strummed the strings, the most beautiful sound filtered throughout the room.

"Looks like me brother wasn't lyin'." I looked up with a big smile to find Thomas's charming grin. He leaned against one of the tables and crossed his arms. "Let's hear it then."

"This is set up for a right-handed person, but I think..." I adjusted it in my arms again. One year, I'd broken my arm, and I was determined to keep up my lessons. I couldn't play as well, but I could get by.

I practiced for a minute before slowly strumming the chords to one of my favorite songs: Ulysses by Josh Garrels. It may not have been as popular as some others, but the words had always stuck with me. They'd gotten me through some of the most challenging times, and my fingers knew this was exactly what I needed.

The song flowed through my body until my eyes closed, drenched in the feeling of comfortable familiarity. Finally, *finally*, I could sing this song and not feel like I was still waiting for my journey to start. Because this time, I was on my journey and had the people I needed to help me carry it out. I no longer had to wonder why my biological family let me go. I received my answers, and it was time for me to start living my life.

I let the words pour out of me, unaware how I was affecting Thomas or even caring if he enjoyed it. This was for me.

My voice reverberated through the room, wading through the instruments and poring over the building, until I felt it seep from my pores with each lyric. The end came quickly, and with it, a deep calm settled over me.

I opened my eyes slowly to find intense green ones boring into me. My skin flushed with the emotions the song evoked as much as what this man did to my mind, body, and soul.

"Ye continue to amaze me, gypsy."

I bit my lip and shook my head while gently putting the guitar back. I continued to look at the instrument even as I felt him draw near. My body froze with sweet anticipation.

Fingers lightly brushed my own before bringing them to his warm mouth. I watched in wonder as he pressed his lips to each one of my fingertips in the gentlest way. My breath caught in my chest as heat pooled in my lower belly. I let out a small gasp when he sucked my index finger into his mouth, and my toes curled as he let out a deep chuckle that went straight to every nerve in my body.

"Thomas," I whispered, and his eyes found mine as my finger popped out of his mouth. I swallowed, suddenly nervous. "I have something to admit to you."

He wrapped a strong arm around my waist and pulled me in, simultaneously skimming the tip of his nose up my neck before reaching my ear. "I love me name on your lips."

I repeated it on a breath, trying and failing miserably to find my bearings. His hands squeezed my hips and pulled my body flush with his hard one, every one of his muscles making my mind short-circuit. "Thomas..."

His lips found my own as his tongue explored the seam of my mouth, making me whimper. "Did ye have something to say, a ghrá?"

My eyes closed as my hands fisted his shirt in an attempt to hold him back, even as my lips pressed against his again. I couldn't help myself. The man was damn irresistible.

"I knew who you were before I came to your time," I said quickly before I could get lost in him. He froze for a fraction of a second, so briefly that I could have imagined it. "I mean, just an old photograph of you and Michael. I knew your names but not much else. So I came to this time looking for you to help me." Something told me not to tell him about the pub.

Thomas pulled back just enough to see my face. "And did ye like what ye saw?"

I slapped his chest. "I'm being serious!"

"So am I." He went back to exploring my body with his lips, his hands gliding up my sides before circling my breasts. I inhaled deeply, enjoying the sensation of his large hands cupping me. "How often did ye think about me, gypsy?"

"Every day since I was a kid."

His mouth paused on my throat, the only clue I had shocked him before his fingers deftly unbuttoned my top and pulled it open. A quick pull of my shift and my breasts were exposed to the cool air.

"Did ye ever imagine me doing this?" Before I could ask him what he meant, he bent me backward, cupping my head with his hand as he sucked my nipple into his mouth.

I groaned embarrassingly loud as I denied it.

A quick swirl of his tongue and he pulled back. "No?"

My hands shot to his head, holding him to me as he laughed and kept up his slow torture.

"I never expected this," I admitted. "The pictures were old, but you were obviously... well, you." My cheeks flushed as I looked at the instruments over his shoulder.

His hand found my other breast as he kept up his assault. My knees weakened, and Thomas had to practically hold me up.

"Me?" he asked, my breast still in his mouth.

"Yes," I smiled shyly though he couldn't see it. "I don't think I have to tell you that you're attractive."

Thomas stood, and I almost shivered with the loss of his heat. I watched him scan my body and nearly purred at the look in his eyes at the way I affected him.

"I didn't bring ye here for this." His words were gruff, reminding me of the night we spent together. If he kept it up, I was about to drop to my knees and beg him to reenact it. "Come upstairs with me."

I pouted, making no attempt to close my top. His fingers skimmed over my breasts, causing a shudder to travel up my spine before he began to button them himself. He paused, his gaze caught on the rosary around my neck, before finishing the last of the buttons.

"What are we here for then?" I asked.

I watched in wonder as the look of nervousness I'd seen earlier reemerged. I reached up and rubbed my thumb over the crease between his brows.

"It's a surprise."

"A surprise," I repeated.

"Aye, lass."

He grabbed my hand and the lantern and whisked me to the stairs in the back of the shop. They were steep and small, and I would have tripped over my skirt if Thomas hadn't kept a hold of me, but when we finally made it to the landing, and he moved out of the way, I forgot everything that led up to that point.

CHAPTER THIRTY-THREE

Emilia

"You did this?" I asked, looking at the candles, lanterns, and fire burning in the grate, all giving the apartment a warm glow. A small table with white linen draping was set in the center of the room. It looked like someone lived there, and I wondered who he had been kicked out of their place.

"I had some help," he admitted. "Didn't want to burn the place down tryin' to get ye here. But I helped set it all up, aye."

"It's beautiful." And it was. Realization dawned on me, and my mouth popped open. "Did that older man help with this? Is this his place?" I spun around, taking in the small area that was the kitchen and sitting area. Another room was shut off in the front of the shop.

Thomas shook his head, eyeing me quizzically. "What man, lass?" I explained to him the man I saw down the street, but Thomas shut that down. It was a younger couple who owned the shop. They were to stay with family for the week. It seemed that the man enlisted and

"

would be leaving soon. His wife would have to run the shop on her own.

Thomas shifted on his feet, looking somewhat uncomfortable. "Ms. Banks helped light the candles while I brought ye over here."

Shay. Of course, she helped. How she kept this secret was beyond me. It explained why she was so adamant about leaving with Rose earlier. If the bakery wasn't busy, I'd have asked her more questions, ultimately leading to her admission. I shook my head, smiling at how well they planned this.

Thomas led me to the table, and I had to do a double take. Were those *burgers and fries*? I looked closely and found some red sauce and gasped. *Literally gasped*—loudly and unashamedly. *Ketchup!*

"Is it not how ye like it?"

My wide eyes found Thomas watching me worriedly. "How did you do this?" I asked.

Thomas shrugged. "Ms. Banks explained, and we had some help from Rose."

This had to cost a fortune. This meat was far rarer than the other forms of beef due to its cut. Believe me, I looked into it after a month here. One could only eat the same thing so many times. It didn't take long before I discovered my low income didn't provide many culinary options.

Before I could respond, he went on. "It might not be what ye remember, but she said it was quite popular where ye're from. Does it not look right?"

"It looks amazing."

Thomas pulled out the chair for me, and I plopped down, ready to devour it. Screw manners. Though, it seemed that Thomas's were exceptional. I was vaguely aware of him taking his hat off and sitting while I formed my plan of attack. Savagery was not beneath me. I was going to make the burger my bitch.

I dug in and groaned. The taste was somewhat different, probably from the type of beef they ground and the spices they used, but my God, was it delicious. I wanted it every night for a week.

"If I would have known that it would make that sound come out of ye, I would have fed it to ye months ago."

I looked up from my food to see Thomas smirking at me, heat in his eyes.

"If you fed this to me months ago, I would have ended up in your bed a lot sooner." I waved the burger at him while he leaned back in his chair, amused. "But then that would be embarrassing."

"Embarrassing?" One dark brow rose.

I nodded, face serious. "I mean, for you. Especially when the burger makes me moan louder."

Thomas slowly leaned his elbows on the table, his features turning feral. "Do ye want to test that out?"

"Can I eat this while we do it?"

That had him laughing, the sound loud and deep, sending goose-bumps across my flesh. He didn't laugh often, but when he did, it was magnificent.

"While I want to test out that theory very much," he admitted, "I think we should just try to enjoy it before it gets colder."

I stuffed more into my mouth as Thomas inspected his. When he lifted the bun and flipped the meat, it dawned on me that this would be the first time he ate a hamburger.

"Just try it." I smiled and tried to act like I wasn't waiting for him to take the first bite.

I watched in fascination as he put the burger into his mouth and his teeth clamped down. His eyes sprung wide, finding me before looking back at the food.

"Do you like it?" I asked, almost nervously.

"I—" He shook his head, and my stomach sunk. "It's nothin' like I ever had before." Another bite into his mouth, and he spoke around the food. "But I think I could get used to it. Although I must admit, I questioned Ms. Banks once or twice when we made it."

My grin faded, and I looked down at my plate as a rock seemed to fall into my stomach. "She helped you," I stated.

"Aye, lass. I didn't think ye would mind."

Shit. I was a terrible friend. Here I was, flirting and eating burgers that my pregnant friend helped make while she was at the bakery eating stew for the umpteenth time. What was wrong with me?

"Emilia." The seriousness in his voice had me looking up. "What is botherin' ye? Do ye not like it?"

My eyes fell back to the food, but I couldn't seem to eat anymore. "I love it."

"Then why are ye poutin'?"

"I'm not pouting!"

He just raised a brow and sat back, studying me as I sulked in my seat. Not only was I a terrible friend, but I was ruining this nice date Thomas had planned. I was the worst.

I leaned back in the chair and felt my corset tighten around my midsection, even without finishing the burger or trying the fries. And yet, I had absolutely no regrets about devouring what I did.

I sighed. "I'm sure you know how pregnant women get."

"Aye." Thomas eyed me as if I had some explaining to do. "Have ye been with a man I didn't know about, gypsy?"

I tried to smile, but I wasn't sure I succeeded, and my following words tumbled out of me. "It's just that Shay had been craving cheeseburgers, and now I'm here enjoying one. I feel bad."

Thomas nodded, scraping his nails across the scruff on his jaw. "I thought ye might think that."

"You did?" I asked, surprised.

"Aye. I made sure Ms. Banks had one herself. Rose as well, for helping."

Relief flooded my body until I almost collapsed onto the table. Tears threatened to spill over.

"Is that all that was troublin' ye?"

"Yes, thank you so much."

"No need to fret. She even made a horrible white concoction that looked like curdled milk from a cat's tit."

"What?" I laughed.

"She put some spices in it, I think."

My mouth popped open. "Did she call it ranch?"

"Aye. Do they tend to make that on ranches?"

"Umm." I drug the word out, puzzling over that for a minute. "I have no idea who invented it or if it was on a ranch, but it's delicious, and a lot of people eat it."

I sighed with relief, and my hunger returned. Shay deserved to indulge her cravings, though I wish I had put more effort into finding out how to make them for her.

We ate in pleasant silence until the seams of my dress threatened to pop, and each delicious fry was devoured off of my plate. And then, Thomas finished mine off when I couldn't eat another bite.

"No wonder why I'm thicker than your women," I joked, patting my stomach. "I could fatten them up in no time. I swear, I think my dress is going to bust."

Thomas ran his fingers through his dark hair, eyes never leaving me. They traveled to where my hand was placed over my stomach and slowly raised over my breasts and neck until meeting my burning face again.

"If these are the results, I'm not complaining, a ghrá. I particularly like the idea of your dress busting."

I stared at him, amazed at how comfortable he made me feel in my skin. I didn't have to try to lose weight or worry about how I looked because he always made me feel beautiful. I could be myself and not have to worry; that kind of power was intoxicating.

Unable to go another minute without touching him, I stood up and made my way around the table. Thomas's eyes tracked my every moment until I stood before him.

I pushed his shoulders farther back into his chair and slid onto his lap, wrapping my arm around his neck before kissing his cheek. I reveled in the scratch of his beard against my soft skin. He wrapped his arms around me, and, at that moment, I had never felt more protected.

"Do you do this for all your women?" I teased.

Thomas shifted me on his lap while his large hand squeezed my thigh dangerously high, sending a jolt through me.

"Ye are really lookin' to be punished tonight. Aren't ye, lass?"

I smiled and pressed a kiss to his lips. I kept them there when my next words came out raspy. "I've been good my whole life. I found that I like being bad with you, Thomas. Very." Kiss. "Very." I crushed my lips to his. "Much."

When I went to pull back, his hand wrapped around my head, holding me in place as he deepened the kiss. The warm stroke of his tongue had me instantly opening for him, and I let out a heady moan.

I held on tighter as our tongues danced, exploring each other leisurely until warmth flooded all the way to my toes. We stayed that way until my lips were numb and swollen, and even then, we couldn't seem to stop.

Eventually, when the candles were considerably lower, Thomas pulled back and kissed the tip of my nose.

"I never courted another woman, gypsy. Ye are the only one I would do this for."

Lava seemed to rush down my head and over my shoulders. I shivered at the sudden sensation.

I bit my lip, wanting very much to kiss him again.

"If ye keep starin' at me like that, we will never leave. And I can't guarantee I won't ruin ye this time."

"Oh." I sighed and squirmed on his lap, suddenly much hotter and even more bothered. "I would love for you to ruin me, Thomas. *Please.*"

A growl rumbled deep in his chest as he grabbed my waist. "Ye are going to be the death of me, woman."

With one swift movement that had me gasping, he lifted me off him until I swayed on my feet and looked up at him.

A crooked grin and a flash of mischievousness in those deep green eyes nearly had my knees buckling.

"I told ye, a ghrá. Tonight, I just wanted to care for ye."

I pouted. "I know other ways that you can care for me."

With a deep laugh, he guided me back to my chair and began cleaning up the table, commanding me to relax. That gesture and everything he did to prepare this night for me—and the extra cash he'd spent when he barely had any extra to spend on himself—was so overwhelming that tears pricked my eyes. Especially during a time when it was rare for men to go out of their way to do this type of work. I eyed the man before me, thanking the stars that he didn't follow societal standards and made sure my happiness was an absolute priority.

My heart squeezed painfully because I knew it wouldn't last. Couldn't. Not with each of us enlisting. Even if by some miracle we both survived, I would go back with Shay.

And yet, my gut twisted. Because deep down, I already knew.

I didn't want to leave.

"Thank you for this." I smiled at him, knowing all my happiness was beaming out of me. We had just locked up the store and headed down the front steps back to Rose's.

"I wanted ye to do something ye enjoyed before we did all this, a ghrá." His rough hand gently pulled me to a stop and swung me into his embrace. "Ye deserve so much more. If we had more time, I would show ye just how much ye're worth." His hands cupped my face, his thumbs brushing decadent circles over my cheeks. A shiver ran up my body as he leaned down to press his lips against mine.

My heart soared as Thomas kissed me in the middle of the street, in front of anyone to see. I grabbed his arms and held on as I deepened the kiss. Making sure that if only one person saw us, they'd know I claimed this man.

He was mine. And I was his.

Our kiss was soft and exploring, without care of time. When we finally broke free, Thomas captured my hand in his, and we continued our walk towards home.

We had just turned the corner when someone jarred my shoulder. I was knocked back a little, but Thomas kept a hold of me.

"Pardon me, mademoiselle," an accent floated over to me, causing all the hairs to rise on my body. There was something odd about it. A warning almost...

"Feckin' gobshite," Thomas mumbled. I turned, but the man had already disappeared between the buildings.

"Are ye all right, gypsy?"

I turned back towards Thomas, already forgetting about the jostle, and smiled. "Yes. It will take a lot more than that to take me down," I joked.

"Aye," he grumbled reluctantly. "Ye sure ye still want to go through with this?"

I bumped his shoulder with mine. "You aren't getting rid of me that easily, O'Connor."

Thomas mumbled something in Irish, making me laugh, even though I didn't know the meaning. I found I loved irking him. And just the thought that I didn't need to stop anytime soon made me far happier than I wanted to admit.

I almost had whiplash from his indecision of whether to push me away or pull me close. But that was how it had to be. I, too, was in a constant state of indecision. We never knew when it would be time for me to go back home.

The next few months would be hard. I knew I might not be able to see Thomas, but I would still be in the same century. I could find him if I needed to. No time or barrier could prevent me from going to him.

And I decided that I wanted to spend as much of it with him as I possibly could. We could worry about our hearts later.

Besides, Thomas already had mine. And I wasn't sure if I ever wanted it back.

Epilogue

Eighteen Years Ago

A large fire roared to life in the dark of the night, big enough to give the trees a golden hue around the edges of the clearing. I was low to the ground, the view of a child, as the women danced circles around the fire, covered in vibrant skirts and flowing shirts. Dark hair and olive skin moved around me. Those not dancing swayed to the music and laughed. They didn't yet know what had happened. What my father did not dare tell anyone but my Nonna.

This place felt safe. Before I would have jumped in and joined the dancers, music already on my lips, but something happened that made me retreat into myself. Something I wouldn't dare to remember again.

"It is time." An older woman, face just starting to wrinkle from years in the sun, spoke in Romani and knelt down. She looked up at someone standing behind me. "Are you sure?"

I could understand Romani and Italian interchangeably without a single thought that the languages were mixing.

"Sì, madre. È troppo pericoloso restare." It was too dangerous to stay.

She nodded sadly. "Already so much pain for such a small child."

"We need to move fast." My father grabbed my shoulder with a shaking hand. I knew he had already cauterized the other and was currently hiding it in his coat. "They're not far behind. I don't want to bring trouble to our camp. To you."

The older woman nodded, frowning. She turned to me, face softening with nothing other than love.

"Come here, piccolina. All will be okay."

I went to her, feeling comfort in her strong arms after being afraid for so long. The rosary with the pretty stones fell over my neck, and with it a light coating of dust swept me and my memories away.

The big thing flew by, making me cry out in fright. Everything looked so different, and it was all so *loud*.

"Mammina?" I cried. "Papà?"

A man passing by kneeled next to me, acting as if he wanted to soothe me, but I couldn't understand what he was saying.

I clutched my necklace in my hands, holding onto it as if it was my lifeline. Nonna told me not to lose it. Ever. So, I held on tight, in a dress of another time, and screamed in the street until the man took pity on me.

The unfamiliarity of it all, and the sudden loss of my parents, put a burden on my younger self that I couldn't handle. My developing mind shut out my old life, and erased everything I had known about that world.

It was a misbegotten reprieve. Each tick of the hand unknowingly brought the hounds closer to my heels. Because he searched for eighteen long years and would no longer wait to claim what was his.

I wish I had known then that time was quickly running out.

Glossary

1. A Dhia – Dear God

2. Ar chaill tú d'intinn – Have you lost your mind

3. Cíochas – Breasts

4. Comrádaí – Comrade

5. Deartháir daor – Dear brother

6. Elle est belle – She's beautiful

7. Ghrá – Love

8. Le do thoil – Please

9. Mo dheartháir – My brother

10. Mo stoirín – My "little darling"

11. Ná bí buartha – Don't worry

12. Ná fág fós – Don't leave yet

13. Ní iarraim mórán, a dheartháir – I don't ask much, brother.

14. Níl gach rud caillte – Not everything is lost

15. Oíche mhaith – Goodnight

16. Pardonnez-moi – Pardon me

17. Sì, madre. È troppo pericoloso restare – Yes, mother. It is too dangerous to stay.

18. Suimiúil – Interesting

19. Tá brón orm – I'm sorry

The author translated these to the best of her ability. However, she is not fluent in either language and apologizes for any mistakes.

Author's Note

The characters in this novel are purely fictional. The author has taken liberties using the names of those on the Vigilance Committee, though they had not conducted the meeting during Chapter Two's events. However, the speech at Tremont Temple, the presentation of the regimental flags, and various events throughout the novel occurred, told by the fictional characters of *Back to You*.

[1] (The New York Times, 1860) In Chapter Four, the events at Tremont Temple were written as close to their natural occurrence as the story permits, including the dialogue and speeches of the men on the podium as well as the audience's outbursts. However, the author used specific characters to incite the incident rather than what Frederick Douglass described as a "gentlemen's mob." The fictional characters created by the author had no part in it and were only used to tell the tragic occurrence through Thomas's viewpoint.

(Macnamara, 1899) Chapter Twenty-One. Speech given by Governor John Andrew.

Acknowledgments

First, I must thank God for guiding me and teaching me everything I needed to get to this point. This world is a dark, dangerous, beautiful place, and I couldn't navigate it without Him.

To my parents, who helped shape me into the person I had become. For allowing me to watch *Jurassic Park* at the age of 3, *Aliens vs. Predator* at 6, *Buffy the Vampire Slayer* at 7, and all the late nights we spent watching all the classics (*Rambo* and *Rocky* are classics, right?). Thank you for showering me with all the love and affection you could. It taught me my worth, and I will forever be grateful. Oh, and thanks for making me my weird self. Love you to the moon and back!

To all the family who have encouraged me to chase my dreams. Your devotion to me (even for my not-so-spectacular work) has kept me going. And my Grandma Gwen, who trades series with me every time I see her. I love that we can talk about the same crazy books. It was a blast talking to you about *Outlander* and *Throne of Glass* (and the hundreds of other books)! Our love for our Scottish and Irish ancestry greatly influenced this story. Thank you from the bottom of my heart for all the stories of your immigrant mother and immediate family. I wish I could have spent time around them while immersed in their lives and lovely accents!

A big shout out to all of my friends who are as close to me as Shay is to Emilia. Without you, my life would be extremely boring! It just goes to show that your family is not always blood. You're my family now! (Insert evil laugh) You know who you are, but I should name a few! Katie, Shelby, and Kelley, who listen to me daily, thank you for suffering with me!

I want to thank everyone who read the earlier drafts. Your input and new eyes helped shape this story. Without Shelby, Emilia's hat would have reappeared on her head eight times in one chapter as if she was in Hogwarts. Thank you for all your input and witty, detailed remarks in the attached document! I swear I'll start paying you soon. (Awkward cough)

Thank you, Hailie Camarillo for editing this book! Your hard work and advice were so appreciated. I loved working with you. And to my readers and everyone on TikTok and Instagram who've encouraged me, asked for more, and interacted with my content! You make me want to bring my characters to life. This journey is so fun to go on with you.

And last but not least. Thank you to my husband, Andrew, who may or may not know this is here because he doesn't read. This will be the only time I tell you to skip to the end! You have always encouraged me to chase my dreams while you kept a roof over our heads! Thank you for keeping our family alive on this adventure of ours.

About Author

Tara Nolan was born and raised sandwiched between The Great Lakes, where she has dwelled in the Mitten state ever since. She occupies a house with her three gremlins, a husband she has known since the first grade, and their various creatures. Tara has been an avid reader since childhood and went to college for English with a minor in history. She began writing her senior year of high school but put that novel aside to attend college and write short stories and poetry before finally starting *Back to You*. Eventually, she no longer put her dream on hold and decided to self-publish. Tara plans on finishing the *Fearless Sons of Erin and the Time-Traveller Series* while returning to her Fantasy Trilogy: *Fallen Kingdoms*, which started this journey. You can find her on TikTok and Instagram @author.taranolan or her website authortaranolan.com.

9 798987 820308